Other books by Leonard St. Clair

THE SEADON FORTUNE

THE EMERALD TRAP

A FORTUNE IN DEATH

Obsessions

Leonard St. Clair

SIMON AND SCHUSTER
New York

DESIGNED BY JEANNE JOUDRY
MANUFACTURED IN THE UNITED STATES OF AMERICA
1   2   3   4   5   6   7   8   9   10

LIBRARY OF CONGRESS CATALOGING IN PUBLICATION DATA

St. Clair, Leonard.
Obsessions.

I.   Title.
PZ4.S135Ob   [PS3569.A43]   813'.5'4   79–24079
ISBN 0-671-24732-8

Acknowledgments

The author expresses his gratitude to those persons and organizations that gave of their time and specialized knowledge so that this work of fiction might be enriched by authenticity of detail and historical accuracy. Among them are:

Catherine St. Clair, the author's wife, for her invaluable knowledge of Costa Rica, its people, customs and topography.

Elizabeth Shaw, Vice President for Public Relations of Christie, Manson & Woods International, Inc., New York City, for information on Christie's of London in the year 1927.

The Very Reverend Archpriest George Grabbe, Secretary to the Synod of Bishops of the Russian Orthodox Church Outside of Russia, New York City, for his guidance in portraying Russian religious services and for certain personal memories of the Russian Revolution.

The staffs of the Gemological Institute of America, Inc., and the Diamond Dealers Club, Inc., both of New York City.

Scores of histories and memoirs were drawn upon for the account of the Russian Revolution, life at the Palace of Tsarskoe Selo, the execution of the Romanov Family, and the hidden fortune in Imperial jewels. Most valuable among those sources were: *The Life and Death of Lenin*, by Robert Payne; *The House of Special Purpose, An Intimate Portrait of the Last Days of the Russian Imperial Family*, by J. C. Trewin; *Nicholas and Alexandra*, by Robert K. Massie; *Black Night, White Snow*, by Harrison E. Salisbury. The account of the assassination of Ambassador Voikov is from *The New York Times*, June 8, 1927.

*For Phyllis and Dorothy
and Catherine*

Prologue

Monte Carlo
July 1958

MONTE CARLO, on that warm and luminous evening in July, was, in the words of the commentator for the British Broadcasting Corporation, "a midsummer night's dream." Men and women and children by the thousands lined the winding streets along which the motorcade would pass. Still more thousands stood or sat on the bluffs and cliffs above the harbor; others stationed themselves on the seaward terraces of the famous Casino; more waited in hundreds of small pleasure craft until time to escort the bridal launch to the great white yacht, the *Diana*, which rode at anchor beyond the breakwater.

9

Monte Carlo was used to spectacle; two years before, it had witnessed the marriage of Monaco's Prince Rainier and the American actress Grace Kelly; it was a veteran of the galas of Aristotle Onassis, of the annual Monte Carlo auto races, of famous ballets and symphony concerts. But this evening's occasion would be still more memorable, for Orsino di Ascoli had willed it so. The radio-television commentator for the German broadcasting network who had covered the wedding ceremony itself had described it as "the uniting of one of Europe's three richest men with the beauty and talent of America's favorite actress. At the behest of Herr di Ascoli, guests have flown in from half a world away. Wherever the di Ascoli empire operates—London, Paris, Zurich, Rome, New York, Tokyo, Rio—the elite of society, of industry and banking, the brightest movie stars of Hollywood, have sent their delegates to do honor to tonight's bridal couple."

So much for Teutonic euphoria. The wedding ceremony was over, and now a vanguard of police motorcycles, sirens screaming, cleared the narrow streets for the motorcade of limousines bearing the guests toward the harbor and the wedding reception aboard the *Diana*.

Orsino di Ascoli, grizzle-haired, powerful of build, smiled vacantly from the window of the lead limousine at the lines of people waving and cheering and pelting the car with rice and confetti. Holding the hand of the woman beside him, he felt more than the usual elation of a bridegroom; it was the special sense of triumph which a man feels who weds a woman twenty-five years his junior and has routed all his youthful competitors—not, he told himself, because of his great wealth, but because he and Erin Deering were two of a kind. Both magnetic, mercurial, demanding the best of everything in life.

For di Ascoli, it was more than a wedding—it was the anniversary of a great secret. He was the lone survivor—yet he dared not admit to anyone exactly what it was that he had survived. It accounted for the bodyguard who sat in front with the chauffeur, and the second guard in the limousine directly behind, and the third who would be aboard the launch going out to the *Diana*. Soon, sometime on the' honeymoon cruise through the Greek Isles, there would be an end to these precautions; they would be needless.

He smiled at the auburn-haired actress beside him, and she said, "Who would have thought—"

"Yes, my dear?"

"Oh, nothing, really." She waved through the window to a child who was being held up in her mother's arms. Who would have thought, she completed in her mind, that she was the same Erin Deering, desperate and poor, who had hunched over a typewriter in the basement of a Hollywood radio station? The newspapers had called it "a Cinderella story." It had been anything but that. There had been no fairy godmother, no glass slipper. It had been sheer guts and drive and talent which had brought her to the public's attention. Now this was her big scene, more satisfying than any role she had ever played, and no matter what Tony Brullov had predicted, by God, this show would never close out of town.

The motorcade began to slow as it reached the harbor *quai* and approached the loading platform where the *Diana*'s launches waited. Lisa di Ascoli peered through the window of the second limousine and saw a helicopter with pontoon floats taking off from the waters of the harbor. It was the television aircraft which would cover the departure of the bridal launch and its arrival alongside the *Diana*. One would suppose they were reporting on a royal coronation, Lisa thought bitterly, or the installation of a new Pope. She could accept any tribute paid to her father, but not if it included Erin Deering. It was unthinkable that now she would have to share her father's love and wealth with a stepmother. How could he so diminish his only child? But not for long, Lisa vowed to herself. She would fight Erin to the bloody end, and she would win. Lisa knew men, she knew women, and how they could be manipulated.

She had done it with her body; now she would do it with the ruthless cunning of a di Ascoli. Tonight was no more than a false armistice.

She was conscious that the two men in the folding seats of the limousine—Aly Khan and Porfirio Rubirosa—were smiling at her curiously. "What's amusing you two?" she asked.

"Your expression," Aly Khan replied. "It reminds me of those lines of William Blake: 'Tiger! Tiger! burning bright/ In the forests of the night.' I forget how the rest goes. Can you remember, Tony?"

Tony Brullov, beside Lisa, completed the quotation. " 'What immortal hand or eye/ Could frame thy fearful symmetry?' "

"That's it!"

"Except," Tony added, "the word should not be *fearful*. It should be *lovely*. A tiger with green eyes burning bright, and every movement feline grace."

Lisa laughed. "Thank you, darling." A troubled look came into her eyes. "Tony, I'm worried about you. You don't look well."

"Just hung over."

"Is it still Erin?"

"You asked that just before the wedding."

"And you didn't answer me."

Nor did he now. It was impossible to explain why he looked as he did. Liquor was not part of it, nor fatigue, nor Erin. It was an almost suffocating sense of dread. During the wedding ceremony, when all the cameras were focused on the bridal couple, he had thought: You're all aiming in the wrong direction. *I'm* the story. The biggest you will ever have. And you'll never know it.

Dan Coopersmith peered with field glasses through the glass bubble of the helicopter and began speaking into the microphone strapped to his chest. It was to be a running commentary which would be broadcast by the American radio and television networks. Beside him Luke Bailey operated the television camera with a telephoto lens and gave directions to Michel, the pilot.

"There they are, ladies and gentlemen. The bridal couple is stepping into the first launch. It's like daylight down there, with all the flashbulbs going off. Now the launch is starting to move and— Wait a moment. Luke, did you see a second couple jump aboard just as the launch pulled away?"

"Yeah. Got 'em in the viewfinder. Think it was di Ascoli's daughter and some man."

"Okay. There they go out into the harbor, heading for the breakwater. Michel is going to give us some altitude and we'll take you out for a preview of the yacht. . . . That's it in the distance. Isn't she a beauty? Almost the size of an ocean liner. . . . We're coming up on her fast. See those searchlights aimed up at the pennants in its rigging? Luke, can you give us a tight shot? . . . That's it. Now we're almost overhead. Luke, those crew members bunched on the aft deck—what are they doing?"

"Looks like they're getting ready to fire off skyrockets."

"Of course! The royal welcome aboard. . . . Wow! There goes the first one! Michel, how about getting us out of here? Wouldn't want to connect with one of those babies. . . . Now we're heading back toward the harbor. You can see the second launch trailing the di Ascolis. And more coming up behind. Those are the guests to the wedding reception. And farther back, there's a whole flotilla of little boats filled with well-wishers. Reminds me of a regatta."

Then Dan Coopersmith's voice tensed. "Hold on! Eric! Eric on the BBC boat! Did you see that?"

Eric's reply crackled over the radio. "Yes! Somebody fell out of the di Ascoli launch. Somebody's in the water!"

"I thought so. But how could it happen?"

Eric's voice crackled again. "Hard to say. It's a high-speed launch. If somebody was standing up and the boat hit a swell head-on, it would be easy to lose balance. No worry, though.

The second launch is slowing down. They've switched on their searchlight."

"I can see it, Eric. There's a head bobbing. Whoever it is ought to be out of the water any second now. Luke, can you bring us in on a close-up?"

Luke grunted. "Let BBC have it. I'm staying with the di Ascolis. I can't figure what their launch is doing down there. First it veered to port, now it's swinging the other way. Maybe they've got rudder trouble. Michel, can you drop down a bit?"

After a moment Dan picked up smoothly. "The launch must be in radio contact with the yacht. The *Diana*'s got her searchlights on it. And there's a skyrocket bursting right over-head. What a dramatic sight, ladies and gentlemen. We're about a hundred yards forward of the bridal launch, and I can see somebody—" His words were lost in a thunder of noise. The helicopter swayed violently, the propellers snarled as the shock wave hit. Then the commentator moaned into the microphone. *"Oh, God! Oh, my God!"*

On shore, the thousands massed along the cliffs of Monte Carlo stared dumbly across the water. Skyrockets from the yacht were still bursting into the night; but now their streams of color gyrated from the shock waves, and on the mirroring sea where they had watched the bridal launch, nothing remained but a towering pillar of fire.

One

•

Petrograd, Russia
January 1918

IT WAS the third day of snowfall. The River Neva and the canals of the great city were iced over. The red flags atop the Winter Palace, the Admiralty Building, the Fortress of Peter and Paul had lost their revolutionary color and were cloaked in white. The onion-shaped domes of the churches were filmed with frost, and icicles dribbled from the marble window ledges and porticos of the former palaces of the grand dukes along the Nevsky Prospect. There was little traffic except for a rare streetcar or automobile on urgent business or an ambulance carrying wounded soldiers from the train depots to the city's hospitals. The war was all but over. Everyone knew that the German armies on the Polish border to the west were poised for a final push to Petrograd. Everyone knew, and yet hoped that somehow there would be a saving miracle. Perhaps Lenin and his commissars could arrange an honorable peace; perhaps there would be no more street riots and shooting; perhaps a way could be found to supply Petrograd with enough food and fuel to get through the winter. Perhaps.

Such hopes little concerned Yuri Dimitrovich Solenko. What would be would be. Everything was a result of luck, and luck was a matter of being in a certain place at a certain moment, which could make one's life a glorious affair or end it on the spot. Certainly luck, kind and steadfast, had been Solenko's. He had fought the Germans and Austrians for three years and had suffered only a sprained ankle and a few colds —until at last a bullet had pierced his lung. Even that had proved fortunate; it had sent him back to a base hospital and the ministrations of a doctor who was disgusted with the war. He had written Solenko a medical discharge and whispered to him, "Let the fools die for nothing. Go home and find work and a wife and give Russia children." Solenko had ignored the latter part and asked, "When will I be strong enough for work?" The doctor laughed. "For anyone else, three months. For you, three weeks. You've got the body and stamina of a fighting bear." It was scarcely an exaggeration: his chest was mighty, his legs powerful, and his arms could crush a man's ribs with ease. Yet there was a contradiction, too. For all his bulk and strength, his face was mild of expression; intelligence shone from his black eyes and humor shaped his mouth.

So on the third day of the snowfall Solenko returned to his native Petrograd. Clad in his army greatcoat, with his duffel bag slung over one shoulder, he strode through the Nikolaevsky Railroad Station and out into Znamensky Square. A streetcar filled with passengers from the train was already in motion. Solenko swore to himself. No telling when there would be another, and the droshkies lined up in front of the station were already hired. No, there was one possibility, a horse-drawn sleigh. He sprinted toward it.

The *izvostchick*, muffled in his greatcoat, frowned down from the driver's seat and shook his head at Solenko. "No soldiers," he grunted, thinking of his tip.

Solenko dug into his pocket and held up a fistful of rubles. "To Vyborg. Double your fare."

The man brightened. "Can't go the short way. A lot of drunk soldiers and shooting on the Alexander Bridge."

"Then the long way," Solenko said and climbed into the sleigh and covered his lap with the sheepskin robe. They proceeded up the Nevsky Prospect past the ducal palaces, and Solenko played again in his mind the game of his boyhood. In which of those great mansions did his father live? Or perhaps his mother? As long as one did not know one's parentage, one could imagine great beginnings. Why think of oneself as the offspring of some porter and scrubwoman? As for the name "Solenko," it was the gift of a sympathetic nun at the Orphanage of the Holy Virgin; she had included "Dimitrovich," "the son of Dimitri," to cloak the fact that he was a bastard. . . .

The sleigh glided across the Fontanka Canal bridge and the Ekaterininsky and approached Palace Square. Directly ahead were the great Admiralty Building, the fifteen-hundred-room Winter Palace and the Hermitage. Nothing had changed, everything had changed. Solenko gazed at the walls of the Winter Palace, now pockmarked from Bolshevik gunfire, and remembered a night in 1914 when he, just turned sixteen, had seen Tsar Nicholas appear on one of the balconies after the declaration of war against Germany. He remembered the cheering thousands in the square and their cries of "On to Berlin!" He remembered the marching bands and the companies of mounted Cossacks in red tunics and black fur hats and their lances tipped with waving pennants. Solenko remembered another evening, in December, 1916—scarcely more than a year ago—when he had been on leave from the front. Tsar Nicholas and Empress Alexandra rode in the Imperial carriage to the Marinsky Theater for a night of ballet. This time there were no marching bands, no cheering crowds, only sullen glares; and the Cossack escort rode with sabers drawn and ready. Now the Cossacks were gone, the Romanov Family imprisoned in Siberia, and Palace Square was dotted with armored cars and groups of soldiers huddled around bonfires.

The droshky crossed the Neva at Trinity Bridge, passed the Peter and Paul Fortress, crossed another bridge over the Little Neva, and reached the workers' section of Vyborg. Solenko directed the driver to stop at the first lodging house that displayed a sign of rooms to let. The room he took was cramped and cold, but it would suffice. He ate supper at the boardinghouse—thin borscht, an aged sausage and cold pirogi—and pondered the problem of work. Where might he find it? After three years in the army he was out of touch with the labor situation. The men in his regiment had known no more than he. They did little but grouse about food and incompetent officers; in the hospital the talk had been about pain and nurses and bowel movements. He must find out where civilians worked, what they were thinking and saying. "The Club Charoshka is what you want," the landlady advised, when he explained his need. "It's expensive, black-market prices, but for information one must pay. It's one street over. You'll see the sign."

Charoshka proved to be a single large room in a basement. The tables were huddled together like frightened mice. In one corner a dispirited *yolka*, a Christmas tree, flickered with candles. The far wall was lined by a counter laden with beer and vodka bottles and a brass samovar that dispensed tea. The customers were male, apparently laborers, students, and several who looked like writers or professors. The air was sour with the odor of unwashed bodies, soiled clothing and cheap tobacco. A brunette in gypsy costume sang songs of the joy and sorrow of love and accompanied herself on a three-stringed balalaika. At Solenko's table the talk was of the coming new order. Farmlands would be seized from the greedy peasant landowners, the kulaks. Industry would be nationalized. Money would be abolished. One would ride the streetcars and trains without paying a kopeck. Everyone would be given cards for food and clothing and lodging. Solenko glanced toward the gypsy singer: would there even be a card for her?

Suppose money did become only scraps of paper—what then? Solenko studied the men who talked so glibly of cards for food, clothing and lodging. That was their collective goal, to be cared for like cattle. They were gutless; they did not believe in themselves; they did not believe in luck, the convergence of the right moment and the right place. That, Solenko decided, was his advantage. He would wait and watch, and meanwhile work at whatever came to hand. Perhaps there might be an opening at the railroad, perhaps at the Finland Station, where he had been employed before the army. At least the great steam locomotives, radiating heat from their iron skins, would warm him through the winter. And if old Sasha was still doing the hiring, surely he would remember Yuri, the engine wiper.

"Yuri, my boy!" The old man laughed, embracing him. "How you've changed! You're a giant now!"

"That's the difference between seventeen and twenty, Sasha."

They were in the yard superintendent's shed situated between the main line and the switching tracks. A bucket of coals glowed beside the desk, which was littered with schedules and reports and dirty tobacco pipes. "Of course we have a place for you," Sasha said, when Solenko explained his visit. "We're nothing but white beards and crippled veterans. We need sound young muscles. How about apprentice mechanic?"

Solenko took a breath and a gamble. "A foreman. I want to give orders, not take them."

"Have you had such experience?"

Solenko drew out his service record and deposited it on the desk. The superintendent leafed through the papers. "Hmmm . . . private, Regimental Transport. Motor maintenance. Then corporal. Then sergeant. Then—" he frowned—"then regiment disbanded. Why?"

"Too many killed, too many deserted. I was transferred to a new unit. Infantryman. Front-line service. It's all there."

The old man tugged at his frayed moustache. "For such a position as you ask, I must talk to someone." He picked up his telephone, then paused. "Wait outside, please."

Solenko leaned against the side of the shed and stared with expert eyes at a passing switch engine. Its boiler plates were rusted, water leaked from the fittings, the forward truck wheels were out of alignment. It too was a war casualty. Then Sasha tapped the window and motioned him inside again.

"You will be foreman of a maintenance crew. Six men."

Solenko started to burble his thanks but Sasha cut him short. "For one week only. That is the trial period. Then someone will talk to you."

"Someone?" he echoed.

"That's all I can tell you. It's a different world, my boy. A very strange world."

Solenko's work crew was composed of men past military age who, despite their disparity in years, accepted his orders with respect, for they recognized that he understood machinery. Solenko himself enjoyed the feeling of authority; at the end of a day's work he was not required to leave by the ordinary laborers' gate; he could walk through the great vaulted station hall where once had trod tsars and grand dukes; he could push through the glass doors into the former Imperial Waiting Room and sit and read the newspaper—the same waiting room where a few months earlier Comrade Lenin had been welcomed by the cheering throng on his return from exile in Switzerland. It was in this same waiting room, five days after Sasha had hired him, that Solenko was approached by a man in a long coat and an astrakhan hat.

"Meet me outside in the square," he said.

Before Solenko could ask the reason, the man turned away and disappeared through the glass doors. Brief as the encounter was, Solenko thought that he recognized the man; he had seen him hovering about the station platform in days past. Perhaps a railroad official, perhaps the "someone" that Sasha had mentioned so mysteriously.

He found him on the opposite side of the snowy square, waiting beside a droshky. As Solenko came near, he indicated that they should stroll about the square.

"My name is Latsis," he began. "I am assistant to Comrade Dzerzhinsky, Director of the Extraordinary Commission for Combating Counterrevolution and Sabotage." He spoke through thin lips with an accent that Solenko recognized as Lett. "You have heard of us?"

"No."

"We are also called the Cheka. A new organization." He eyed Solenko closely. "The yard superintendent tells us you are a good railroad man; that you are intelligent and ambitious."

"Very intelligent, very ambitious."

"And well placed for our purposes. The Revolution depends on speedy and safe rail transport. If you work for us, you will be well paid, in addition to your regular wages."

So money was not to be abolished. At least not yet. "What do I do for this pay?"

Latsis pointed an index finger at his eyes, then at his ear.

"An informer?"

"A defender of the Revolution against its enemies. You will report anyone you suspect might be a Tsarist or otherwise against us—especially anyone who might sabotage our trains." Solenko stared at the steam caused by their breath, at the people trudging through the snow, at the droshky and the horse stamping its hooves. "I'll think about it."

"And we shall talk again. Here. The same time tomorrow."

Solenko spent the evening pondering Latsis' proposal. The Cheka was clearly the Bolshevik secret police, a version of the Tsar's dreaded Okhrana. If he refused to be recruited, they likely had the influence to bring about his discharge by the railroad. On the other hand—and this thought was exciting with promise—he was being offered a chance to join Russia's new order. To be next to power was power itself.

The following afternoon Latsis was waiting in the square. "Well?"

"There is a man I overheard the other day," Solenko said. "He was arguing with someone I do not know. He said he does not think the Tsar should have abdicated. He does not believe the Tsarina was a German spy, or that she was lover to the monk Rasputin."

"Who said these things?"

"The assistant station superintendent."

"He is one of us."

Solenko bit his lip. So the assistant superintendent was a *provocateur*. What an innocent he was. And more deflating, he was not alone; there were others at the Finland Station. He was not special, after all.

Latsis read his thoughts and smiled encouragingly. "To-morrow you will do better."

The next day they met again in the square and Solenko gave Latsis the names of two men in the locomotive sheds who had declared that Lenin was a false leader who would betray his promises to the Russian people. Latsis jotted the names in a notebook, and the next evening when Solenko returned to his lodging house, there was an envelope slipped under his door. Inside were ten rubles. The two men at the locomotive sheds were replaced by others and never seen again.

In the following weeks Solenko became aware that the Finland Station was thronged with Cheka men. Some were railroad personnel, others posed as passengers waiting for their trains. All showed an uncommon interest in travelers with manicured fingernails. These were hurried into lavatories and their clothing inspected for hidden gold rubles and gems; if found, they would never reach Sweden and freedom.

On March 3, 1918, the Bolsheviks signed humiliating peace terms with Germany and gave up Poland and the Baltic states. A few days later Latsis appeared again at the Finland Station and escorted Solenko into the square for his first meeting with the director of the Cheka. Felix Dzerzhinsky spoke with a Polish accent. His face was slightly effeminate, with soft eyes and a delicate mouth; but his manner was coldly authoritarian.

"Comrade Lenin is moving the government to Moscow," he said without preamble. "You will leave Petrograd with us."

Solenko felt his pulse pound. He was being chosen by the director himself. "To work in the Moscow depot?"

"Yes. It is necessary to have men who are not identified with us. Men without families or friends in Moscow, with no memories of the city, nothing to compromise their actions."

Solenko disliked Moscow. After the Parisian beauty of Petrograd, Moscow was ugly, the Kremlin vast and depressing, the people sullen. Moreover, the Bolshevik government was faltering. Lenin had banned all opposition newspapers, yet adverse news still leaked out. The Socialist Revolutionary Party was denouncing the surrender to Germany and gaining strength; the German Ambassador was assassinated; bridges were bombed; there were rumors that a huge White Army in far eastern Siberia was fighting its way westward. Cheka squads roamed Moscow to round up suspected Tsarists and black marketeers and shoot them in alleyways. Hundreds of the lesser nobility suffered "bloodless execution"; they were herded into freight cars, without water or food or heat, and shipped to the coldest region of Siberia, where their frozen bodies were dumped into common graves.

Solenko tried to close his eyes to the situation. He was, he told himself, simply a foreman at the railroad station who must occasionally report subversive activities. His real work, he rationalized, was the maintenance of the railroad yard of the most important depot in Russia. Time itself would bring an end to the Bolsheviks and the Cheka. After that, Fortune would surely smile again on Yuri Solenko.

Instead, it frowned on him. In the second week of July two bombs exploded under the depot's main tracks. Immediately Solenko was summoned to Latsis' office at Cheka headquarters on Lubyanka Square.

"You have disappointed us! You have failed us!" Latsis began in a shrill voice. "What do we hear from you? The names of a few lazy workers. A man who steals coal from a locomotive. Someone who reads a Socialist manifesto. But when bombs are put under the tracks, you see nothing!"

"No one else did, either, Comrade."

Latsis was not listening. "There are enemies everywhere. They must be exterminated! Sent to the firing squad!"

It was the tirade of a frightened man, Solenko thought. "Do you wish me to resign?" he asked hopefully.

"No one resigns—except one way." Solenko understood the meaning; he had heard whisperings about the deep cellars below headquarters and the machine guns that provided instant solutions.

Latsis scowled into space for a moment, then pushed back from his desk. "Wait here." He opened a side door and closed it behind him. Solenko could hear muffled voices. Then Latsis opened the door again and beckoned him into the adjoining office. A man stood staring out the window. It was the director of the Cheka, Felix Dzerzhinsky. He spoke over his shoulder to Solenko.

"It has been decided to transfer you to another area. A new duty. Something to test your mettle, to harden you. What do you say to that?"

"I would be most grateful," Solenko replied, knowing he had no choice.

Dzerzhinsky turned and faced him with a smile that was

soft, almost feminine. "Then we talked at the right time. I am looking for a man, a railroad man, to send to the Urals. It will be a brief mission, but most important. What do you know about Ekaterinburg?"

"It is on the line from Petrograd to Omsk, and also served by a branch line from the Trans-Siberian Railroad. A mining town, I think."

Dzerzhinsky grunted approval. "You will report to Yakov Yurovsky at Cheka headquarters in Ekaterinburg. Yurovsky will be in charge of the matter of the Romanov Family. The military situation to the east is unfavorable and requires that the prisoners be moved to a place more secure. You will be aboard the Romanov train. You will see that there is no sabotage. And no more bombs, understand?"

Solenko glanced at Latsis, who still wore a sour expression. He was being promoted!

"I understand. Shall I send reports directly to you?"

"No reports. Only watchfulness. You will leave on tonight's train."

Ekaterinburg, Siberia
July 16, 1918

At exactly four o'clock in the afternoon the prisoners were allowed their daily walk in the dusty and withered garden. They came out of the stone house by twos; first, a pair of guards with rifles; then the two elder Grand Duchesses, the sisters Olga and Tatiana; then the younger Grand Duchesses, Marie and Anastasia, followed by Nicholas, the father, and Yuri Solenko, with a revolver tucked into his belt. Bringing up the rear pattered the two particolored spaniels, Jamie and Joy. The guards took up stations about the garden and the machine gunner on the rooftop swung his weapon to cover the street and the square beyond. The machine gunner was chiefly for psychological effect upon the prisoners, for the street and square were guarded by companies of Red troops to prevent the approach of any would-be rescuers.

If anything, the House of Special Purpose, as it was officially termed, was more depressing than a conventional prison. Formerly the residence of a prominent merchant, it had been enclosed by a high wooden stockade to shut out all view of the town; and on the second floor of the house, where the prisoners were quartered, the windows had been barred and made opaque with whitewash to further increase the sense of isolation. But it was an isolation that also weighed upon the captors, especially Solenko. In the railroad yards he had been able to move about freely, to joke with his co-workers, and to go home at night. Here he must sleep in the guardroom on the ground floor. When he had arrived in Ekaterinburg, three days earlier, Solenko had expected Yakov Yurovsky to unfold his plan for the removal of the Romanovs to some new place of confinement. Yurovsky had dismissed the subject. "You'll hear when the time comes. Meanwhile, you are simply Moscow's liaison. You will report to Comrades Medvedev or Nikulin whenever I'm away on other matters." And away he was, from breakfast till supper.

So Solenko stood guard in the garden, sweltering under the July sun, and watched Nicholas Romanov walk slowly arm in arm with Olga and Tatiana, while Anastasia and Marie amused the spaniels by tossing a ball for them to retrieve. They were, he thought, a strangely confident family considering their situation. Did they sense that the White Army was near? Perhaps that priest, Father Storozhev, who had come to the house to conduct religious services, had whispered that rescue was near.

Solenko's musings were interrupted by a voice beside him. "Which one would you take?" It was Vasili, one of the guards —small, pinch-faced, bandy-legged and cocky. He nodded toward Anastasia. "The pudgy one could be fun."

26

"If you like children." Solenko knew all their ages—Anastasia, sixteen; Marie, eighteen; Tatiana, twenty-one; Olga, twenty-two. Tatiana was the most appealing to Solenko. She was both pretty and tall; her eyes were a deep gray that shaded into brown when she was excited. Even in her worn and patched summer dress, he thought her manner was more aristocratic than her father's. On that particular afternoon, Nicholas Romanov, once the most powerful ruler in the world, appeared anything but regal. His khaki tunic and trousers were frayed and patched, his boots scuffed and worn. He might have been a soldier straight from the trenches, weary-eyed and gray, except for one contradiction: the face that bore such a startling resemblance to his cousin, King George the Fifth of England.

Vasili still stared at Anastasia. "That one is not such a child, if she had a lover. They all did, you know. Four whores doing everything their mother did with Rasputin. Or do you think those were just stories?"

Solenko shrugged. He disliked the attempt to draw him out. Vasili was like the other members of the Cheka squad; they resented the new man from Moscow, so obviously their superior.

"Get back to your post," he muttered to Vasili as he saw Nicholas approaching as if he wished to speak.

As Vasili moved off, Nicholas said, "I have a complaint to make to Commandant Yurovsky."

"He's away on special business."

"I know. But I wish you would be good enough to relay my words to him. Our cook is upset because the kitchen boy was taken away this morning. The cook says it is very difficult to feed us all without the boy's help. He would like him to return."

"I will give the Commandant your message."

"Thank you."

Finally a buzzer sounded within the house. It was time to

27

escort the prisoners back to their quarters. The four daughters filed upstairs to their bedroom and Nicholas entered the room which he shared with the former Empress and their fourteen-year-old invalid son, Alexis. Solenko glanced in and saw the boy in his wheelchair and Dr. Botkin, the bearded former court physician, examining his crippled leg. Behind them, gray-haired Alexandra looked sadly at Nicholas and raised her hands in a gesture of despair. Solenko passed on to the bedroom of the four daughters, hoping that he might catch a view of the girls changing their dresses. Especially Tatiana. But no, they were simply sitting on their metal camp cots, as if waiting for something. Their room never failed to interest Solenko, so unlike the perfumed cubicles of the prostitutes he had frequented. Here there was an atmosphere of deep religiosity. On the dressing table were icons of Christ, and on the wall dozens of photographs of family picnics, of favorite members of the Imperial Guard, of aunts and uncles laughing and waving at the camera. Seeing these mementos of family produced in Solenko one of his rare pangs of envy, the envy of the parentless.

The four Grand Duchesses watched him calmly, until the spaniel Jamie began to growl and Anastasia swept him up into her lap to quiet him. "We'd like to be alone," Tatiana said coolly.

But he made no move. He stood there and surveyed Tatiana's figure and thought of the soft white body beneath her ragged dress. Then the buzzer in the hallway sounded twice; Commandant Yurovsky had returned and was in his office on the ground floor.

Solenko knocked on the door, waited a moment, then entered. Yurovsky was at his desk, lighting a cigar. He was stocky of build, with hair, beard and moustache black and unruly. He wore a permanently sly look, as if enjoying some private joke. He drew on the cigar and asked, "Anything to report?'

"Nothing. Except that Citizen Romanov says the cook is

making a fuss about sending away the kitchen boy this morning. Romanov wants him returned."

Yurovsky shook his head. "He's too young. Just a boy. The guards like him, and I don't want any hesitation." He saw Solenko's puzzled expression. "Close the hall door." When it was done, Yurovsky went on. "The Ekaterinburg Soviet has made a decision, which is also authorized by Moscow. We are to shoot the Romanovs, all of them. The servants as well." Yurovsky announced it as casually as if he were saying, "Tonight we shall play a game of cards."

Solenko thought rapidly. So there had never been a plan to move the Romanovs elsewhere. Director Dzerzhinsky had sent Solenko to Ekaterinburg for a different reason—he was to be Moscow's subtle warning to Yurovsky: You are being watched. Obey orders. And it was another proof of the growing Bolshevik weakness; the White Russians were gaining and might rally the nation behind Nicholas Romanov. If he were still alive.

Solenko saw that Yurovsky was waiting for his reaction. "When will it be?"

"Tonight. I've scouted all the hills around the city for a place to dispose of the bodies. There's an old mine shaft in the woods. Abandoned. I'm sure you will approve." Solenko noted the recognition of his importance. "This is just between us, understand. I will tell the others at the last minute, so they won't have time to think about it."

After the guards had eaten supper in the downstairs mess, Solenko and the guard Vasili posted themselves in the prisoners' dining room to oversee their evening meal. It was a gloomy room, paneled in dark woods, with a central chandelier that cast a yellowish light over the long table. Trupp the footman and Anna Demidova, who was the Empress's tall and husky personal maid, brought the first course to the table, and Nicholas said the grace and made the sign of the cross, which was repeated by the others. Solenko leaned against one wall and smoked and regarded the diners with an interest sharpened by knowledge of their fate. What would it be like to kill these people? He had shot his share in battle, but they had been enemies and strangers; he had never been a party to an execution. It would not be pleasant; but he had no choice. Until the Bolsheviks collapsed, Solenko himself was, in effect, a fellow prisoner of the Cheka.

It was a leisurely meal. The four daughters spoke lightly to each other in French; Dr. Botkin and Nicholas took turns cutting up the meat for Alexis. Mother and father exchanged remarks and called each other "Nicky" and "Sunny." Then footman Trupp and Anna Demidova entered with the dessert. Solenko considered them; no, he would not waste bullets on servants. He would shed only royal blood. There would be a distinction in that, an act of historical importance. As these thoughts passed through his mind, he saw Tatiana's luminous eyes meet his. She frowned and glanced away. Very well, she would be his special target. His bullets would bridge the gap between high-born privilege and lowly bastardy.

After supper the family went as usual into the drawing room. The daughters played bezique, Alexandra picked up her embroidery and Nicholas read James Fenimore Cooper to Alexis. Solenko alone remained on duty in the hallway outside while the rest of the Cheka gathered in the guardroom to hear Commandant Yurovsky's plans for the night. Vasili was the first to return.

"Well?" Solenko prompted.

Vasili wrinkled his nose and muttered, "They wasted a lot of good food tonight."

At ten-thirty the family went upstairs to their bedrooms. Solenko listened to their exchange of goodnights, posted a guard outside each door, then returned to the Commandant's office to smoke and drink vodka with Yurovsky.

In the long Siberian summer, in the far northern latitude of Ekaterinburg, twilight lasted until almost midnight. It was at that hour, when darkness finally came, that Yurovsky and Solenko heard the growl of motorcars drawing up outside the compound. "Right on time," Yurovsky said and motioned Solenko to follow him upstairs.

Nicholas, in his dressing gown, was the first to answer their knock. "Get dressed," Yurovsky said. "We're moving everybody to a safer place."

"Safer?" Nicholas echoed, still half asleep.

"The enemy is just outside the city. Wouldn't do for us to lose you, would it?"

Solenko noted the sudden spark of hope in Nicholas' eyes, and in Alexandra's, standing behind him. "Don't bother to pack your things," he said. "We'll send them along to you."

The deception was accepted without question. Nicholas, in uniform and wearing his military cap, carried the crippled Alexis down the stairs, followed by Alexandra in her heavy traveling coat. Anastasia bore the spaniel Jamie in her arms, with Joy bouncing beside her. Following the daughters came the servants. Maid Anna Demidova was last, bearing two pillows. Yurovsky gestured them into an unfinished basement room which adjoined the supply room. There they must wait a while, Yurovsky said. Nicholas looked about, noted that there was no place to sit and asked for chairs. Solenko beckoned several guards and relayed the request.

Still no one suspected. Alexandra seated herself on one chair, a pillow at her back; Nicholas took the second chair and Alexis reclined on the third, with his head resting on his father's shoulder. The four daughters ranged themselves behind, with Dr. Botkin, footman Trupp, cook Kharitonov and Anna Demidova, still clutching one of the pillows.

"We won't be long," Yurovsky told them and went with Solenko into the hallway and closed the door. The rest of the squad, ten in number, had assembled around a turn in the hall, and there Yurovsky gave the final orders. "Draw your revolvers, but hold them behind you. When we go in, wait till

I fire. And remember, the honor of killing Citizen Romanov is mine." Then he led the way back to the basement room and the squad filed in behind. The prisoners were as before, no one had moved; they looked, Solenko thought, like a group waiting at a railroad station for the arrival of their train.

Yurovsky stepped toward Nicholas. "Your journey is over," he said. "By order of the Soviet Council, we are to shoot you."

Nicholas started to his feet and Yurovsky fired into his face. As he toppled, Solenko, determined to share in it, sent a bullet into his chest. He swung his revolver toward Alexandra. As she made the sign of the cross he fired twice, then took quick aim at Tatiana and pressed the trigger three times. Everyone was firing now; the basement was a roar of explosions. Bodies pitched forward and convulsed on the floor. Only Anna Demidova still stood, unhurt. *"Kristos! O Kristos!"* she shrieked and began running from wall to wall. Revolvers aimed at her and clicked harmlessly; the ammunition was gone. "Bayonets!" Yurovsky shouted. The squad pushed into the supply room and returned with rifles. Demidova, still screaming *"Kristos!"* backed away, holding the pillow to her chest. Solenko forgot his resolution to shed only royal blood and lunged with his bayonet. The blade deflected against something solid within the pillow and he thrust again, lower, and pierced her abdomen. She cried out, flung herself sideways and met more bayonets.

For a moment there was silence. Then a scream, and Anastasia struggled to her knees. She had escaped the bullets and had merely fainted. She flung up an arm at the descending bayonets, then crumpled backward. Jamie leaped onto her body with a howl of grief and Vasili brought his rifle butt down on the dog's skull.

It was over. The sole survivor was the spaniel named Joy.

Commandant Yurovsky ordered that the House of Special Purpose be cleared of all evidences of the Romanovs. Some of the squad carried clothing and photographs and icons to the various stoves and burned them. Others wrapped the bodies in canvas and took them to the waiting truck. Solenko and Vasili and a guard named Pyotr were detailed to clean and scrub the execution room. It was there, while Vasili and Pyotr were carrying out the chairs, that Solenko gathered the remnants of the pillow which Anna Demidova had held to her chest. What was inside, he wondered, that his bayonet had struck? Then the answer tumbled out at his feet. A small metal box. The lock had been sprung by his bayonet point and the lid yielded readily. Solenko gasped, sank down on his knees and gaped at the astounding contents—a dazzle of diamonds, rubies, emeralds, sapphires, jeweled medals, and a strange flat jewel, brown in color and shaped like a domino.

"We're partners in this," Vasili's voice said behind him.

"Sssh!" Solenko hissed, hearing Pyotr's footsteps in the hallway.

"Partners?" Vasili's fingers were already closing on a handful of jewels.

"Yes. But shut up."

When Pyotr entered, the box was empty and their pockets filled.

By dawn the motorcade reached the clearing in the woods and the abandoned mine known as the Four Brothers. They were an hour's drive from Ekaterinburg and could work without danger of observation. The eleven bodies were unloaded from the truck and carried to an area of bare clay near the vertical mine shaft. Then Yurovsky led the men into the brush where he had cached axes and saws and drums of gasoline and vats of sulphuric acid. These were brought into the clearing, then pine trees were felled, cut up, and a bonfire lighted. Now it was time to strip the bodies. Solenko went directly to Tatiana, who lay face up, her gray-brown eyes still open, a trickle of dried blood on her lower lip and chin. He knelt down and ripped away her jacket, her blouse, her corset. Between the cups of her blood-soaked brassiere, pinned to the joining, he

33

discovered a small golden figure, a mermaid clasping a black pearl in its hands. Of little value, he thought, except that it had belonged to Tatiana. He added it to the treasure in his pockets. Now, at long last, he was to see her breasts. He pulled the torso upright and unfastened the brassiere. As he did so, he saw something tiny fall to the earth and flash in the sunlight. An unset diamond.

He decided that it must have come from the brassiere. He inspected it with trembling fingers and found a bullet hole, his bullet hole, in the cup for the left breast. A second diamond tumbled out. The brassiere must have a false lining. He ripped at it with his teeth and there was a cascade of rubies and emeralds and more diamonds. He tore open the hem of Tatiana's skirt. More jewels. He twisted off the cloth-covered buttons of her jacket. Sewn within were still more.

He heard whoops of glee all around him; others were making similar discoveries. Yurovsky held up a handful of gems he had found in the clothing of Alexandra. "We're rich!" he shouted. "Put everything in one pile! We share evenly!"

Solenko had no such intention. He would make a token contribution and say nothing of the treasure from the metal box.

By now the bonfire, fueled with gasoline, was a superheated blaze. It was time for the dismemberment. Axes swung, bit through flesh and bone, and severed heads and arms and legs joined the flames. Solenko's stomach churned at the stench. He gazed at the slender defenseless body at his feet and started to turn away. Yurovsky saw his action and kicked an ax toward him. "Get on with it."

He picked up the ax and looked downward again. Tatiana's eyes seemed to be staring at the blade. He tried to close his mind to the sight, to concentrate on the glittering fortune in his pockets. It was useless.

Yurovsky stepped closer, enjoying his discomfort. "You surprise me, Comrade. All you have to do is think of the centuries her kind has done things like this to us. Then it's merely an eye for an eye, a head for a head."

Solenko took a deep breath, raised the blade high, then swung it flashing downward.

That night the men slept on the ground. When Solenko thought everyone was asleep, he slipped into the woods and transferred the jewels from his pockets to the toes of his boots. When he returned he saw Vasili sitting up and grinning at him. He had guessed. "You know what I'm going to do?" he whispered. "I'm buying a fur coat and a farm and cattle—and a dozen virgins! What about you?"

"Don't know yet." But Solenko did know. His jewels would buy a greater prize—his escape from the Cheka. They would be his passport to safety and a magnificent future somewhere outside Russia. . . .

They labored at the site for two days to complete their work. The bonfire, even augmented by gasoline, could not destroy the thigh bones and knuckles and pelvises; they had to be dissolved by sulphuric acid. The final residue was dumped down the mine shaft, along with a miscellany of corset stays, false teeth, and the body of Jamie, which was not considered worth the trouble to burn.

On the third morning a messenger from Cheka head-quarters arrived with alarming news. The White forces, augmented by a Czech army, were one day's march to the south of Ekaterinburg. The Red garrison had been ordered to en-train and move south along the rail line to Chelyabinsk and make a last-ditch defense. Hearing this, Yurovsky ordered an immediate return to Ekaterinburg. "And when we get back," he added, "tell no one what you've been doing here. Even under torture."

They found the city preparing for siege. Shopkeepers were locking up, people were hurrying toward their homes; com-panies of Red troops with full fieldpack were marching toward

the railroad depot; at Cheka headquarters in the Hotel Amer-
inskaya men were carrying files into the street and burning
them. Solenko had already decided on his own course of action. He followed Yurovsky into the hotel, lost him in the
crowd and confusion, then found him in his office, clearing
out his desk.

"Commandant, I want new identification papers. False, if
possible."

"Why?"

"Your squad dislikes me because I'm their superior. I'm
Moscow's man. They would enjoy telling that to the Whites."

Yurovsky sniffed. "Probably. But from now on it's every
man for himself."

"Is that what I am to take back to Director Dzerzhinsky?"

"*If* you get back." Yurovsky hesitated and frowned; the
name Dzerzhinsky still carried weight. "You intend to hide
out?"

Solenko nodded.

"Where?"

"I'll find a place."

"All right. Go down the hall to the end room. Perhaps they
haven't burned those files yet."

The room was deserted and the filing cabinets still intact.
But for how long? Solenko raced from drawer to drawer,
dumping out the contents and pawing through the folders.
Finally he found what he needed: a file on one Serge Malinkov, a merchant of Omsk, suspected White agent, jailed and
awaiting sentence. There was a Red railroad pass, probably
forged, and a White railroad pass, probably genuine. Solenko
took both. But Malinkov's identification card posed a problem; his height was given as five feet three inches. Solenko
erased the "five" and typed in "six." The final step was to pry
off Malinkov's photograph and substitute Solenko's from his
own identification card. Then he moved down the hallway,
joined the stream of men carrying files out into the street,
crossed to the other side and walked rapidly away.

Lest he be seen and recognized, he approached the railroad depot through the deserted alleys of the warehouse district. It was there, in one of the alleys, that he heard footsteps behind him. He swung around but saw no one. He walked faster, and again heard the footsteps; they, too, had increased their speed. Again he turned, and again saw no one. And the footsteps had stopped. He increased his pace to a half-run. When he had gone a little distance, he whirled again. This time he saw a man's figure disappear into a doorway. He reached inside his coat for his revolver; it was gone. Then he remembered; he had used it to hammer the lock on one of the file drawers and laid it aside. He began to sweat and feel panic. No one must rob him of his jewels, his chance for a new life.

He saw that just ahead the alley was intersected by another. When he reached it, he turned into the side alley, ran toward a pile of packing crates and slipped behind. He listened. The footsteps were still following; then they were almost to the crates. As he heard them pass, he sprang. One blow knocked the revolver from the man's hand, then Solenko's thumbs jammed against his carotid arteries. In a few seconds he sagged to the ground.

It was Vasili. Dead.

Solenko's leaving the hotel had been noted after all. Vasili had wanted Solenko's jewels, just as Solenko now wanted Vasili's. He retrieved the revolver, pulled the body behind the screen of packing crates and searched the coat. He found only a Cheka card, which might come in handy. He went through the trouser pockets; this was better—there was a surprising amount of rubles, paper and gold and silver. Where had Vasili gotten so many? Had he managed to loot the Cheka safe at the hotel, or had he already sold his jewels? Then Solenko remembered the boots and pulled them off. Yes, there was a knotted handkerchief stuffed into one toe. Solenko grinned contentedly and transferred the handkerchief to his own boot. Two lots of Romanov jewels—now he was incredibly rich, powerful, invincible.

At the train depot the last of the troops were boarding the boxcars. Solenko was not in uniform, he was without rifle and fieldpack; therefore he would have to act boldly. He strode toward the nearest boxcar. "You, there!" a Red captain shouted and came toward him. Solenko's first inclination was to bolt; then he recovered and advanced on the captain. "What's the meaning of this? Who are you?" he demanded coldly. The captain was taken aback and Solenko pushed his advantage. He waved Vasili's identification card. "I'm Cheka. On secret orders. Interfere and I'll take you in." The captain paled, mumbled apologies, escorted him to the boxcar and saluted.

One hour passed, then two, then three; and still the train wound its way southward through the hills. The soldiers in Solenko's car became restive; how far were they going? According to reports, the enemy was only a day's march south of Ekaterinburg, yet the train had already passed that point. Clearly, the reports had exaggerated; perhaps the enemy was only then leaving Chelyabinsk. Just when everyone had agreed on that supposition, the train jolted to a halt and the troops were ordered from the cars. They were, Solenko noted, in a rocky defile. The light of day was fading, it would soon be midnight. Surely they would not make camp at that hour in such dangerous terrain. Then there was another flurry of orders bawled out: Form up! March out! Quick step! Solenko loitered until the final squad grouped up, and fell into place in the last line. When darkness was complete, he simply stopped marching and the troops disappeared before him into the night. Then he clambered up one side of the defile until he found a boulder large enough to shield him, stretched out behind it and went to sleep.

He woke to the sound of artillery fire and then rifles. It was to the south and not far distant. The sun was already high. In a while the firing ended. Solenko peered cautiously around the border and saw soldiers running northward through the defile.

The Reds were in full rout. A few minutes later the vanguard of the advancing Whites appeared, and behind them a *broneviki*, an armored train with iron sheeting on the sides of the boxcars and sandbags on the rooftops to shield the machine gunners.

In midafternoon Solenko judged it safe to leave the shelter of the boulder. He reached the railroad tracks and struck south. He walked the balance of the day without sighting another troop train, and those humans he saw were dead and already drawing flies. By evening he had reached the plains. He was desperately hungry and thirsty. He sighted a rabbit and killed it with one shot of Vasili's revolver. As he picked it up, he saw the wide, surprised eyes, so like Tatiana's. And there was blood dripping from its mouth. Then hunger won out over memory; he twisted off the head and devoured the raw flesh and drank the warm blood.

On the evening of the third day he saw the rooftops of Chelyabinsk and the white flags of the anti-Bolsheviks. He waited until darkness to enter the town, for his stubbled cheeks and filthy clothing might arouse suspicion if he met a police patrol. He skulked down alleyways toward the railway depot until he located a house where men were going in and out and balalaika music could be heard. The madam of the brothel opened the door, stared at the unpromising figure before her and shook her head. Then she saw Solenko's handful of ruble notes.

That night, for the first time in a week, he slept in a bed. In the morning he gave a silver ruble to the maid and asked for a razor and soap and directions to a store that might sell used clothing.

"You must be off one of the refugee trains," the merchant said glumly, surveying his filthy garb and worn-through boots. "Any money?" Solenko produced more of Vasili's rubles and the merchant turned cheerful. "At least you saved something. I've seen some families down at the depot whose farms had been burned out. All they brought with them was maybe a goose or a goat to sell in our markets. They were all anti-Bolsheviks, so why would our troops do that to them?"

"That's civil war," Solenko answered absently. His eyes were fixed on a newspaper on the counter. The headline on the front page shouted: EKATERINBURG IS OURS! A second headline read: SEARCH FOR ROYAL FAMILY.

By now, Solenko thought uneasily, the Whites must have discovered the basement room in the House of Special Purpose. The bullet-shattered walls would suggest the worst. There would be questions, perhaps torture, and somebody would talk. Possibly Yurovsky. It would be like him to say that the killings were carried out by order of Director Dzerzhinsky's agent from Moscow. Then a description would be circulated. Not only in Ekaterinburg, but throughout White Siberia.

At the railroad depot the ticket seller shrugged; train schedules were meaningless. Chelyabinsk might originate a train eastbound on the Trans-Siberian Railroad tomorrow, or possibly the next day. Who knew?

For the following two days and nights Solenko secluded himself at the brothel and waited. In the afternoons he played cards with the girls in the parlor, drank endless glasses of tea from their burbling samovar and chose one of the group to go up to his room; in the evenings, more cards, more tea (but no vodka lest he grow loose-tongued) and finally another girl. He slept soundly, except on the second night, when he awoke with a shout, bathed in sweat. The hall door opened and a girl peered in.

"What's wrong?"

"Nothing. A nightmare."

She laughed. "We don't permit nightmares here." She entered and sat on the bedside and saw the sweat on his brow. "What could frighten a big man like you? What could you dream about?"

He dared not tell her. It was only a rabbit he had shot. With wide, surprised eyes.

On the third day an eastbound train was readied and he bought a second-class ticket to Omsk, the provisional capital of White Siberia. There he changed to another train that carried him through vast wheatlands to Irkutsk; thence, on another train, through endless timberlands, over mighty rivers and past the great inland sea of Lake Baykal, to Chita and Khabarovsk, and finally south to Vladivostok, on the Sea of Japan.

At last Solenko felt secure. Vladivostok was thronged with Japanese marines, with French and British and American troops readying for their push westward against the Bolsheviks. Whenever a military patrol stopped Solenko, they glanced casually through his papers and accepted without question that Serge Malinkov, merchant of Omsk, was in Vladivostok to import Chinese rice for the hungry of Mother Russia. It was a noble humanitarian mission, the Provisional Siberian Customs and Immigration Officer agreed, and stamped his exit permit and wished him well.

His first view of Shanghai was from the ferry that connected the railway depot to the west bank of the Whangpoo Channel of the Yangtze Kiang. The city was a surprise. It did not appear to be an Oriental metropolis of three million Chinese; rather it resembled a European city much like Petrograd. A broad boulevard ran along the river embankment, with a serpentine of autos, trucks and streetcars. Beyond, on the far side of the boulevard, was a massive array of stone buildings with copper domes and awninged windows. This was the famous Bund of the International Settlement and the adjoining French Concession with its tree-lined avenues and splendid residences. It was not until Solenko turned his eyes to the south that he saw a portion of the Old City, the native quarter, and its miles of go-downs and shipping docks.

The docks were Solenko's goal, which he reached by street-car. Then, on foot and sweating under the August sun, he made his way along the wharves and inspected the Chinese coastal junks, the freighters and passenger liners that flew the flags of Australia, France, Britain, the United States and Japan. Surely one of them would sign him on as a deckhand. And just as surely, some member of the crew would go through his clothing while he slept and find the jewels hidden in his boots. His own safety would be to travel as a passenger in a private cabin. But to where? And how could he pay for his passage, even third class? Vasili's few remaining silver and gold rubles would not carry him past Yokohama. The Romanov jewels were too fine and too large to sacrifice to a local moneylender; he would not fritter them away as most dull-witted thieves would do. There was, of course, the little gold mermaid with the black pearl which he had taken from Tatiana's brassiere, and yet he hesitated; it had meant something special to Tatiana, and so to him. He must, if at all possible, keep it as a good luck piece, a talisman.

Then, as if the mermaid were rewarding him for his decision, he heard a voice call out, *"Tovarich!"* For a moment he thought it was his imagination; perhaps it was not a human voice but the whine and chatter of a loading boom aboard one of the freighters. Then he heard it again: *"Tovarich!"* It was a woman's voice.

He glanced over his shoulder; a coolie and his rickshaw were bearing down upon him. Seated in back was a woman holding a parasol above her blond head. As they came abreast, Solenko saw that she was young and rather plain, but her brown eyes and her smile were warm and winning.

"How did you know I was Russian?"

"Your clothes. Also I was guessing. I'm Sonya."

Solenko was puzzled; her voice was educated, upper-class, her skin fine; yet it was clear that she was a street girl. "Do you fancy me?" she asked, as if to remove doubt.

"I've just arrived," he temporized. "I haven't even looked for a hotel."

"I can help you. I know Shanghai well. And if you fancy me—" She let the sentence dangle. "Would you pay in taels?"

"Rubles."

She made a face. "They are only paper."

"Then a silver ruble?"

At that she brightened and patted the seat beside her in the rickshaw.

Solenko was bewildered by the sights and sounds and smells as they moved through the humid alleys of the Old City. Vendors ran alongside the rickshaw and shouted their wares; coolies by the hundreds streamed past with sweatbands across their foreheads and mountainous cargoes strapped to their backs; women in black pajamas gossiped in doorways and laughed in high singsong voices; old men carried cages with pet canaries and crickets; boys played bamboo flutes and relieved themselves in the gutters; dogs barked, chickens cackled, pigs squealed. And everywhere there was the smell of cooking.

Sonya's room was on the top floor of a rickety wooden building close to the French Concession. It was, she said, "the temporary home of many from Mother Russia." The room itself was immaculate and the bed turned down. Beside the tin washbasin on the chest was a silver icon and a framed photograph of two men in military uniform, one with gray hair, one with dark. "My father and my brother," Sonya said, seeing Solenko's interest. "My father was a general. The Bolsheviki shot him. That's why Andrei and I left for Vladivostok. When we came to Shanghai we had a good deal of money, but Andrei wanted more and gambled away everything. Now he's dead too. The smallpox."

"So you took to the streets."

"Not at first. I went to the big ballrooms where the rich Chinese men go. But there were already too many Russian girls, too many pretty ones."

43

Solenko picked up the photograph and examined it more closely. He recognized the ribbons on the father's jacket; he was definitely a general. Then he noted, in the background, waves breaking upon a beach. "Odessa?" he asked.

"France. The Riviera. We went every year until the war. Oh, it was so beautiful! And everybody was friendly because we Russians spoke French and spent money like water. Cannes was our favorite because there were so many villas of our grand dukes and their mistresses, and they entertained Papa and Andrei and me as if we were family. They all admired Papa and they'd invite him along when they went to mass at our Cathedral in Nice, or to gamble at Monte Carlo."

"What about your mother?" There had been no mention of her.

"Oh, another man. Many men. She was like me."

She began to undress and the monologue continued without break. "Some day I will live on the Riviera. When I have saved enough. After every sailor, I put aside a little. Except the times when they cheat me, and I get nothing. But some day, oh, yes!"

Finally she stretched herself naked on the bed. She was very thin, Solenko noted, and there were bite marks on her thighs. Still, it was an inviting body, much like Tatiana's. Sonya giggled, seeing his own nakedness. "Mother of God, what will I do with you? You are more than *two* sailors! You are an entire navy!"

For the first time in months, Solenko laughed.

Afterward they propped against the pillows and smoked cigarettes. Unlike Solenko's other women, Sonya showed no inclination to dress and return to the streets. Perhaps, he thought, he had exhausted her; or perhaps she was glad to be with a fellow Russian. In any case, he decided, she could be useful. She was a general's daughter, a girl of breeding. Her present life aside, she represented a world which had been beyond his reach. But soon, no longer. Yes, he could learn from her.

"Suppose, Sonya," he said, "that you did not have to wait for sailors. Suppose I paid you to stay with me, and no one else."

She stared at him. "I was that good?" He nodded. "You could afford?"

"If I can sell a few things."

She glanced toward the small satchel on the floor which carried his belongings. "What kind of things?"

"Would you do it?"

"Perhaps." Then suddenly she was radiant. "Yes! I will show you where we Russians sell everything that we smuggle out. The Chinese buy our furs, icons, silk stockings, rings, brooches, even guns if they are worked with silver." She stopped and shook her head thoughtfully. "No, I could not be that good. I am not beautiful. What can I do for you that other women cannot?"

"You can teach me French."

"Ah! And then you will go away to France?"

"To the Riviera. You and I, together."

The following weeks were Solenko's first experience of domesticity. They slept together, went about the city together, ate *dim sum* together in the open-air restaurants, and strolled together along the Bund in the evening cool. And everywhere, hour after hour, Sonya conducted her French lessons. "I can do nothing for your bad Russian," she said. "It is a laboring man's Russian—but your French and your French accent will be very high-class. When we go to the Riviera, no one will suspect. You will be a gentleman."

Her confidence was justified. Solenko proved to have an ear for languages and an eye which quickly mastered the Western alphabet, so unlike the Cyrillic symbols of Russia. Moreover, he demonstrated a gift for figures; with ease he converted versts into kilometers and miles, rubles into francs and pounds and dollars. And there was progress in another direction. Sonya confessed her love for Solenko; she called him *dushki*, "my soul," and would no longer accept his rubles. Instead, she dipped into her own savings for their daily expenses. "Whatever you have to sell," she said, "must wait until we leave China. We must not spend the money foolishly or risk being robbed. Nothing, *dushki*, must keep us from the Riviera."

Still, she was curious as to what he wished to sell, and one time her questions hit upon the truth. Was it jewels? He laughed. Had she found any in his satchel? No. In his clothing? No. It did not occur to her to inspect what lay beneath a loose floorboard under their bed. In the end, she contented herself with the idea that her lover was waiting for the arrival of a friend from Russia, some unknown who was to smuggle out something of great value.

In reality, Solenko was waiting on the shipping news, which he followed each day in the pages of the English-French edition of the Shanghai *Mail*. In late October the front page headlined a report from Paris that the German front was crumbling, the war would end in a matter of weeks; and on the back page, in the shipping announcements, there was a notice of the Messagerie Maritime d' Extrême Orient. The *St. Michel*, arriving from Yokohama, would sail that evening for Singapore, Bombay and Marseilles.

"Tonight, my love," he told Sonya, "let us celebrate. Let us go to the finest restaurant in Shanghai. You will wear a beautiful new dress, a new handbag and new shoes."

Her eyes went wide. "*Dushki!* He's come!"

"Who?"

"Your friend from Russia!"

"Ah, you've guessed it. Now see what you can buy with these rubles." They were gold, his last two, but they would guarantee that Sonya's afternoon would be spent in the shops.

When she was gone, he took up the floorboard and sorted through his jewels. The least valuable, he decided, the one which would cause the least curiosity, was a sapphire. He placed it in his pocket and was about to transfer the rest to the security of his boots—then he paused. Something was missing. He spread out again the sparkling bits of red and green and blue and brilliant white. *Where was the golden mermaid?* He groaned and struck his forehead with his fist. The bitch! The little bitch! She had found his treasure. She had suspected what he might do to her, and had taken the mermaid to tell him she was not such a gullible fool after all.

Speed meant everything now. Within an hour Solenko sold the sapphire to a Chinese pawnbroker for nine hundred taels, which he converted at a bank into French francs.

The first lights of the evening were winking along the Bund as the *St. Michel* swung out into the Whangpoo Channel. Solenko stood at the railing, smoking and watching the city grow dim in the gathering fog. He wondered momentarily if Sonya was still waiting in her room for his return—the thieving whore. Then he dismissed the subject. He flicked his cigarette over the side and went below.

Two

New York City
July 17, 1927

IT WAS a sultry summer morning. On Fifth Avenue men in straw hats and women in summer dresses were already promenading the avenue of high fashion. Some paused to window-shop or to greet friends and repeat the latest jokes of Will Rogers and Fanny Brice; they gossiped about the newest speakeasies and "hot" review up in Harlem, about the next "sure thing" on Wall Street and tomorrow's ticker-tape welcome to Commander Richard E. Byrd and his flight crew for their feat of flying to France with the first official trans-atlantic airmail. A few on Fifth Avenue were even making their way to St. Patrick's Cathedral for late mass.

Farther uptown, at the corner of Madison Avenue and 121st Street, which in 1927 had not yet been engulfed by Harlem, another religious service was in progress in the Russian Cathedral of St. Nicholas. Within the vast interior, barren of pews and seats in the Russian manner, the congregation stood in devout silence while the bearded bishop and priests in resplendent robes and bearing golden crosses and smoking censers made obeisance before the gallery of icons, and the voices of a hidden choir rose and sank away and rose again in the pontifical liturgy. It was a scene which might have been plucked from *Boris Godunov*, were it not for the worshippers' American clothing and hair styles. For the most part, the congregation consisted of upper-class White Russians, emigré college professors, doctors, scientists and owners of fashionable shops; here and there a man of towering height and muscular build suggested a former Cossack officer.

Of all those present, the Brullov family was easily the most fashionably dressed. Fyodor (Ted) Brullov's suit was cut by one of Saville Row's finest tailors; his blond American wife, Helen, wore a French lace, and seven-year-old Anton was garbed in a junior adaptation of Brooks Brothers. A further distinction was that Helen, alone among the congregation, showed no interest in the services. She shifted her weight from one foot to the other, sighed with impatience, and cast glances of annoyance at her son, so full of childish piety, so desirous of his father's approval. The pontifical liturgy drew to a close, there was a moment's silence, then the silvery tinkle of a handbell. The bishop handed his staff to an altar boy and began to distribute lighted candles to the priests, who then moved to the center of the church and formed a circle. At the same time, the congregation filed to a counter at the rear of the Cathedral, dropped their contributions into the church box, accepted candles from attendants, lighted them and returned to their former places. The deep basses of the choir joined the soaring of sopranos in the opening passages of the *Repose of the Saints*. It was the beginning of the memorial

49

service for the Romanov family and their loyal servants on the ninth anniversary of their execution at Ekaterinburg.

The bishop and his priests faced toward the iconostasis and the bishop began to intone the names of the souls for whom prayers were to be said. Nicholas Alexandrovich . . . Alexandra Fedorovna . . . Alexis Nikolaevitch . . . Olga Nikolaevna . . . Tatiana Nikolaevna . . . Marie Nikolaevna . . . Anastasia Nikolaevna. . . .

At the mention of the Grand Duchess Tatiana, Ted Brullov's throat tightened and his intense brown eyes misted. His candle in his left hand, he crossed himself and sank to his knees and bowed forward to touch his brow against the floorboards. He heard a sob beside him; his son, too, was kneeling, bowing and touching his forehead to the floor. Overwhelmed, the father reached out an arm and clutched the boy and together they wept openly.

The memorial ended and the congregation began to move down the Cathedral's steps. As the Brullovs reached the pavement a square-faced man with thinning sandy hair thrust himself in front of Ted.

"Fyodor!"

For a moment, his thoughts still on the service, Ted Brullov did not recognize the man; he was out of context. Then: *"Andrei!"*

The two embraced each other and Brullov demanded, "What are you doing in New York?"

"On my way to Halifax and back to London," the man called Andrei said. "My brother died out in Chicago, and I came over to settle his affairs. I was going to stop by your store tomorrow for a talk." He smiled toward Helen. "But this is even better, because now I get to meet this lovely lady."

Brullov turned to his wife. "My dear, you've heard me talk of Andrei Katchin. The one and only Andrei . . ."

Helen nodded politely.

"And this is our son Anton."

The boy stared up at Katchin with an awed expression. "Sir,

did you really break your leg and hide diamonds and emeralds inside the cast so you could sneak them past the Bolsheviks?" Katchin chuckled. "So your father has been making a hero out of me, has he? Yes, it happened. But your father's way was a lot less painful—no broken bones, just a crutch with a hollow leg."

Before the boy could ready another question, Brullov threw his arm around Katchin. "This calls for a celebration. Tonight you're having dinner with us."

"Afraid I can't, Fyodor. I've already made an engagement. But I do want to talk to you. That's why I was coming to your store." He lowered his voice. "It's important."

"Then lunch? Now, at the Plaza."

"No. In private, please."

Brullov caught the urgency in Katchin's eyes; he turned to his wife and gave her the car keys. She was to drive home with their son. He would join them later.

The two men boarded a Fifth Avenue bus and ascended to the open-air upper deck for the ride downtown. At Thirty-sixth Street they left the bus, crossed to the east side of the avenue and walked to the middle of the block, where a marble-fronted store bore the legend above the bronze door:

BRULLOV & COMPANY
Fine Jewels

Ted Brullov unlocked the door, switched off the burglar alarm and led Katchin through the salesroom with its display cases empty of the usual weekday display of jewelry, then past his office and into the workroom in the rear. It was a high-ceilinged room dominated by a massive black Mosler safe, where the store's merchandise was kept overnight and on weekends. Alongside was a smaller safe that contained bars of gold and silver and platinum as well as boxes of loose gems waiting to be mounted into rings and brooches and necklaces and earrings. The center of the room was taken up by benches

51

with high stools, where Brullov's artisans worked with modeling clay and blowtorches and engraving tools and burnishing wheels.

Brullov made a sweeping gesture. "This is where I feel really at home. Not in my office or the showroom. The workroom is where everything begins, just as Papa Karl always told us." The reference was to Karl Fabergé, court jeweler to the Imperial Family in St. Petersburg. Brullov's father had been a work-manager for Fabergé and had brought Ted into the company as a junior designer, where he had met Andrei Katchin. They became the closest of friends, both seventeen at the time, and twenty-four when they had fled Russia—Katchin to London and Ted Brullov and his parents to New York City. Financed by the gems which the Brullovs had smuggled out of Russia, father and son opened a small jewelry store in Maiden Lane. It had prospered modestly until 1925, when Ted's parents were killed in an automobile accident. The proceeds of their life insurance, plus heavy borrowing, had enabled Ted to make his debut on Fifth Avenue, only a block south of the prestigious Tiffany.

Katchin gazed about the workroom with approval. "Makes my place look like pretty small beer. But in London we don't have big buyers, no stock market millionaires or rich bootleggers."

Brullov smiled at the rueful tone; Katchin was as competitive as ever. "You're doing all right, from what I hear. But what's this that you want to talk about?"

Katchin glanced about the empty workroom, as if there might be some invisible eavesdropper. "Would you have something to drink?"

"Of course." He guided Katchin back through the corridor to his private office. It was a simply furnished room with a large desk, an easy chair and a leather sofa. On the desk were the accouterments of the jeweler's trade—a dustproof glass case containing a pair of gem scales, a microscope, gem tweezers and a loupe. The wall opposite the desk was lined with framed photographs: the largest was a group photograph of Tsar Nicholas and Empress Alexandra and their five children; a smaller photograph was of the Grand Duchess Tatiana by herself. There was a street view of the granite-faced Fabergé store on Morskaya Street in St. Petersburg, and an interior view of one of the workrooms with Ted Brullov smiling into the camera.

Brullov gestured Katchin to the easy chair, opened a desk drawer and withdrew a bottle of vodka and two shot glasses. "Hard to get genuine vodka," he said. "Sometimes takes my bootlegger three months." He poured the liquor and the two men raised their glasses to each other and said *"Nazdorov'e!"*

Brullov studied his friend for a moment. Katchin's manner was nervous, almost apprehensive; his light-blue eyes seemed even paler than usual. "And now?"

"To begin with, do you still have the list?"

"The list?"

"The one we made in St. Petersburg."

"Oh. *Our* list. Certainly I have it."

"In the safe?"

"Hardly. It's not the sort of thing I'd want one of my staff to stumble onto."

"I think we should look at it."

Brullov's heavy eyebrows lifted momentarily. "Very well." He unlocked the center drawer above the kneehole of his desk, emptied the contents onto the blotter and turned the drawer upside down. Thumbtacked to the underside was a sheet of paper bearing a handwritten list of names. The first was Yakov Yurovsky, with an X preceding the name; the second, Yuri Dimitrovich Solenko, bore a question mark; the third, Vasili Kolodin, carried another X.

Katchin ran his eyes down the list. "On my copy I've gone into a little more detail. Yurovsky I marked 'liquidated by Stalin'; Solenko, 'whereabouts unknown'; Vasili Kolodin, 'strangled Ekaterinburg. Presumed robbery.' "

"You always were fond of details." Brullov smiled. "The

important thing is that of the twelve Cheka, seven have been killed so far. More mercifully, I regret, than the murders they committed in Ekaterinburg."

Katchin tapped his finger on a thirteenth name which had been added to Brullov's list, also with an X and a date in June, just three weeks past. "I don't have this one. Voikov wasn't Cheka."

"That's splitting hairs," Brullov replied. "Voikov supplied the gasoline and sulphuric acid to destroy the bodies. Nicely rewarded, too, as Soviet Ambassador to Poland. I was delighted to read of his assassination."

"The fellow who shot him—the London papers say he was a student, the son of one of the Tsar's officials. Could he be one of us?"

"Not likely. He'd have been more careful. He wouldn't shoot Voikov right in the Warsaw railroad station and then let Voikov turn around and empty his revolver at him. Lucky Voikov was a lousy shot."

"The next one may not be," Katchin said glumly. "That's what I want to talk about." He ran his finger down the names and stopped at Pyotr Pagodin. "This one will be in London next month."

"How do you know?"

"From one of our Moscow friends. Pagodin is now an assistant commissar in the Treasury. He's with the Soviet commission coming to London to auction off some of the crown jewels and art objects. You got the announcement from Christie's, didn't you?"

"And threw it in the wastebasket. Damned if I'll go over there and give those bloody murderers any dollar of mine."

"That's the way I feel," Katchin agreed. "Here's what I think we should do. We ask every important member of the Russian communities, here, in England, on the Continent, to sign a letter of protest to the London newspapers. We point out that the Imperial treasures are the loot of a gang of murderers. We ask the public to boycott the auction, not to give them one pound or franc or mark. We might even picket the auction." Katchin was about to elaborate when he saw the angry fire in Brullov's eyes.

"So *that's* what you wanted to talk to me about? A whimpering letter to the papers? A boycott?" Brullov's voice was cold with scorn. "Andrei, we swore an *oath*. On our sacred honor."

Katchin winced. "I was afraid you'd take it that way. But, Fyodor, we were young hotheads then. Now we're married, we have children. You have Anton; I have John and Anna. I have the responsibility of my brother's family. This Pagodin will be on guard after what just happened to Ambassador Voikov. We've got to be sensible. If we stir up public sentiment, we'll have done a very good thing."

"That's the way you'd sell it to the rest of our friends? 'A good thing'? Is that what you'd tell Boris in Stockholm, Leonid in Brussels, Igor in Paris?" Brullov tapped the list of Cheka names. "How many of these would have been eliminated by writing letters to the papers? They happened because men risked their lives to fulfill their oaths." Brullov paused to pour himself a second vodka. He downed it and made a decision. "I'll see you in London."

Katchin's face registered alarm. "Then what? Fyodor, you've always been reckless. Let some of the others do this."

"No! This will be my pleasure."

"All right. But don't try to involve me in your fanaticism."

"All I'll want from you is information."

Katchin rolled his eyes. "What kind?"

"I want to know what Pyotr Pagodin does in London. Where he goes, the people he sees, the hotel where he stays."

"An inquiry agent?"

"No! No detective. Nobody who might get to wondering and go to Scotland Yard. Just you and only you."

Brullov locked the bronze door of his store and watched Katchin disappear into the pedestrian traffic of Fifth Avenue.

He thought sadly how the years had altered the man. When the news of the tragedy at Ekaterinburg had reached Petrograd —the wartime name of St. Petersburg—Andrei had been the first to embrace Brullov's grand design for vengeance. Now prosperity and family had sapped his nerve. Perhaps it was too much to expect. It was Ted Brullov, not Katchin, who had been presented to His Majesty the Tsar, and so felt a personal loss. It was Brullov, not Katchin, who had spent those few golden moments with the Grand Duchess Tatiana and had fallen in love with her.

"Did he want to borrow money?" Helen asked, when her husband returned to the apartment on Washington Square.

"Oh, no. Just wanted some advice. He has a problem."

"A woman problem?"

Brullov smiled. "Andrei's married. And happily."

"Then if it's not money or a woman, it can't be much of a problem. Why was he so melodramatic about wanting to talk in privacy?"

"Oh, that's just Andrei."

Helen accepted it. "By the way, Tony and I went ahead and ate lunch without you. But we left plenty of chicken salad in the icebox."

"Where is Tony?"

"Taking a quick nap." She placed a kiss on her husband's ear and murmured, "I've talked him into going with the Bronson kids to the Harold Lloyd matinee."

Brullov noticed for the first time that his wife had changed into a housecoat and that she was wearing fresh perfume. "A trade, hmm? A matinee for a matinee?"

Another kiss, this time on his lips. "We'll have two whole hours."

Their lovemaking did not go well. Brullov realized that his caresses were almost perfunctory; he told Helen it was the sultry afternoon, which she did not entirely believe. "Maybe if we nap for a few minutes, it'll be better," she said. But Brullov could not nap: his mind was on London and Pyotr Pagodin. When Helen began to fondle him again, he could not respond.

"I know what it is," she decided sourly. "That damned memorial service this morning. Who wants to screw after a funeral?"

"You, for one," he said, attempting to be light.

"There's one thing I've decided," she went on, unheeding. "Next year I'm not going through another memorial. Nor Tony, either. I watched him this morning, imitating everything you did. Crossing himself, praying, kneeling, bowing to the floor, being the perfect little White Russian, instead of a normal American boy."

"He *is* normal. He just thought it would please me."

"Ha!"

Helen rose from the bed and sat naked before her vanity mirror and began to comb her blond hair. "You've filled Tony's mind with fantasies of a Russia that never was. From the very beginning it was bedtime stories about the Snow Maiden and Baba Yaga and the house that walked on hen's legs, about great balls in marble palaces with beautiful princesses and Cossack heroes and sleigh rides on the Neva. Nothing about the real Russia, the corruption and tyranny and . . . and . . ." She broke off abruptly.

"Yes? What else?" Brullov's voice was steely. The last time they had had such an argument, Helen had called Tsar Nicholas a weakling and a fool, a henpecked husband, and he had slapped his wife. And, by God, he'd do it again.

She veered away, as if remembering that incident. "All I'm saying, Ted, is that I'd be grateful if you'd stop living in your lost paradise. It would be far healthier for Tony if he heard about pirates and Daniel Boone and Tom Sawyer." She softened further; her tone was almost apologetic. "It's just awfully hard for a Philadelphia Yankee to understand you foreigners."

"And yet you chose me."

She sighed and smiled into the mirror. "Because I couldn't help myself. You *are* a remarkable man, you know."

The squall was past. Brullov slipped into his dressing gown, lighted a cigarette and went to the window and stared down into Washington Square. Young couples were walking hand in hand; children were skipping rope and blowing wheezy tunes on kazoos; a cotton-candy man pushed his cart through a flock of feeding pigeons. To the north, past the Arch, a marching band was practicing in readiness for tomorrow's official welcome for Commander Byrd. And tomorrow, Ted Brullov decided, it would be wise for him to double his life insurance.

The *Mauretania* moved in a cocoon of fog for most of the passage to England. Even at high noon it was cold and bleak when one walked the decks. Brullov was especially lonely, for on the last Atlantic crossing Helen and Tony had accompanied him. He had explained that the present trip would be no more than several days in London to restock his jewel inventory, with no time for sightseeing and social activity. Helen had accepted it at face value, which increased Brullov's sense of guilt. Each day he went to ship's Radio Room and sent home a message, a daily "I love you" or "I miss you." After several such messages, Helen had replied with her own radiogram: "What's wrong? No shipboard romance?" His wife's humor was followed the next day by another in a confessional vein: "The home fires are burning and so am I." Reading it, Brullov's spirits improved. Whatever their disagreements, the sexual attraction between them was an unbreakable bond. That, and their mutual love for Tony.

Throughout the tedious voyage he turned over in his mind the problem of Pyotr Pagodin. Brullov had no experience in assassinations; in his youthful days, when he had first conceived the notion of vengeance, the thought had a glamorous appeal. But now, faced with the proposed actuality, he realized that this was not the project for an amateur. He was no romantic revolutionary who could toss a bomb and go gladly to his own death. Life was far too pleasant to gamble away. And there was Helen, there was Tony....

It was late afternoon when the boat train from Southampton reached London. Brullov checked into his hotel, Brown's, on Dover Street, then took a taxi to Hatton Garden, which was the London counterpart of Maiden Lane. Jewel dealers, mostly Jewish, wearing fedora hats, stood about on the sidewalks showing one another papers of diamonds and haggling over prices. Andrei Katchin's shop was exactly as Brullov had remembered it from his last visit, two years before. It was on the ground floor of a Victorian brick building; there was but one window facing onto the street. The lettering in the window read:

KATCHIN JEWELS
Manufacturing & Wholesale

Brullov opened the glass front door, which was reinforced with iron netting. A warning buzzer sounded. Almost simultaneously a door at the rear of the tiny showroom opened and Katchin's head appeared. "Oh! It's you." He advanced toward Brullov, looking decidedly unhappy, and whispered, "Mind stepping outside a minute? Walk around the block, then come back."

"What's wrong?"

"My assistant's in the workroom. I'll tell him I'm shutting up."

It was clear that Katchin did not wish a witness to the meeting. Brullov did as instructed, and as he approached the shop a second time he saw an elderly man with a stoop leave and walk off in the opposite direction. Katchin locked the door behind Brullov, pulled down a blind over the door and another over the window. "It's only two days till the auction," he said. "I thought maybe you'd given it up."

"Didn't you get my letter?"

"Yes. But I was still hoping." He led Brullov to the rear of the shop and gestured him toward a chair which flanked an old rolltop desk. Katchin himself remained standing, as if he might decide to make a quick exit. He made polite inquiries about Helen and Tony and the Atlantic crossing until finally Brullov interrupted.

"Did you do what I asked?"

"As well as I could. I'm not a professional at this, you know." He unbuttoned his jeweler's waistcoat, which was designed with the pockets on the inside of the garment to foil pickpockets, removed a fold of paper and handed it to Brullov. "Wherever you read the initial *P,* that means Pagodin. And *S* stands for the Savoy, where he's staying with the rest of the commission. His room number is four twenty-one."

"How did you get the room number?" Brullov asked.

"I handed an envelope to the room clerk and watched which box he put it in."

"I hope you put something in the envelope."

"I'm not stupid," Katchin said, looking miffed. "I slipped in a girl's photograph and wrote a phone number on the back. If he calls the number, he'll find it's the Salvation Army."

Brullov laughed. Then: "You know if the other members of the commission are on the same floor?"

"They are. I took the elevator to Four and walked about. There were several chaps stationed along the hallway. Not from Scotland Yard; Russian faces and clothes. OGPU, most likely."

Brullov's eyes skimmed Katchin's report and noted that Pagodin had been the typical tourist. He had visited, along with his fellow commissioners, the Tower of London, the British Museum, Westminster Abbey. He had had a conversation with a streetwalker, but the bodyguards had interfered and sent her off. He had shopped at Harrods and Liberty's, alone except for a bodyguard. He had gone to four different custom bootmakers in Bond and Oxford Streets.

"I followed him into the first shop," Katchin said, "and saw the clerk measure his feet. I ordered a pair of shoes myself so I could watch. Pagodin ordered three pairs—and probably more in the other shops, too. But I didn't dare go into them, or the bodyguard might have recognized me."

"Sounds like he has a shoe fetish," Brullov mused. "Or just wanted some high-class English gear. I see that you didn't follow him this morning or afternoon."

"Because I thought you'd given up the idea. And I do have a business to run."

"Where do you think he will go tonight?"

"Nowhere. The whole group eat in the hotel, then take the elevator upstairs. I'd say the OGPU has warned them about making targets of themselves."

"Can you describe Pagodin?"

"Overweight. Fat, really. High forehead, starting to bald. Wears glasses with heavy rims. Oh, and quite short. Probably why he goes to custom shoemakers. He wears extra lifts in his heels."

"Vain, then. What about his bodyguard?"

"It's a different man each time, so I can't tell you. One other thing: Pagodin and the others carry furled umbrellas. They look a little heavier than usual. Might be a pigsticker inside." Katchin shook his head. "Give it up, Fyodor. Nobody can reach him."

"That's what I want him to think." Brullov folded the report and tucked it into his billfold. "I may want to phone you this evening. Will you be home?"

"Yes. I'll write you the number." Katchin did so and added, "If my wife or the kids answer, don't give your real name."

It was a sensible precaution, yet it irritated Brullov. Caution could easily turn to cowardice.

During dinner at Brown's Hotel, Brullov read through Katchin's report again. The incident with the streetwalker was intriguing. Pagodin might be vulnerable to a prostitute—but that meant involving a third person, which was out of the question. And the buying spree for shoes with built-up heels suggested nothing.

After dinner Brullov strolled down Bond Street and up Piccadilly to the Circus and watched the crowds and the circling traffic beneath thousands of light bulbs advertising Guinness Stout and Players Cigarettes and various nostrums for indigestion and constipation. Somewhere, he told himself, there must be a chink in Pagodin's armor, an Achilles heel. But nothing came to him. He turned north into Regent Street and gazed into the shop windows. Outside an antiquarian shop he paused to admire a display of dueling pistols and Victorian watches and antique brooches. A small announcement card caught his eye. SPECIAL COLLECTION OF MEDICI JEWELRY. INQUIRE WITHIN. Brullov gave a snort of triumph. *Medici!* Medici and built-up heels. Medici and the Achilles heel. . . . *Yes. Why not?*

He glanced at his wristwatch. Just past nine. Too early; he would have to put in some time. A cinema on Piccadilly helped him while away the next two hours. Then he hailed a taxi and directed the driver to the Savoy Hotel.

As he stepped off the elevator on the fourth floor he saw the first OGPU man. He was seated on a straight-backed chair directly opposite the elevator. To the right, down the hall, sat another; and to the left, still another. Brullov gambled that Room 421 was to the left and set off humming lightheartedly and twirling his room key from Brown's. As he drew near, the guard stood up, eyed Brullov carefully, then relaxed at the cheery smile, the hearty "Evening!" and watched the supposed hotel guest go humming down the hall and around a corner.

He had guessed correctly; Room 421 was to the left of the elevator. There was a pair of black shoes with built-up heels outside the door. A few steps beyond was the cross-hall, and down the hall a door that bore the word "Linens." Brullov tried the door; it was locked. He examined the keyhole and decided that it would accept a skeleton key.

A final bit of information he gleaned from the white-haired chief porter in the lobby. "I expect to be out until the small hours," he said. "Can you tell me how late I can have Boots polish my shoes?"

"He picks up around three A.M., sir. If it's after that, you can always ring down for special service."

"Thank you."

"You're welcome. And a pleasant evening, sir."

At seven o'clock the next morning Brullov telephoned Andrei Katchin and asked him to give his assistant the day off. Brullov would be at the shop at nine o'clock.

It was a repeat of the day before; the blinds on the front door and the window were drawn, and Katchin, at his rolltop desk, looked painfully uncomfortable. He listened in silence to Brullov's plan and studied the diagram Brullov had inked with a fountain pen on a sheet of hotel paper.

Finally Katchin spoke. "Reminds me of a Medici poison ring."

"That's where I got the idea. Dissolve crystals of cyanide of potassium in water and it will kill within seconds."

Katchin glowered at the word "cyanide." "And you expect me to supply it?"

"You're the best source—a manufacturing jeweler who uses it in gold refining. You've got the equipment to make the pressure plate, the steel needle and a powerful spring. You can even make me a skeleton key." Brullov watched the growing expression of resistance. "Don't say you can't do it. You were one of the best metalworkers in St. Petersburg."

"Then is not now."

"You can do it. Andrei, there's absolutely no way to trace it back to you."

"And if I say no?"

"Then the oath you swore with me and the others was a lie." Brullov's dark eyes turned cold, his voice grew guttural. "Justice must be done, or you will be a traitor to the memory of the Anointed Father of all the Russias, the Empress, our

Maturshka, to their children. Is *that* what I'm to tell the rest of our friends—that you're a coward, a betrayer of our vows?"

Katchin winced at the tirade. "Fyodor, this is not vengeance, this is religious mysticism. I spied for you, and that's as far as I go. I won't be an accessory to murder."

"An *execution!*" Brullov corrected. "An execution for one who killed the Royal Family, destroyed their bodies and denied them Christian burial." He waited for Katchin to surrender; but he did not. "Very well, then I'll find someone else to help me."

"Then do it!"

Brullov turned stiffly and strode to the shop entrance, banged the door behind him and started rapidly down the street, which was just beginning to come to life with jewel dealers. Then he heard Katchin's voice. "Fyodor! *Don't! I beg you!*" He caught up with Brullov and tugged on his arm and whispered, "Go to someone else, and they'll turn you in to Scotland Yard. I'll make the damned thing for you, God help me!"

It was what Brullov had hoped for. They returned to the shop and went over his design again. Katchin said he could complete the device that day and promised to deliver it at eight o'clock that evening in the safety of the gardens of the Victoria Embankment. "But even if I do my part," he concluded, "I still say you can't get away with it. It's just too goddamned dangerous."

Brullov smiled complacently. "That's why it's safe. Dare the impossible, and it becomes possible."

Meanwhile there were purchases that Brullov must make. He took a bus to Caledonian Road and turned off into the side streets, going from store to store in search of the necessaries—a cobbler's hammer, a small chisel, a needle-nosed pliers, a briefcase, a box of chalk sticks, an apron with spacious pockets and a cloth laundry bag with a drawstring. In a shabby secondhand shop he bought two pairs of shoes that a man in menial work might wear; and lastly, horn-rimmed eyeglasses with minimal correction for distance vision.

At eight o'clock that evening Brullov wandered along the paths in the gardens of the Victoria Embankment until he saw the figure of Andrei Katchin. "Before I give this to you, Fyodor," he said, "I want you to swear that if you're caught, you'll never mention my name."

"On my word of honor. I'll say I made the thing myself."

"Then *mazel und brocha*," Katchin said, using the Jewish jewel dealers' traditional wish for good luck and success, and transferred a small packet from his coat pocket to Brullov's hand. "So what will you do first?"

"Go back to the hotel and practice."

"But when?"

"Tomorrow night. After the auction."

"Two thousand pounds on my right. . . . Now against you, sir, at three thousand. . . . Four thousand in back. Any more? All through? Five thousand. Thank you, madam." The auctioneer, in evening clothes, presided over the bidding with the flair of an orchestra conductor.

Although Ted Brullov had no intention of bidding, he attended for dual purposes: to view with nostalgia the items from the land of his birth and to observe the man he intended to kill. When Brullov arrived at Number 8 King Street, St. James's Square, he found every seat in the hall aleady occupied and he was forced to join the standees in the rear. There was more than the usual tension of an auction, for there had never been such an offering of genuine royal Russian treasures. Collectors, dealers, society people, all shared a common gleam in their eyes—the lust to possess. And if not to possess, at least to behold the trappings of Imperial power and wealth.

Before the beginning of the bidding, the auctioneer had announced from the stage the terms of sale and had introduced the Soviet commissioners, who sat in the first row of seats. The three men had stood up and faced the audience and

65

bowed. Brullov immediately singled out Pyotr Pagodin; fat, balding, glasses, a doughy face of minimal intelligence. And on either side of that first row, Brullov had noted a pair of burlys standing with folded arms as they scanned the audience. The OGPU.

Brullov turned his attention to the catalogue. Most of the important jewelry was reserved for the latter part of the sale, the climax of the evening. Much of it was attributed to Catherine the Great and her succeeding empresses. Few articles were ascribed to the various tsars; still fewer had been the property of Nicholas and Alexandra Romanov, and most of these were limited to the famed *objets d'art* created by the studios of Karl Fabergé. It was these which opened the auction; a gallery assistant displayed the articles, one after another, under a spotlight against a black velvet screen—a dazzling parade of gold chess sets, rock-crystal peacocks with sapphire eyes, miniature dragons in gold and enamel, letter openers glittering with emeralds.

"And here," the auctioneer announced, "we have a magnificent malachite-and-gold cigarette box, ornamented with diamonds, the property of Nicholas the Second."

Brullov borrowed a pair of opera glasses from the dealer standing beside him. Yes. It was the same cigarette box he had seen on the Tsar's desk on that afternoon of all afternoons. October 1915. The dark days of the war with Germany. Karl Fabergé had invited Ted's father to accompany him to the Imperial Palace at Tsarskoe Selo. It was young Ted's twentieth birthday, and in honor of it, he, too, had been included by Fabergé. Every detail was engraved in Brullov's memory. *The carriage ride through the vast Palace Park . . . the escort of mounted Cossacks, scarlet uniforms, black fur headpieces, drawn sabers . . . white-bearded Fabergé pointing out the sights . . . there eight hundred acres of lawn, there the lake, there the drill ground for the five thousand Imperial Guards, there the Catherine Palace, now a hospital for wounded soldiers. And here, the Alexander Palace. . . . Through the great*

66

portals to the bowing equerry, red cape, yellow ostrich plumes streaming from his hat . . . more corridors, and a huge Negro in crimson silks and white turban flinging open the door to the Tsar's study . . . the Autocrat of all the Russias advancing to welcome them, to shake their hands. A simple man in a modest gray tunic . . . Fabergé opening his portfolio and displaying an artist's sketch of the proposed Imperial Easter egg that would be presented to Empress Alexandra the following year. . . . A side door opening and the four grand duchesses and the Heir entering. Anastasia and Marie and Alexis, still children; Olga and Tatiana, grown, in white nurses' uniforms, circles of fatigue under their eyes; they had come directly from the hospital operating room. . . . Fabergé again delving into his portfolio and bringing forth designs created by Ted's father for possible Christmas presents from the family to the Empress. A miniature golden spaniel, like Joy and Jamie, a prayer book with gilded leaves, a nightingale with ruby eyes in a crystal cage. "There must be no rubies," Nicholas said. "Rubies remind me of blood, of which we've had enough." Some time during the conversation, Tatiana turning to the younger Brullov. "What do you think?" And he answering, "Yes, by all means"—not knowing to what she referred, not knowing if his answer was appropriate. Lost in her amber-gray eyes, hypnotized by her gentle smile. . . . Yes, by all means. He, Fyodor Brullov, would design a secret gift, a personal tribute, for this loveliest of the grand duchesses. It would be tiny, it would be solid gold, with some gem of simplicity and purity. No matter that it would cost his entire savings; he would ask nothing in return, except another smile. . . .

"Ninety-five thousand pounds! Your last chance, ladies and gentlemen!" the auctioneer's voice echoed through the hall. Brullov came out of his reverie. Ninety-five thousand English pounds meant four hundred and seventy-five thousand American dollars, a fantastic price even for a shimmering necklace of diamonds. The audience gabbled excitedly. "Once! Twice! Third and last time!" The hammer dropped. "Sold to Mr.

Orsino di Ascoli!" There was a wave of applause and a man in the second row rose and bowed in acknowledgment.

Brullov turned to the man who had lent him the opera glasses. "I remember the name di Ascoli from somewhere. Who is he?"

The answer was: "Europe's Man of Mystery, the newspapers call him—although there's nothing mysterious about his millions. One of the richest of the new rich."

He was walking up the center aisle now, and Brullov examined him with interest. Well over six feet tall, with a powerful chest that seemed about to burst out of his tuxedo jacket. "Looks like a wrestler to me," Brullov commented.

"That's his wife behind him. A baroness. Part German, part Dutch."

Brullov's eyes focused professionally on the diamonds circling her throat; they were the equal of any he had seen on the auction stage. Someday, when he was a famous international jeweler, he would see to it that Brullov jewels adorned that throat.

At 1 A.M., two hours after the final sale of the night at Christie's, Ted Brullov, carrying a briefcase, strolled through the lobby of the Savoy. The two night clerks at the registry counter were deep in conversation and failed to notice him pass and glance quickly at the bank of key compartments behind the counter. The key for Room 421 was absent. Pagodin had claimed it and gone to his room.

Rather than risk encountering an elevator boy with a memory for faces, Brullov chose to take the stairs to the fourth floor. A few paces along the cross-hall brought him to the door of the linen room, which opened with a twist of his skeleton key. He did not turn on the light until he was inside and had placed several bath towels along the floor to block any leakage of light. He checked his watch; it was 1:09. He opened the briefcase and put on the secondhand shoes; he removed his coat and vest and donned a blue-and-white striped apron. He shook talcum powder into his palms and applied it to his dark sideburns. He put on the secondhand pair of distance glasses, which caused only a slight blurring of his vision, slung the empty laundry bag over an arm and stepped out into the cross-hall. It was 1:14.

In the main hall the three OGPU guards were stationed as before. Brullov went toward them, working the even-numbered rooms, picking up pairs of men's shoes and women's pumps, chalking the room numbers on the soles and slipping them into the laundry bag. He passed the first OGPU guard, then the one opposite the elevator, then the third. At the end of the hall he reversed direction and attended the odd-numbered rooms. Thank God, not every room had shoes outside, for his laundry bag was almost crammed to capacity. He neared Room 421 and heard footsteps behind him. He quickly bent down to pick up another pair of shoes; as he straightened up, she was standing beside him, squinting. A night maid, gray-haired, matronly. Brullov started to tremble; his stomach churned; she would know he was an impostor.

"New?" she asked.

"Yes."

"I like it."

"Like what?"

"The new apron." Then she bustled on.

His eyes followed her: Was she going to the linen room? She reached the cross-hall and turned into it, but to the left, away from the linen room.

Finally Room 421. Pagodin's same black shoes with the built-up heels were at the door; then they were in Brullov's hands, were chalked, and went into the laundry bag. The OGPU guard, not two feet away, watched impassively and belched.

Two more pairs and Brullov turned into the cross-hall and sprinted to the linen room. It was 1:20. The longest six minutes of Brullov's life.

He emptied out the rest of the contents of the briefcase and

69

went to work. First, with his penknife, he loosened the lining of the innersole directly above the heel; then, with his chisel, he pried off the heel and inspected the thickness of the leather separating the heel and innersole. One-quarter inch. He chiseled a one-inch-square window in this leather separation and turned his attention to the heel itself. Luckily the buildup was very thick, which allowed him to chisel a hollow sufficiently deep and wide to accommodate the spring, the steel needle and the metal pressure plate. He broke open the ampule of liquefied cyanide and drained it into the rubber sac attached to the needle. He installed the whole assembly into the hollow, hammered the heel back onto the shoe, and glued down the inner lining over the pressure plate. Finally he sprinkled clear polish over both shoes and buffed them with a hand towel. Comrade Pagodin must have no cause to complain that Boots had shirked his duty.

Boots! he thought, and went cold. Good God, he had over-looked the greatest danger of all. At 3 A.M., when the genuine Boots started down the hall, the OGPU would surely tell him that another had done the work already. Even if they spoke no English, they might pantomime the situation. Brullov leaned against a linen shelf and tried to think it through. Boots could hardly suspect that an impostor was at work; but how *would* he react? Step by step, Brullov analyzed the probable working of the menial's mind. First of all, the Savoy was a large hotel; no one man could polish anywhere up to a thousand shoes in, say, three hours before the guests awakened. There would have to be at least two Bootses, perhaps three. The man would conclude that one of the others had serviced the wrong floor. Or, more likely, he would react with the typical menial's insecurity—he was about to be replaced. The service superintendent had not yet told him. Perhaps if he said nothing, the boss might relent. Keep the mouth shut, and maybe the ax would not fall.

Brullov clung to that hope, for he had no other. It was 1:54

A.M. Too soon to return with twenty-one pairs of shoes, presumably polished; such speed would be noticed by the guards. He would wait in the linen room for a few more minutes and actually perform the duties of a Boots.

At 2:15, he began depositing the shoes outside each door, smiled a goodnight to Pagodin's guard and hurried back to the linen room. He stuffed his equipment into his briefcase, slipped into his vest and coat, and descended the stairs to the lobby.

After breakfast, Brullov walked to Piccadilly and found a telephone. He called Katchin at the shop and reported his success.

"Thank God!" Katchin breathed. "But how will we know if it worked?"

"I'll phone the Savoy and ask to speak to Pagodin. If he comes on the line—well, it failed."

But it had not failed. The hotel operator told Brullov she would have to connect him with another member of the Soviet commission. And the early edition of the *Evening Standard* carried a small box item that Commissar Pyotr Pagodin had suffered "heart failure." The body would be returned to Moscow for burial.

The next afternoon Brullov was to take the boat train for Southampton, there to board the *Leviathan* for his return to New York. Before leaving London, he decided, he should buy a handsome present for Helen. Perhaps an unusually fine antique perfume container for her collection. But where should he look? Perhaps Andrei Katchin might have a dealer friend whom he could recommend. Besides, he should stop by anyway to say goodbye and to thank Andrei in person for his invaluable help of the past few days.

As the taxi turned into Hatton Garden and drew near Katchin's shop, Brullov noticed the unusual number of jewel dealers standing about on the sidewalks. None were showing each other papers of diamonds; all were talking and gesticulating excitedly. Then he saw the constable posted at Katchin's door. Suddenly he felt weak.

"Sorry, sir. The shop is closed," the constable said when Brullov approached.

"But why?"

"You might ask at the station, sir."

"What's happened? Andrei Katchin is a friend of mine, a very dear friend. Tell me, for God's sake!"

The constable hesitated; then Brullov's agitation conquered official restraint. "Afraid he's been strangled, sir. Must have surprised a burglar. If you go round to the station, ask for Inspector Harrison. . . ."

Brullov walked blindly down the crowded street; then he bent over the gutter and vomited.

He did not visit the police station to see Inspector Harrison. It was best to keep distance between himself and the tragedy. But had it been the work of a burglar, a simple coincidence? Possible, but not likely. The OGPU must have discovered the cause of Pagodin's death. And analysis of the cyanide of potassium, the skilled workmanship of the steel needle and spring might have suggested the work of a jewel craftsman. But how had they linked it to Andrei? Where had he blundered? Then Brullov remembered the shoes Andrei had ordered at the custom bootmaker while the bodyguard stood watch beside Pagodin. The OGPU saw everything; they were thorough and tireless. . . .

On the boat train to Southampton, Brullov wrote a note to the widow, expressing his sympathy.

> *I would consider it a privilege, if you would allow me to buy an interest in Andrei's business. I would see that it prospered and insure that when your son John reaches manhood he would be given a post in my planned London branch of Brullov & Company. I can do no less for the dear friend of my youth.*

Three

San José, Costa Rica
Summer 1936

ERIN DEERING, violin case under one arm, hummed softly to herself as she strolled down the Calle Esperanza. She was in a lighthearted mood, for her violin lesson at Señora Verdugo's was over and she was not due to join her mother at the Gran Hotel for almost two hours. She sniffed pleasurably the morning air, cool and thin due to San José's high altitude—air, moreover, that was perfumed with the aroma of the nearby chocolate factory. Should she visit the factory and enjoy a free bonbon? But it was almost too far to walk, and if she took the streetcar, the fare would cancel the benefit of a free chocolate. Then she remembered old Pablo and his fruit cart, just past the French convent. Pablo was always good for a bunch of grapes; besides, it would be interesting to see if he was aware of something different in the fit of her sweater. At Señora Verdugo's, after the violin lesson, Erin had slipped into the bathroom and stuffed toilet paper into her brassiere. Señora Verdugo had not noticed the sudden transformation; but she was old and her eyesight was poor. Pablo would be a far better test.

A housewife was examining the bananas and mangos and papayas piled high in Pablo's cart; and so distracted his attention from Erin's arrival. Then he saw her and bobbed his head. "Buenos días, chiquita," he said. *Not* "señorita." Erin bit her lip in disappointment; his eyes had seen nothing. Of course, Pablo had known her ever since her family had arrived in Costa Rica three years before; he knew she was only fourteen and did not merit inspection. Very well, forget Pablo.

"Chiquita!" he called after her, holding up a bunch of grapes. "No, *gracias*," she called back and quickened her pace. It would be different when she reached Carrie Wyatt's.

Erin's violin lessons were invariably followed by visits with Mrs. Wyatt. If Señora Verdugo meant music and concentration, Mrs. Wyatt meant frivolity and a delicious sense of wickedness, and, like a chocolate sundae, was not to be rushed at. The goal was to be approached roundabout, in ever growing anticipation. It was so this morning, as Erin sauntered block after block, past *pulperías* and notion stores, past the foreign embassies, and along the broad avenue which permitted a view of Monte Irazú, soaring in the hazy distance. A wisp of smoke was curling from its volcanic peak, which was a reassuring sign. "When Irazú smokes, all is well," went the native saying. "When Irazú does not smoke, there will be an eruption or an earthquake." Today all was well.

Finally Erin could bear the suspense no longer, and made

straight for Mrs. Wyatt's house. As she neared it, she spied another sign as propitious as the smoke from Irazú. The American flag was flying from its staff on the second-floor balcony of the Wyatt house. It meant that Carrie Wyatt's husband was out of town and that she was "receiving."

The Wyatt house was much like the others in the better part of San José. It faced directly onto the sidewalk without interruption of garden or lawn: there were no windows on the ground floor; admittance was gained by pulling on the bell chain alongside the towering cedar front door. As this door swung inward, Erin was greeted by the Wyatt house-boy, Joselito, giggling and bowing, and explaining in Spanish that the Señora was still in bed.

"Naturalmente," Erin said, for she could hear the boom of male laughter floating down the mahogany staircase. How many would there be this time? she wondered, and paused to regard herself in the great gilt mirror in the entry. Why did she always have to appear before Carrie's gentlemen callers in the same schoolgirl outfit? The same tatty white sweater, the same gray skirt that needed shortening, the same white socks and saddle shoes. Monotonous as poverty, she told herself. But at least her auburn hair was freshly bobbed. Short hair, she considered, magnified the size of her eyes, which were an intense blue, a color much admired by brown-eyed Latin Americans.

She climbed the mahogany staircase and went along the corridor toward the master bedroom. She could smell the rich aroma of expensive Havana cigars, not like the cheap things her stepfather was forced to smoke. There was another chorus of male laughter, and above it a soprano whoop of glee.

"Erin, my dear! Come in," Carrie called from the bed. The scene was as Erin expected—blond, buxom Carrie in a French negligee, reclining voluptuously against a mound of pillows, a long cigarette holder in one hand, a demitasse of chocolate in the other. Ranged around the bed were wicker chairs in which her three callers lounged. Erin recognized two—a section head of the German Embassy and one of the officials of the Allied Fruit Company. The third man, unknown to her, was introduced by Carrie as Señor Gutierrez, an engineer on the Pan-American Highway. Carrie examined Erin with shrewd eyes. "My dear, you've filled out since the last time. Yes, quite an interesting shape."

Erin blushed and bent down to kiss Carrie's waiting cheek. As she did so, there was a slight crinkling sound from the toilet paper within her brassiere, and Erin's blush deepened.

"I first met Erin when her family lived at the Gran Hotel," Carrie explained to Señor Gutierrez. "They came down from the States to start a coffee and banana finca. Bob Howell— her stepfather—bought raw land fifty miles out of town and had to build a house and plant everything from scratch. Never occurred to the poor soul it would take a while before it would grow into a cash crop. Meanwhile, what does one live on?"

Such a detailed history pained Erin. Fortunately Carrie was ignorant of her stepfather's prior background, which would have been an even greater embarrassment. Howell had drifted from one job to another in St. Louis, until he was run down by a streetcar and received a generous settlement from the insurance company. Suddenly flush with money, Howell had the ill luck to fall in with a drunken stranger in a bar who assured him that a fortune was to be made as a planter in Costa Rica. From that day on, folly compounded folly.

Carrie turned back to Erin and asked if she would like a cup of cocoa and a plate of *pan dulce*. Erin said yes and helped herself from the silver tray at the foot of the bed. She settled herself in the one vacant wicker chair and sipped and munched contentedly while Carrie and her guests continued their gossip. Julio Martínez had lost heavily at cards the night before. Juan Sepulveda's affair with Elena was cooling off; his next prize appeared to be Lupe. Young Rafael

Zamora would be leaving soon for English schooling. Oxford, of course. All the Zamora boys go to Oxford. And afterwards, Paris, to learn the finer points of love. Erin listened dreamily. This was how, Carrie had told her, all the great ladies of Europe spent their mornings: in bed, circled by their admirers, playing one against the other, and saucing the flirtations with information which could cause governments to topple. In Carrie's own case, she was among the first to know of future price changes in coffee and cocoa and bananas—courtesy of the Allied Fruit executive—which she turned to advantage in dealings on the commodity exchange.

It was the Allied Fruit visitor who was first to look at his wristwatch and declare that he must make an appearance at the office for at least a few minutes before the lunch break. The German diplomat followed suit, and finally, after a few last sallies and winks, Señor Enrique Gutierrez added his adieus. Carrie looked after him with a wistful smile. "Enrique reminds me of the pasha, when I was in Egypt."

"Egypt?" This was new intelligence to Erin.

"Such a romantic country. Moslem, of course, so they don't allow liquor. But the pasha had developed the thirst when he was abroad, so I made him gin in his gold-plated bathtub. The same recipe I used during Prohibition, back in the States."

"Where was your husband?"

"Oh . . . away." She lighted another cigarette in a long holder. "Can you imagine what it's like to have your whole body delicately stroked by the tip of a peacock feather?"

"The pasha?"

"The pasha."

Erin remembered it as being an Indian rajah in the previous telling.

Carrie suddenly grimaced. "You know, I think that crown on my wisdom tooth is coming loose again. I'll have to see a dentist."

"The one in the Canal Zone?"

"Naturally. He's the only one I trust. But it's such a bother. Three whole days just lost out of my life." Erin started to giggle and Carrie looked at her reproachfully. "It's not what you're thinking. I'm sure Enrique is faithful to his wife. Besides, he has no excuse to go to the Canal Zone." Erin's giggling increased and Carrie lifted a haughty eyebrow. "If you insist on being all that sophisticated, my dear, you should know better than to stuff your bra with Costa Rican toilet paper. American paper is softer and doesn't make those crinkling sounds."

Carrie's advice was interrupted by footsteps in the hallway; then a florid-faced man appeared in the doorway. "Carlyle! How delightful!"

Carlyle Williams was a junior secretary at the American Embassy and a frequent visitor to Mrs. Wyatt. He bestowed the ceremonial kiss on the cheek, and then to Erin, "A man stopped by the Embassy this morning and asked where he could find your stepfather. I told him he was probably at the finca, and since there was no telephone, he'd have to take the train, which won't be till tomorrow."

"He's not at the finca," Erin said. "He's in Balboa."

"Too bad. I gathered that the fellow had some important business. Said he was from New York. His name was Brullov, as I recall. Anyway, he's put up at the Gran Hotel, so you might tell your mother."

"Whatever would he want with Bob?" Grace Howell wondered aloud, when her daughter repeated the information that afternoon in their room at the Gran Hotel.

"Maybe it's about money," Erin suggested.

"It usually is." Mrs. Howell sighed and looked worried, an expression which had become habitual with her. Aside from this expression, she was an attractive brunette with refined features. "A lady through and through" was Carrie Wyatt's favorite description.

"Well, I suppose since he's staying here at the hotel I might phone him. I just hope it *isn't* about money."

"May I offer you a cocktail?" Theodore Brullov asked, when Grace Howell met him as arranged at the registration desk in the lobby at 4:30.

"That would be nice, thank you." She was agreeably surprised by the appearance of this stranger. He was distinguished-looking, she thought, with cocoa-brown eyes and a touch of gray in his sideburns. His white seersucker suit indicated that he was probably a frequent visitor to the tropics.

"I have taken the liberty of reserving us a table," he said and escorted her across the marble lobby to the area set aside for the daily *thé dansant*. The Cuban band, in red satin blouses with ruffled sleeves, was playing "The Peanut Vendor" and shouting *Olé*s as the dancers snapped hips and shook shoulders. Several of the couples smiled at Grace Howell and others, at tables, waved a welcome.

"I see you are well known, Mrs. Howell," Brullov commented as he drew out a chair for her.

"The foreign colony is very small," she said. "Most of the people here are from the embassies. The Ticos—that's what the natives call themselves—come in the evening to . . . to . . ." She paused in mid-sentence. Directly behind Brullov was a potted palm, and behind the palm was her daughter Erin.

The waiter arrived and Brullov, ordering champagne cocktails, was oblivious of Mrs. Howell's gestures to Erin to go away, which Erin ignored.

"Now, as you were saying?"

"Oh, nothing important. As I told you on the phone, I don't know where my husband can be reached in Balboa. But I'd be glad to give him your message when he returns."

"I'd appreciate it." Brullov began to rummage in his coat pockets. "I should explain that I am a jeweler. I've been in Colombia buying emeralds. I've stopped off here in response

79

to your husband's letter." He saw Mrs. Howell's look of surprise. "He didn't discuss it with you?"

"No. But that's not unusual."

"In any event, I cabled him that I would see him here in San José and I gave him an approximate date, depending on ship sailings from Colombia. Possibly he never received the cable."

"But *why* did Bob write to you?"

"Oh, I'm sure he wrote similar letters to other jewelers. But I doubt they would have had as compelling an interest in the merchandise he had to offer. This is the photo he enclosed in his letter to me." He handed it across the table.

Mrs. Howell stared at the photograph of a small golden mermaid which held a pearl in its clasped hands. "My anniversary present!"

"Yours?"

"Yes. Bob gave it to me several years ago when he got the insur—when we were moving to Costa Rica."

"Then it is your own personal property?"

"Of course it is!" There was anger in her voice. It was one thing for her husband to be a failure; quite another to secretly peddle one of her few possessions.

"Then I'd like to make you an offer of purchase. What would you consider a fair price?"

She frowned at the palm tree behind Brullov and Erin's wide-eyed face pushing through the fronds. "I'm not quite sure I want to sell it."

"Two thousand dollars?"

She caught her breath at the figure. "Mr. Brullov, why would you come all the way to San José for one little piece of jewelry?"

"I have sentimental reasons." He paused, as if to gauge the wisdom of saying more. "I designed that mermaid when I was a very young jeweler in Russia. I designed it for a certain young lady with whom I was in love."

"I see. And she married another and sold it?"

"No. I have reason to believe it was stolen." Brullov held up his hand as if to ward off an objection. "Please. I am not suggesting that you have come into illegal possession. Somehow the mermaid was taken out of Russia, probably pawned, and then went from jeweler to jeweler. I'm sure your husband bought it in good faith, which I shall respect." By now the champagne cocktails had been consumed, and Brullov ordered a second round. "At least, Mrs. Howell, I hope you will allow me to see my little mermaid."

"I don't have it with me. It's home, at the finca."

"Still, as a great favor, please?"

"I don't know what to say, Mr. Brullov."

"Then say nothing for now." He smiled ingratiatingly. "Meanwhile, 'La Cumparsita' is my favorite tango. Would you join me?"

He proved to be an expert dancer, and she followed his steps with a sureness which surprised her, almost as much as the sudden increase in the figure which he would pay for the mermaid. Three thousand dollars would go a long way to solve the Howells' financial problems.

On the way back from the dance floor she saw Erin standing to one side, signaling frantically. Grace excused herself from Brullov for a moment and walked Erin toward the lobby elevator.

"He's the handsomest man in the world!" Erin whispered. "Invite him to the finca and show him the mermaid."

"While Bob is away? What would Mr. Brullov think? And the servants? They'd tattle to Bob."

"It might be a good thing if they did." She watched her mother waver. "This man likes you, Momma. I could see it. He could even be your lover."

"Erin! I am *not* Carrie Wyatt."

Mrs. Howell had long been aware that Erin detested her stepfather. Whatever happened, she would be on her mother's side. And three thousand dollars . . .

She returned to the table. "Mr. Brullov, our finca is half

a day's trip from San José, and there won't be a return train until the next day. But if you can spare the time . . ."

"Gladly, Mrs. Howell. Gladly."

The following morning Grace Howell, Erin and Brullov boarded the *Ferrocarriles Nacional* for the long descent from the high plateau on which San José was situated. The train wound through dark green forests and crawled along the brink of gorges where rivers tumbled a thousand feet below. With every passing hour the air grew more humid and the scenery more tropical. Giant blue butterflies fluttered past the train windows; wild parrots and macaws flashed past in flurries of green and blue and yellow. Finally the train shuddered to a halt in a clearing which Mrs. Howell said was the junction for the finca. "And that's Juanito waiting for us with our own private train." She pointed toward an elderly native in cotton trousers and shirt who stood beside a horse-drawn conveyance that ran on a narrow-gauge track. The conveyance was no more than a platform with two benches bolted to the flooring. Mrs. Howell and Brullov seated themselves on the forward bench, Erin on the rear; Juanito mounted the horse, tossed the reins, and they moved off into a forest of banana trees. They had scarcely gone a mile when the banana trees began to thrash in a rising wind. Then there was a low drumming sound of approaching rain. "Juanito, quick!" Mrs. Howell called out. Juanito reined in the horse, jumped down and drew a machete from the saddlebag. With rapid strokes he cut three wide banana leaves from the nearest tree and presented them to the passengers. "Our umbrellas," Mrs. Howell explained, and lifted the leaf over her head. A moment later a moving curtain of water pounded into view and engulfed them. "Does this happen often?" Brullov shouted over the deluge. "Every afternoon," she shouted back. "All we can do is wait it out. It'll be over in a few minutes."

And so it was. An hour later they reached the limit of the

banana thicket and Mrs. Howell pointed across a ravine to the Howell finca. As far as Brullov could see there were rows of cocoa and coffee bushes, and in the center, on a hillock, a rambling one-story house completely circled by a screened veranda.

They were met on the veranda by Pedro, the houseboy, and Beatriz, the cook, bowing and smiling shyly at the sight of their mistress with a strange man. Mrs. Howell issued orders in a flurry of Spanish: Pedro was to take Mr. Brullov's case to the guest room, Beatriz was to cook her special "company" dinner and to lower a bottle of white wine into the water well. Then she returned to Brullov. She would go freshen up and return with the golden mermaid. Meanwhile, Erin would show him around the house.

There was little to show, Erin realized with embarrassment. A living room with bare floors, a few secondhand wicker chairs, a center table of bamboo, a windup Victrola in one corner. "That's Harold," she said, pointing up at a ceiling rafter where her pet monkey was gleefully munching on a small lizard.

"Very homey," Brullov said wryly.

She went to the Victrola, wound it, and put on a record, Fritz Kreisler's "Caprice Viennois." "It's my favorite," she said. "I practice it every night. We have a radio, too, but the batteries are dead. When it works, we can get Cali, Colombia, and Caracas, Venezuela."

"And when it doesn't work, what do you do for entertainment?"

"We read books. But not at night, because our electricity comes from a generator, and it's awfully weak."

Brullov looked thoughtful. "What about your schooling?"

"Oh, I went to the French convent in San José while we were waiting for this house to be built. And next year, my stepfather says I can go back to board when the cocoa and coffee start bringing in some money." Then she added defensively, "But I'm always learning. When Momma goes to San

83

José once a month to shop, I take a violin lesson, and Carrie Wyatt gives me magazines she gets from the States. I know all about Clark Gable and the Stork Club and King Edward and Mrs. Simpson."

"What about Hitler's occupation of the Rhineland and Italy's conquest of Ethiopia?" Erin looked blank. "Don't fill your head with frippery, my dear. Pay attention to the important things, some good, and some bad and frightening that are pushing us toward a second World War." Brullov's advice was interrupted by the return of Mrs. Howell, white-faced and weeping.

"*Momma!* What's wrong?"

She threw up her hands in despair. "The mermaid! It's gone. Everything in my jewel box. My mother's diamond ear studs, her ruby ring, everything."

The room was silent except for the phonograph doggedly repeating the last bar of "Caprice Viennois." Finally Brullov spoke. "Do you think it was the servants?"

"Oh, no. We've had them for years. I'd trust them with my life. My husband did it."

"Mrs. Howell!"

"I'm positive. I should have known something was wrong when he rushed off to the Canal Zone. He's sold or pawned everything I own. Without asking my permission." She broke into fresh sobs. "We need money, but not that badly. It has to be blackmail." Brullov gave a startled laugh at the accusation. "It has to be. Bob is more than a fool and a failure. He likes men."

This time Brullov did not laugh. "You're sure? A homosexual?"

"Yes. I didn't know it when I married him. Not really till we came to Costa Rica. They don't approve of that sort of thing down here. It exists, but it's hidden away in nasty places. . . . Oh, Erin. What are we going to do? What are we going to do?"

She sank down into a chair and buried her face in her hands. Erin, tears in her own eyes, knelt down beside her and stroked her head. Brullov watched uneasily, then went to the Victrola and silenced the broken record.

Dinner was a somber affair. Grace Howell ate with a look of tragedy in her eyes, and her daughter, usually of robust appetite, did little more than toy with her food. The stillness seemed intensified by Erin's macaw scrabbling along the bare floor in a circle around the table. Erin fed it a bit of mango and it waddled off clucking contentedly. Pedro served the coffee—cocoa for Erin—and withdrew.

Finally Brullov spoke. "Mrs. Howell, I'm still willing to make you an offer. If you can find out where your husband pawned or sold the mermaid, I'll pay you five hundred dollars. And if you can learn where he bought the mermaid originally, I'll pay you another five hundred. All you have to do is drop me a line in New York. Is that agreeable?"

She nodded. "It's better than nothing."

"Good." He finished his coffee and spoke again. "Mrs. Howell, you've taken me into your confidence about your situation, and so I'm curious. You have ample grounds for divorce; why stay on here in this jungle prison?"

She considered his question with a detached calm. "I'm a coward, Mr. Brullov. I married Carl Deering, Erin's father, because I wanted someone to be responsible for my life. After he died, I met Bob. I think he married me to appear respectable. Protective coloration, I suppose. And again, I wanted someone to be responsible for me. All I am, all I'll ever be, is a consumer of days and weeks and months and years . . . until finally there won't be any more." She glanced at Erin, who was listening with an expression of alarm. "I'm sorry, darling. I shouldn't talk this way. But today has been a terrible shock."

"Shock can be valuable if it leads to action," Brullov said.

"You've an attractive woman, Mrs. Howell, and you're well liked. I saw that at the Gran Hotel. There must be some unattached man. . . ."

She shook her head. "The people you saw were mostly in the diplomatic corps. The last thing an embassy man wants is to be linked with a woman who's gone through a messy divorce. His career comes first, as it should."

"Then what about a Costa Rican?"

"It's just as hopeless. The Tico families are a closed society. The young men go off to universities abroad. When they come home, they marry one of their own, girls of seventeen or eighteen. They get them pregnant, then go looking for mistresses. I hardly fit into that category."

"Then return to the States. For your sake and for Erin's. She's a very bright girl, and she'll be an attractive woman. But that will mean little unless she gets the proper education." He smiled at Erin. "When my boy Tony was your age, my wife and I were already planning for him to go to Harvard, which he will, next semester. Fight for education, Erin, it's the great key to life."

"Señora! Señora!" the houseboy cried, bursting into the room, followed by Beatriz. There was a babble of Spanish about *la culebra grande* and much arm waving, which Mrs. Howell explained to Brullov. "It seems there's a boa constrictor in the poultry yard. Pedro wants permission to use Bob's rifle. If you'll excuse me." She rose, as if glad for escape from the conversation.

"Let me help," Brullov said, also rising.

"There's no danger. All Pedro wants is for me to watch and applaud his bravery. Please stay and talk to Erin." With that, Mrs. Howell hastened off.

The air in the dining room was still and sultry, and Brullov suggested that they move to the veranda where they might find a breeze. They seated themselves in wicker chairs and gazed out at the night through the screening, which was crawling with insects and the bats that feasted upon them.

Brullov glanced sympathetically at Erin's downcast expression. "There will be better days."

"I know." She spoke without conviction. She had never felt so frightened. For the first time she realized the desperation of her mother and her own predicament. She had been too wrapped up in the adventure of life in a foreign land, in the fantasies of Carrie Wyatt, the amusements of her pet monkey and her macaw. She had accepted her mother's faith that somehow something would turn up, the *mañana*-sickness of the tropics. Now reality had savaged it all. Today an era had been brought to an end by a stranger in search of a golden mermaid.

Coming out of her introspection, she was aware that Brullov was speaking to her. What was it about? Oh, the jewelry business.

". . . So how do we know that these beautiful jewels were not once ornaments on the body of some great Pharaoh? It's possible that a woman's wedding ring may contain some fleck of gold from the mummy case of a Rameses. The grave robbers never destroyed what they stole. Everything of value was sold or bartered and passed down through the centuries, and it exists today, whether in national treasures or as the pride of princesses and queens, or even some simple housewife." Brullov broke off and patted Erin's knee. "But enough about that. Let's talk about you."

"Not yet, please. There's something I've been wondering about."

"Yes?"

"You told Momma you'd pay five hundred dollars to know where my stepfather bought the gold mermaid. Why do you care?"

Brullov smiled. "You're a shrewd girl. Jewelers keep records, Erin. Pawnbrokers, too. I want to trace the mermaid back, owner by owner, until I find who took it out of Russia."

"But why?"

He hesitated. "Because it was stolen from the young lady I

loved. And very possibly the thief is the same one who murdered her and her whole family."

"Murdered!"

At that moment, as if melodramatic underscoring, three rifle shots rang out in the distance. They listened intently, and there were two more shots. "Could there be more than one boa?" Brullov asked.

"No. Pedro is just clumsy with a gun."

Now there was a new sound, a distant drumming and the whine of wind. It was the approach of yet another rainstorm. "So what do you want to be, Erin?" Brullov prompted.

She frowned with thought. "Oh, to live in New York. To travel, to know the people everybody's talking about." She tossed her head with determination. "And I will, when I'm a world-famous violinist. I'll travel everywhere and be soloist with all the great orchestras." She looked doubtfully at Brullov. "You don't think it will happen?"

"Anything is possible, Erin. But you should be realistic. Most women violinists wind up fiddling in the orchestra." By now the rain was marching across the plantings of cocoa and coffee and pounding toward the house. The bats on the screening chittered with alarm and darted off into the night. Brullov rose from his chair, lighted a cigarette and leaned on the veranda railing. "It's a good idea, Erin, to have a second goal, maybe a less glamorous career, but something that might turn out to be more satisfying in the long run. Any ideas?"

"Oh, yes. Of course." It was flattering to have a man of the world treat her as an adult. But what should she tell him? Then, desperately, she decided. "I'll be a courtesan!"

"A *what?*"

"Like Carrie Wyatt! I'll have secret lovers. We'll go to the Canal Zone, to Balboa. We'll walk along the sea front at night and watch the waves crash. Then we'll go back to our hotel suite and drink champagne and smoke long cigarettes in golden holders and dance naked on the balcony!"

For years afterward Erin Deering remembered Brullov's reaction—standing on the veranda, his back to the water sheeting down from the eaves, his dark-brown eyes crinkling with amusement. And above all, his words.

"Forget the violin, my dear. Your fame and fortune are on the stage."

Much later that evening—in fact, near midnight—Erin left her bedroom and slipped out onto the veranda. The rain was long past and a near-full moon cast its magic over the hillock and the distant groves of banana trees. It was not a jungle prison at all, she thought. It was beautiful; it was nature, refreshed, waiting for the morning sun and another day to grow. . . . She stole along the veranda toward the window of the master bedroom. She knew it would be wrong to watch what must be in progress within; but it, too, must be beautiful and therefore to be admired. She drew her face to the edge of the window and peered in. The mosquito netting that surrounded the bed glowed with light. Inside the netting her mother sat propped up beside a kerosene lamp and leafed through pages of a magazine. She was wearing her best negligee, Erin noted, her makeup was fresh and there was a red ribbon in her hair. And she was alone.

Erin sagged with disappointment. Had she misjudged Mr. Brullov? Surely on such a night, in such a situation, he could at least show gallantry. Unless, perhaps, because he was married, because he was a man of old-fashioned standards, too much a gentleman. . . . That had to be it. And how Erin must have shocked him with all that silly prattle of being a courtesan.

She sighed and turned away and gazed once more at the moon. It was useless to be sad about her mother, she decided; the young could not solve the problems of their elders. Then, suddenly, she realized that she was humming to herself, that she was happy in a strange new way. A happiness that centered on Mr. Brullov. Suppose, just suppose, that he had correctly foreseen her future. An actress. A famous actress. How old would she have to be? She ticked off the years on her fingers. Six might do it. A famous actress at twenty. Then, God willing, Mr. Theodore Brullov would come to *her*. And he would not be too much a gentleman.

Four

Zurich, Switzerland
August 1939

THE GREAT mansion set in its twenty-acre park on the
slopes of the Dolder, high above Zurich, was commonly
called by the locals the "Gold Schloss," because of the enormous wealth of its owner. But the name on the plaque attached
to the massive wrought-iron gates was simply "Bellevue."
The view was beautiful indeed, surveying the many-spired
city below and the Zurich See beyond, whose blue in the
month of August was freckled with hundreds of white sails.

On this particular afternoon few of the guests at Bellevue
paid heed to the view, but a great deal of attention to each

other's guesses as to Orsino di Ascoli's motive for such a lavish garden party. Some thought it was to announce a new corporate merger, which would account for the number of Swiss bankers present, as well as company heads from London, Paris and Berlin. Others suspected it was to celebrate di Ascoli's winning of that oil concession in Arabia, for three of the guests wore flowing robes and kaffiyeh headdresses. A few cynics whispered that the gala was in honor of di Ascoli's newest mistress, the blond Parisian film star Odile Lebrun. That would explain the strange absence of his wife, Gerda, the Baroness von Duzee. All agreed on one point: everything Orsino di Ascoli did was for a purpose. A second point, unspoken but understood, was that when di Ascoli issued an invitation, it was an order to be obeyed.

"It is merely a simple little affair to amuse my friends," di Ascoli himself repeated each time he shook hands or kissed a cheek. Those who were meeting their host for the first time were impressed by his towering height, his powerful chest and piercing black eyes. And when they were introduced to his eleven-year-old daughter Lisa—"my joy, my pride, my harshest critic"—they remarked on the girl's dark beauty and poise.

As for the "simple little affair," it included a dance band that played jazz on the tennis court and a string quartet that rendered Vivaldi from a float in the center of the immense swimming pool. It included, in the topiary garden, a fountain that cascaded champagne over a Venus carved from ice; from the pool of bubbling wine at her feet waiters in powdered wigs, blue livery and white gloves ladled up glasses for the thirsty, which seemed to be everyone. The guests drank and danced and joked with an almost frenetic intensity, as if to forget for a few hours the ominous march of events beyond the walls of Bellevue and the borders of Switzerland. Reichsführer Hitler had annexed Austria, had humbled Britain and France at Munich, had swallowed Czechoslovakia, had signed a friendship pact with Stalin, and now, in the month of August, 1939, was demanding control of the Free City of

Danzig. And after Danzig, would it be Poland? Was another European war inevitable? So the guests at Bellevue drank and danced and joked that the view from the guillotine was truly breathtaking.

As Orsino di Ascoli took his leave of one group of guests and was about to join another, his confidential secretary, Constantine Durer, moved alongside and murmured, "Sir, the chauffeur has returned. He inquired at all of madame's favorite shops. No one has seen her."

"Then telephone all of her friends."

"But they are here, sir. Every one."

Di Ascoli scowled in bafflement. He had not seen his wife since lunch, four hours earlier. The chauffeur had reported that he had taken her to an office building on the Ramistrasse, had picked her up a few minutes later and she had directed him to the Rieterpark and then dismissed him.

"I hesitate to suggest this, sir," Durer said, "but perhaps madame has disappeared unwillingly. This might be a police matter."

"No, no. I can't believe that. Let's wait a while."

The wait proved short. Durer reported back that madame had returned to Bellevue in a taxi. The butler had seen her go up to their bedroom suite.

Di Ascoli found her seated on a red velvet bench in the alcove of the bay window, gazing vacantly toward the Zurich See. He noted that she was still dressed in the tweed suit which she had worn at lunchtime; but her chestnut hair, which had been coiled at the nape of her neck, now hung loosely about her face, giving her an almost emaciated appearance.

"What is the explanation of this?" di Ascoli demanded, advancing toward her. She sighed and continued to gaze into the distance. "Gerda! All afternoon I've made excuses for you. This is your party as well as mine."

"No. Only yours. Always yours." She turned her eyes toward him and he saw that she had been weeping.

He seated himself beside her. "*Liebchen,* what's happened? Where have you been?"

"Walking. Thinking."

"But surely not all day."

"I went to St. Peter's. I prayed. I asked forgiveness."

"As if you had done anything. Gerda, tell me . . ."

"First I went to see Dr. Winklemann."

"Yes?"

"There is no hope. He's positive."

Di Ascoli placed his arm around her waist. "Winklemann isn't God. There are other specialists."

"I've been to the last one. Five is enough for any woman. If you insist on another child, I'll give you a divorce and you can find yourself a brood mare. I'm sure Odile Lebrun will be happy to oblige. Or any of the dozen others."

"Gerda! That is unkind."

"But the truth. When we married I knew that I could not hold you for long. My value to you was that I was a baroness. Romance was not part of our bargain. But I did hope for many children. They would be my consolation. Instead I had Lisa." She spoke her daughter's name with bitterness. Then she nodded her head vigorously. "So divorce me. But one word of advice, Orsino. Do not marry again until your new woman has proved herself with a son."

Her husband's face hardened. "There will be no divorce. I will not marry again. I will not bring in a stepmother over Lisa. That is final." Gerda bowed her head and her shoulders shook with sobs. He caught one of her hands in his. "Listen to me, *Liebchen.* Other men have had this disappointment; they, too, have wanted sons to carry on the name, the business. With me, it will have to be Lisa. She will be both daughter and son, and some day, one of the richest women in the world."

Gerda gave a strangled laugh. "One of the richest old maids. You'll see to that."

"And I say, Lisa *will* marry. I shall find her the right man. And she will give me a grandson. He will be my posterity." Di

Ascoli got to his feet. "Now, fix your face and change into a dress. I want our guests to see you."

"No."

"Gerda, I require it. You will pay special attention to our German guests. Be particularly gracious to Gunther von Falke. Draw him out concerning Danzig and Hitler's intentions. I wish to know if he will go to war this year."

"Then ask Hitler himself. No one else knows."

"Ah, but they do. If there is to be war, the General Staff has already made its plans. Others close to the Führer will know. Von Falke, for one. It is already August. An attack on Danzig, and perhaps Poland, must come soon, before the rains."

Gerda regarded her husband with sudden understanding. "So that is the reason for this party."

"Yes. If there is to be war, I must act one way; if there is to be peace, I shall act another. Now, ring for your maid and change."

"No."

"Gerda, I order it."

"I will not."

He glowered at his wife for a moment, then shrugged and stalked from the room.

It was Gunther von Falke's first visit to Bellevue, although he had transacted business in Berlin with Orsino di Ascoli. He was a German of the Junker class, which permitted him that particularly relaxed confidence of the well placed. He was not only one of the Third Reich's most influential industrialists; his brother-in-law was a general on the staff of Air Marshal Hermann Göring. Physically he was almost as tall as di Ascoli, but more slender of build. His eyes were dark gray in color, lively and humorous. He was exchanging quips with Odile Lebrun in the topiary garden when di Ascoli nudged his elbow.

"Gunther, my friend, you must not monopolize this beauty. Permit others to share the pleasure."

"Such as you, perhaps?" Von Falke smiled.

"Unfortunately, no. Please excuse us, my dear." He took von Falke's arm and murmured, "Allow me the honor to show you my library. There we can talk confidentially."

Von Falke eyed him shrewdly. Di Ascoli had something on his mind. The two men bowed to Odile and crossed the garden to the house. They entered by way of the fernery, which was kept at the proper degree of humidity for di Ascoli's collection of African and South American specimens; then along a marble corridor which was lined with suits of armor. At the end of the corridor di Ascoli threw open a double door that gave into the paneled library.

"A cognac, perhaps?" di Ascoli asked.

"Nothing, thank you." Von Falke surveyed two tables on which were displayed miniature models of steam locomotives.

Di Ascoli saw his interest. "When I was a boy, I dreamed of being a locomotive engineer. Engines seemed alive, panting with power. They symbolized speed and faraway places." He strolled from table to table, identifying the miniatures. The locomotives on the Flying Scot, the Orient Express, the Twentieth Century Limited, the Trans-Siberian Express. "I never saw one of the great trains, only the local, which passed through the Turkish hills where I tended my sheep. But in imagination I saw it as the Orient Express."

Von Falke looked thoughtful. "Then the stories we read are true?"

"Of me? Yes. I was a shepherd boy. Illegitimate. A bastard." Di Ascoli had learned long ago that men born to privilege could be seduced into trust by one's confession that he is not so fortunate of birth, or that he had shabby beginnings.

"But you do not look Turkish. More Slavic. Perhaps Czech or Yugoslavian."

"You are not far off. Let me show you where I was born." He guided von Falke to a group of framed photographs on the library wall. "This is the village of Polonezkoy, in northern Turkey. It was settled by Polish refugees after the uprising

96

against the Russians in 1830. I assume one of my great grand-parents was one of those refugees, because I've been told my mother was Polish."

"And your father?"

"Italian. A strong man with a traveling circus. They passed through Polonezkoy and my father met the Polish girl. The strong man went on his way and the Polish girl left me in a blanket beside the village well. A family took me in, and when I was old enough, they gave me their sheep to tend. Here I am." Di Ascoli pointed to a photograph of a boy holding a lamb in his arms. "I never learned my mother's name. I think the village protected her because she was probably of good family. And all I know of my father was that he came from Ascoli—so I chose the name di Ascoli. And Orsino, meaning 'the bear,' because it fitted my strength."

He moved along the wall and indicated another photograph. "This one was taken when I joined Kemal Atatürk's revolutionary army." Von Falke saw a youth with an indistinct face in soldier's uniform. Another photograph showed a well-dressed young man standing beside a Mercedes touring car. "My first automobile," di Ascoli said proudly. "I bought it with my first profits from running guns to the Greeks just before the Turks massacred them at Smyrna. After that, everything came easily. I smuggled my money into Switzerland, and used Swiss gold francs to buy up German businesses in the great inflation of Twenty-two and Twenty-three. After that, the American stock market. I got out a week before the Crash. The rest you know. Not bad, eh, for a poor shepherd boy?"

"Remarkable." Von Falke shifted impatiently. "You said you wished to talk confidentially."

"Of course." Di Ascoli paused, as if to choose his words carefully. "You know that I have a reputation as a collector. . . ."

"Jewels, I hear."

"The very finest. But my most important collection is—

people. It is they who are the real secret of my success. There is someone I want you to meet. She is waiting for you upstairs."

"She? A lady?"

"A very beautiful lady. A French lady." Di Ascoli winked suggestively.

Von Falke beamed with anticipation. "She has asked to meet me?"

"Not asked; but I am certain that you will lose your heart to her. Shall we go?"

"By all means!"

The two men left the library, retraced the corridor and ascended a great curved staircase to the second floor, followed another hallway to a door which di Ascoli opened. "This is my private study," di Ascoli said, and ushered von Falke into the room. The German glanced around expectantly, seeing only a desk, lounge chairs and a wall hung with paintings. "She is gone!"

"No. She is very much here. Looking down at you."

Von Falke's eyes followed di Ascoli's outstretched arm. The French lady gleamed down at him in painted nudity. Von Falke's face fell with disappointment. Then he removed his monocle, polished it, replaced it and studied the painting. "A Manet. A fine one. Yes, magnificent!"

"And there are more. The finest museum quality. Manet, Pissarro, Degas, Renoir. All to be had at distressed prices."

"Where?"

"Paris. The owner must raise money very quickly. That is what I wished to talk to you about. I propose that you and I visit the gentleman and take our pick. Since Marshal Göring is a great collector of art, perhaps you might wish to present him with a painting or two. Or through your brother-in-law, the General. I'm sure the Marshal would appreciate the gesture."

The German's eyes brightened. "Most definitely. And I, that you would be willing to share with me."

"That is the test of friendship." Di Ascoli opened the cigar case on his desk and offered a Havana, then lighted one for himself. "Shall we meet in Paris, say, in the second week of September?"

"I'm afraid I have several board meetings that week."

"Then the first week?"

"No. I'm sorry."

"Perhaps next week? The last week in August?"

Von Falke pursed his lips. "Would the owner of the paintings permit us to take delivery immediately?"

"On the spot. I have been assured of it."

Von Falke's face relaxed and he extended his hand to di Ascoli. "Make the arrangements and let me know when and where to meet you."

"Consider it done." Di Ascoli smiled gently. He would make no arrangements, for the owner of the paintings was nonexistent. But now he knew what he desired. Europe's peace would last through August. Hitler's war would begin in early September.

The following morning Orsino di Ascoli went to the bank on the Bahnhofstrasse in which he owned a large interest. He gave orders to sell immediately his vast portfolio of German stocks and to invest the proceeds in gold bullion, South African industrial diamonds, and commodity futures in Cuban sugar and Argentine beef.

As he left the bank he paused in the lobby to chat with one of the executives who had been at the garden party, then he went down the steps onto the sidewalk of the Bahnhofstrasse. His limousine was waiting at the curb. Dieter, the chauffeur, saluted and opened the car door. At that moment a woman's voice called out in English, "Sir! Oh, sir! Wait, please!" Di Ascoli glanced around; a middle-aged woman in a flowered hat was running down the bank steps. "Sir," she panted, coming up to him, "you dropped this in the lobby." She thrust out something which appeared to be either a postcard or a photograph.

"I'm afraid you're mistaken, madam. It must be someone else."

"But I saw it happen, sir. Surely you recognize it." She held it up to his gaze; it was a photograph of a blond young woman in a Chinese rickshaw. Beside her stood young Yuri Solenko.

Di Ascoli recoiled as if he had been struck by a blow. He stared into the woman's face, a face gone to fat, hair from blond to muddy gray, brown eyes that burned with meaning. "Forgive me, madam," he managed. "It must have fallen from my pocket. Thank you."

"You're welcome." She smiled, then turned and walked away.

He stared after her until the flowered hat disappeared among the noonday crowd. She was cunning, he thought. She had known she could never breach by telephone or letter the protective shield of his secretaries. But how had she found him? How many days or weeks had she tracked him until the right moment presented itself?

He entered his limousine and the chauffeur swung it out into the traffic of the Bahnhofstrasse. When Dieter's eyes were concentrated on a truck ahead, di Ascoli slipped the photograph from his pocket and examined it carefully. Why wasn't she dead, or rotting in some Shanghai prison? He turned the photograph over and read the message inked on the back.

Dushki: I will be at home August 29—the afternoon. Number 4, Rue de Roche, Menton. S.

The address Sonya had given proved to be a seedy cottage in the poorer section of Menton, at some distance from the beaches and the villas of the wealthy. It was situated at the end of a lane, without close neighbors. The walls of the cottage were a faded pink stucco; the roof was missing a number of red tiles and the bare spots had been patched with metal sheeting. Potted geraniums, drooping and dusty-leaved, lined the dirt walk that led to the front door.

At di Ascoli's first knock, Sonya opened the door and smiled at his vacationer's costume—walking shorts, rope sandals, a sweatshirt, sunglasses and a straw hat. A cloth duffel bag was slung over one shoulder.

"So the famous Orsino di Ascoli is now a beach rat," she said, closing the door behind him. "What is in the bag?"

"A business suit. I changed in the depot rest room."

He glanced appraisingly around the parlor at the stained sofa and the chairs with sagging bottoms. On a sideboard he saw a silver icon and a framed photograph of two men in military uniform—her father, the general, and her brother; he remembered them from Sonya's room in Shanghai.

"How long have you been here?" he asked.

"A month. Renting, of course."

"And before here?"

"Hong Kong."

"Do you live alone?"

She understood his meaning. "There is no one to listen. Yes, I am alone. As always." She seated herself on the sofa and lighted a cigarette. "So here we are on the Riviera, at last. Not as I had hoped and you had promised. But still here. Twenty years too late." There was a bitter edge to her voice. She went on, speaking some sentences in French, some in English, and all with the authority of a woman in control of the situation. "First I will tell you my story, then you will tell me yours. You remember a bit of gold jewelry which you hid under the floorboards in Shanghai, with the diamonds and emeralds and sapphires? The one I stole?" He nodded: the golden mermaid. "I sold it for many taels and bought myself very fine dresses and shoes. And when I wore them at the ballrooms, I was admired, even though I was not beautiful like the other girls. My fine dresses told the men I must be unusual, an experience, so they all wanted me and I made them pay double the price of the beautiful girls. After that I had a big apartment and other girls working for me. Soon I will have enough money for the Riviera, I told myself. I did not know I would have the tuberculosis and spend everything in the hospital. When I was well again, I started over. This time I was robbed by my number one girl, and I had to begin once more. Two years ago I was certain I had saved enough; I was ready to leave. That was when the Japanese bombed Shanghai and I lost everything again. I got away to Hong Kong, where I learned English, and went back to walking the docks and charging almost nothing because all the Chinese girls were so young. Then one day—yes, one very lucky day—I saw your picture in a magazine, with your baroness wife and your daughter, and I knew I would see the Riviera after all. I would have a fine villa and a proper dowry to find a husband."

During her recital di Ascoli watched her intently. In appearance she might be any middle-aged housewife gone to fat; but in her eyes he thought there was a hint of madness.

"How did you know it was me in the photo?"

"We had been lovers."

"Still, after so many years . . ."

"You are not every man. Older, yes, but not changed." She lighted another cigarette and he noticed that her fingers shook as she did so. "And now, tell me how you became the very important Orsino di Ascoli. All those diamonds and emeralds and sapphires could not buy what you have become."

"They helped. The rest was brains."

"That does not tell me. How did you get to France? What did you do?"

There was no harm in telling her. For twenty years there had been no one to whom he could divulge the truth and be admired for his exploits. "I came by ship to Marseilles. I bought false identification papers and went to Nice which, as you know, has had a Russian colony since the old tsarist days. I was a bit homesick for Russia, you see, and I wanted to live near my own people, at least for a while. I went to a bank and rented a safe-deposit box for my jewels. From time to time I sold a diamond or an emerald to a dishonest jeweler—sometimes in Nice, sometimes in Cannes. There was civil war in Turkey at the time, and I used my money to buy guns and bombs, which I smuggled to Kemal Atatürk. After that, there was war in Morocco and I ran guns to Abd-el-Krim. Wherever men fought, I sold, and always under a different name. When I had my millions, I became Orsino di Ascoli. The financier, the art patron, the friend of Europe's great." He concluded with a sardonic smile. "I wait for your applause, Sonya."

She frowned and lighted still another cigarette from the stub of the previous. "We have both lived bad lives. But at least I have never pretended."

Di Ascoli seated himself on the sofa beside Sonya. "I suppose that photo you gave me, the one with the rickshaw, is not your only copy?" She laughed comfortably, which was answer enough. "I can deny everything, of course. It is my word against yours. Who would believe a whore?"

"Perhaps only your enemies. But there is something which would interest even your best friends. After you left me there was something you may not know about, which I read in the Shanghai newspapers. It was about the murder of our holy Emperor and his family." She paused and watched his face; it revealed nothing, and she continued. "When the White Russian Army took Ekaterinburg, which we now call Sverdlovsk, they made an investigation. They asked questions of the Cheka, who did the killings. There were confessions, there was talk of many fine jewels which were found and then disappeared. You see, *dushki,* there is a difference between selling stolen jewels and selling jewels which were robbed from the bodies of our beloved Imperial Family. There is horror in that. It is a very terrible thing."

Di Ascoli rose and went to a french window and stared out into the withered garden. He was weary, so very weary. "I know what you are thinking," Sonya went on, behind him. "I have prepared for it. This morning I wrote a letter. A very long letter, with most interesting details."

Di Ascoli tensed and turned to face her. "Are you threatening me, Sonya?"

"Why should I do such a thing? I thought merely you should know."

"This letter—to whom did you send it?"

"Oh, not to the police. They aren't to know unless—well, you understand."

He nodded; then with forced casualness, "Then to some friend?"

"I have no friends. I wrote it to myself. I wrote that if I am missing or found dead, it is by the hand of Orsino di Ascoli—and why." She watched his eyes dart about the room. "Oh, no, it is nowhere in this house. I mailed it at the post office."

"Then it will be delivered here. Tomorrow morning."

"Yes. Then if something happens, the police will come and open the letter."

Di Ascoli gazed at her with an expression of profound sadness. "Sonya, Sonya—you've been through such bad times that you expect only the worst of people. You must not hate me so. I want to be your friend. That's why I've come."

"You have come to find out what I will do."

"No. What you need. You want a villa on the Riviera. It shall be yours."

She dwelt on his words for a moment. "A fine one? Like my father had before the war?"

"Finer! Anywhere on the Côte d'Azur. And you want a dowry for a husband. Tell me how much it shall be." He watched hope kindle in her eyes—hope that was fragile, that needed encouragement. "When I left you in Shanghai, Sonya, I was very unhappy. I had to do what was necessary. Just as you had to take to the streets again. But I owe you so very much, and I pay my debts."

She sniffed; her eyes began to glisten. "You will come visit me sometimes?"

"If your husband permits."

She laughed. "Or my lover. When one has money, there are many arrangements."

"Exactly. Now, let us have a drink to seal our friendship."

She went into the kitchen and returned with a bottle of *vin rouge* and two glasses. She poured, they touched glasses and he took her into his arms and kissed her on the lips. She broke into sobs of happiness, which turned to strangling sounds as his thumbs pressed against her carotid arteries.

He guided her body gently to the floor. "My poor Sonya," he murmured sorrowfully to the unhearing ears. "The Riviera was never meant for you."

Then he went into the kitchen and selected the canned goods which he would eat for dinner. Later he would sleep, and in the morning he would wait for the postman and Sonya's letter.

Five

Hollywood, California
Summer 1940

THE LUNCHTIME crowd at the Brown Derby was trick-
ling out into Vine Street, on the way back to rehearsals
at the various radio stations. A number of the lunchers were
film stars; others were agents, directors, producers and writers;
almost all were working on that Monday evening's dramatic
and variety broadcasts. Waiting for their appearance outside
the Derby was the usual crowd of autograph seekers and
tourists who hoped to be able to tell the folks back home
that they had "almost touched" their favorite star.

Erin Deering had no favorite; every actor and actress received her admiration, which on this Monday focused on the blond Carole Scott. As she and her agent came blinking into the sunlight of Vine Street, Erin detached herself from the waiting fans and held out her pen and autograph book. The actress scribbled her signature, Erin thanked her and then added shyly, "Miss Scott, could you tell me how I can get into the movies?"

Carole Scott raised her eyebrows in mock surprise. "How? Gimme a dollar, kid, and I'll tell you."

Erin flushed; at age eighteen no one should call her "kid." "I don't have a dollar. Not with me."

"Then you'll never make it."

"I don't understand."

"Anybody who doesn't have a dollar can't be lucky. It's luck that gets you into the movies. Let's go, Joe."

Erin watched the actress and her agent turn away; then Carole Scott looked back at her. "Hey, kid!"

"Yes, Miss Scott?"

"You really want to know how?" she called. "You fuck your way in."

There was a moment of silent shock among the crowd, followed by snickers as Erin, white-faced and trembling, tore Carole Scott's autograph from her book, shredded it and dropped the fragments into the gutter.

On the bus to downtown Los Angeles, where Erin was to work the afternoon-evening shift behind a food counter at Clifton's Cafeteria, she mulled over the problem which had obsessed her for months. How did one get "discovered" by the studios? Certainly not every actor and actress had the benefit of a Broadway stage background. Several girls she had known in her drama class in the final year at Hollywood High already had signed film contracts. Erin herself had caused no enthusiasm in the school's commencement show, *The Pirates of Penzance.* But that, she told herself, was because she had been relegated to the role of a maiden in the chorus.

"Tapioca pudding, Waldorf salad, Jell-O, lemon, orange

and pineapple," she recited to the customers who pushed trays past her counter. Oh, to be back in Costa Rica, with the luxury of servants on the finca; the carefree days with her pet monkey and macaw, and those delicious visits with Carrie Wyatt in San José. All that had ended with the disappearance for good of Erin's stepfather, the mortgage on the finca foreclosed and Grace Howell drawing on the American Embassy's distress fund to pay passage back to the States and St. Louis. For three years she and Erin had endured the humiliation of having to live with Mr. and Mrs. Deering, the parents of Erin's father. While the daughter crammed courses at high school to make up for the lost education in Costa Rica, the mother worked as a seamstress in Alterations at a local department store; but the few dollars a week she earned fell far short of paying their board with the Deerings. "I don't know how much longer I can take it," she said one day to Erin. "Eating on charity is like mud in the mouth." It was then that Erin came up with what she considered a dazzling solution, a move to Hollywood. Surely seamstresses must be needed in the film studios, and Erin would enroll at Hollywood High; she would take the drama course and be discovered by a movie producer. But she had not been discovered and her mother was again a seamstress in Alterations. And instead of living in the spacious house of the Deerings, they went home each day to a bungalow court—one room with a let-down bed and a kitchenette and quarreling neighbors.

That evening when Erin returned from the cafeteria, she sat on the steps outside their room and repeated to Maggie Griswold, who roomed next door, the advice she had received outside the Brown Derby. Maggie was a chunky woman with dyed red hair who worked occasionally as a crowd extra in Western movies.

"Carole Scott said you should sleep your way to the top?"

"Well, words to that effect."

"Uh-huh. I'll bet she said 'fuck your way.'" Erin flushed and stared up at a sentinel palm whose fronds rattled in a hot dry wind. "Sure, she did. I know Scott. She's a dirty talker, and a dirty doer. That's what it takes." She patted Erin's shoulder. "Honey, you ain't hard enough for the racket. You ain't mean enough. You're stuck with what you are."

"What's that?"

"A lady. Like your mother. And in Hollywood that's being up shit creek without a paddle. So forget acting. Be a normal girl and live a normal life."

But "normal" for Erin meant acting. The following Monday, before taking the bus to the cafeteria, Erin went again to Vine Street. This time she did not loiter outside the Brown Derby—what was the use of autographs? They merely emphasized the chasm between winners and losers. This time she walked south to Sunset Boulevard and turned eastward past NBC and CBS until she came to the studios of RBC.

"How fast can you type?" the man behind the desk asked.

"Eighty words per minute," she lied. Forty was nearer the truth, but at least Hollywood High had taught her that skill.

"Know how to cut stencils?"

"Of course." What in the world were stencils?

"Well, we got three girls out with summer flu. We'll give you a try." The man scribbled his name on an employment slip. "Take this down the hall. You'll see a stairs to the basement. Show it to Trudy in Mimeo."

The Mimeograph department, which produced the broadcast scripts for all the radio shows, was four concrete walls surrounding the clatter of typewriters. Eight women, all overweight, all masculine-looking, all wearing eyeglasses and with cigarettes drooping from their lips, hunched over their machines and cut the purplish stencils, which were then fastened to the drum of the Mimeograph machine, the handle was cranked, and copies of the script pages sifted out into a tray. Trudy, the supervisor, was operating the Mimeograph when Erin produced her employment slip. She looked skeptically at the tall titian-haired girl with sparkling blue eyes.

"Sure you know what you're getting into?"

"Yes. A radio station."

"The *basement* of a radio station. We're galley slaves, and those—" gesturing toward the bank of typewriters—"are our oars. Okay, that Underwood at the far end is yours."

"At least I've got my foot in the door," Erin told her mother that night. "I'm actually inside a radio station. It's just a question of time till somebody notices me, then I'll be upstairs and behind a microphone. After that, the movies."

But getting "upstairs" proved to be another of Erin's fantasies. The only upstairs employees who saw her were the girls who shuttled scripts back and forth between Mimeo and the broadcast studios. Every workday was a challenge to physical endurance; eight hours of typing meant bloodshot eyes, eardrums numb from the incessant noise of the machines, lungs aching from cigarette fumes. In addition, there was loneliness. None of the other typists attempted to be friendly; Erin was too young, too pretty. Still, she was learning. She began to recognize good dramatic scripts from bad; she grew familiar with the names listed on the credit sheets, the producers and directors, the radio actors and actresses who worked in support of the film guest stars; the usage of cues for music and sound effects. In the bungalow court, in the evenings, she listened to the broadcasts of the scripts she had typed and decided if the whole ensemble effort had succeeded or fallen short.

Three months passed, and Erin was no nearer her goal. Then, one afternoon, Betty, the snub-nosed redheaded script girl for "Hollywood on Parade," dashed into Mimeo with a stack of scripts. "Have we ever got rewrites!" she announced to Trudy. "Seven whole pages just to please his honor Gary Trumbull." Erin came to attention; Gary Trumbull was the current romantic star of Ajax Studios.

"What's he like, Betty?" she called out.

"Gary? A wolf in wolf's clothing. We've got five girls in the studio. Me, the harp player, three actresses. One of us is going to get the red rose for sure."

Trudy deposited the scripts at Erin's desk and saw her look of perplexity. "Hadn't you heard? Every time Gary does a show, he looks over the girls. The one he gives the red rose to is *It* for the night."

"You mean—?" Erin gaped.

"I mean! Now snap to it."

Erin typed with a speed that almost equaled the rapidity of her thoughts. *What if? Why not?* Anything to be noticed. If she could somehow get upstairs to the broadcast studio . . . Trudy had promised the new script pages within forty minutes; Erin finished them in twenty-five. Then, on the excuse of going to the washroom, she hid the pages under her blouse and flew upstairs, out the employees' entrance and across Sunset Boulevard to the florist shop.

"What's going on across the street?" the florist asked. "You're the third girl wanting a single red rose."

"The third?"

"Yeah. That'll be twenty-five cents."

"I'm sorry. I've changed my mind."

Original ideas were hard to come by, Erin thought bitterly, and trudged back across Sunset. Then, in a flash, she saw how to outwit her competition. She raced across Sunset again to the grocery-delicatessen where she daily bought the ingredients for her lunch. "Hey, Hank," she called to the grocer, "one bunch of radishes. And don't bother to bag them!"

She walked bravely onto the stage of Studio B and crossed toward the table where Gary Trumbull and the cast were trading anecdotes. One of the actresses, Erin noted, was sporting a single red rose. So was the harpist. So was Betty, who marched toward her with mayhem in her eyes. "What the hell are you doing here? Where the hell are my scripts?" Then she saw the radish corsage pinned to Erin's blouse. "Why, you little creep!"

There was a gust of laughter behind them. "Your rewrites, Mr. Trumbull," Erin said, laying the sheets on the table.

Gary looked up at her with his famous boyish grin and the bedroom eyes which had set millions of female hearts aflutter. "You've topped them all, baby. What's your name?"

"Erin Deering. I'm an actress."

"She's a typist in Mimeo!" Betty corrected hotly. "And you damn well better get back there!"

Gary nodded to a white-haired man with a world-weary expression who hovered beside the table. "Jim, get Miss Deering a chair."

"Jim," Erin realized with awe, was Jim Gittel, the famous agent. He was getting her a chair, seating her beside Gary Trumbull, and Gary was saying, "I like girls with a sense of humor. Tell me about yourself."

She remembered that everyone she had met in St. Louis and Hollywood had been intrigued by her having lived in Costa Rica, so why not Gary Trumbull? There was her life at the finca, her time at the French convent where none of the girls spoke English and she no French and she had had to pantomime everything. That was her first "acting experience." And afterward Hollywood High, and *The Pirates of Penzance*. For Gary's benefit she promoted herself from the chorus to second lead. Then she began to falter; she realized Gary's attention was not on her words but on the front of her blouse —and that Fred Gallo, the director, was glaring through the glass window of the control booth and making a slashing gesture across his throat. *Cut it.* "All right, gang," Gallo's voice boomed through the talk-back speaker, "let's do a run-though."

Erin rose from the chair. "It was wonderful to meet you, Mr. Trumbull."

"Sure." Gary glanced toward his agent and flickered his eyelids. Jim Gittel acknowledged the look with an almost imperceptible nod.

As Erin pushed through the soundproof door that separated the studio from the hall outside, she heard Jim Gittel's voice behind her.

"What time you get off work?"

She turned. "Five o'clock."

"Well, I won't finish till nine-thirty." She knew that: Gary's broadcast for the East Coast was at six, and the Pacific repeat was at nine. "Think you could meet me outside the artists' entrance?"

"You?"

"Who else? You want to act. I'm an agent. Unless you're holding out for William Morris."

Suddenly she was lightheaded. "I'll be there. Thank you, Mr. Gittel. Thank you very much."

Several minutes after nine-thirty Erin watched the members of the show exit into the studio parking lot; first Gary Trumbull, who drove off in his Rolls-Royce; then the cast members, including the actress who was wearing the single red rose; then the harpist and Betty, the script girl, also with red roses. All three women got into a Yellow Cab. Finally, Jim Gittel appeared and guided Erin to his Cadillac, a convertible with the top down.

He swung the Cadillac up Vine Street to Hollywood Boulevard, which he followed west toward Graumann's Chinese Theater. Erin supposed that they were driving to Gittel's office, although he had not indicated it. In fact, he had not spoken a word since leaving the parking lot.

"Where is your office?" she asked finally.

"Wherever my head is. Tonight it's at Gary's."

He turned north off Hollywood Boulevard onto another street, then onto a road which would go up into the Hollywood Hills.

Erin felt a twinge of nervousness. "Mr. Trumbull is married, isn't he?"

"He is."

"Will his wife be there?"

"She will."

Finally, high above Hollywood, the convertible entered a private driveway and stopped in front of a two-story Spanish-style house. Erin counted over a dozen other parked cars; there must be a party in progress, she suggested to Gittel.

"You might call it that."

A white-jacketed houseboy opened the front door and they crossed the entry hall toward the sound of laughter and piano playing. Then they were in the oak-beamed living room and Erin understood the nature of the party. The three girls with red roses were reclining on sofas and men were kissing them and groping inside their blouses. "Mr. Gittel," she said, turning to him, "can you tell me where there's a telephone?"

"What for?"

"To call a taxi. I'm going home."

He scowled at her. "I thought you wanted to act. This could be your break."

"The only break I want is because I'm good. I don't intend to cheat my way."

The following morning Erin entered the Mimeograph room and Trudy leered at her. "Well. Seems like we got your name all wrong. It's not Erin Deering, it's Miss Erin Cement Panties."

So Betty had spread the story. By now the whole building probably knew.

At noon, when Erin left for her lunch break, she chanced to pass Fred Gallo, the director, in one of the upstairs corridors. "Congratulations," he said, smiling.

"Please. I don't want to talk about it."

"Okay. But have you got a minute?" She wavered. Gallo's smile was not like Trudy's leer. It was kindly, fatherly. "Come in the office."

When they reached it, Gallo leaned back in his swivel chair and locked his arms behind his bald head. "I got a daughter about your age," he began. "If she got roped into what you did last night, I'd have beaten Gary's brains out."

"Nothing happened, Mr. Gallo."

"So I heard. I want to talk about something else I heard—in the studio yesterday. I was in the control booth, but we had a microphone open when you were telling Gary about yourself. How do you know you can act?"

"Because I've got talent."

"Anybody tell you so?"

"Yes. A man in Costa Rica. A gentleman I admired. He was an international jeweler."

"A jeweler. He'd know talent, of course."

Erin felt a surge of defiance. Then her eyes fell on a radio script on Gallo's desk. She picked it up, leafed through the pages until she found a bit of woman's dialogue. She read it aloud, with all the feeling she possessed. Then she read it again, this time translating the words into Spanish.

When she finished Gallo looked impressed. "Not bad for a sight reading. Although I liked it better in Spanish." He laughed. "Think you could do baby cries?"

"Baby cries?"

"There's a scene in next week's script that includes a nine-month-old. Let's hear what you can do."

Erin thought of the baby in the bungalow court that had kept her and her mother awake night after night. She took a deep breath and launched into an imitation. When she finished, she asked: "How was it?"

"Like wet diapers. Okay. Now let's hear pleasure." Erin cooed and prattled. Gallo nodded. "Pretty fair. Work on it a bit and report for rehearsal Monday morning."

"What about Mimeo?"

"Let me worry about that."

The next week, at dress rehearsal, Gallo increased her assignment to include walla-wallas, the term for crowd noises in the background. The following week, the director told her, she would be cast for two lines of dialogue. "Oh, and by the way," he added, "Mimeo is firing you. But you'll pick up just as much money working for me one day a week. All you have to do now is go around to AFRA and get yourself a union card."

"How can I ever thank you enough?" Erin bubbled.

"By being good," Gallo retorted. "You know you're not really an actress yet. You need professional training. Can you afford it?"

"Not unless I can find a part-time job."

"You could, but I hope you won't. You need to spend all your energy on training." Gallo thought a moment. "A friend of mine is a drama coach; he takes on an occasional free kid who's got talent and ambition like a rocket up the ass. He trains primarily for film acting." Gallo saw Erin's eyes gleam with excitement. Then her arms were around him and her lips were distributing kisses. "I'm not doing this for you," he said when he disengaged himself. "I'm doing this for my own reasons. The first, to repay the debt I owe to the guy who gave me my first job. The second, because I can go on throwing cues in that glass fishbowl for the next ten years, and when I'm washed up, nobody will remember me. Unless maybe, just maybe, they can say, 'Fred Gallo? Sure. He's the guy who discovered Erin Deering.' "

Rheinhold Hoffman glared at Erin through his horn-rimmed spectacles and emphasized every point with a toss of his white mane and an index finger that jabbed the air before him like a bayonet. "First—there vill be no boys. There vill be no beach picnics. There vill be no trash magazines. Ven you read, it vill be Ibsen, Shaw, Shakespeare, Oscar Vilde. You vill learn ballet from my vife, and you vill dance good or she break your legs. From me, I vill teach you to valk, to sit, and stand, to breathe from your belly. I vill teach you to sing—not much, not fine, but to place your voice so nobody holds his ears. You vill obey me in everything, or I break your head and kick you out. Understand, agree, promise, *ja?*"

"Oh, I promise! I swear!"

"So ve give it a try. In six months, ve shall see."

Six

France
July 1945

ERIN SAT hunched on her army cot and smoked another cigarette. Her hair was in curlers, her face cold-creamed, her shoulders covered by her dressing gown. Overhead she heard the drum of rain on the tent canvas. Didn't it ever stop raining in France? They had never warned her about that when she volunteered to join the Army Special Service Troupe to entertain the GIs overseas. About diarrhea, yes; about fleas and bedbugs, yes; about the khaki fatigues and boots she would wear except at show time, yes; about lugging her heavy barracks bag without help and eating out of a mess kit after standing in line behind a hundred GIs—yes again. But not the rain. Absolutely nothing about that.

She heard a groan from the cot across from her. Madge Carson, the red-haired comedienne of the troupe, was propped up on one elbow. "Erin, one more smoke and you'll turn to a side of bacon. For crying out loud, go to sleep."

"I can't. I'm waiting for that phone call."

"Why the hell does your husband always call you at one in the morning?"

"Why the hell does the connection always break?"

There was a moan from the third cot, occupied by Trixie Winters, the dancing starlet. "Will you two knock off the yakking? I'm dead."

"Promises, promises!" Madge said.

The women were exhausted and edgy. In the afternoon they had given a show at a different army camp, then a bone-jarring Jeep ride to their present location, a regimental base somewhere near Strasbourg. There had been an evening performance followed by endless jitterbugging in the officers' mess. And tomorrow it would be repeated all over again.

Erin lighted another cigarette and ran over in her mind what Ben had said on the phone before the connection had broken off. He had reported that Erin's mother wanted her monthly allowance increased and she needed the down payment for a new house at the beach. Erin had told Ben, who was not only her husband but her agent and personal manager, to pay over whatever would make her mother happy and Ben had grumbled that "nothing will make that woman happy," and then rambled on about inconsequentials, which meant that he was leading up to something unpleasant. Erin pictured Ben twiddling with his hair, what there was of it, and shifting his feet about on the desk, either at the office or in the den of their Beverly Hills home, while he tried to approach the main subject. Then he had launched into it. "What I'm really calling about, baby, is the studio. It's absolutely urgently important that—" And there the call had broken off.

Everything with Ben was absolutely urgently important. It was refreshing, Erin thought, to be away from the insularity, the claustrophobia of Hollywood, where everybody ate dinner at the Derby, went to the same parties at Malibu, exchanged the same lovers, saw the same shows at Mocambo and Ciro's, were buried in the same Forest Lawn cemetery. In the months that Erin had been on camp tour she had reacquainted herself with reality. She had heard the crump of shellfire, the screech of falling bombs before the Nazi collapse; she had seen the pain and loneliness of the wounded in base hospitals, the charred and gutted remains of villages and the fortitude of the homeless.

"Miss Deering, are you awake?" a corporal asked, peering into the tent. "We're ready with Hollywood again. You can take it in the officers' mess."

Ben picked up exactly where he had left off. "Baby, it's absolutely urgently important that you be back here no later than July twenty-fifth. I've signed you for the new Spencer Tracy. You're scheduled for costume fittings on the twenty-sixth and—"

"Ben! I am not leaving the troupe. I've told you that before."

"I know, I know. But listen, baby, the shooting is over in Europe. You've got to pick up your career before the audiences forget you."

"Ben, I've *got* an audience. The most important in the world. Our boys may not be dying, but they still need entertainment. Everybody wants to go home and they can't. Morale is shot to hell."

"Are you saying you won't come home?"

"I'm saying it."

"Okay," he sighed. "I'll call you again in a couple of days. Love and gooses."

Ben expected she'd still come around, Erin decided. He had been all for her camp tour in the beginning. "Every GI who sees you will be a fan for life," he had predicted. Then he had been outraged at the discovery that the troupe would include Madge Carson and Trixie Winters. They were nobodies. Erin Deering, the sensational star of *Fire and Ice*, and *Hedda Gabler*, the actress *Variety* had hailed as "the volcanic glacier," in recognition of her controlled intensity, would be slumming with a troupe of pork-and-beans players. But Ben had not foreseen the craft and cunning of his wife's performances. Erin had chosen to be completely different from Betty Grable exhibiting her legs, Martha Raye making with the gags, and those starlets who played straight for Bob Hope. Instead, Erin had sung songs of home—"Carolina Moon," "My Old Kentucky Home," "Back Home in Indiana"—and the GIs had taken her to their hearts. *Stars and Stripes* had run photographs of Erin in half a dozen editions and praised her as the American Marlene Dietrich.

"Guess where we're going next," Madge Carson challenged Erin several days later as their Jeep bumped its way to another airfield. "The Riviera!"

"Where did you hear that?"

"Straight from the Colonel's mouth. Pays to play footsie with the top brass. Anyway, it's Nice and an honest-to-God hotel. Guests of the French Government. We play the hospitals for four days, then it's Stateside."

So the tour was almost over, and Erin would be back in Hollywood by the time Ben had specified. Was it possible, she wondered, that he had pulled strings? Or that the studio had? In any case, the Riviera was the Riviera. . . .

But not as Erin had envisioned it from travel brochures. The famed gaiety of Nice, the queen city of the Côte d'Azur, was muted by the presence of too many women in black, too many Frenchmen on crutches or with empty sleeves pinned to chests. There were no vacationers save those Allied military on rest and recuperation. And when Erin went shopping on her first day in Nice, she found that wartime austerity meant bare shelves. Only by diligence and luck could she find one sundress and one swimsuit left over from prewar stock.

The troupe's first performance was in the evening in the ballroom of the Hotel Négresco, before an audience of French, British and American ambulatory patients from the local hospitals. Before they went on stage Erin proposed to Madge and Trixie that after the show they should stay dressed in their evening dresses and taxi to Monte Carlo and the fabled Casino.

"What'll we use for money?" Madge asked. "You cleaned us in that last poker game."

"I'll lend it back to you," Erin said. "It'll be worth it to see how the real thing stacks up against our studio imitations."

The real thing proved to be a confection of white stone with twin towers, perched on a cliff above the moonlit Mediterranean. As Erin and her friends paused to buy their admission tickets in the foyer, they caught a glimpse of the main hall with its massive crystal chandeliers, marble walls and gilt mirrors. "Damn, there's hardly anybody here," Madge commented, looking at the few elderly women at the tables and a scattering of men in Allied military uniforms. "Where are all the ritzy people?" The answer was that they were mainly bankrupt, wounded or dead, or on their way home from concentration camps.

"Maybe it'll be better in a *salon privé*," Erin said hopefully. "The Kitchen, as they call it, is just for the two-bit players."

"Huh? Where'd you hear all that?"

"Research, honey. I boned up for a movie I did with a Monte Carlo scene. The big players pay extra and go into a *salon privé*. Want to give it a try?"

Madge and Trixie declined. If the Kitchen was cheaper, they would have extra francs for the tables. Very well, Erin said, she would see them later. Erin paid for her ticket to a *salon* and turned to enter the main hall. As she did so, she noticed a young man in evening clothes limp past, leaning heavily on a cane. The lower part of his face was lost in a dark beard and fierce drooping moustache; a black eye patch covered his left eye. Just before he reached the main hall a gray-haired man in tails, obviously a casino attendant, hurried up to the man with the cane and tapped him on the shoulder. There was an exchange of words, the younger man threw back his head in laughter and surrendered his cane to the attendant. Weren't canes allowed? Erin wondered, or was there the possibility that it was a weapon of some sort? Then an even stranger action followed: the younger man tugged at his beard and it came away in his hand. Then the moustache, then the eye patch. He handed them to the attendant, who grinned in satisfaction. Erin wished that she could see the young man's face, but his back was to her. Then she did see it, reflected in one of the great gilt mirrors. She caught her breath. Where had she seen that face? When? Not recently. Not in years. Or perhaps never. Perhaps he simply reminded her of someone. Then her speculation ended as he strolled into the gaming hall and linked arms with a handsome young woman.

The *salon privé* which Erin entered was a miniature version of the main gaming room, with its own bar and dining area. There were only three players at the roulette wheel, which Erin preferred to baccarat or chemin de fer. She bought her chips and settled into a chair next to the croupier's post. She lost the first four bets and began to grow anxious. This was not a movie scene; she was not wagering with play money—it was real, it was her own. The croupier chanted, "*Les jeux sont faits. Rien ne va plus.*" The ball whirled again before she gathered courage to place a fifth bet. This time she recouped a small amount and was about to try again when she saw the young man who had engaged in the strange scene in the foyer seat himself across from her at the roulette table. In a flash it came back to her—the intense brown eyes, the firm mouth, the high cheekbones—all were the same, but in a younger version of the man who had inspired her to a theatrical career. The jeweler, Theodore Brullov.

He placed a bet, lost, placed another, then saw Erin's eyes fixed upon him. He smiled politely. *"Bon soir."*

Erin was disappointed. "Do you speak any English?"

"Sure. What would you like to hear?" The accent was faintly Harvard.

"Well—I saw you coming into the Casino. That was a very odd scene, the fake beard and moustache and eye patch. What was it all about?"

He grinned. "Just trying to fool Victor. But he sees through me every time. He's the Casino's *physiognomiste.*"

"What in the world is that?"

"A face man. Every casino has one. His job is to spot card sharpers and gamblers who have worked out a system to beat the house. But I've never been able to fool Victor. His memory is a catalogue of hundreds of thousands of faces, or so he claims, and I believe him."

"But why would you want to fool Victor?"

"It's a game, for laughs." He paused to watch the roulette ball drop into a numbered slot. He shrugged at his second loss. He signaled to the waiter in the background and ordered a glass of champagne. "How about you, Miss . . . Miss . . . ?"

"Erin Deering. And yes, a glass, please." It irked her that he did not recognize the face known to millions. "Don't you ever go to the movies?" she asked.

"Not willingly. They bore me." Then he looked puzzled. "Why do you ask?"

"It's unimportant, Mr. Brullov."

His puzzlement increased. "How did you know my name?"

"I took a chance. Your face is almost a carbon copy of one I've never forgotten. Would your father be Theodore Brullov?"

He nodded. "So you know Dad. You must be from New York."

"Hollywood. I met your father when I was fourteen. He was my first big crush—partly, I suppose, because he told me one day I should be an actress, which I am; but mostly because he was the most charming man I had ever met, or probably ever will meet."

He laughed. "That sounds like a challenge." He regarded Erin with added interest. "My name is Tony, incidentally. How about skipping the wheel here and taking our champagne out onto the terrace. We've got lots to talk about."

Erin agreed readily. They strolled along the seaward terrace with its breathtaking view of the moonlit Mediterranean. They flew from subject to subject, like two friends meeting after long separation. How was Tony's father? Fine, as always. Mother not too well. How long had Erin been in Europe? Four months this year, two months last year. And Tony? A year and a half. He was a major in the OSS, had been wounded in a parachute drop behind the German lines, had been discharged from the hospital and now was on rest and recuperation. Erin sketched her meeting with Tony's father in Costa Rica, highly dramatized, and her experiences on the army camp tour and her husband's insistence that she return to Hollywood for the new picture.

"Damn it to hell!" Tony interrupted.

"What's wrong?"

"I was hoping you weren't married."

"Didn't you see my wedding ring?"

"Sure. I figured you might be wearing it as a hands-off thing. A lot of girls over here use a ring to avoid complications. I didn't see you with a husband, so I thought there wasn't one."

His words startled her. Tonight, she realized suddenly, she felt distinctly unmarried. "Are you?" she asked.

"No." He frowned at the sea for a moment, then: "Tell me about your husband."

What could she tell? She had married Ben more or less out of gratitude. Ben had been her first and only agent; he had hawked her talent around from studio to studio, and when he had secured her first major role, he immediately proposed marriage. He had hitched his wagon to a star and intended to enjoy the ride for the balance of her career.

None of this Erin would admit to Tony. Instead she said, "Ben is my agent and my personal manager. His whole life is Hollywood."

"And Hollywood is six thousand miles away." Tony's words were loaded with implication, Erin thought; then he disarmed them immediately. "I mean, we're here on the most beautiful coastline in the world. It's a warm night and the moon is out. I think two friends deserve to enjoy it. How about a drive along the Corniche?"

She hesitated. "I came with friends. How will I get a ride back to Nice?"

"Tell them you've got a ride." He took her arm as if it were settled. "I'm sure I can pick up a bottle of champagne in the Casino."

"No, thanks," Erin said. "The night is intoxication enough." Why did she have to say that? Then she remembered: She had spoken that line in her last picture.

The car—borrowed, Tony said—was an aged convertible which he drove as though it were a souped-up racer. With the throttle pushed to the floorboard, he flashed along the Corniche Inférieure, passing the occasional auto or bus as if it were standing still. Once Tony rounded a blind curve and almost collided with an oncoming vehicle. Erin ducked her head in fright. "Tony! For God's sake, I want to live to see the sunrise."

"You will," he shouted back. "Tomorrow I'll see if I can rent us a plane at the Nice Airport. Wouldn't that be a kick?"

"In the head, yes. Count me out."

They roared through the outskirts of Beaulieu sur Mer and then Tony swerved onto a side road and bore south onto a cape heavily wooded and dense with expensive villas, most of which nestled behind stone walls. Erin caught a glimpse of a road sign which announced it to be Cap Ferrat.

"Tony, do you know where you're going?"

"We're there," he said. He braked the car to a stop outside a high iron-filigreed gate. The villa inside the gate, behind the wall, he said, belonged to an English lord. Tony had been a house guest the winter before; he had met the son of the lord at Oxford, when he was doing postgraduate studies after Harvard.

"It's hard to believe," Tony said, "at this time last year this villa was the cozy hideaway for some Nazi general. Cap Ferrat swarmed with German brass until the Allies made their southern invasion."

He helped Erin from the car and peered through the gate. "No use ringing the bell. The place is closed for the summer. I know, because I phoned yesterday, and all I got was the caretaker." He took Erin by the arm and guided her along the bouldered wall until he located a spot that suited him. "Okay, give me your pumps and I'll boost you up."

"Tony! That's trespassing."

"Not when I'm a friend of the family. Come on."

"No. Unless you tell me what this is all about."

"It's simple. They've got a swimming pool, one of the best on the Riviera. And there are swimsuits and towels in the bathhouse."

"You mean you brought us all the way here just to go swimming?"

"Sure. Could there ever be a better night for it? Let's go."

"I don't know why I'm doing this," Erin sighed, removing her pumps. Seconds later she was teetering on the top of the wall and watching Tony scrabble for a foothold among the cemented boulders.

They dropped down into a rustic garden and Tony led her to a path that descended steeply past a wooden promontory on which Erin made out the dark silhouette of the villa. When they reached the lower portion of the path, the swimming pool came into view.

"Oh–oh," Tony muttered. The pool was an empty shell of concrete; it had been drained during the owner's absence.

"Well, that's that," Erin said.

"Maybe not." Tony went to the bathhouse and disappeared inside. When he returned he had two beach towels. "A bit musty but clean," he pronounced. "But no swimsuits. Let's try down at the cove. Nothing beats salt water anyway."

"But you said there were no swimsuits."

He grinned at her.

"Tony, what makes you think I'd swim naked with a man I've barely met?"

"Pretend you're doing a movie scene."

"No. Absolutely not."

"Okay. Back in a while."

She watched him start down a series of steps which apparently led toward the cove. The man was insane, she told herself, and then decided that she did not care to be left alone in strange surroundings. When she caught up with Tony he was already at the water's edge. He shucked his dinner jacket and shirt and piled them neatly atop his beach towel on the pebbly shore; then his shoes, socks, trousers and shorts. He glanced back at Erin, who was watching intently, waved to her and waded into the water. When he was waist-deep he threw himself forward and began to swim toward a float far out in the inlet.

Erin picked up a small rock and threw it into the water; she felt both irritated at her prudery and excited by the sight of Tony's athletic body. Then abruptly she smiled to herself. What was it she had blurted out to Tony's father all those years ago at the finca? She would be a courtesan in tropical Balboa and dance naked with her lover on the hotel balcony. What adolescent bravado—or was she being adolescent now? Or worse, a coward? She kicked off her pumps, slipped off her evening dress and deposited it on her towel. She stepped to the water's edge and dipped her foot in. The water was wonderfully warm and inviting. "Oh, what the hell," she muttered. She unfastened her brassiere, stripped off her panties and waded in.

She swam lazily, enjoying the foaming caress of the salt water. She felt unbelievably free, a strange primitive excitement. After a while she trod water and tried to locate Tony. She saw the flash of his arms farther out and she swam toward him. "I knew you would," he shouted as she drew near, and then they swam side by side, like two playful otters. Finally they reached the swimming float and caught hold of its anchor chain.

"Are you always this crazy?" Erin demanded.

"Always. Crazy is what keeps you alive."

Tony grasped the edge of the float and pulled himself aboard. "A friend of mine wasn't crazy enough," he shouted down to her. "We did a parachute drop together. The Nazis were waiting for us. I was crazy and ran for it. He played it safe and surrendered. They hung him on a meat hook until he was dead."

She shuddered and tightened her grip on the anchor chain. "Thank God that's behind us."

"There are still the Japs. I'm waiting for a transfer to the Pacific."

"*Oh, Tony!*"

He stared up at the sky. "God, what a beautiful night. One I'll never forget."

Nor would Erin. "Tony," she called, "pull me up."

He crouched at the edge of the float and gave her his hand. She clambered aboard, trying not to appear to ungainly. Then she faced him squarely, boldly.

"Christ, you're beautiful," he said in an awed tone.

"I feel beautiful." She laughed. "And shameless."

They stretched out on the float and gazed at the rind of a

quarter-moon and the blazing stars. At first Erin felt chilled as the sea water dripped from her skin; then shortly she was dry, and warmth returned.

"A penny," Tony said finally.

"Oh . . . I'm just surprised at myself. All my years in Hollywood I was so damned respectable. I never let myself get into compromising situations. Or on this tour. Every day a new camp, new invitations. But I was always the irreproachable married lady—until tonight."

"I feel flattered."

"Don't be. I told you how I felt about your father. This is acting out a schoolgirl fantasy. I'm fourteen again. Back at the finca. It's a tropical night like this. And your father is beside me."

Tony chuckled. "I must remember to thank Dad."

"Oh, by all means."

They were silent again; the only sound was the slapping of the water against the float. Erin wondered to herself how many other women had swum naked with Tony. So many, she decided, that he had probably forgotten their names. At least, she hoped he *had* forgotten.

"At the Casino tonight," she said, breaking the silence, "I saw you with a blond girl."

"Oh—Karen. We met in Switzerland. Bern was the command station for OSS-Europe. Karen liaised between the station and the guys going on assignment. She'd pretend to be dating us, give us our orders, then we'd slip off to some little airfield in France, and on to Germany."

Tony described the parachute drops at night in the dark of the moon, with the countryside below barely visible by starlight. Sometimes the drops were unlucky, when a man landed in a river or lake and drowned. Or before dynamiting a bridge or powerhouse, there might be guards to be dealt with, by knife or strangling wire.

"Weren't you ever frightened?" Erin asked.

"Hell, yes. The man who isn't frightened is the one who

makes mistakes. So you stay frightened, stay a little crazy, and live to enjoy a night like this."

Tony was enjoying it in a way that was becoming very noticeable. The sight of his growing erection did not offend Erin, as it might with some other man. It was a tribute; it made her wish to reach out and caress it.

Tony saw the direction of her gaze and smiled. "They say this always happens to a man just before he's executed. An affirmation of life." He paused, but Erin made no reply. Then he bent over her and brought his lips down to hers.

"Tony . . . please," she whispered weakly.

"Only if you want to."

If! She sighed deeply and her arms went about his neck. "I said 'Please,' didn't I?"

The next afternoon the USO troupe appeared at a different Nice hospital and Erin gave one of her rare poor performances. She missed her opening song cue, sang "My Old Kentucky Home" off-key, and absentmindedly walked off the improvised stage before her closing number. "What's wrong with you, honey?" Madge asked afterward. "A hangover or your period?" Memories, Erin was tempted to tell Madge. The delicious delights of adultery. First on that swimming float, then again on the slow, dreamy drive back to Nice, when she had begged Tony to pull off the road and she had climbed onto his lap.

"What you need is to bake it out," Madge counseled. "What say we all grab a couple of hours on the beach?"

"Count me out," Erin said. "I'm allergic to the sun."

A few minutes later she rendezvoused with Tony at the harbor, and he led her to the small sailboat he had borrowed. It was remarkable, she thought, how easily he could produce cars and boats; it was certainly an advantage to be the son of an international jeweler who knew the right people.

They sailed eastward along the coast until the wind died and the sails went slack. "Thank God," Tony said, grinning, as he left the tiller. "Now we can get down to more important business." He pressed his mouth against Erin's throat while his hands busied themselves with her dress and she tugged at his trousers.

After they had made love, they sunbathed on the foredeck and Tony napped briefly. Erin gazed at his naked body and compared him to her husband. Tony, surging with animal vitality, gay, amusing, confident; and Ben—how could she describe him? Humdrum. Even in sex. It took love to bring people alive, she thought, and then was startled by her conclusion. Was she in love with Tony? Was he with her? The question frightened her. Love meant surrendering her freedom, her happiness, her peace of mind, into another's keeping. It was a form of bondage. Then she had a disturbing vision—the memory of her mother that night in Costa Rica, reading in bed, wearing her best negligee, with a ribbon in her hair, waiting for Ted Brullov, who never came. God spare her that same scene, that she should ever wait in vain for the coming of Ted Brullov's son. . . . Still, she told herself, better to avoid that word "love." Call it an "episode"; that was easier to deal with. Two bodies simply bent on self-gratification. If simply that, she was still grateful and eager for more. Sex with Tony had become an obsession; her brain was filled with memories of the last lovemaking and anticipation of the next, with ideas for new positions, new arenas—in elevators, on hotel balconies, on park benches, wherever there might be the added spice of discovery. "Never turn away from the feast," Carrie Wyatt had declared on one of those mornings in far-off Costa Rica. Dear, wise old Carrie. If she could see Erin now.

That evening when she rejoined the troupe, Madge raised her eyebrows at Erin's blazing sunburn. "You're allergic, all right"—she sniffed—"especially to those who thought they were your friends." Erin shrugged off the barb; all she cared about was meeting Tony after the performance. He drove her to a movie house on the Promenade des Anglais, which was showing the latest Erin Deering film. Someone must have recognized the Hollywood star and called the newspapers, for when Erin came out of the theater, laughing, on Tony's arm, they were met by the popping of flashbulbs.

"I guess the movie was a stupid idea," she said to Tony, in his car. "We've got to be more discreet."

"How? By not seeing each other?"

"No, silly! But you can't spend tonight at my hotel, and I can't spend it at yours. We've got to get the bloodhounds off the scent."

They would have breakfast together the following morning, they decided, at a modest café that Tony knew just off the Flower Market. When Erin joined him she said she was positive that she had not been followed. Halfway through their meal they heard the rapid clicking of a camera. A moment later a man ducked out into the street. That evening the leading newspaper in Nice carried a photograph of Erin and Tony with their hands linked across the table.

In the middle of the night Erin was awakened by the telephone beside her bed. The operator apologized for the hour, but there was a telephone call from Hollywood, California. Then Ben was on the line, icy-voiced.

"The studio wants you back immediately. They're arranging air space for tomorrow."

"I can't do it, Ben. I won't. Make up some excuse."

"Like what?"

"That's your department. Say I'm sick."

"They know that already. Have photographic proof, you might say." Ben's voice altered to a pleading tone. "Erin, for Christ's sake, think of your career. Don't throw it all away because of some foreign cock."

Erin slammed down the receiver and shouted at the disconnected phone, "He's an American, damn you! An American major in the OSS!"

There was no longer any point in secrecy. The following day Erin and Tony went about openly, embraced in public, and thumbed their noses at the clicking cameras. It was the final day of the tour, and Erin told the officer in charge that she would not return with the troupe to America. The officer insisted; no one could leave his charge, her space on the transport was reserved. "I told him I didn't give one lousy damn," she repeated afterward to Tony. "From now on, it's just you and me."

One day they motored to the perfume village of Grasse and picnicked beside a field of carnations. They were followed by a motorcade of photographers and reporters demanding Erin's views on love and lovers. Tony shouted obscenities at them and threatened to break their skulls. The next day they evaded the press by slipping out of Nice early in the morning. They drove to Villefranche, where Erin was enchanted by the crescent harbor veiled in soft blue haze, by the pastel houses clinging to the hillsides and the narrow stone streets dating back to the fourteenth century. Then again someone recognized Erin, and the press descended in full cry. Tony smashed a photographer's camera and Erin obliged the other photographers by saluting them with an upraised finger. At sunset they registered at one of the local hotels and asked for adjoining rooms but slept the night in only one—Tony's.

The following morning Tony told Erin he had to be back in Nice before noon; he had an important engagement. The lack of detail bothered her; it must be connected with the OSS, she thought, which was hardly a comfort. When they reached Nice, Tony dropped her off at her hotel and promised to return in time for lunch together. They would dine in style, he said, at the Hotel Ruhl. That, Erin decided, meant they would have something to celebrate.

But at the Ruhl, Tony made no explanation. He seemed, Erin thought, in a somber mood. Finally, unable to curb her curiosity, she asked, "Did everything work out all right?"

"Work out?"

"Yes. Your engagement, or whatever."

"Oh. I went to church."

Erin choked back an impulse to laugh with relief. She could

not picture Tony, the passionate lover, the OSS saboteur, in a house of worship. "Church!" she echoed. "Why in the world didn't you take me along?"

"Because those damned photographers and reporters would have traipsed after us. Hollywood hoopla has no place at a memorial service." He saw Erin's look of bafflement. "It's a Russian Orthodox cathedral. It was a memorial service on the anniversary of the murders of the Tsar and his family."

"Nicholas and Alexandra?"

"And their children and their retainers."

"I see," Erin said, although she did not. "Tony, I know you're half Russian; but the Romanovs died years before you were born. How could they possibly matter to you?"

Tony paused; the expression in his eyes was as if he were closing a door between Erin and himself. "They mean something to my father, a very great deal. That's what matters."

The rest of the afternoon went badly. Tony, for once, did not propose a new amusement; rather, he suggested that Erin might like some free time in which to visit the local shops. For a moment she felt panic. Was he slipping away from her? No. She must be logical; she must accept that Tony might be surfeited with what he had called "Hollywood hoopla"; he would be in a better mood by dinner.

But he was not. They ate at a seafood restaurant overlooking the harbor and Tony barely spoke until their coffee. "I've got my orders," he said. "Tomorrow I'm leaving for New York and then on to Hawaii and Guam."

Erin was silent. She had known it would happen; Tony had told her that on their first night at Monte Carlo. But she had pushed it into the darkest closet of her mind—had never introduced the subject into their conversation. Finally she said, "How long have you known?"

"A couple of days." He had camouflaged it well.

"Maybe the Japanese will surrender before you get there."

"No chance."

"Well," Erin said finally, "there's no point of my hanging

135

around the Riviera by myself. I'll tell the studio to get me out. There's one thing I want you to know, Tony. When I get back to Hollywood, I'm filing for divorce from Ben."

He frowned at her announcement. "Not on my account, please."

"*Tony!*" She thought frantically for the right words. "Darling, I'm in love with you. And I have every reason to think you are with me."

"I am," he admitted gravely.

She went weak with relief. "Well then? I'll get the divorce the quickest way possible. A Mexican divorce. Then I'll fly the Pacific and we can be married wherever you're stationed."

"No."

"Darling, *why not?*"

"Because I won't be Mr. Erin Deering."

Erin's jaw sagged. "Tony! It would never happen. You're too strong for that."

"Let's say, strong enough to say, No, thank you. We've had our fun. Let's leave it at that."

That night, their final night, they made love with an intensity that approached desperation. Afterward, as Erin lay exhausted in Tony's arms, she thought to herself, *At least there's one love that will never desert me. Hollywood or Broadway, I'll always have my audience.*

Seven

New York City
Winter 1950

TONY BRULLOV made his way past the display cases in the new Fifth Avenue store of Brullov & Company and counted the number of salespeople busy with customers. Six out of eight. Business was good for a mid-morning in January. At the rear of the store Tony took the elevator to the third floor and went down the corridor to his office. As he entered, Trisha, his secretary, was placing the morning mail on his desk. She was a woman with prematurely gray hair, a prominent nose with flaring nostrils and a permanently sardonic expression. She eyed Tony shrewdly as he sank listlessly into his desk chair.

"Coffee, *mon capitaine?*"

"Please."

"And maybe two aspirin?"

"Thank you, Mother." He had taken aspirin when he had awakened, but without noticeable effect on the pounding in his forehead.

Trisha lingered in the doorway. "It went well last night?"

"Till three this morning." Tony propped an elbow on the desk and rested his forehead on one hand. "Damn these charity affairs. Always too much liquor, too much dancing, too many old biddies."

"But?"

"But Mrs. Wellington-Sims should stop by later this week. She wants her diamond lavaliere reworked. I'll tell the shop to add twenty more carats."

"Only twenty for Mrs. Wellington-Sims?"

"It's a beginning. The word is that her daughter is about to be engaged. I danced two sets with her. That ought to shut out Tiffany and Cartier on the engagement ring."

"Bravo!" Trisha disappeared and returned with the coffee and aspirin. "Incidentally," she said, "your father wants to see you."

"Okay. After the coffee."

Trisha retreated to her office and left Tony to his thoughts. His father probably wanted to go over again the proposal to switch the London manager to Zurich, where sales had fallen off rather sharply. Tony had suggested hiring a new man from outside, which would be a perfect excuse for him to cross the Atlantic and do the interviewing. His real reason for wanting to go was the possibility of skiing in Switzerland, and, if the timing was right, he might enter the elimination trials at Gstaad and perhaps come home with another trophy to add to the collection on his office wall. Tony's awards extended beyond skiing; there were silver and gold cups for championship yacht racing, speedboating, steeplechase, and point-to-point sports-car rallies. Tony enjoyed competition, and the publicity connected with his wins had meant handsome business for Brullov & Company. His father was proud of Tony's successes in sports and as a society salesman for the company; but he was unhappy that there was no framed photograph of a wife on Tony's desk—only that of Tony's late mother. At age thirty, Ted Brullov reminded his son, it was time that he provided grandchildren and heirs for the business.

The intercom rasped on the desk and Tony flipped the switch. "Can I see you?" Ted Brullov's voice boomed.

"Right now, Dad."

Tony went down the corridor to his father's office and found him in conversation with a man who appeared to be in his mid-fifties. His hair was gray and straggly and his face a craggy ruin; there were bags under his eyes, a wrinkled double chin and hollows in his cheeks. Despite all this, there was still a sense of strength and determination; the mouth was firm and the eyes an electric blue. He might possibly be a member of the English landed gentry, Tony thought, although his father introduced him as "Doctor Serge Kohlski."

"If you don't mind, Doctor," Ted Brullov said, "would you repeat what you've told me. I'd like my son to hear it from the beginning."

"Certainly." Dr. Kohlski nodded. "I'm an art dealer in Rio de Janeiro. Import and export. Next week I leave for Moscow to buy Russian icons, nineteenth-century jewelry, *objets d'art* —especially the work of Karl Fabergé. I thought perhaps your company might wish to commission me to make purchases on its behalf."

Tony glanced toward his father to gauge his attitude toward the proposal. Ted Brullov replied with an almost imperceptible lift of his eyebrows, which signaled cautious approval.

"I presume that you will have Soviet approval to export your purchases?"

Dr. Kohlski smiled comfortably. "There will be no problem. All I wish at this time is an indication of the size of your commitment, and an agreement to forward thirty percent of the total due me to a mutually satisfactory bank in Stockholm."

Tony's eyes returned to his father, and again there was a delicate lift of the eyebrows. It was confusing; if Brullov Senior was in favor of the proposal, why did he not make the commitment? Somewhere, Tony decided, he was expected to find a flaw in the arrangement.

Tony tried again. "I was under the impression that everything worthwhile and exportable had left Russia years ago, with the refugees from the Revolution. Are you saying that the Soviet government is willing to sell off some of the treasures which they confiscated, as they did in 1927?"

"No," Kohlski said. "I am speaking of articles of value which have gone underground, so to speak. There are still many closet tsarists inside the Soviet Union, and with whom I have contacts. How the merchandise will leave Russia is my problem and my secret."

Ted Brullov intervened in the dialogue. "May I suggest, Dr. Kohlski, that you elaborate about those contacts for Tony's benefit."

"With pleasure. My name, Serge Kohlski, is an alias. My baptismal name was Serge Andreivitch Romanov. A shirt-tailed cousin, so to speak, of the late lamented Imperial Family." Tony saw his father's smile; this was apparently the crux of the matter. "As a Romanov, I have invaluable contacts with tsarist sympathizers, men and women who will be willing sellers to one of the royal blood. And through them, incidentally, I hope to locate some of those criminals who murdered my relatives."

There was a moment's silence. From Ted Brullov's startled expression, it was clear to Tony that the mention of the Romanov murders was a surprise.

"To what purpose?" Ted asked finally.

Kohlski-Romanov gazed from father to son with an air of calm dedication. "To mete out justice, gentlemen. The Jews are hunting down their Nazi exterminators and the world applauds. Why should there not be similar vengeance for Ekaterinburg? It was just as infamous as Belsen and Buchenwald. Time does not dim the Bolshevik horror, nor my intention that blood must be paid for in blood."

Ted Brullov sat back in his desk chair and pulled absentmindedly on an earlobe. "I presume that you know I am Russian-born, that I worked for Fabergé, and was loyal to my Tsar."

"I do. That is why I speak so freely."

"But I am now an American citizen, and I wish that the tragedies of the past should remain in the past. As a Romanov, I realize that is difficult for you to accept. But I am afraid our company cannot make a commitment to you which may, if matters should go wrong, implicate us in an international incident." He turned to Tony. "Do you agree?"

"I do, Dad."

Kohlski-Romanov shrugged philosophically and rose from his chair. "At least, gentlemen, I hope that you will do me the favor of silence."

"You have our word," Ted said.

"Then thank you for your time."

After the departure of their visitor, Brullov drummed his fingers on the desk and frowned at his son. "I don't like it."

Tony agreed. "It doesn't smell right. He didn't have to throw in about Ekaterinburg. A man who says that blood will be paid for in blood doesn't advertise his intentions to strangers. Unless he's a mental case."

"I thought of that. But everything else made sense, good commercial sense. Unless . . ." Brullov broke off and pushed the button on his intercom. "Miss Wilson, would you get me Mikhail Sazonoff? He's listed in my personal phone book." Miss Wilson called back in a moment that Mr. Sazonoff was on line one.

Tony listened curiously as his father exchanged pleasantries and then came to the point: Had Sazonoff been contacted by a Dr. Kohlski who claimed to be a surviving member of the

Romanov family? Tony watched his father's expression turn grave as he repeated "I see . . . I see," as if he did *not* see. Brullov hung up and turned to his son. "He saw Sazonoff yesterday. But he used a different name. He was Boris Karlinsky, a mechanical engineer. He's going to Moscow and wants to be sales representative for United Foundry. Then he went into the Romanov routine and said he was out to avenge Ekaterinburg."

"Then he *is* a mental case," Tony said.

"Or very clever." Brullov consulted his watch and pushed the intercom button again. This time he asked Miss Wilson to make a transatlantic call to London; he wished to speak to Leonid Pavlovitch. Because of the time difference, he added, Pavlovitch would probably have already left his office and Miss Wilson should try his home number.

"Who's Pavlovitch?" Tony asked.

"An emigré like myself. Editor of a Russian-language monthly on scientific subjects."

"And you want to know if Kohlski may have approached him, too?"

"He's the likeliest. Pavlovitch is the grand old man of the White Russian colony in London."

It was a few minutes before the connection was completed. Ted Brullov repeated the questions which he had asked of his New York friend, and the answers were similar. Two weeks earlier a man who claimed to be a Romanov was going to Moscow; he wished to be commissioned by the London editor to write a series of articles on Soviet scientific advances. And he intended to hunt down the killers of Ekaterinburg.

"This time," Brullov told Tony, "he used the name Kohlski, but he was a professor, not a doctor. Whatever his real name, it's not Romanov. He's someone on a fishing expedition. He hopes that someone he talks to will say 'bravo' to the vengeance idea. He figures one of us may come forward and say he's a member of the group who killed Pyotr Pagodin and the others."

Tony glanced about nervously. "Shouldn't we be talking about this somewhere else? Maybe in Central Park?"

His father chuckled. "Hell, Miss Wilson is stone-deaf, except on the phone or the intercom." Even so, he lowered his voice. "What we have to find out is if Kohlski, or whatever his name, is acting on orders from Moscow. Or he could be one of the few surviving members of the Ekaterinburg firing squad."

Tony pondered the idea. "In other words, he may have escaped from Russia and is trying to flush out the people who want his head. Know his enemies and then remove them."

"Exactly. Or he may be the agent for such a man. A hired executioner." Ted Brullov tilted back in his desk chair and permitted himself a small smile. "Whatever, he's bound to surface again. I'll make it happen."

"How?"

"I'll talk to the U.S. Immigration people and give them a description of the man. I'll say we suspect him of burglarizing our store."

"That means you'll have to make a police report. A false one at that."

"I couldn't care less. The main thing is to flush our man into the open. Then I can act."

Tony looked anxiously at his father. "I think you should follow your own words to Kohlski. Let the tragedies of the past remain in the past."

"We'll argue that when the time comes."

Ted Brullov's stratagem failed. The immigration authorities could not match the jeweler's description of "Kohlski"; neither could the Police Department from their mug shots. As a last resort, Brullov visited the New York City Diamond Dealers Club and posted a description of the man on the bulletin board, on the chance that he might approach some jeweler of White Russian background. And there the matter of Dr. Serge Kohlski appeared to end.

Eight

Paris
September 1957

THE PEOPLE of Paris had returned from their August vacations; shopkeepers had unlocked their doors and the city had resumed its accustomed bustle. The annual automobile show was about to open, the great couture houses were displaying their new collections for the fashion editors of America and England. The City of Light was as self-satisfied as a dowager who looks the other way when confronted with life's items of unpleasantness—such as the bodies of the Algerian revolutionaries which each morning were hooked from the waters of the Seine. Small matter that the Fourth

Republic was tottering; that black-market peddlers of francs did business on every street corner, or that there had been a drop-off of American tourists due to the economic recession in the States. Life was still good, whether one was a midinette or a lady of *le gratin*.

The Paris branch of Brullov & Cie, in the Place Vendôme, was in the midst of remodeling to bring itself up to the luxuriousness of the great jewel houses—Van Cleef & Arpels, Mauboussin and Chaumet—which ranged the side of the Place opposite the Ritz Hotel. Tony Brullov, fresh from New York, strode from showroom to showroom giving orders to the architect and contractors. This wall was to be upholstered in suede, that one was to be redone in marble; in the salon where Argentine cattle millionaires and Arab oil sheiks bought their jewels, spotlights were to be installed to illuminate the recently acquired Beauvais tapestries. With it all, dark-suited salesmen managed to attend to the wants of customers who expressed them in a half-dozen languages. A few complained because the police had barred auto parking in the center of the Place, where the monumental statue of Napoleon gazed down from its towering column. The prohibition would be just for this afternoon, Tony explained to a Venezuelan lady, to allow a motion-picture company to shoot a scene outside the entrance to the Ritz Hotel.

The scene, as far as Tony could see from the jewelry store, was a yawning bore. A Rolls-Royce limousine would drive up to the hotel entrance, an actress would step out and disappear into the Ritz; later she would reappear, enter the limousine and drive off.

It seemed ludicrous to Tony that such a small action should require a shooting crew of more than a score of men and women—cameraman and assistant cameraman; director and assistant director, script girl and gaffers and makeup woman and costumer and others who simply lounged about and spit on the pavement. "No wonder movies cost so much to make," Tony commented in French to Pierre, the store's errand boy.

"Any piece of film junk runs as much as our whole inventory."

"But this is not junk, m'sieur," Pierre protested. "They say this is a grand romance. It must be, to star Mademoiselle Deering."

Tony looked sharply at Pierre. "Who?"

"Mademoiselle Erin Deering. It is she who steps in and out of the Rolls-Royce."

Tony felt a tightening in his chest. *Erin.* How long had it been? Nineteen Forty-five to 1957. My God, twelve years.

"M'sieur Brullov, about the spotlights," the architect said, approaching Tony.

"In a moment," Tony said and strode from the store onto the sidewalk. She was coming out of the Ritz again, the camera-man panning her action. From the distance she could be any-body—a woman in a sable coat and hat. She got into the limousine, it started to drive off, then stopped and backed up. "Encore!" Tony heard the director call and Erin stepped from the Rolls-Royce and returned to the Ritz Hotel.

Tony debated. Should he? There had been no communication between Erin and himself since that last night in Nice. He had gone faithfully to see every Erin Deering film during those intervening years, had watched her mature as a woman and an actress—the critics now hailed her as "the American Ingrid Bergman"—but Tony had never written her so much as a congratulatory line. He had seen an item in the New York papers—when? last year?—that she had been divorced from Rayburn Grace, the industrialist, which Tony presumed meant that she had another bridegroom in her sights. But so far, he had not read of another marriage. What did it matter, anyway? She had been married when they had first met. It was enough that after twelve years, Erin was here in Paris, less than two hundred meters away.

He hurried back into the store, intending to telephone the company's florist and order a box of roses to be rushed to Erin on the set. Then Tony reconsidered. Perhaps the filming was almost over; the flowers might arrive after everyone had left.

Very well. Expediency would have to substitute for style. Tony went quickly from salon to salon, surveying the various bouquets in their epergnes. In the Beauvais Room he gathered up a bouquet of four dozen red roses and called out to Pierre. "Wrap these in our best paper, and bring them back to me immediately."

Pierre hastened off with the bouquet while Tony sought a gift card and envelope. He wrote Erin Deering's name on the envelope and on the card: "Our reservation at Tour d'Argent is for nine o'clock. Where shall I pick you up? Tony." Then, as an afterthought, in case there were other Tonys in her life, he added in parenthesis "Brullov."

"You are to give the bouquet and this note to Mademoiselle Deering and no one else," Tony instructed Pierre. "And wait for her reply, understand?"

Pierre nodded and trotted across the Place while Tony watched from the entrance of the store. Pierre circled about the movie group like a puppy looking for its owner, then headed for the Rolls-Royce. A few seconds passed, then Pierre reappeared, without the bouquet, and hurried back toward the store.

"She read my note?" Tony asked.

"Yes, m'sieur."

"And what is her message?"

"Nothing, m'sieur."

"Nothing?"

"She thanked me, that is all."

Tony scowled at the rebuff. Yet he could scarcely blame Erin. He had walked out on her in Nice; he had humiliated her by refusing marriage; he had never, during the intervening twelve years, attempted to contact her. Why should a woman of pride do other than ignore him? He deserved it.

Tony turned back into the store and sought out the architect and took up the problem of the spotlights. They were deep in discussion when a young woman in owlish spectacles and carrying a clipboard approached them. "M'sieur Brullov?"

"Yes?"

"Mademoiselle Deering asked me to give you this." She held out the same envelope which he had addressed to Erin. Inside, below his own words on the card, he read Erin's reply. "Hotel Raphael. 8:15 tonight."

Tony thanked the message bearer and turned back to the architect. "That's all for today, François. See you tomorrow."

"But the spotlights?"

"Tomorrow."

He was both elated and puzzled. Erin wished to see him three-quarters of an hour before the dinner he had promised her at the Tour d'Argent. The drive to the restaurant would take no more than fifteen minutes, which suggested to Tony that she wished to talk—or have it out—before she accompanied him to dinner. If, indeed, she would accompany him. Still, it was worth a gamble to phone in the reservation. . . .

The Raphael, on Avenue Kléber, which had been the wartime headquarters of General Eisenhower, was a dignified residential hotel, now a favorite of motion-picture stars and producers. The lobby was small and quiet, with the desk of the concierge almost at the entrance. Tony nodded to the man with the crossed keys on his lapel, looked about for the registration desk and found only a small American bar. The Raphael apparently refused such a cliché as a registration desk. He returned to the concierge, who surveyed him sternly. "You are M'sieur Brullov?"

"I am."

He picked up his desk telephone, murmured into it, hung up, and favored Tony with several more words. "Mademoiselle Deering's suite is on the fourth floor. Number two." His gloved hand rose in the air and twitched. In a moment an elderly elevator operator materialized and escorted Tony to the *ascenseur*.

At Tony's knock on suite number two, the door opened and a young woman in maid's uniform ushered him into the sitting room. The furniture was Louis Quinze, an Oriental carpet on the floor, a crystal chandelier overhead; on a commode gleaming with brass ormolu a vase held Tony's four dozen red roses. He was contemplating the bouquet when he heard a door open behind him, and Erin Deering strode into the room. She wore a blue velvet dinner suit that accentuated the blue of her eyes; her hair was swept up into a corona and fastened to one side by a spray of small diamonds.

"Good evening, Tony," she said formally, extending a hand on which Tony noted a magnificent ruby.

"How are you, Erin?" he inquired in the same formal tone.

"Very well, thank you. And your father?" *Not* "How are you?"

"Couldn't be better, thanks."

"Won't you sit down?" She gestured toward a tapestried love seat and positioned herself catercorner on a small *fauteuil*. For a moment they surveyed each other, as if cataloguing the changes of the past dozen years. To Tony, Erin's radiance of her early twenties had given way to the cool sophistication of a woman of the world. Perhaps *too* cool, he thought uncomfortably, and was grateful at the sight of the maid approaching with a silver tray bearing two glasses of apéritif.

Tony raised his glass to Erin. "To old times," he said.

She nodded and said, "I'm having dinner with a friend. I hope you won't mind."

It was the most crushing put-down Tony had ever experienced. "I understand," he heard himself say. Then he added quickly, "I want to congratulate you, Erin, on your success. I've seen every one of your films, and with each new one you seem to top yourself."

"Because I intended to." She smiled quietly.

The conversation was dying a painful death, and Tony cast about for a means to revive it. "How long will you be filming in Paris?"

"Two days more. We're just doing pickup shots for a picture already in the can. Then I'm over to England to visit some friends." She paused, then asked with studied casualness, "I presume you are married now." Tony shook his head and she showed her surprise. "Divorced?"

"I've never married."

"Really?"

Full stop. Tony was tempted to rise and take his leave; then he decided on one more attempt to bridge the chasm. "Erin, I've had years to regret my mistake. In Nice, I mean. It all went wrong because we rushed into things too fast. Everybody did during the war; but it was wrong. We didn't give ourselves time to get to know each other, to really know. In any case, the fault was mine." He thought he detected a gleam of amusement in her eyes. Or was it satisfaction?

"Perhaps you're right," she conceded. She picked up a small handbell on the coffee table and tinkled it. A door opened and the maid appeared. "Martha, I'll be taking my alligator handbag."

Martha nodded and disappeared. Tony rose awkwardly and held out his hand. "It's been good to see you again, Erin. If there's anything I can do for you while you're in Paris . . ."

"Thank you."

Martha returned with the alligator handbag and Erin turned to Tony:

"Shall we go?"

Tony blinked his confusion. "But you said you were having dinner with a friend. . . ."

"And so I am."

She smiled and took Tony's arm. "All I wanted was to hear you apologize. Everything hung on that." She turned to the maid. "Goodnight, Martha. Don't wait up for me."

At the sight of Erin Deering, the Hollywood *vedette*, the maitre d' at the Tour d'Argent escorted his guests to the window table that afforded the best view of the floodlit flying buttresses of the Cathedral of Notre Dame. Erin and Tony went from champagne to oysters to pressed duck and a bottle of Romanée-Conti—all of which were consumed with no more thought than if they had been hamburgers and Cokes. Their real nourishment was conversation, the jumbled stories of lives apart.

"My second husband," Erin said, "hardly counted. Bax was just another Hollywood producer with ulcers. We lasted six months. Rayburn Grace was different. He had everything a woman thinks she wants. Millions, a beautiful estate down the Peninsula from San Francisco, a villa at Acapulco, a penthouse on Park Avenue. I was his fifth wife, which should have been a warning. All he cared about was having a famous actress on his arm. His real love was that damned railroad of his."

"Which railroad?"

"Oh, not the real thing. A model railroad, a miniature. An engine and six flatcars and a caboose. He had tracks laid all over the ground. When people came down from San Francisco, he'd put on that stupid engineer's cap and hoist himself onto the locomotive and take everybody for a ride. Most people were bored silly crawling along at two miles an hour through the gardens and the stables and the miniature golf course. One day Rayburn and I had a fight—a real dilly—and when he took off for lunch with some of his cronies I decided to fix that fucking railroad. I relaid the tracks with a crowbar and hammer. I routed them to the edge of the swimming pool, hitched up the whole train, set the locomotive on wide-open throttle, and in she went, chug-chug, toot-tootle and splash. God, it was lovely! The next day Rayburn filed for divorce."

Tony laughed so uproariously that diners at the nearby tables turned to stare; then when he had caught his breath, he asked, "Anyone new on the horizon?"

"No," Erin said, "but enough about me. I want to hear about the many fractures of Tony Brullov." She made an impish face. "Didn't you break your leg in the Monte Carlo auto rally a couple of years ago?"

He admitted it with a grin. "I would have come in second except for a misunderstanding with a stone wall."

"Wasn't there another misunderstanding while slaloming at Garmisch-Partenkirchen?"

"A broken arm and collarbone. But not until *after* I'd won a first. Did you hire a clipping service to keep track of me?"

"No. In case you've forgotten, you made the pages of *Life* magazine, and footage in some of the television news. If I were a psychiatrist, I'd say you're looking for a peacetime substitute for the OSS."

"Except now I'm not killing anyone," Tony rebutted. "I just like the challenge of competition and the kick of winning. Life's got to be an adventure or it's nothing."

Erin looked thoughtful. "And you don't think marriage could be an adventure? Surely in all these years you must have met some woman who could take your mind off all these high-wire acts."

"Oh, for a few weeks, yes. But I like my independence, not having to worry about neglecting a wife or kids." He paused. "Speaking of children, you haven't mentioned any."

Erin studied the glass of burgundy in her hand and frowned. "I had a string of miscarriages, and then I stopped trying. Besides, I'm not sure I'd be a good mother. I'm selfish." She laughed lightly. "A real brass-plated bitch, according to a couple of my producers and directors. So what? It sells tickets."

After the dessert, while they sipped cognac, Tony described the remodeling of the Place Vendôme store and his dual role as society salesman and roving supervisor of the Brullov chain. Then he switched subjects: Would Erin like to finish off the evening with a drive in the Bois de Boulogne? She reacted with mock disbelief: "A drive in that little gadget we came here in?"

"That 'little gadget,' " he retorted, "is a Jaguar XK150, with dual carburetors and a speed of one hundred and twenty miles an hour."

"Then thank God we're out of range of the Grande Corniche. I may be a fast woman, but not on wheels."

"Okay. Then the Bois in a *fiacre*?"

"Provided you get me home by midnight, or one o'clock at the latest. I'm a working woman, you know. Shooting doesn't begin till noon, but I can't show up with circles under my eyes."

Luck was with them. In the Bois, outside the restaurant in the Pré Catalan they found a *fiacre* with an ancient rheumy-eyed cabby and a horse to match. With the lap robe tucked about them—for the night had turned chilly—they went slowly along the Route de Suresnes and watched the trees drifting down their autumnal leaves. It reminded Erin, she said, of certain passages in Marcel Proust's *Remembrance of Things Past*—as if the ghosts of an earlier Paris were accompanying them in invisible carriages, the great ladies and their gallants, when all the world seemed young. Tony interrupted her fancy with a practical question. "Dinner tomorrow night?"

Erin smiled. "I thought you only intended this one evening."

"I did. Now I want more."

"But not tomorrow night. I'm having dinner with my producer. You know," she added, "I really did have an engagement tonight. A big bash that I didn't much care about, or to be bothered with an escort. When you came to the Raphael I had already cued Martha. If I asked for my alligator handbag, that meant I was going with you, and she was to phone my host that I had a headache. If I asked for my suede handbag, that meant I was dumping you and going to the party. Pretty sneaky, hmm?"

"Very," Tony said. "Then dinner the night after next?" He

saw she was tempted. "I'll pick you up at eight. And don't wear anything fancy or high heels. We'll be roughing it."

"How rough?"

"Wait and see."

Tony maintained the mystery when he called for Erin two nights later. He drove the Jaguar through the Bois de Boulogne, then past the apartment complexes of Suresnes and westward until he picked up the northern loop of the Seine near Bougival, where surburban houses and farms came into view. Tony turned right onto a side road that led down to the water's edge where a number of houseboats were anchored. The Jaguar halted beside the floating dock where the largest of the houseboats was moored. Erin surveyed the darkened vessel with an amused eye. "Let me guess," she said to Tony. "You've rented your own *bateau mouche* and we're going for a cruise on the Seine."

"Half right," he answered, leading her out onto the dock. "I've rented it for my stay in Paris. It's a hell of a lot more fun than a hotel. Even if I have to make my own bunk and take the laundry out." They went up the short gangplank onto the deck and Tony opened a door and flicked on the lights in the main cabin. The furnishings were cosy and nautical in theme, with a bar forward and a radio-phonograph combination aft. "And through here," Tony said, guiding Erin along a companionway, "is the dining saloon." The table was already set for two, there was a bottle of champagne in a wine cooler and a bouquet of roses on the sideboard. "That door aft—" Tony pointed—"leads to the galley, where you're going to watch me rustle up dinner."

Erin laughed. "A cook yet! Lord, the man is talented."

"I hope this isn't a letdown for you," Tony said with a tinge of apology.

"It's delightful," Erin protested. "I couldn't ask for a lovelier surprise."

"Good. Then all hands forward for martinis."

Over their cocktails in the main cabin Tony observed Erin's change from their first evening together. Then she had been the worldly sophisticate in couturier velvet and jewels. Tonight she was simple and unaffected; her dress was a light-blue jersey fastened in front with oversized buttons of jet, and instead of an expensive handbag she carried a modest affair of split cane. But the most noticeable difference, he thought, was in her voice; it was lower in register and the brittleness was gone. She was the Erin Deering of another time and place.

She insisted on helping with the dinner. Donning an apron, she tossed the salad, while Tony, also in apron and in shirt sleeves, shucked the Belon oysters, which they consumed with the champagne. Then back to the galley, laughing and chattering inconsequentials, Erin oversaw the hashed brown potatoes while he attended to the steaks and opened a bottle of red wine. They voted against dessert and for mugs of coffee, which they carried out onto the deck and up to the wheelhouse.

There was no moon, and clouds covered the stars, so that the Seine ran darkly with only a faint ripple against the hull of the ship. Dogs barked in the distance and accordion music floated across the water from one of the other houseboats.

For a while they sipped their coffee in silence; then Erin said, "I can't tell you how much good tonight has done me. And the other night, too. It's made me feel young again."

Tony snorted. "Really, Grandmother?"

"I'm almost thirty-five. It's a scary age. There are so many bright young things coming along. Kids out of television. One day unknown, next day a star—and all of them ready to elbow me out of the key light."

He was surprised that she should feel insecure. "Erin Deering has nothing to worry about."

"Ha!" She balanced her coffee mug on the railing and stationed herself behind the ship's wheel and turned it idly from side to side. "Why do you suppose I rush from film to film? To keep myself before the public. I count the number of lines in

Variety of every review of my newest picture. To see if there were as many lines as the last time. I go through my scrapbooks and count up the interviews I've given this year, and how many I gave the year before. I'm like a boxing champion always having to defend his title. But one day I'll take the count."

"You can always play character parts."

She shuddered. "Oh, God! That's like the tunnel at the end of the light."

Tony moved up behind her and kissed the nape of her neck.

She sighed. "Five years. With luck, that's what I've got." Tony's mouth moved to the side of her neck and he felt her pulse surge in response. "It's strange, isn't it?" she mused, "I always associate you with water. And your father. That night in Costa Rica, on the finca. Your father standing on the porch, the rain pouring down behind him, looking at me with those wonderful eyes and telling me that my future would be the theater." Tony turned her head so that he could kiss her throat. "Water . . ." she went on dreamily, "first on that swimming float . . . then the sailboat . . . now here." His arms went about her and his hands moved up to cup the fullness of her breasts. Trembling, she twisted around in his arms and looked up into his face. "Do I take it that you brought me here for immoral purposes?"

"Completely immoral."

"Oh, thank God!" She laughed and went up on tiptoe to kiss him, deeply, hungrily.

That night was the first of many. Their mutual attraction, they told each other, was even more passionate than twelve years before—"only the curtain raiser," as Erin put it. She postponed her planned visit to England and spent her days, when Tony was at the jewelry store, viewing the new fall fashion collections and visiting the Louvre. On their first weekend together they drove to the chateau country in the valley of the Loire. They picnicked beside the pond in the gardens of Azayle-Rideau and made love in the forest approach to Chenon-ceaux. It was there, as they lay side by side in the grass, that Erin said: "I'm glad we're not married. This way, we're to-gether because we want to be and don't *have* to be. There are no strings, no commitments." Even the word "love" seldom en-tered their conversations, as though it were a cliché to be avoided; it was enough that their mouths and bodies declared their feelings.

The openness of their affair—the luxurious dining at Max-im's and Lapérouse and Lucas-Carton, then returning nightly either to Erin's suite at the Raphael or Tony's houseboat—quickly attracted the attention of the journalists and photog-raphers. *Paris Match* ran a three-page spread of Erin and Tony together, and compared their photographs of the present with those twelve years before on the Riviera. Erin was child-ishly pleased and bought herself a new scrapbook in which she pasted the pages from *Paris Match* and the clippings of the gossip columnists. It both amused and irked Tony. "I hope I'm not just another leading man in your newest feature." Erin took it with a laugh. "You're my *only* leading man, darling, and the biggest feature in my career and my whole life." That mollified him and, for the first time, Tony lost his resentment of the trail of photographers. "They're part of your life," he told Erin, "just as parties and receptions and squiring around rich old bags are part of the way I sell jewels." And sell he did. Business boomed at the store on the Place Vendôme; wealthy women of half a dozen nationalities, attracted by the publicity, requested that Tony personally aid them in the selection of jewelry. Erin, too, benefited; she was offered the starring role, and accepted it, in a French-German co-production film which would shoot on the Riviera.

One Sunday afternoon they attended the horse races in the Bois de Boulogne. It was the big race of the month at Long-champs and attracted the cream of Parisian racing society. The women appeared in their smartest ensembles and many of the men—such as Aly Khan, Porfirio Rubirosa and the

French Rothschilds—wore cutaway coats and gray top hats. "I wish we had dressed more formally," Erin said to Tony as they posed for press photographers in front of the grandstand. "You'd be a smash in a topper and cutaway."

"I'm a smash anyway, with you on my arm," Tony said. He waved to the photographers. "Thank you, boys. No more photos." He took Erin's elbow and escorted her through the milling crowd. "Would you like to meet Aly Khan?" He nodded toward that celebrity, who was attracting the attention of still other photographers.

"You know him?"

"Sure! He's a sports-car buff, too. We run into each other at most of the European rallies." As they approached, Tony bent close to Erin's ear. "Lay on the charm to the people Aly is talking to."

Erin peered through a break in the ring of photographers and saw a gray-haired man of imposing height and build. On his arm was a young brunette of striking beauty.

"Who are they?"

"Later," Tony murmured and guided her past the photographers. "Aly!"

"Tony!"

They embraced like long-lost friends, and Tony introduced Aly Khan to Erin. "You are my favorite motion-picture star," he said gallantly, then added with a wink, "after my former wife, of course," referring to Rita Hayworth. He turned to the couple beside him. "Permit me to introduce my friend Orsino di Ascoli."

Di Ascoli kissed Erin's hand. He was delighted, he was enchanted, and it was a pleasure to meet Mr. Brullov. "And this is my daughter Lisa," he added. She nodded and managed a bored smile.

"Now I get the connection," Tony said. "The favorite in the big race is Princess Lisa. It is *your* horse, Miss di Ascoli."

"My father's."

"The same thing. I've bet a bundle on her. And Erin has a side bet that Princess Lisa wins by at least four lengths."

"In that case," di Ascoli beamed, "let us watch our win together. Won't you and Miss Deering share our box?"

Tony made a gesture of disappointment. "Oh, I *am* sorry. We have already accepted another invitation." He moved as if to leave, then hesitated. "Am I correct, sir, that your racing colors are green and gold?"

"They are."

Tony's hand flashed to his tie and removed his gold tie tack shaped in the form of a miniature horseshoe and set with tiny emeralds. "Then accept this as a hostage to our mutual good fortune." He paused and turned to Lisa. "Better still, permit these emeralds to be flattered by the green of your eyes."

He fastened the tie tack to Lisa's lapel, grinned at her pleased surprise, gave his arm to Erin, and moved away.

When they were at a safe distance, Erin sniffed, "I thought I was the one to lay on the charm. What the hell was that all about?"

"Orsino di Ascoli happens to be one of the richest men in Europe. He buys jewels for his women like they are candy mints. Dad's been angling for his business for years; but it's always gone to Van Cleef and Arpels or Cartier. After today that may change."

"*If* he knows you're the Tony Brullov of Brullov and Company."

"He'll check first on you, my dear. Di Ascoli has a thing for actresses. He'll read up on you in *Paris Match* and your grand romance with a certain playboy and jewel dealer." Tony saw Erin's frown and added, "How do you think I rake in the business? I checked the racing news yesterday and saw that di Ascoli's horse was running today. His colors were listed as green and gold, so I grabbed the tie tack at the store and had the rubies switched to emeralds." Erin was still frowning. "I'm sorry I had to use you, baby. Am I forgiven?"

"Well, I suppose," she grudged. "But sometimes I do think your scheming is a bit unnerving."

One of the few subjects in life over which Orsino di Ascoli appeared to have no control was his daughter in one of her sulky moods. Such was the case as they sat in their box at Longchamps shortly before the beginning of the main race of the day. Lisa chain-smoked cigarettes, fiddled with her field glasses, and occasionally peered through them to view the surrounding boxes and the throng below the grandstand.

"See anyone of interest?" he asked finally. She shook her head silently. "There never seems to be with you. Not today, certainly. Your performance was disgraceful."

"Really?"

"You were barely civil to anyone. Your position in society does not allow you to go around ignoring people; not the people who count."

"You mean Aly Khan?"

"I mean young Rothschild. One of the most eligible bachelors in Europe, and you almost yawned in his face."

"Father, I wish you'd stop planning my life for me."

He had to, di Ascoli told himself. How else would she make the proper marriage? Lacking a son, his daughter was his one hope of founding a dynasty. Somewhere he would have to find a man whom Lisa would marry and give him a grandson, a future head of the Ascoli empire. So far nothing had worked—not even Portugal, where di Ascoli had bought a magnificent estate outside Lisbon in the hope that Lisa might capture one of the exiled royalty who had settled in the region. A prince of the blood might have a vacuum between the ears, but if he were effective in bed, there would be a title to pass on.

The public-address system blared; the horses were at the starting posts. The spectators in the grandstand and the boxes rose expectantly to their feet. But not Lisa. She was studying her face in the mirror of her compact.

Di Ascoli glared down at her. "Lisa! This is our race!"

"Good. Then we can go."

"In God's name," he exploded, "doesn't anything in the world matter to you?"

She returned the compact to her handbag and glanced down at the tie tack that Tony Brullov had pinned to her lapel.

"Perhaps emeralds," she murmured thoughtfully, but her words were lost in the blare of the public-address system. The horses were off and running.

Nine

Paris
September 1957

THE FOLLOWING afternoon Tony and Jacques Verdier, the manager of the store on the Place Vendôme, were closeted in the business office on the second floor to review the sales figures for the previous week.

"Most satisfying," Verdier declared. "We are up twelve percent over the same week last year. It's surprising—we've run no advertising since the beginning of the month."

Tony smiled at his manager, an ascetic-looking man in his

mid-fifties. "No *paid* advertising, Jacques, but reams of the free stuff. The best kind, in my book."

Verdier cleared his throat in embarrassment; he had overlooked the matter of Erin Deering. The intercom on the desk buzzed, Verdier flicked a switch, and a male voice spoke in hushed tones. "M'sieur Verdier, Mademoiselle di Ascoli is in the front showroom."

The manager's eyes widened, but before he could answer Tony spoke into the intercom. "Is her father with her?"

"No. But she has asked for you, Mr. Brullov."

"I'll be right down. Show her into the Beauvais Room." He glanced at Verdier. "If she's buying, I'll want you for back-up. Count to fifty and join us."

Verdier nodded. "What about music?"—referring to the store's practice of supplying background harmonies whenever a customer entered the inner sanctum.

"Nothing distracting," Tony decided. "Nothing likely to be hummed. Perhaps Chopin piano etudes."

The Beauvais Room was small, its walls hung with the tapestries from which it took its name. There were no showcases, nothing to indicate the possibility of crass commercial transactions. Centering the room was a large circular table of black marble, flanked by two love seats in gold velvet. One of the love seats was occupied by Lisa di Ascoli.

At the sight of her Tony sucked in his breath. She was stunning. A toque of crimson silk crowned her raven hair, a sable jacket dropped casually over the shoulders of her suit. But it was her countenance that set her apart from other beauties—a fact which Tony realized he had not properly appreciated at Longchamps because he had so focused his attention on her father. It was a strong face, with Orsino di Ascoli's high cheekbones and full sensual lips. The green eyes he had complimented at the track were even deeper of hue.

Tony accepted her gloved hand and declared his pleasure to

see her again. "And my congratulations on your win yester-day. I'm only sorry that Princess Lisa did not finish by four lengths."

"Perhaps it might teach Miss Deering that side bets can be treacherous."

Tony nodded. "May I offer you tea, or an apéritif? Perhaps champagne?" She shook her head. "Then how may I be of service?"

She pursed her lips as though this were a weighty question. "Is it possible that you might have emeralds in something be-sides tie tacks?"

Tony smiled and went along with her. "Barely possible," he said, and beckoned to Jacques Verdier, who was hovering in the doorway. "Emeralds, Mr. Verdier."

Verdier pressed a concealed button and the tapestried wall slid silently to one side to reveal a walk-in steel vault. He disappeared inside and returned in a moment with two trays which he set down on the marble table. "Mr. Verdier is our manager," Tony explained, "and a connoisseur of emeralds."

Lisa examined the contents of the velvet trays. Emerald earrings, emerald pendants, emerald rings, emerald brooches; some cabochon, some square cut, all highlighted by diamonds. Finally she sighed. "I had in mind something important."

Tony swallowed and glanced at Verdier. "The Castagna necklace."

Verdier went to the vault again and brought forth a square box of white velvet. Tony opened the lid and Lisa stared down at a circle of green fire set off by a clasp of canary diamonds.

"May I?" Lisa asked Tony.

"I insist."

She shrugged off her sable jacket and opened the collar of her suit blouse. Tony fastened the emeralds around her neck. She viewed the effect in the table mirror, first head-on, then from side to side. In complete silence. Tony and Verdier ex-changed glances: Was she serious or simply passing the time?

Tony tried to concentrate on the Chopin etude in the background. It was too lugubrious, too melancholy. If only it were a Sousa march. . . . Finally, after a small eternity, Lisa spoke. "It's rather nice, isn't it?"

"The finest in all Paris," Verdier interposed.

Tony raised his eyebrows in warning. Let the merchandise speak for itself. One does not praise the Venus de Milo or the Apollo Belvedere; the ultimate is beyond words.

Lisa nodded to herself. "I think my father would approve. Emeralds, diamonds, rubies, sapphires are an absolute passion with him."

Tony chose his words carefully. "Then this would be his gift to you?"

"No. Mine to myself." She considered a moment. "Shall I open a charge or give you my check?"

"Quite unnecessary in your case," Tony said. "We shall send you a statement at the end of the month." Was she never going to ask the price? he wondered. Three hundred thousand dollars was not taxi fare.

She pondered again. "I have more shopping to do. Could the necklace be delivered to my house?"

"Whenever you wish."

"And the insurance?"

"The necklace is covered by the store policy. When we receive your check, the title will pass to you, and then you should contact your insurance company."

She nodded. "Could you deliver the necklace personally?"

"With pleasure. If you'll give me your address . . ."

She wrote it on a card, turned to Verdier and thanked him for his assistance, then Tony escorted her through the front showrooms and out to the sidewalk. A limousine was waiting at the curb. As the chauffeur opened the door, Lisa turned back to Tony. "It just occurred to me—could you bring the necklace at eight tonight?"

"Certainly."

"Good. Then perhaps you might be able to stay awhile. I'm having a small supper for some friends. I think you might find them amusing."

"I'm sure I shall."

"Oh, and informal dress, please."

Tony was elated by his coup. Three-hundred-thousand-dollar sales were rare enough; but to sell to a di Ascoli was a milestone for Brullov & Company. Tony glanced at his wristwatch and computed the time differential between Paris and New York City. Then he placed an overseas call to his father's apartment.

"I was just about to leave for the office," Ted Brullov's voice came over the wire. "What's up, son?"

Tony recounted the sale of the emerald necklace to Lisa di Ascoli and his father cackled with glee. "Magnificent work, boy. I'm proud of you. Where the di Ascolis lead, others will follow—if we publicize it properly."

"It's got to be done subtly, Dad. Verdier here has solid contacts with the newspapers and magazines that we advertise in. He could feed the story to their society columnists."

"That's the ticket." Ted Brullov's voice went from jubilation to sobriety. "By the way, Tony, is the telephone on that houseboat of yours out of order?"

"Not that I know of. Why?"

"I called you last Friday—night, your time—but all I got was a busy signal. I tried three times." Tony remembered— Friday night Erin had spent on the boat and he had taken the phone off the hook. Ted went on, "What I had to say wasn't something to put in a letter. You remember a few years back that fellow who came into the office and wanted us to commission him to buy jewelry in Moscow?"

"The man who claimed to be a Romanov?"

"That's him. Seven years ago. Nineteen-fifty. Anyway, a police captain stopped by to see me with a report from Interpol. Seems they had just found the guy's body. In a basement

166

in Amsterdam. Actually, it was a skeleton inside a suit of clothes. He was hanging from a chain. According to a hotel bill they found in his pocket, he'd died shortly after he came to us."

"Suicide?"

"An execution, according to Interpol. They got in touch with New York and New York with me because they found a wad of paper in what was left of his gullet. They think he swallowed the paper before he was killed."

"What was on the paper?"

"Names and phone numbers, including mine. The police wanted my explanation, but I had an instant attack of amnesia."

"Interpol have any idea who the man really was?"

"Yes. There were three passports in his suit. One turned out to be genuine. His name was Bartolozzi. A professional killer."

"Jesus! Who do you think did him in?"

"Somebody who wanted that paper he swallowed."

The conversation between father and son drifted off into trade gossip and then finally to the subject of Tony and Erin Deering. "I've seen some of your photos in *Life* and *Look,*" Ted Brullov said. "How serious is it?"

"Too soon to tell, Dad. The main thing is we're having fun."

His father chuckled. "That's what Paris is all about. Fun . . . and emeralds."

Lisa di Ascoli's house on the Île St. Louis was one of the series of seventeenth-century structures on the Quai de Béthune, facing onto the Seine near the Pont de la Tournelle. It was a narrow house, its four stories topped by a mansard roof and a forest of chimneys. A white-haired butler answered the front door, and when Tony Brullov gave his name, he was escorted into a small foyer and up a steep winding staircase to the second-floor corridor. Tony could hear music and laughter filtering through closed double doors directly opposite the landing. Would he wait there, please? the butler requested, and slipped through the double doors. A moment later the doors opened again and Lisa, in black lounging pajamas and gilt sandals, came toward him with her arms extended.

"How thoughtful of you, Tony!" she exclaimed, seeing him holding a package wrapped in gold paper. "Let me guess. It's a box of bonbons. Right?"

Tony understood her and grinned. "I heard you had a sweet tooth."

She sighed hopelessly. "My besetting sin." She handed the box to the butler. "Marcel, would you take this box of chocolates to Zara? Tell her she is not to open it, but to put it in my bedroom." Then Lisa linked arms with Tony and they went through the double doors.

His first reaction to the party was disappointment. The decor of Lisa's drawing room was starkly modern—chrome-and-glass tables, chrome-and-leather chairs and sofas, Giacometti metal sculptures and bare walls. It might have been a reception room at IBM. The guests struck Tony as being as functional as the furnishings; they were uniformly handsome, talked with animation, laughed with brittleness, and fawned on their hostess. Several recognized Tony Brullov's name, for as Lisa guided him from guest to guest, he heard whispers in his wake: "You know . . . Erin Deering."

When dinner was announced, the guests trooped into an adjoining room to a group of small circular tables. Tony found himself seated between two blond young women with the emaciated faces of fashion models; the man opposite him, breathless-voiced and dramatic of gestures, announced that he was the interior decorator who had "done" Lisa's house, and launched into a monologue of the problems and his solutions which lasted through the entree. Just before the dessert Lisa came up behind him, whispered into his ear, and he rose and surrendered his chair to the hostess.

"I've recently returned from India," Lisa said, addressing Tony. "I was fascinated by the jewelry the women wore."

"Peasant women, I imagine," Tony said. "The upper class wear jewels much the same as European women."

"Of course. I liked the nose rings some of them wore. And their toe rings. Do you think they might catch on here?"

"Certainly not nose rings."

"Then toe rings? Perhaps with an important jewel?"

"Possibly. For evening wear or at resorts." Tony smiled thoughtfully. "I think you've given me an idea for a new line of fad jewelry."

Lisa's green eyes sparkled at him. "Then you must see that Lisa di Ascoli gets the credit. You shall design me a toe ring. With a cabochon ruby."

She had barely finished speaking when Tony felt something brush his knee and then Lisa's bare foot deposited itself in his lap. He glanced quickly at the two blond women on either side of him; they were debating in French the rival design talents of Balmain and Givenchy, unaware of the action beneath the table.

"Do you accept the commission?" Lisa purred and made a thrust with her foot.

"With pleasure." Tony's right hand slipped beneath the tablecloth and closed about the bare foot. Gallantry must be observed, especially toward one's hostess.

"You will have to take measurements, of course."

"Of course." Tony dropped his left hand below the tablecloth and with his right removed his class ring and deftly slipped it onto her little toe. It was a perfect fit. Lisa acknowledged it with a secret smile and thrust her foot forward until her toes wriggled against Tony's crotch. He felt color coming into his cheeks; Erin was the only woman who had been so bold with him—but, after all, they were lovers.

Suddenly one of the blond women shifted in her chair and reached under the tablecloth, as if to retrieve a fallen napkin. Her hand must have discovered Lisa's outstretched leg, for she gave a startled *"Oh!"* Then she recovered and smiled at her hostess. *"Très charmant, ma chérie."*

But it was not charming to Tony. He cut short his embarrassment by pushing back his chair and rising.

"Excuse me," he said to the table. "I think I'll take some fresh air."

He wandered into the drawing room and found a door which gave onto a balcony. He lighted a cigarette, leaned on the railing and watched a freight barge move darkly up the Seine. He stared down at his class ring which he had retrieved from Lisa's toe. She was a game-player, he decided. Like so many wealthy people, it amused her to test the power of her money—who could be bought, and what was the price. In Tony's case, was it a three-hundred-thousand-dollar necklace?

He heard footsteps behind him and then Lisa joined him at the balcony railing. "I'm afraid my party is a failure," she said ruefully.

"How so?"

"The people. Complete bores. Except for you."

"I'm flattered."

"They're the sort my father calls vacuums dressed in clothes. But then, I don't approve of his associates, either. All they talk about is mergers and schemes to ruin their competitors. What do I care about tanker rates, or the price of Bolivian tin, or Malaysian rubber?"

Tony was tempted to say those very matters allowed her to live in luxury and to buy emerald necklaces. Some day, when her father was gone, she would have to shoulder those concerns, or marry and hear the same sort of talk from her husband.

"Money is a barrier to a life of feeling," she went on doggedly. "Money is an invisible cage against which one beats one's wings in vain. Outside, somewhere, there must be friends —not sycophants and camp followers."

The tenor of her talk intrigued Tony. It might be the genuine complaint of a woman adrift in a world not of her choosing, or it could be a veiled explanation for her actions at the dinner table. Or both.

"There is an unwritten rule in my home," she went on. "The guests are permitted one cognac or highball, a bit of conversation, then it is goodnight. But I'd like you to stay on." Tony looked at her sharply. "For a few minutes, perhaps?" Her tone was almost pleading.

Tony looked down at the barge. In his mind he heard again his father's jubilation over the telephone; at last Brullov & Company had snared the di Ascoli account. Oh, what the hell? What were a few minutes? They might be educational. Even an adventure.

"I'd be delighted," he said.

Lisa's house rule was strictly obeyed. After the one drink and a short while of talk, the guests departed, singly and in pairs, until only Tony remained in the drawing room. Then the elderly butler approached him. "Will m'sieur follow me, please." They went up a narrow stairs to the third floor and then the fourth. The butler knocked on a heavy oak door, bowed to Tony, and started down the stairs. A moment later the door opened and a brown-faced young woman in a striped caftan said, *"Buenas noches, señor."* Tony noted the slash mark on her forehead and decided she was a Spanish Berber, of which there were many in Paris. As she closed the door behind him, Lisa's voice floated into the room over some hidden speaker. "I'll be with you in a moment, Tony." In Spanish, she added some instruction to the Berber, who immediately crossed the room and disappeared through a beaded curtain.

Tony strolled about with growing astonishment. It was an enormous room with a single window which afforded a view of Notre Dame in the distance. The floor and walls were of white marble veined with green. In place of chairs and sofas there were silken puff pillows and body-length reclining pads in rainbow colors. Low brass tabourets served as occasional tables. Illumination was provided by hanging lamps of pierced brass, and heat by a brass brazier of glowing coals. At one end of the room, a sunken pool floated lotus blossoms on its surface and a marble fountain spouted mistily and gave off the scent of jasmine. At the opposite end was the bed, a huge affair of Indian lacquer that swung from brass chains fixed into the mirrored ceiling. Along one wall was a series of alcoves. In one, a sulphur-crested cockatoo, chained by one leg to its perch, preened itself and surveyed Tony with a wary eye. Another alcove sheltered a large Tibetan bronze, a Yamantaka, with four bull's heads, lolling tongues, and myriad arms, embracing a female figure in sexual union. Still another alcove displayed on its three walls a collection of photographs: Lisa astride a camel, Lisa in a howdah atop an elephant, Lisa with a rifle and one foot on the corpse of a tiger. In every photograph, Orsino di Ascoli stood to one side smiling, not at the camera, but at his daughter.

Tony heard a rattle of beaded curtains and the Berber reappeared bearing the gilt-wrapped "box of chocolates" and placed it on one of the brass tabourets. Now Tony thought he understood why Lisa had asked him to stay on; there was to be some sort of a ceremony of unveiling the emeralds. Or—an unsettling thought—she was going to return them.

While Tony was pondering the latter possibility there was another rattle of beaded curtains and Lisa di Ascoli entered the room. She was completely transformed in appearance. Her jet hair was combed out and hung loosely over her shoulders. The outer edges of her eyelids were accented with kohl, and the upper lids glistened with gilt. She wore a flowing robe of white moiré silk that reached to her bare feet and was fastened at the waist by a sash of gold mesh. Above the waist, the robe parted sufficiently to expose the half-moons of her breasts.

Lisa made a gesture to indicate the room. "I call this my Scheherazade fantasy. One needs fantasy to insulate oneself from the ugliness of the world." She prodded one of the puff pillows with a bare foot. "Please sit down."

Tony did so, sitting cross-legged, while Lisa arranged herself alongside on a second pillow. "Zara!" she called and the Berber came forward with a small brass tray on which there were two crystal glasses filled with a colorless liquid. "It should be raki to go with this setting," Lisa said, "but I think you will enjoy this more." She raised her glass to Tony's. "To pleasure."

It was not pleasure that scalded Tony's throat and brought tears to his eyes. Lisa laughed lightly. "Your first taste of absinthe, I see. Pre-World War One. One hundred and fifty proof. Distilled before the French government banned it."

"I can see why," Tony gasped.

Zara knelt before them again with another brass tray on which were cigarettes, two long ivory holders and a lighter. Lisa selected a cigarette, fixed it into its holder, and Zara held the flame to the tip. Tony followed suit, and on his first inhalation he realized it was not conventional tobacco; he recognized the scent from his travels in the Near East. It was kif.

He was conscious that Lisa was watching for his reactions, and so he kept his face expressionless. Still he was puzzled. He had been at several parties in New York where a few smoked hashish or used the needle. He had understood their unhappiness, their need to retreat into dream worlds; but here, Lisa had constructed her own solid three-dimensional fantasy. Why should she require absinthe and kif? Then he abandoned the question. The customer is always right, especially a three-hundred-thousand-dollar customer. Besides, he was intrigued. Tonight was an adventure beyond racing or skiing or even parachute drops.

Lisa drained her absinthe, inhaled deeply from her cigarette, then rose to her feet. "It is time," she said, and went to the tabouret and began to unwrap the gilt box. She opened the lid, withdrew the emeralds and held them up for Zara to see. The Berber's eyes went wide; she clapped her hands and exclaimed *"O la, la, la, la, la!"* Lisa turned to Tony. "Would you, please?"

He rose from the pillow and fastened the necklace at the nape of her neck. "Tell Zara to bring you a mirror," he said. Lisa turned to face him, spread back the top of her robe and exhibited the glowing green nestling between her breasts. "There is no need," she said. "I can see their beauty in your eyes."

They returned to their pillows and Zara replenished the absinthe and lighted fresh cigarettes. "I think I'll pass," Tony said. But Lisa tapped a finger to her lips. "Ssssh! Drink. Smoke."

He began to feel a floating sensation. He was aware that Zara had left them; that the lights in the brass lanterns had dimmed, that Arabic music, probably recorded, was coming from one of the alcoves. Hand drums thumped, stringed instruments whined in a minor key, bells and gongs punctuated the rhythm. There was another rattle of beaded curtains and Zara glided into the room. She had loosened her black hair and discarded her caftan in favor of a minimal dancing costume. She wore no brassiere and the nipples of her full breasts were heavily rouged. Golden bracelets circled her wrists and her ankles were bright with tiny brass bells. Her skirt, banded at the girdle and hem in crimson, was a haze of white over her fawn-colored legs; at her loins, where one would have expected a dark nest, the hair had been artfully teased and gilded.

Zara bowed slightly to Lisa and Tony and began to dance —slowly at first, her arms outstretched, finger cymbals tapping lightly, hips gently slipping sideways, feet barely moving. The tempo of the music increased and Zara's arms began to twist and writhe like twin cobras. Belly and navel circled and pushed, feet stamped, anklets jangled. Then faster and faster, muscles seething in rhythm and counterrhythm. A male voice began to sing in quavering quarter-tones. The rhythm quickened again. The drums thundered, bells tinkled, a new instrument joined in, making cracking sounds like a bullwhip. Zara, her face and body glistening with sweat, made little cries as if to encourage herself to still greater frenzy. Only an arm's length now from her audience, she unfastened her skirt and danced naked; she tossed her hair from side to side, shook her breasts, thrust her gilded nest first at Lisa, then at Tony.

His throat was dry and taut, his stomach churned from the drink and Zara's sensual appeals. He glanced at Lisa. She was sucking excitedly on her empty cigarette holder; her green eyes glittered and followed every movement of the dancer. Then abruptly, the music stopped. Zara shuddered as if waking from a trance and sank to her knees before Lisa and kissed her bare feet. It was, Tony thought hazily, the finale of the performance. But not quite. Zara sat back on her haunches and looked at Lisa like a pet dog waiting for its mistress's command. Lisa nodded faintly and Zara, still on her knees, crawled forward, and Lisa kissed her mouth, then her nipples. In Tony's fuddled state, it seemed hardly more than a pretty gesture. It was appropriate. Fitting. And only mildly unusual when Lisa rose from her pillow, released the sash of gold mesh at her waist and slipped off her robe. Tony gaped at her magnificent breasts, her total nudity, save for the emeralds, and thought she was the ultimate in sensuality. Then she extended her hand and guided him to his feet. Zara was behind him now, removing his jacket and waistcoat. Lisa was undoing his tie, unbuttoning his shirt, drawing down his zipper with impatient fingers. This, too, was appropriate. Fitting. Utterly desirable. When he was naked they went hand in hand to the huge swinging bed beneath the mirrored ceiling and sank into its perfumed softness. And were joined, moments later, by Zara.

Shortly before noon the next day Erin Deering stopped by the jewelry store to beg off their dinner date for that evening. "I have to fly to Munich to talk to the director of my new film," she said. "I want some changes made in the script. Any chance you could get away for five days?"

"I'm afraid not, Erin. We're winding up the remodeling here, and I should be on hand."

She nodded understanding. "I'll be glad when you're done. You need a rest. I've never seen you with such circles under the eyes." She kissed him. "I'll miss you, darling. When I get back, let's spend a few days with my friends in England. They've got a lovely place down in Kent. It'll make a new man out of you."

"I'm ready for that," Tony agreed.

Erin had barely left the store when Lisa di Ascoli telephoned, bubbling with enthusiasm. "Tony dearest! I have the most magnificent idea. I want to match my necklace with emerald earrings and a bracelet. How soon can I have them?"

He told her it might take a month or two to assemble emeralds of equal quality and cut, and he could give no estimate of the probable cost.

"I didn't ask you about cost. Just can you do it?" Certainly, Tony said. "Marvelous! And tomorrow evening, I have tickets for *Norma*. It will be the perfect debut for my necklace. And we can have an early dinner at Maxim's." He stared at the telephone in his hand. How could he get out of it? No way. At least Erin would be safely in Munich, thank God.

"Tony! Are you listening?"

"Yes. I'll make the table reservation at Maxim's."

"Thank you, love!"

He prudently requested of Albert, the maitre d', a banquette in an inconspicuous corner of the restaurant, but his caution went for nothing. All during their meal they were interrupted by a stream of Lisa's acquaintances and even by an associate of her father's.

At the opera house Tony was dismayed to see photographers snapping photos of those mounting the marble grand staircase to their boxes. And, of course, Lisa insisted on posing radiantly on Tony's arm. Fortunately, he rationalized, the photographs would be published in the press and forgotten by the time Erin returned from Munich. Besides, he told himself, he had a perfect defense: he was entertaining a valued customer of Brullov & Company. She knew that was one of his duties; they had even discussed it.

After the opera, Tony escorted Lisa home to the Île St. Louis and dubiously accepted her invitation to come in for a nightcap. The inevitable followed, this time without absinthe or kif or the participation of Zara. Instead there was Lisa's cabinet stocked with every conceivable device to heighten sensations and to prolong climaxes.

Two days later the Brullov store swarmed with women customers, some from society, some merely wealthy or with wealthy "gentlemen friends." Best of all, they bought.

"Jacques, you've done a fantastic job," Tony congratulated Verdier. "You must have planted the Castagna emeralds with every damned gossip columnist in town."

The store manager winced unhappily. "I cannot take the credit. The stories which I gave out will appear in fashion magazines which will not be on the newsstands for at least two months."

"Then what's the explanation for this stampede?"

Verdier shifted uneasily. "Perhaps word of mouth. Yesterday's papers did carry photographs of Mademoiselle di Ascoli at the opera. The emeralds were very visible."

"But there was nothing about their being from the house of Brullov." Tony frowned at Verdier. "I think you're holding something back."

Verdier sank down into his desk chair and studied his fingernails. "There are certain types who sell unsavory information to the more unscrupulous columnists. My advice is to ignore the yellow press."

Tony planted both hands on Verdier's desk. "Do you have clippings? If so, I want to see them."

Verdier gave a Gallic shrug, opened his desk drawer and handed Tony three clippings from newspapers of the previous evening. Tony glowered as he translated the French of the columnists. *It is said that the fabulous emerald necklace being worn by the heiress of one of Europe's great fortunes is a gift from an American jeweler doing business on the Place Vendôme.* The second item: *Has that American sportsman abandoned fast cars and ski slopes for a more intimate sport with the lady known as "L"?* The third was more pointed and cruel: *We hear that the famous American actress seen about our city has lost the starring role in her big off-camera romance. Her understudy is doing splendidly, thank you.*

That dinner at Maxim's and the opera were too innocent and aboveboard to inspire such smirking lines. Tony was positive on that score. Then he remembered that first evening at Lisa's apartment. The last of the parting guests must have noticed that Tony was remaining on and had drawn conclusions—and paychecks from the gossip columnists. Lisa had called them sycophants and camp followers. Traitors and dirt peddlers would have been more accurate.

Erin Deering returned to Paris on schedule and telephoned Tony at the store. She wanted to see him at the Raphael immediately. "I'm tied up right now, Erin," he said. "But I can make it in about two hours."

Erin's voice turned icy. "I said immediately. Unless you want me to come to the store and have an audience for what I have to say."

Tony arrived at the hotel fifteen minutes later. He saw Martha, Erin's maid, loitering in the lobby, which he deduced was on orders of her mistress to stay clear of the suite upstairs. An ominous sign. And worse, when Erin opened the door and turned her face away from Tony's kiss.

"I must compliment you on your sense of timing," she began, stony-eyed. "Right when I'm in the middle of talking script changes with my producer and director you have to splash that garbage all over the Paris papers." She held up her hand to silence Tony's reply. "Oh? You didn't think Munich would hear about it? Christ, they started yammering that I was a loser, bad box office, and I damn near lost the film—all because you had to fuck that green-eyed cunt."

Tony recoiled at her language. "Who the hell believes everything in print?" he retorted hotly. "Do you swallow everything in *Variety* or what you read in Hedda Hopper and

Parsons?" He saw her waver. "Yes, I took Lisa to Maxim's. Yes, I took her to the opera, on her tickets, at her request. I was escorting a customer who had just bought a three-hundred-thousand-dollar emerald necklace."

For a moment Erin seemed mollified. She moved aimlessly about the sitting room; then she faced Tony again. "What did she say about me?"

"Why, nothing. Not one word. Not even a question."

"Smart, I'll give her that. Tony, don't you see what's going on? She doesn't care about you. She's using you to get at me. *I'm* the one she's after. Oh, yes I am. I saw her at the race-track, the way she watched Aly Khan and her father making over me. It would be quite a notch in her gun to bring down Erin Deering before the public. *She's* the one who planted that filth in the papers."

Tony was silent. Was it possible? Was this whole unsavory mess a battle of woman versus woman?

"Just tell me one thing," Erin went on. "Tell me on your word of honor that you didn't sleep with Lisa." She waited. "Then it's true."

Tony realized he should have denied it instantly; instead he added a second mistake. "Erin, may I remind you that it was you who said you were glad we aren't married. You were glad there were no strings, no commitments. . . ."

Erin cut him off with a scream. "You fucked her! You fucked that scheming bitch. That lousy cunt."

"I was drunk."

"My God, how original. It forgives everything."

"Jesus, Erin, keep some sense of proportion. It was a mistake, I admit—but the crazy thing is it's turned out to be damned good for business. Lisa and her friends have bought over a million dollars in stuff at our store this week alone. Now Lisa's talking about commissioning us to make a solid-gold dinner service for her father's yacht."

"So she's bought you. She owns you lock, stock, barrel and cock."

"Not bought, not owned—*rented* is the word," Tony corrected ruefully. "All I can do is wait for Lisa to get bored with me."

Erin snorted. "Are you telling me you're afraid of her?"

"Of the situation, yes. If I break off with Lisa on my own, she'll look like a loser—the very thing you were complaining about. But there's a difference with Lisa. She uses people, she's got to be the winner. And her father is Orsino di Ascoli. If I make his daughter look like a loser, Lisa, the idol of his life, he'll turn vindictive. I know his reputation. He'll stop at nothing. He could ruin our company with one word to the bankers. Paris, London, Zurich, New York. They'll cut off our credit. He'll see that no magazine or newspaper will run our ads. I can't let that happen to my dad." He paused for breath. "So all I can do is wait until Lisa finds a new plaything."

Erin ran a hand over her brow hopelessly. "Well, then, this is it, isn't it? I'm going on to England and see my friends. And maybe *I'll* find a new plaything."

"Erin—"

"Goodbye, Tony."

Ten

London
October 1957

ORSINO DI Ascoli swiveled his club chair and peered through the window of his private DC-6 at the starry night, and below, at the blanket of fog. He consulted his wristwatch. 7:35 P.M., English time. He picked up the telephone and pressed the button which would connect him with the cockpit.

"Martin, how much longer?"

The pilot answered, "Can't tell, sir. London tower control says there are four planes ahead of us in the stack-up."

"Tell the tower we must have priority. Don't they know whose plane this is?"

"They do, sir. But they got to go by the book."

Frustrated, di Ascoli rose from his chair and began to pace about the cabin, which resembled a library in some exclusive men's club. Besides books, the shelves were furnished with framed photos of oil tankers, steel foundries, office buildings, chemical works, in all of which di Ascoli owned controlling interest. In addition there were miniatures of his daughter Lisa, from those in her first childhood rompers to those in adult equestrienne habit and ball gown. Go by the book, did they? He'd see about that when he got to London. Tomorrow he'd lodge a formal complaint with the airport authorities and demand that henceforth Orsino di Ascoli's plane receive the same priority as a transatlantic craft with near-empty fuel tanks.

He glowered at his wristwatch and pressed the intercom button again. "Call the tower and tell them I want to put through a phone call to London. Say it's absolutely urgent."

"Don't think they'll take personal calls, sir, but I'll try." A few moments later the intercom buzzed and the pilot reported, "The tower says they're sorry, sir. But, anyway, they've just moved us up into third position to land."

Small consolation, that. This entire flight had been jinxed. At Monte Carlo, which was di Ascoli's headquarters, the plane had been delayed in takeoff for two hours because of a faulty radio transmitter, then they had encountered a line of thunderstorms over France, and now heavy fog over the London area.

The intercom buzzed again. "Sir, we're in second position. We'll be landing in three minutes."

That was better. Ascoli went aft to his bedroom and into the bathroom to relieve his bladder. As he washed his hands he examined his face in the mirror to see if he needed a quick once-over with his electric shaver. No, he looked almost as fresh as when he had left Monte Carlo. He looked damned good—for a man of fifty-nine going on sixty. No bags under the eyes, a full head of hair only beginning to grizzle, and not even glasses to sharpen the gaze of his intense black eyes.

On the ground, he was whisked through Customs without examination, a courtesy extended to visiting multimillionaires whose luggage carried the *X* mark of honorary diplomatic immunity. Then he went directly to a bank of public telephones in the waiting room and put through his telephone call to the auction gallery. Yes, the operator at Sotheby's said, she would page Mr. Osborn in the auction hall. In a few moments, di Ascoli's London legal adviser came on the line. "Isn't the Rolls at the airport, sir?" he began anxiously.

"I haven't checked. I wanted you to know I just landed. With traffic and this damned fog, I probably can't reach Sotheby's for an hour or more."

"That's all right, sir. I'll tell Cartwright to bid just as you instructed."

"Fine. One other thing—have you seen Miss Erin Deering in the audience?"

"Couldn't miss her, sir. The press has got her surrounded. I'm sure she's going to bid on the diamond."

"See that she doesn't get it. Or anyone else. Tell Cartwright to drag out the bidding long enough for me to get there."

"Very good, sir. But I don't believe we discussed the limit which you would pay."

"Because I thought I'd be there in time. Go to the equivalent of one-half million dollars."

Di Ascoli heard Osborn catch his breath at the figure. Then: "Yes, sir. That should certainly discourage any competitors."

"It better, damn it. I want that diamond."

Di Ascoli's covetousness for great jewels went beyond the usual collector's desire to possess. Great gems, diamonds, sapphires, emeralds, rubies were an almost mystical symbol of purity to him; for only the great stones were "pure" in a gemological sense. The deeper motivation, again associated with purity, was to own jewels which had not been stripped from murdered corpses; jewels that he, di Ascoli, had honestly paid for in dollars, pounds, francs, lire or marks. Never mind that those currencies might have been acquired by devious and unethical means. "Money has no smell," a Roman sage had once said of the tax on urinals—a philosophy with which di Ascoli heartily agreed.

Erin Deering, who usually enjoyed London, found her present visit dispiriting. The news of her breakup with Tony had preceded her, and when she dropped backstage to see old friends with whom she had worked in Hollywood or New York, she was greeted with such elaborate kindness that it bordered on pity. Or so it seemed to Erin. "It's all in your head," Josey and Eric Hemmings had told her when she went down to Kent to spend a weekend with them in the country. "Nobody is pitying you," Eric had insisted. "We've all had affairs go sour on us. The thing to do is to fill your mind with positive things." Which meant, for the Hemmingses, endless rubbers of bridge and tennis sets played every bone-chilling afternoon.

Erin had never felt so adrift, so alone. No lover, no husband, no children, and her mother in a Los Angeles hospital with a serious heart condition. All she had was her work. And that French-German production was still many weeks away. How to fill the time? She considered an African safari, a cruise on the Mediterranean, and had discarded both. Work was what she needed; but the only openings on short notice would be New York television specials. Television. The elephants' dying ground for fading film stars. Absolutely not.

Then, quite by chance, she read in the *Times* of London of the coming jewelry auction at Sotheby's which would include the famous Rose of India diamond. According to the account, it was a rare rose-pink color, pear-shaped, weighing sixty-eight carats, and would fetch the equivalent in English pounds of at least a quarter of a million dollars. Suppose its new owner should be Erin Deering? Twice she visited the auction gallery to inspect the diamond during its display period. On her second visit, whether by chance or by inspiration of Sotheby's publicity department, news photographers had been on hand and had recorded the noted American actress admiring the great stone. Questions flew. Would she be bidding on the Rose of India? Possibly.

It was more than "possibly." The Rose of India would clearly outclass Lisa di Ascoli's emerald necklace. And bought with her own sweated-for money; not a handout from a rich daddy. It would announce to the world that Erin Deering was confident of the future and far more wealthy than imagined. It would raise her in the esteem of those nail-biting producers in Munich and Paris. And, not the least, be an up-yours to Lisa.

Every seat in Sotheby's auction hall was taken, and there were scores of standees in the rear. The audience was evenly divided between jewel dealers and collectors and society folk, many with illustrious titles, there to be seen and entertained. Erin Deering, in her aisle seat, third row, smiled prettily for the news photographers and surveyed the salesroom. It appeared, she thought, a curious blend of a concert hall and a judicial court. The two great crystal chandeliers, the vaulted ceiling with a glass roof, the olive-green walls, the rows of tiny gilded chairs might well be the setting for a musicale. In solemn contrast was the auctioneer high in his circular wooden pulpit, a bank of microphones before him, and flanked by a row of clerks with pens poised as if to note down testimony to be given—although in reality to record prices and names of successful bidders.

At first the auction went slowly as assorted offerings of routine jewelry went under the hammer. Erin ignored these and concentrated on a card which gave the currency-conversion rates from English pounds to American dollars. It was important that she not confuse the two when the time came. Finally the moment arrived. A porter in a gray uniform crossed the stage bearing a box of white velvet. The auctioneer held up the box, tilting it so the audience could view the rose-pink fire within. He recited the provenance of the famous stone, the names of its former owners, and announced that he would not entertain an opening bid of less than fifty thousand pounds. The actual opening was sixty thousand, made by a portly gentleman with a fringe of white hair who gave his name as Jared Cartwright. Other bids followed quickly— 65,000 pounds . . . 70 . . . 75 . . . 80. Erin shifted uneasily in her seat; the price in dollars was already 224,000. It was time that she make her own bid. "Do I hear ninety thousand pounds?" the auctioneer asked. Erin raised her hand. Another bidder topped her at 95,000. "Do I hear one hundred thousand pounds?" Jared Cartwright nodded. The figure was approaching 300,000 dollars, which was the limit Erin had set in her mind—the exact amount of her savings in U.S. Government bonds. "I have one hundred and five thousand pounds," the auctioneer intoned. "Do I hear one hundred and ten?" Erin signaled again and was immediately topped. At 130,000, Jared Cartwright returned to the contest. Erin responded with 135,000. Now she would have to sell some of her IBM stock and her General Motors. The other bidders began to drop out until finally it was a duel between Jared Cartwright and Erin Deering. "One hundred and sixty from Mr. Cartwright. Will you go higher, Miss Deering?" She hesitated; she dared not appear a quitter. She was the star of the evening; she had her audience with her. She could control them, not by brilliant dialogue and emotional fireworks, but by the simple act of bidding higher and higher. "One hundred and sixty-five thousand!" she called. She would have to borrow from her business manager against the salary from her next film. Cartwright went to 170,000; Erin to 175,000; Cartwright, 180,000. Erin, 185,000. She felt lightheaded with excitement; this was her biggest scene yet; the night was hers; it *must* be—even though it meant she would have to put a second mortgage on her Malibu house. Then Cartwright topped her again. One hundred and ninety thousand pounds. They were approaching the half-million-dollar mark. "Do I hear one hundred and ninety-five thousand?" Erin raised her hand. The auctioneer peered at Cartwright, who was wiping his mouth with a handkerchief. "Will you go higher, sir?" Cartwright grimaced and his voice was almost a croak. "Two hundred and seven thousand pounds." One-half million dollars. "I'm sorry, sir. The bidding is by increments of five thousand pounds. I suggest that you lower your bid by two thousand pounds." Cartwright agreed. The auctioneer turned to Erin. "Miss Deering?" It was madness to go on; but she must have the Rose of India. The audience wanted her to have it; they were rooting for her, waiting for her big scene. She would dare one more bid, a shutout. "Five hundred and fifty thousand American dollars!" she cried.

The auctioneer raised his eyebrows. "I have just advised Mr. Cartwright that the bidding is by increments of five thousand pounds. We do not wish our clientele to be carried away by emotion."

"Five hundred and fifty thousand American dollars," Erin repeated firmly. "I insist on it."

The auctioneer smiled. "The terms are English pounds; but we shall accept your bid at the current conversion rate." He turned again to Jared Cartwright. "Will you top it, sir?" Cartwright took a breath, then threw up his hands in a gesture of defeat. The auctioneer's gavel fell. "The Rose of India, sold to Miss Erin Deering!"

The auction hall resounded with applause for Erin's victory. She rose from her seat with the intention of going to Sotheby's business office to write out her check. As she stepped into the aisle, a man of great height and powerful physique blocked her passage. Orsino di Ascoli held out his hand: "It is a pleasure to meet you again, Miss Deering. I wish you great happiness with your purchase."

"Thank you." Then she eyed him shrewdly. "Would I be correct that it was you who made me pay such a high price? That Mr. Cartwright was your agent?"

Di Ascoli looked at her blankly. "Who is Mr. Cartwright? I

arrived at the gallery just moments ago. But now that I am here, may I take you to supper to celebrate your victory?"

Supper with the father of the hated Lisa? Never! "I'm sorry, but thank you just the same."

Di Ascoli persisted. "May I ask, are you here with friends?"

"No."

"Did you come in your car? No? Then permit me to offer the use of my limousine."

"Thank you again. But I'll take a taxi. Now, if you'll excuse me. I'm sure Sotheby's is anxious to see the color of my money."

"Of course. I understand."

When Erin reached the sidewalk outside the auction gallery the fog was almost impenetrable. Automobiles were pulling to the curb and whisking away the auction-goers; but a taxi was nowhere to be seen. It didn't make sense; an event such as at Sotheby's should have attracted a flotilla of taxis. The alternative, Erin decided, was to walk to her hotel. No sooner decided than she saw a black Rolls-Royce pull up at the curb. The rear door opened and Orsino di Ascoli loomed beside her.

"Alas, there are no taxis, Miss Deering. Won't you reconsider?"

She hesitated a moment, then surrendered. "I'm staying at the Connaught, on Carlos Place."

Di Ascoli gave her his arm, helped her into the rear seat and relayed their destination through the speaking tube to the chauffeur behind the glass partition.

"Do you suppose all the taxi drivers are on strike?" Erin asked, making conversation.

"I doubt it. But quite a few are happily on their way to their pubs to spend their ten quid." Di Ascoli's black eyes danced with amusement. "I paid them off in order to enjoy the pleasure of your company."

Erin eyed him sharply. "You must always get your way, is that it?"

"Always." Di Ascoli leaned forward to the burled walnut cabinet built into the back of the front seat and opened its sliding doors. It was a miniature bar, stocked with liquor and glasses and assorted cigarettes and cigars. "A brandy perhaps?" Erin shook her head. "Then a cigarette? I recommend my special Turkish blend." Erin accepted it; he flicked a lighter at its tip, then lit another for himself, and asked casually: "Miss Deering, how often do you suppose one could earn a quarter of a million dollars without any effort whatsoever and within the space of thirty minutes? That is the bonus I am offering you for the Rose of India."

"Then Cartwright *was* bidding on your account."

He ignored that. "So far as the public need know, you will still be the owner of the diamond. You will still enjoy the prestige that goes with it, because I would give you my word never to publicize my purchase."

Erin pondered a moment. "The 'prestige,' as you call it, wouldn't last long unless people see me wear the Rose of India."

"Then I shall have an exact duplicate made for you."

She shook her head. "*I* would know it's a fake; that's what counts. I'm sorry. The diamond is not for sale."

"I see that you are more than a beautiful woman, Miss Deering. You have character, integrity, and I honor you for it."

At that moment Erin noted that the limousine had passed down Bond Street and turned onto Piccadilly, in the opposite direction from the Connaught Hotel. "Where are you taking me?"

"Do not be alarmed. It is merely a little conspiracy which I have made with my chauffeur. To the Connaught Hotel, yes; but first a little drive through Hyde Park. And a little conversation."

Erin's lips tightened. He was wily and determined. But like it or not, there was an electric magnetism about the man, an aura of power which was attractive.

Di Ascoli interrupted her thoughts. "Allow me to tell you a small story. When my daughter was quite young, she used to come into the bedroom suite each morning to watch my barber shave me. One time, when she saw the barber's razor at my throat, she broke into tears. 'What is the matter, Lisa?' I asked. And she said, 'I'm afraid.' 'But of what?' And she said, 'That man might cut off your head.' The barber and I laughed, of course. 'Lisa,' I said, 'you must trust someone every moment of your life. Without trust nothing is possible.'" Di Ascoli paused and stubbed out his cigarette in the ashtray built into the back of the seat. "Tonight, Miss Deering, I wish to give that trust to you."

His words startled her and she waited for his explanation. Instead, he gazed broodingly out the car window at the flare of headlights approaching through the fog. He lighted a second cigarette, then abruptly faced Erin. "Whatever you tell me shall go no farther than this limousine. And what I ask of you is asked in trust of a woman of character and honesty. You also may speak freely, for that glass partition between us and the chauffeur is double thickness. He can hear nothing."

Erin frowned. Why all this circular talk? All this flattery, this *misterioso?* Then di Ascoli cut through her wondering.

"I wish your opinion, your evaluation, of Mr. Anton Brullov."

She stared blankly. *"Tony?"*

"Let me explain. My daughter Lisa, for more years than I care to say, has associated with men and women totally lacking in integrity. For the first time, in Mr. Brullov, she was with a man of responsibility, solid business experience, with a distinguished war record." He smiled. "You see, I investigate everyone who comes into contact with Lisa. She is never without a detective somewhere in the background."

"Let's go back a bit," Erin replied. "You said that for the first time Lisa *was* with a respectable man. You used the past tense. Has something happened?"

He nodded. "Mr. Brullov has gone back to New York. Business comes first with him, as it should. Lisa does not appear too concerned, perhaps because her attention span is very limited, or perhaps because Mr. Brullov will shortly return to Europe. That I have no way of knowing."

"In spite of your detectives?"

"Their purpose is not to read minds or hearts. Lisa is under surveillance because she is a perfect target for kidnappers. I fear that more than all else. I'd gladly pay any ransom; but paying does not guarantee her life. Of course, there have been numerous attempts at blackmail by various men and women. But those are of little consequence. Orsino di Ascoli pays blackmail once, but never twice."

Erin felt a chill at the implication of his words, then turned her mind away. "What do you expect me to say about Tony? You know we've broken up. Everybody does."

"That does not alter the fact that you would speak the truth of him, as you know it, without spite. I cannot be so wrong about human character."

"Very well. Tony is a fine man. A strong man. But perhaps too vulnerable to beautiful women."

Di Ascoli chuckled. "I share that failing. It is of no importance." He stared thoughtfully out at the fog-draped trees of Hyde Park, then back at Erin. "Then you can suggest no other flaws in his character?"

"None that I'm aware of."

"So you believe that Mr. Brullov would make a suitable husband for my daughter?"

Erin twisted her fingers in irritation. She was not about to give a Good Housekeeping Seal of Approval for the benefit of that bitch Lisa. "I don't know your daughter except by hearsay. How could I know if Tony is suitable or not?"

"I was attempting to put my question as delicately as possible; but I see there is no easy way. I wish to know if Mr. Brullov is potent—that he is capable of siring a child."

Erin's anger washed away in laughter. "Very capable. In other words, you want to be certain of an heir."

"Above all else."

"Then perhaps first you should learn if Lisa is fertile. Has she had miscarriages, abortions?"

She saw a cloud pass over his face. "I know she has gone to various doctors. But those may have been for routine checkups. The physicians refuse to tell me."

"Understandably. I'd say your basic problem, as it stands now, is how to get Tony and Lisa together again. That shouldn't be too difficult for the famous maestro of mergers."

He smiled at her irony, then, seriously, "You have been most helpful, Miss Deering. Believe me, I shall find some way to show my gratitude."

"You can. Just drive me to my hotel."

He put the speaking tube to his mouth. "Charles, the Connaught, please."

Sleep eluded Erin that night. She was exhilarated by the thought of the Rose of India, which she would take possession of as soon as she had paid for it in full and had arranged for insurance coverage. On the whole, it had been a most satisfactory evening. And informative. Tony was out of the clutches of Lisa di Ascoli, however briefly. Perhaps just long enough for a reconciliation with Erin. A very big perhaps, now that Daddy Orsino saw Tony as his son-in-law.

She punched her pillow and told herself to forget Tony Brullov. All that mattered now was sleep. She rose and went to the bathroom and swallowed a Seconal. Should she take another? Before she could decide, she heard the jingle of the telephone beside her bed.

"Miss Deering?" a male voice inquired. "This is Doctor

Smiley, at Good Samaritan Hospital in Los Angeles. I'm sorry to call you at this hour but—"

Erin interrupted. "It's about my mother, isn't it?"

"She passed away a few minutes ago. If you have any wishes about final arrangements . . ."

"I'll take care of them, Doctor. I'll take the first plane out in the morning."

Now she was truly completely alone.

Eleven

*Hollywood and Monte Carlo
December 1957*

THE FUNERAL services for Erin's mother and burial at Forest Lawn were attended by a pitiful few—her nurse, several old neighbors and Erin's agent, who accompanied Erin for diplomacy's sake. The next day she empowered her attorney to file her mother's will, which would result in the sale of her house, her furniture, her automobile and furs. The most difficult part was sorting through the mementos of a life of brave hopes and sad disillusionments, which filled bureaus, trunks in the attic and cardboard boxes on the top shelves of closets. There were faded photos of Grace and Carl, her first husband, others of Grace and her second. Erin's baby bootees, her silver food pusher, her first report card. A snapshot of the freighter that had borne the family to Costa Rica. Erin with her violin case on the steps of Carrie Wyatt's house. Erin at the finca, playing under a banana tree with her pet monkey and her macaw. She had looked like such a happy child then, believing her mother's declarations: "Your stepfather will change; he'll find himself once the coffee and cocoa crops start to bring in some money." Then Hollywood and a snap of that wretched bungalow court . . . a copy of a radio script Erin had typed in Mimeograph . . . a review from *Variety* of Erin's first film, lumping her name with "also in the cast."

But how was Erin to fill the empty weeks until the beginning of shooting of her new film on the Riviera? She attended a few Hollywood parties and found them boring; she preferred drive-in movies, where she would not have to make small talk. Her agent suggested guest appearances on TV shows, but she refused. Finally she looked up Rheinhold Hoffman, her first dramatic coach, and worked on scenes from Ibsen and George Bernard Shaw and Arthur Miller. He drove her hard and she was grateful for the total absorption he demanded.

Then, a week before she was to return to Europe, she had an inspiration. She would look up Madge Carson, the red-haired comedienne who had trouped with her on the wartime camp tour. But where to find her? Erin's agent hadn't heard Madge's name in years. Finally Erin called Central Casting, which gave her a telephone number.

"It's the old Hollywood story, kid," she told Erin when she called. "When it's too long between jobs, you become contagious. Nobody wants to breathe the same air you do. So now I'm a receptionist for a pack of lawyers. And bored out of my skull. I'm thinking of joining a trained-dog act and maybe recruiting some talented fleas for a circus of my own."

The same old Madge, Erin thought. "Before you do that, would you be free for the month of December?"

"Free for what? A red suit and ho! ho! ho!?" Then she turned serious. "Why you asking?"

"I'm doing a film on the Riviera. I think I can talk the producers into writing in a couple of scenes for you. Your usual bit, the gum-chewing, wisecracking broad who gets stranded in Europe. The script needs some humor. And I need an old familiar face on the set. An American face. It just might mean your comeback. What do you say?"

"I'll sing it for you, hon. Yippee! Hallelujah!"

The weather on the Riviera that December was made to order for the film: days of brilliant sunshine for the upbeat sequences and occasional rain or a gusty mistral to fit the somber episodes. Much of the shooting was to be in a rented and picturesquely run-down villa in the La Condamine area of Monaco, the residential and business section adjoining the city of Monte Carlo. It was an area little frequented by the tourist hordes, who were drawn to the shops and cafés of Monte Carlo, the Casino, the Palace of Prince Rainier and his bride of a year, the actress Grace Kelly.

Erin's mood was buoyant; she had a family again, however temporarily. From the first crack of the clapsticks to the final wrap, she would be related to everyone—actors, stand-ins, director, cameraman, script girl; dressers, makeup people, grips and gofers. She liked and respected the English director, Rex Carmichael: ruddy-faced, with a handlebar moustache which, when he wore a wide-brimmed straw hat, reminded her of a nineteenth-century African explorer. Marcel Le Clerc, who played her husband, was as dignified as an archbishop, which was the required contrast needed for Jerry Helprin, the Canadian actor who was cast as Erin's lover and former partner of Madge in a variety of slippery confidence games.

But even the most congenial company and the most professional productions run into problems. In the present case it was script trouble. Scenes which had read well did not "play." The writers, one from Paris, one from Munich, arrived and quarreled and made the scenes worse. An English writer was imported. While he labored over rewrites, Erin and Madge found themselves excused for a day and immediately decided on a shopping spree in the Monte Carlo boutiques, followed by an evening at the Casino, which neither had seen since that night in 1945. The gaming halls, which had been so sparsely peopled twelve years before, now were massed with gamblers. Victor, the *physiognomiste* who had so easily seen through Tony Brullov's disguise, was still stationed in the lobby. He had grown bald and one eye twitched with a tic—yet he instantly recognized Erin and described the evening gown she had worn twelve years earlier. "But it's impossible," she protested. Victor chuckled. "How could I not know the face of a famous actress? My brain is a catalogue of a quarter of a million faces—but your gown, Mademoiselle Deering, I remember as a matter of personal interest. It was cut very low in back, very daring, exactly as the gown that I had once forbidden my daughter to wear."

The following day shooting resumed with one of the rewritten scenes. The action was set in the cypress-bordered garden of the villa, where Erin was to be discovered by her husband in the act of embracing her lover. It was a warm day, very nearly hot. While the director and cameraman enjoyed the shade of umbrellas, the three actors were required to work in full sun and battle against perspiration and the persistent attention of gnats. At the end of the third take, the actors glanced at the director for his approval. Carmichael appeared to have forgotten them entirely; he was lost in conversation with a tall heavyset man in white yachting attire, who waved to Erin and bowed. It was Orsino di Ascoli.

"I heard that you were filming in Monaco," he said, when he approached Erin. "I came to pay my respects as a neighbor and friend."

"A neighbor?" she echoed. "You live nearby?"

"Everybody in Monaco lives nearby. The Principality is but four hundred and fifty-three acres. My offices and penthouse are just around the hill." His black eyes twinkled. "Tell me, do you still like your diamond?"

"Well enough not to sell it." Erin smiled.

"Good. It is unfortunate when one has regrets. Especially half-million-dollar regrets."

Rex Carmichael joined them, tugging thoughtfully on his huge moustache. "I'm sure I can clear it with the production office, Mr. di Ascoli. We can shoot around Erin and Marcel and Madge. It'll give Jeremy time to finish the rewrites, and my assistant can shoot the chase scenes while we're gone."

Erin rolled her eyes at the director. "Gone? Gone where?"

"On the cruise. I thought that's what you two were talking about. Damned if I'll pass up a chance to sail on the world's most famous yacht."

Di Ascoli protested modestly. "I'm afraid that description fits the vessel of my neighbor and competitor, Ari Onassis. Still, I believe you will find my *Diana* quite an experience. So, Miss Deering, will you be my guest?"

"Gladly!" she cried. "When?"

"Tomorrow afternoon. The cruise will be but three or four days, to Corsica and perhaps Sardinia." He raised Erin's hand to his lips. "Shall we say, the harbor at four o'clock tomorrow?"

"My God, this must have been whelped by the *Queen Mary*," Madge Carson murmured to Erin as they followed a steward with their luggage up the gangplank of the *Diana*. The vessel was almost two hundred feet in length, dazzling white, its funnel banded in green and gold. Varicolored pennants flapped overhead from bow to taffrail and the blue peter was flying.

"Welcome aboard," di Ascoli greeted the two women as they stepped off the gangplank. "You are the last to arrive, so we sail immediately. At five o'clock there will be cocktails in the lounge and you will meet the other guests."

Other guests? So the members of the film company were not to be the only passengers.

The women followed the steward down a flight of steps to the lower deck and along a companionway to their adjoining cabins. Erin's was the more luxurious, being, the steward explained, reserved for the guest of honor. A bouquet of yellow roses scented the sleeping area, which was furnished with a full-sized bed; an arrangement of cymbidium orchids graced a cocktail table, and in the dressing room a shelf offered flacons of the leading French perfumes, all unopened. The bathroom itself was a splendor: the washbasin was carved from a solid block of royal green malachite, with fixtures of gold plate. Moreover, off the sitting area, a sliding glass door gave onto a balcony with a deck chair for private sunning. Just as Erin completed her inspection, the cabin was flooded with music from *Tosca*. It startled her; was it coincidence, or had di Ascoli learned somehow that *Tosca* was her favorite opera?

At cocktails in the lounge Erin counted ten guests beside herself. Four were from the film company, four were middle-aged married couples. The husbands, according to di Ascoli, were business associates. A sharp-eyed bald-headed man was introduced as Constantine Durer, his confidential secretary. "And of course you met my daughter Lisa at the racetrack." The two exchanged cool smiles and Lisa locked arms with a lovely blond girl whom she called "my friend Simone." At least there was no Tony Brullov, Erin reflected gratefully.

At dinner, Erin sat at di Ascoli's right, at the head of the long table. Lisa was at the far end flanked by Simone and Rex Carmichael. The conversation was animated, but for Erin's taste, rather too effusively admiring on the part of the two business couples, who had never before encountered the glamour of film folk. It was "absolutely thrilling," according to one of the wives, when di Ascoli announced that there would be a showing after dinner of Erin Deering's most recent film.

Nevertheless, she was tremendously flattered. And afterward, when there was dancing in the bar-lounge to a five-piece orchestra, di Ascoli claimed Erin for the first dance. "You are an actress of great emotional depth," he said as they danced. "But I could tell, during the showing, that you were uncomfortable. Why?"

"I'm always uncomfortable watching myself," she answered. "I always feel I could have done better. I see little mistakes, or opportunities missed. I wish I could do it all over again."

"I hope you will be able to say that of my little cruise—to want to do it all over again."

She realized that he wanted to be complimented and she complied. "It's absolutely perfect. We're all overwhelmed by your hospitality."

Between one of the dance sets she sat at the bar with Madge, who asked, "Have you checked out the boss's daughter and the blond girl friend?"

"In what way?"

"*That* way. There's enough electricity passing between them to light up Times Square. What happened with Tony?"

Erin shrugged. "Maybe nothing, maybe something. I'd say Lisa is a girl who can't live in an emotional vacuum."

"Uh-huh. Could sort of run in the family."

"Again?"

"Well, your cabin, I hear, is next door to Mr. Big. Maybe one of the walls is rigged to slide back. Or at least a two-way mirror in the john."

Erin laughed. "Who needs sliding walls? The balcony outside my cabin runs past di Ascoli's, too. There's a gate that divides it for privacy. But all you'd have to do is slide back the bolt, and bingo!"

Madge nodded triumphantly. "See what I mean?"

Erin's answer was a yawn. "It's been a long day. I'm hitting the sack."

She found the bed in her cabin turned down, the reading

lamp beside the bed lighted, and an assortment of magazines placed on the nightstand. Service aboard the *Diana* was certainly impeccable. Even the sliding door onto the balcony had been opened to fill the cabin with fresh sea air. She stepped out onto the balcony and stared at the calm sea. The night was cloudless and the stars, usually invisible on land, now sparkled on the horizon like myriads of diamonds. Erin stretched her arms wide, inhaling the salt air, and felt her fatigue begin to melt away.

"There's a smell of Africa in the wind tonight," di Ascoli's voice came through the darkness.

Erin gave a start. She was positive that he had not been on his balcony when she had stepped out; now he was leaning his elbows on the railing and staring at the southern horizon. "The Mediterranean is my favorite sea," he went on as if talking to himself. "It is the waterway of history. Phoenician merchant ships knew these waters, and Greek and Roman galleys bound for the port we call Marseilles. Beneath this surface, so calm tonight, rot the skeletons of hundreds of ships lost in battle or storm. And there to the south—" he gestured—"the Barbary pirates plundered as ruthlessly as any on the Spanish Main." He paused and looked toward Erin. "Forgive me. I am boring you."

"Not at all," Erin said quickly. She was intrigued by his mood and surprised by his sense of history.

"Do you know the story of Aimée Dubuc de Rivery?"

"I'm sorry, no."

"The Barbary pirates reminded me of her. She was the cousin of Napoleon's Empress Josephine. She sailed from France to visit her family in Martinique, which was the birthplace of both Aimée and Josephine. Unhappily, a great storm came up in the Bay of Biscay, and the ship, which was small and no match for the huge waves, was on the point of sinking when it was sighted by a much larger vessel, a Spanish merchantman. The Spaniard took aboard the passengers and crew, rode out the storm, and proceeded toward its port, which was Majorca. But now appeared a new threat, a flotilla of the Barbary pirates. The Spanish ship was captured and all aboard her were delivered to the slave markets of Tunis. All except Aimée. The pirates, impressed by her great beauty, presented her to their master, the Bey of Tunis. It so happened that at that time the Bey of Tunis wished to ingratiate himself with the Sultan of Turkey, and what better gift than the beautiful cousin of the Empress of France? So Aimée was installed in the Sultan's seraglio as one of his hundreds of concubines. Her situation seemed hopeless. Her beauty made every other woman in the harem her enemy. And as for the Sultan, he, too, was in effect a prisoner. The palace was filled with the spies of the Janissaries, who were the elite of the Turkish military and the real rulers of the Empire. Yet it came to pass that Aimée—again because of her beauty and intelligence—found favor with the Sultan. She became his First Wife. She bore the Sultan a son, and as he grew, she taught him the progressive ideals of the West and everything she could remember of French culture. When her son came to the throne as Mahmoud the Second, he remembered his mother's enlightened teachings, which, it is said, inspired him to defy the Janissaries and finally to destroy them to the last man."

Di Ascoli paused. "An almost forgotten bit of history, my dear. A woman of beauty and intelligence rose from slave and concubine to be the Queen Mother, the power behind a throne, and helped to bring an empire out of the Dark Ages."

"What a magnificent story," Erin said, meaning it sincerely.

Di Ascoli smiled and took Erin's hand and raised it to his lips. "May you sleep well," he said, and turned and went into his suite.

The next morning Erin was awakened by a male voice booming through the combination radio-intercom beside her bed. The time was 8 A.M., the voice announced, and the *Diana* was at anchor in the harbor of Ajaccio. Breakfast orders should now be given to the cabin stewards. And at nine-thirty promptly, di Ascoli requested all guests to assemble in the gym for the exercise period. Appropriate sweatsuits were now being placed outside each cabin door.

"Who the hell does he think he is, a boot-camp drill sergeant?" Madge muttered to Erin between pushups, which were led by di Ascoli himself. The scene was slightly comical, Erin thought—all those gray-clad bodies heaving up and down and panting with unaccustomed exertion. All except for di Ascoli, who, seemingly without effort, chinned himself on the overhead bars, lifted weights and pummeled a punching bag. It was a remarkable performance for a man of sixty, and intended, Erin suspected, less for fitness than to impress his guests.

"After showers," he announced finally, "there will be deck games and sunning pads for those desiring them. Buffet luncheon on the aft deck will be at noon. For those who wish to see a bit of Ajaccio, our launches will leave at one-thirty. You will return at four o'clock. Please observe exactly all times given. Punctuality is more than courtesy, my friends, it is the pride of princes. And now, enjoy yourselves."

Di Ascoli did not join the party going ashore, nor did the two men who were his business associates, leaving the sightseeing of Ajaccio to their wives. Rex Carmichael speculated on this to Erin as they strolled about the curio shops. "There's more to this cruise than di Ascoli pretends. I think you and I and the rest of us are bugs under the magnifying glass. That's why he showed your movie last night and has another one scheduled for this evening."

"Would you mind translating that into plain Greek," Erin said.

"It's just a hunch; but I think di Ascoli is selling the idea to his two fat friends to buy up your films for television. And maybe a lot of others. I overheard one of the guys use the word 'syndication,' which just might be a clue. Or maybe di Ascoli wants to buy into film production directly."

"A lot of maybes," Erin commented.

At sunset the yacht turned seaward for a leisurely cruise along the coast of Sardinia. The evening went much as had the first—an overly rich dinner, another Erin Deering film, then dancing in the bar-lounge. This time di Ascoli danced with only one partner, his daughter Lisa. It was clear to everyone that they were arguing, for Lisa kept shaking her head angrily, and then suddenly she broke away and left the lounge with Simone, who, Erin speculated, had been the subject of the quarrel. Whatever the cause, di Ascoli withdrew to the bar and sat moodily smoking one Havana cigar after another, until, at his signal, the dance band put away their instruments. The evening was over.

When Erin returned to her cabin she stepped out onto the balcony for a last look at the sea and sky. Again di Ascoli was leaning on the railing, staring at the sea. He did not indicate that he was aware of Erin's arrival, yet he began to speak immediately.

"Sometimes does a person come to you and tell such and such an experience and ask if it would make a fine motion picture?"

"Sometimes," she answered. "But the stories are seldom any good."

"And so you forget them?"

"Yes."

The tip of his cigar reddened momentarily. "Perhaps you will not forget this one." He glanced across the gate separating them, then back at the sea. "There was a young man I knew in Paris many years ago. It was in the very early Twenties. He had no background, he had come from nothing; but by various means he was on his way to becoming rich. He had married a very beautiful girl, a music student at the conservatory. She bore him a son. The father was proud, immensely proud, to be blessed with a son, and this fact goaded him on to make more and more money. But to do this, he had to make many business trips to other cities and countries. At first his wife, who loved him dearly, went on these trips with him and left their baby with a nurse in their Paris home. Soon she decided, however, that she missed her baby too much, and she went on no more trips. But there was a problem, a small problem, at first. She had servants to take care of the house and to help with the baby; there was too much time on her hands and she missed her music, which was the piano. . . ."

Di Ascoli's words became a blur. Few people knew how to tell a story, she thought; they swamped everything in petty details. Erin's eyes wandered to the lights of a distant ship passing in the opposite direction. It was a large ship, probably a cruise liner, she decided, with hundreds of middle-aged tourists gabbling about the bargains they had bought at the last port, or how they had been swindled; fat people who belched complaints that they had eaten too much at dinner; old people having a last fling before the wheelchairs.

Suddenly her attention was wrenched back to di Ascoli's monologue. "This mistress whom the husband took was totally different from his wife. She came from a titled family, she had money of her own. Of course, the husband did everything possible to keep it a secret from his wife, and he thought that he had succeeded. She was, he told himself, too taken up with her music. Every afternoon the teacher, a young man from the conservatory, came to the house and there was the sound of the piano hour after hour. But then one evening the wife said to him: 'You are in love with another woman.' He denied it furiously. 'I know it is so,' she said. 'Every evening when you are dressing to go out, I hear you whistling. You are thinking of her, you are already with her.' The husband was surprised by this; he had never been conscious of whistling at all. 'You will leave me and our son and marry this bitch,' she said."

Erin was listening carefully. There was an emotional intensity in di Ascoli's words that seemed unwarranted in recounting a secondhand story.

"The husband continued his denials, and finally convinced

himself that his wife had believed him. But that weekend, when he was supposedly on another trip, but was actually with his mistress, his wife ran away with her music teacher. And worse, she took his three-year-old son. The husband hired detectives to find them. They were not in Paris. They were not in France. Then, in the middle of one night, the telephone rang. It was the music teacher. He was calling from Rome. He told the husband that his wife had jumped from the hotel window with their son in her arms. They were dead."

Erin gasped, "How horrible! But why? Why would she do such an awful thing?"

"Perhaps guilt because of her affair. Perhaps on an impulse after a quarrel with her lover." Di Ascoli stared down at the sea foaming away from the hull of the yacht. Then his voice turned husky. "I think, I truly think, her motive was more terrible. I think she wished to punish her husband, to make a scandal, and even worse, to destroy the son he loved and for whom he had made such plans."

Erin shuddered at the suggestion. It was Greek tragedy. "Could it be," she ventured, "that her lover was actually the murderer?"

"No. The police said he was not even in the hotel at the time. Also, his grief was too genuine. The husband saw that at the funeral. And there is the final irony. Two men who should have been enemies became friends, united by their loss. Today the lover is one of Europe's great music conductors, and his orchestra is subsidized by one of the husband's companies."

"And the husband's mistress? The cause of it all?"

"He married her. They had one child."

"A daughter?"

"A daughter."

Erin was silent for a moment. Then she reached across the gate which separated their balconies and touched di Ascoli's hand. "It would make a movie, a sad but beautiful movie. But there are some stories too painful to be told."

"Or repeated," di Ascoli added. He raised Erin's hand to his lips. "Good night, my dear."

The following day was much like those that preceded it. The *Diana* cruised the coast of Sardinia, the guests sunned themselves, played cards, and Erin read a movie script which had been sent to her by a hopeful producer. The plot seemed vapid and artificial compared to the tales which di Ascoli had told her evenings before. There was, she decided, a purpose behind his stories. Aimée Dubuc de Rivery illustrated the heights to which a woman could rise when married to a man of great power. The story of the wife's revenge on her unfaithful husband, the loss of his beloved son, explained di Ascoli's fixation on Lisa, the disappointing substitute. But it went further, Erin thought; it was as though di Ascoli wished to deny his image of power and invincibility, a confession of vulnerability and loneliness.

By early afternoon the coastline of Italy emerged from the sea haze. They were heading for Genoa, someone said. An hour later the *Diana* dropped anchor a short distance off the port and the owner's launch, roaring and churning up a trail of spray, sped into the harbor. A few minutes later the launch reappeared and swung alongside the boarding platform. Erin joined the other guests in peering over the side to see who might be coming aboard. Looking down, they saw a youngish man with sandy hair dressed in a business suit and carrying a flight bag and a small case. Not until he stepped onto the deck did Erin recognize him. It was Tony Brullov.

He stared at Erin, his face mirroring her own surprise. Then he grinned awkwardly. "You're the last person I ever expected to run into."

She forced a smile. "Especially with Lisa aboard."

"Is she?" He glanced around at the cruise party. "Where's di Ascoli?"

"Taking his afternoon siesta, I imagine."

A steward interrupted them, took Tony's bags and said he would place them in Tony's cabin. Tony moved to follow the steward, then Erin stayed him with "You've missed the best part of the cruise. Why so late?"

"The whole thing is a mystery to me," he answered. "I was in Antwerp, talking to our diamond cutters, when Dad called from New York. He said di Ascoli phoned him from Monte Carlo and invited both of us to join him for a few days on his yacht. Said he had a matter of mutual interest to discuss. Dad couldn't get away during the Christmas buying rush, but he suggested I might be available. Days went by and I didn't hear from di Ascoli until a radiogram this morning. It said he was sending his private plane to Antwerp to fly me to Genoa. And here I am."

"Ton-nee, darling!" a woman shrilled, then Lisa was throwing her arms around him.

Erin turned on her heels and walked rapidly away. The "matter of mutual interest," she fumed, had been invented by that bitch Lisa.

Minutes later there was a knock on Tony's cabin door and di Ascoli, in white slacks and an open-necked shirt, welcomed his new guest and invited him for a talk in what he termed "my office away from my office." It proved to be a small room, without windows, on the upper deck. The walls were paneled in rosewood. The wall to the left of di Ascoli's desk was largely taken up by a huge sheet of opaline glass on which were etched the outlines of the continents of the world. Small green bulbs glowed behind the glass to mark the location of di Ascoli's interests in Europe, Africa, South America, the Near East and Japan. The overall effect, Tony thought, was that of a military command post. There was no bar, no shelf of books, no personal photos on the desk—only a telephone with a bank of push buttons and, beside the desk, a news ticker that clattered financial dispatches from Reuters until di Ascoli switched it off.

After the usual pleasantries of host and guest, di Ascoli

leaned back in his swivel chair and fixed his black eyes on Tony, who was attempting to look at ease in one of the two lounge chairs.

"To begin with," di Ascoli said, "I have one rule in all business propositions. It must be so simple that it can be summarized in one short paragraph. Complicated propositions merely guarantee unhappy surprises. Do you agree, Tony?"

He nodded. It was the first time that di Ascoli had not addressed him as Mr. Brullov.

"Good. As to the proposal I'm about to make, it must be confidential, known only to you and your father. If you are agreeable, then you may make known the terms to the minority stockholders in Brullov and Company, which, from my investigation, means your comptroller, with five percent of the stock, and the sister of your late mother, with fifteen percent."

Tony stiffened in his chair. "Are you suggesting a buy-out?"

Di Ascoli leaned forward in his chair and planted his elbows on the desk. "The very opposite. The firm of Brullov sells jewels in New York, London, Paris and Zurich. You are an international firm with a high reputation. But you are not exploiting that reputation to the fullest. Brullov should introduce a line of the very finest perfumes, bearing its name, with the highest price tags. You must be aware of the fantastic profits in perfumes. Then, couturier gowns and suits designed by one of the best creators in Paris. There should be Brullov handbags and shoes and quality luggage. Brullov crystalware and fine porcelains. As you Americans say, 'The works.' "

"In other words, we become a general merchandising chain."

"No. Specialists in status goods. You would be the sensation of the fashion world."

Tony felt his pulse beating with excitement. Di Ascoli's vision was breathtaking. And yet. And yet . . . "Your proposal," Tony said, "would mean tremendous expansion. We'd have to triple the square footage of our stores, and build new ones.

The cost would be beyond us, and I doubt the banks would extend us the line of credit necessary."

"Quite possibly not. But Orsino di Ascoli will."

"*You?*"

Di Ascoli permitted a modest smile. "I have a certain influence with various banks on both sides of the water. The money will be provided."

At that moment the telephone buzzed discreetly. Di Ascoli glanced at the opaline glass on the wall with its outlines of the world's hemispheres. A red light blinked behind the name Tokyo. He picked up the phone. "Yes?"

Tony listened, bemused, to the periodic "yeses" and "noes" and considered di Ascoli's reputation. How many strategies—"plots" might be the better word—had been born in this floating office? How many flies had been enmeshed in this spider's web? How many companies swallowed, how many lives ruined?

Di Ascoli hung up the telephone and apologized for the interruption. "I see you have a question."

Tony nodded. "There's no such thing as a free lunch. So, in return for your help, what do you ask?"

"That Brullov become a public stock company, and that my share of the stock be twenty-five percent." Di Ascoli threw wide his hands in a gesture of admission. "Yes! A high price, but think what it means. When Wall Street learns of the alliance of di Ascoli with the Brullovs, there will be a stampede for our stock. The price will soar into the heavens. You and your father will be multimillionaires within weeks, perhaps even days."

It was a heady prospect. Tony the businessman recognized the opportunity, the almost guaranteed success of the venture; but Tony the sometime lover—or prey—of Lisa di Ascoli sensed danger. "Assuming we agree," he said, "are there other conditions? Conditions perhaps not in dollars and cents, but personal expectations."

He was positive that di Ascoli understood his meaning. The black eyes stared unblinkingly at Tony as a cobra might hypnotize its victim. Then, at last, di Ascoli smiled. "No other conditions. But a personal expectation, yes."

"Which is?"

"That we be the best of friends."

Tony joined him in a laugh. "I'll talk this over with my father. But I must warn you that the jewel business is his only love. Gems are his life. Dad is already a millionaire and he may not care to just keep piling up millions upon millions."

"True. But you could persuade him. And you must consider yourself. When your father is gone, you would be master of a high-fashion empire. What a magnificent legacy to leave to your children!"

"If I have any."

Tony saw a look almost of dismay come into di Ascoli's eyes. "But surely—" he began, then broke off with a small laugh. "You will consider my proposal, yes?"

"Of course. But I—or rather Dad and I—won't rush into it."

"Understood. I admire you for your caution—and for standing up to Orsino di Ascoli. It promises well." He rose from his desk. "Meanwhile, let us enjoy our cruise."

When Lisa di Ascoli appeared in the dining salon that evening, even Erin caught her breath at the young woman's beauty. Golden flecks were strewn through her black hair, the Castagna emeralds circled her neck, and her skintight sheath, slit to the hip on one side to reveal the tanned leg and thigh, announced to all that she was naked underneath. She seated herself at the far end of the table, with Tony at her right. From Erin's place beside di Ascoli, she watched the couple with studied detachment. Lisa chattering into Tony's ear, Tony smiling and nodding—Erin could not decide if the romance was on again or if Tony was simply being polite to the daughter of his host. But she did note that Simone was now relegated to neutral territory in the middle of the long dining table.

After dinner there was again dancing in the bar-lounge and on the open aft deck just beyond. Erin was pleasantly surprised when Tony asked for the first dance. "Have you figured out yet why di Ascoli was in a sweat to see you?" she asked.

He nodded soberly. "I can't go into it. It's confidential. But I should congratulate you."

"For what?"

"Being the guest of honor on the cruise. The news ought to be worth a couple of film offers at the very least."

"I hope so."

That was the whole of their conversation, and Erin's only dance with Tony. The balance of the evening Lisa was his steady partner. Rhumbas, sambas, foxtrots, waltzes, swing, she was constantly in his arms, and whenever she caught Erin's eyes upon her, she would twine her bare arms around Tony's neck and press her loins against him.

"Christ," Rex Carmichael whispered to Erin, who was dancing with him, "that's the most public dry screw I've seen outside blue movies."

"At least they make a fantastic-looking couple," Erin answered.

Carmichael eyed her with surprise. "Damned generous of you, considering."

"Why? If I had to lose out with Tony, at least it's not to some third-rater."

Words, she said to herself. The important thing was to play out the scene with class. "All I wish," she thought aloud, "is that that hunk of diamond of mine was here, not in a London bank vault. I'd make that panting slut's emeralds look like dime-store beads."

Carmichael hooted. "That's more like it! You're human, after all."

"You bet I am! Lisa may have ten years on me and half a

billion dollars hanging on a heartbeat, but she's never done a goddamned thing on her own—it's all been handed to her. She never had to scramble out of the muck the way I had to. I'm where I am through guts and brains."

"And a hell of a talent," Carmichael appended and kissed her cheek.

The dance set was over and Erin retreated to the bar and ordered a double Scotch. At the far end she saw di Ascoli watching the dancing couple with the impassive expression of a Buddha. Was he pleased that they were together again, or a bit put off by his daughter's public display of lust? It was hard to fathom the man. His wealth gave him the power of a feudal monarch; at the crook of a finger, people jumped. Yet the tale he had told Erin the night before revealed a private side, a man haunted by guilt over his first wife's suicide, a man still mourning the loss of his son.

Erin finished her Scotch and ordered another double and tossed it down. She felt nothing. She looked searchingly at the dance floor; Tony and Lisa were no longer there. She wandered to the open doors giving out onto the aft deck. There they were. Still dancing. Very closely. Lisa's arms still around his neck. Pelvis to pelvis. Erin wished she could see the expression on Tony's face; then she thought, The hell with it. The hell with everything. Early or not, she was going to bed.

In her cabin she turned indecisive—to undress, remove her makeup and cream her face, or to simply rest awhile and return to the bar and try once more to get stoned. No, that would be a public admission of her distress. Better to ring for the steward and have him fetch a bottle. Or she could take a sleeping pill. Instead, she compromised. She undressed, wrapped herself in her robe, propped herself up in bed, lit a cigarette and brooded over Tony. Why had di Ascoli invited him aboard? Genuine business matters could always wait. Perhaps he was trying to break up Lisa's relationship with Simone and get her back on the track with Tony. Or—and this was intriguing—was it to prove to himself that the romance between Tony *and Erin* was truly dead? Of course it was. It had to be.

She lighted another cigarette and told herself she must think of other things. The film she was shooting. It was going to be good, very good, maybe even an entry at Cannes next spring. She glanced at her wristwatch. Were Tony and Lisa still dancing? Or in Lisa's cabin? It would be Lisa's, of course, luxurious and feminine. She would be naked, hands under her breasts, offering them to Tony's lips, just as Erin herself had done. Or was she on her knees before him? Or . . . or . . . As image after image flashed through her brain, her body responded with prickling desire. A sleeping pill was the answer. Maybe two.

She stubbed out her cigarette and became aware of the aroma of a different kind of tobacco. Di Ascoli's Havana cigar. He was out there on his balcony again.

She left her bed, tightened the belt of her robe and stepped through the open door onto her side of the balcony. In the shaft of light from his own quarters she saw that he, too, was in a dressing robe. He did not turn to greet her; he spoke not a word. His attention seemed focused on the wash of the sea, which tonight gave off a faint glow of phosphorus.

Were there to be no more stories? She shifted impatiently, watching the periodic brightening of the tip of his cigar.

"Orsino . . ." He appeared not to hear. "Orsino!" she repeated more loudly. "I've been wondering about Tony." She saw his head turn slightly. "Is it possible, just possible, that you wanted him on this cruise so I would be jealous?"

Now he looked at her. "For what reason?"

"The oldest in the book. To even the score. Romance on the rebound."

He studied her face for a moment, then tossed his cigar over the railing. "If I understand you, no. I have tremendous pride, my dear. Such a game would be too humiliating. A man in my position does not have to pursue women; it is the reverse." He

214

paused thoughtfully. "Except perhaps in a very special case. Then I may pursue—but only so far. Then it is up to her."

Erin cleared her throat awkwardly. "I see."

"Do you?"

She saw him look down at the bolted gate which separated them, then raised his eyes to hers. She smiled and extended her hand to the bolt and slid it back. The gate swung wide and she stepped onto the far side.

Di Ascoli took her arm and guided her through the door into his private sitting room. She looked quickly about at the luxurious furnishings and the walls with their Picassos, Renoirs and Matisses. Through an open door, she saw the sleeping quarters with the double bed turned down.

"A cognac?" he inquired.

"Perhaps later."

She moved toward the bedroom, paused in the doorway and looked back at him. Then she went boldly into the room and slipped off her robe. She turned again toward di Ascoli and unfastened her negligee, slowly, deliberately, and dropped it to the floor. She stood there, naked, motionless, and watched with satisfaction as the fire of desire came into his eyes. Then he gave a sigh of pleasure, gathered her up in his powerful arms and lowered her onto the bed.

"I never doubted this would happen," he whispered. "It is in our stars. It is destiny."

Erin smiled to herself. Let him call it whatever he wished. The main thing, tonight, and the nights to come, would burn a hole in Lisa di Ascoli's guts.

Twelve

Cannes
May 1958

IT WAS *the* gala week of the year and there was not a vacant hotel room in the whole of Cannes. The palm-lined Croisette, the boulevard bordering the waterfront, seemed to have attracted every Rolls-Royce and Bentley in Europe. The sparkling blue waters of the bay offered anchorage to a fleet of magnificent yachts—including Orsino di Ascoli's *Diana*—while on the wide sandy beach every daylight hour saw would-be starlets posing in bikinis for photographers and repeating endlessly their names, their measurements and the rooming houses where "talent agents" might find them.

But the important action, from breakfast to midnight supper, was centered in the various movie theaters and the bars and conference rooms of the luxurious hotels that lined the Croisette.

It was slightly after ten o'clock in the evening and already everyone in the bar of the Hotel Carlton was either a little drunk or very drunk. They were also fatigued and red-eyed from days of viewing the new films competing in the annual Cannes International Film Festival. From early morning through the afternoon and evening there were screenings of motion pictures made in a dozen languages from studios and independent producers in every part of the globe.

Rex Carmichael braced his back against the bar and, holding a Scotch in either hand, gazed about at the milling stars, producers, directors, press agents and professional hangers-on and pronounced unsteadily to the man at his side, "It's a whole damned convention of tuppenny uprights, that's what it is."

The man he addressed was Gottfried Sachs, the producer of Erin's Monte Carlo film. Sachs had once weighed almost three hundred pounds, one hundred of which he had recently lost by a crash diet that left the flesh of his face hanging in flabby folds and gave him the lugubrious expression of a basset hound. "Please," he said, "what is a tuppenny upright?"

Carmichael gravely consumed one of his scotches before giving his definition. "A tuppenny upright, my dear chap, was a social institution belonging to my father's youth. It stood in London doorways or under a street lamp. 'Only tuppenny, sir,' she'd say, then up skirt, hoist ass, and thank you kindly, sir."

Sachs considered it with heavy solemnity, a warning that one of his elephantine attempts at humor was on its way. "*Ja,* I see. It could be the beginning of a love story. Perhaps as they say it in Hollywood, the meet-cute. How do you see the story line?"

"Through the bottom of a bottle of Black Label." Carmichael launched himself away from the bar and elbowed his way through the crowd. Snatches of talk blurred in his ears. "Oh God, it was a bomb! He'll be lucky to sell distrib rights in Patagonia." . . . "Rome is the only place to shoot. Cinecittà is the new Hollywood." . . . "Sure, I remember you, baby. You were the one with the cute belly button." . . . "My next is a documentary on the end of the world. I'm titling it *Tomorrow Is Not Another Day*." It was a damn shame, Carmichael thought, drawing near the hotel lobby, that his Monte Carlo film with Erin couldn't be an official entry in the Festival. It still needed another month of editing; the print Sachs had shown at an out-of-competition screening was only a rough cut, without the final music scoring. But the distributors had gone for it anyway; the American, British and German rights had already been sold. Not, Carmichael reminded himself, because of the superior quality of the film; it was strictly star appeal—Erin Deering, the much publicized mistress of Orsino di Ascoli.

Carmichael had been the first to learn of the affair. On the last morning of the *Diana*'s cruise, five months before, Erin had told him that she would not be returning to the second-class hotel where the film company was lodging; she would commute to the set from either the *Diana* or di Ascoli's penthouse. And it had been Carmichael who overheard the parting words of Tony Brullov just before he left the yacht: "How in Christ's name can you sleep with that old goat?" To which Erin had retorted, "Just as easily as you can sleep with his double-gaited daughter." Within the first week after the cruise, the international press had seized on the story. There were photo layouts of Erin and Orsino waving from the yacht, dancing and dining at galas in Monte Carlo, Paris, London and Madrid. Both refused to be interviewed about their affair or, for that matter, on any subject whatsoever. It was daughter Lisa who had been happy to volunteer comments. To the London *Daily Mail:* "Daddy loves a practical joke, and Erin

is one of his best. When the laughing ends, so will she." And to
Paris Soir: "I've lost count how many women my father has
been involved with. What's one more?" That had been her last
comment; since then Lisa had been silent. Probably, Carmichael surmised, because her father had threatened to cut off
her allowance.

Carmichael reached the hotel lobby and glanced about at
the groups seated together drinking and smoking on sofas and
lounge chairs. Each group, like satellites, ringed a superstar—
Alec Guinness, Jean Gabin, Rosalind Russell, Henry Fonda.
Finally he located Erin Deering and Orsino di Ascoli seated
beside a potted palm. A bodyguard was keeping the photographers at a distance, which they compensated for by using tele-
scopic lenses on their cameras. Erin was wearing the Rose of
India diamond and an expression of anxiety. Di Ascoli, by
contrast, appeared bored as he absentmindedly rolled a
brandy snifter between his hands.

Carmichael dropped down into a chair beside Erin. "What's
the good word?"

"I wish I had one," she said. "You were at the screening
tonight. The audience didn't clap over a single scene." Erin
was referring to *Enigma Variations,* the film she had completed in Paris the previous October, which was an official
entry in the Festival. "Not one single scene."

"I noticed." Carmichael nodded. "Which is a very good
sign. Nobody wanted to miss the dialogue. They certainly beat
their hands to the bones on the fade-out."

Erin acknowledged this with a nervous smile. "But will I
win Best Actress?"

"You'll know day after tomorrow when the votes are
counted."

"If I can last that long," she sighed.

Orsino patted her hand. "One must keep a sense of proportion, my dear. There *are* more earth-shaking matters. The
Russians are orbiting Sputnik over our heads. Kenya has its

Mau Mau killings. The French Army in Algeria is torturing the fellagha; the Fourth Republic is crumbling and de Gaulle will surely take command."

Erin gazed at him as if to say none of these touched her. "I *want* the Best Actress award," she said quietly.

Orsino frowned and raised his brandy snifter to his mouth. He was clearly losing patience.

Carmichael sensed the tension between the two and said, "All I wish is that *I* had directed *Enigma Variations*, because it's going to win the Palme d'Or, just as surely as Erin is going to walk off with Best Actress."

Di Ascoli looked at him across the top of his snifter. "You sincerely believe so?"

"I do."

Erin seized Carmichael's hand and kissed it. "Thank you, Rex. You've made my day—what's left of it." She laughed. "What do you say to that, Orsino?"

"I say that we should make preparations then. I shall give a party aboard the *Diana* to celebrate Erin's victory. Mr. Carmichael, please set aside the evening after next to be our most favored guest."

"Thank you, sir."

Di Ascoli touched Erin's elbow and reminded her that the hour was late; they should return to the *Diana*.

As the launch sped out into the bay toward di Ascoli's yacht, Erin noted that his enthusiasm had waned. He did not speak a word, but stared broodingly at the spray rising from the stern of the speeding boat. Whatever was on his mind, she thought, he would bring it out into the open once they were in bed. He always had. But tonight proved to be the exception.

No sooner had he locked the door to their suite than he asked gravely, "My dear, let us assume that you are going to win the Best Actress award—what then?"

She puzzled a moment. "Why, it should be obvious. I'll be a

superstar, the studios will pay me double what I'm getting now."

"But you do not need more money. I've given you leave to spend as you please."

"I know. You've been darling about it. But I want it to be money I've earned myself."

"Always the independent." He frowned.

"That's what attracted you to me, isn't it?"

"In part. Also, you are the only woman who has stood up to me in an argument. I admire that." He came close to her and kissed her bare shoulder. "And everything else."

She knew he was referring to their lovemaking. Orsino was amazingly virile for a man of sixty. Whenever he brought her to orgasm, she forgot that he was old enough to be her father. In a way, she had thought frequently, he could be her father, the father she had never known, dead soon after her birth. Her stepfather had never counted; Erin remembered him only with distaste. If Orsino was her father figure, she cared not a whit; in fact, the psychological implication of incest was almost as powerful an aphrodisiac as Orsino's immense wealth.

Di Ascoli raised his lips from her shoulder and regarded her intently. "Let us suppose that you do *not* win the award here at Cannes. How will you take it?"

She laughed nervously. "Badly. But I'll go on and on until I *do* win. And until Hollywood hands me an Oscar."

"And then?"

"Then I'll be on top, the queen of the mountain."

He traced a fingertip across his lips and the brooding expression returned. "My dear, let's get married. I want you for my wife."

For a moment she was too startled to answer. She went to the sliding door onto the balcony and stared out at the stream of lights on the Croisette. Then she looked back at him. "Why? We're lovers. Everybody knows it. We don't have to sanctify our relationship to please the world. What is missing that we don't have now?"

His answer was a sigh and a shrug of the shoulders. Then Erin understood. He was afraid of losing her. Too much success and she might be gone. She was touched by the thought of his vulnerability and went up to him.

"It's been a long day, darling, and we're both tired. Nothing has to be decided now."

The next night they were again in the lobby of the Carlton, but this evening much earlier. Although the voting for Best Actress would not be known until the following day, Erin was too tense to remain quietly on the yacht; she had to hear all the gossip, the rumors, the predictions, which Rex Carmichael —sober, this time—brought dutifully from the bar.

During one of Carmichael's reports, a white-haired gentleman approached, begged pardon for his intrusion, and beamed down at Erin. "I'm sure you do not recognize me, Miss Deering. But I have never forgotten you and your dear mother."

Erin stared up at the face, then leaped to her feet and embraced him. "*Mr. Brullov!* Oh, how wonderful to see you after all these years!"

She turned to di Ascoli and introduced Tony's father. Di Ascoli shook his hand warmly. "Is Tony with you?"

"He is. Wandering around here somewhere. We stopped in tonight to see the excitement. We're looking for possible locations for our new Cannes store. Last month we opened a branch in Nice, and business has been so good we've decided to cover the whole Riviera."

"So you should." Di Ascoli went on smoothly, "And perhaps you now see the wisdom of my proposal?"

Ted Brullov laughed pleasantly. "We are tempted, sir. But give us a bit more time."

"But not another five months, I hope."

Erin looked from one to the other. "What in the world are you two talking about?"

Di Ascoli was about to answer when his eyes lighted on a

chic brunette crossing the lobby followed by a retinue of bell-boys with her luggage. "Lisa!" he exclaimed. "She's come after all!"

Erin's eyes followed di Ascoli's. "Were you expecting her?"

"I invited her last week. But she wasn't sure she could leave Paris; she said friends were giving a party for her birthday, which is tomorrow." He got to his feet, excused himself and hurried after his daughter.

Erin watched him go; it was strange that Orsino had not mentioned the possibility that Lisa might join them at Cannes. Perhaps it had been to avoid upsetting Erin; that would also explain why Lisa was to stay at the Carlton, rather than aboard the *Diana*.

"So at last you two have met," she heard a voice say. It was Tony Brullov, standing alongside his father. "How are you, Erin?"

"Why, fine, thanks. And you?"

"No complaints."

Rex Carmichael remembered Tony from the cruise and pulled up extra chairs for the Brullovs. As they seated themselves Tony stared at the Rose of India glittering at Erin's throat. "I know it's none of my business, Erin, but you're taking a chance wearing a half-million-dollar diamond in a hotel lobby. You're asking for a snatch-and-run."

Erin smiled tightly. "Oh, Orsino has taken precautions. You see that man over there?" She nodded toward a burly figure a few paces away who appeared to be idly watching the passersby. "He's my bodyguard."

Tony surveyed him. "That's something, at least. If he's reliable and not a member of the gang."

Erin laughed. "You weren't always so morbid, Tony."

Ted Brullov interposed with a shake of his head. "I see you haven't been reading the papers. Jewel thefts are at an all-time high on the Riviera this year. The police believe it's the work of Algerian rebels raising cash for their cause. Tony and I have given orders to our store in Nice that all of our really

valuable goods be kept in the bank vault. If we have a customer that we know and trust, then the shop manager goes to
the bank and brings back whatever is required."

"It's really that serious?" Erin asked, impressed.

"Believe us," Tony answered. "I wouldn't even risk keeping
that diamond in a safe on the yacht. Put it in a bank box and
sleep nights."

The conversation was interrupted by the return of di Ascoli
with Lisa on his arm.

Carmichael and the Brullovs rose to greet her, and Tony
offered her his chair. "Later, darling," she said, kissing him
elaborately on the mouth. "First, let's go somewhere for a
drink in private." The last was spoken with an icy smile at
Erin.

Erin returned the look. "So tomorrow is your birthday.
Your thirtieth, I presume?"

Di Ascoli cut in before his daughter could respond. "I have
a splendid idea. Tomorrow night's party on the *Diana* was to
be in Erin's honor; now we have a double cause to celebrate. It
will be a birthday party as well."

Erin's eyes blazed. "I don't split top billing with anyone. It's
my party." She paused angrily. "Or am I mistaken, Orsino?
Did you plan it for Lisa all along?"

"Of course not, my dear. I told you Lisa expected to be in
Paris. But now that she's here, please, let bygones be bygones." He looked pleadingly from Erin to Lisa. "Let us all be
friends. For my sake. Please."

The two women exchanged cold glances; but it was Erin
who appeared softened by his appeal. "You're right, Orsino. It
was petty of me, and selfish. We'll make it a real gala celebration of Lisa's birthday."

"Thank you, my darling."

"And we'll forget whether or not I'll be voted Best Actress,"
she added, warming to the idea. "It will still be a double celebration, Orsino, because we'll announce our engagement to be
married."

Di Ascoli gasped with surprise, then he clasped Erin's hands in his. "Thank you, my love. Thank you." He beamed at his daughter. "Congratulate me, Lisa."

Lisa responded with a wordless glare. Then Carmichael came gallantly to the rescue. "I propose a toast," he said and snapped his fingers for the attention of their waiter.

He approached, carrying a trayful of drinks. "*Oui,* m'sieur?"

"A magnum of champagne, please. And charge it to me."

"Very good, m'sieur."

As the waiter turned, Lisa aimed her elbow at his tray; there was a tinkling of sliding glass, then the tray and a cascade of liquor descended onto Erin's head. There was a moment of silence as the entire lobby turned to stare, then Lisa gave a whoop of delight at Erin's dripping face and shoulders. An instant later Erin was out of her chair, screaming curses, kicking Lisa's shins and grabbing her by the hair. Tony and Carmichael finally separated them; but not before cameras had flashed and reporters were sprinting toward telephones.

The brawl in the lobby of the Carlton occurred too late in the evening to make the next morning's headlines. But the following day every newspaper on the Riviera carried the story with photographs—and added that Erin Deering, who had failed to win Best Actress award, would soon wed Orsino di Ascoli and so become the stepmother of Lisa.

But the main headline concerned another matter: THIEVES LOOT NICE BANK VAULT. HUGE LOSS.

Thirteen

Nice
May 1958

JEAN DUMONT was a ladies' tailor. On this particular
Monday morning he decided to go early to his shop in
order to get a good start on the week's work. He was so early,
in fact, that as he bicycled along the street leading to his shop
there was no one for him to wave to; his neighboring shopkeepers were still at home munching their croissants. He
braked his bicycle and pulled it up onto the sidewalk where
he would chain it beside his front door. That's strange,
Dumont thought, staring at his shop window; he did not
remember pulling down the shade Friday evening. But down
it was, and also down was the shade on the glass front door.

But at age fifty, he told himself, one must expect to be a bit absentminded. He took out his key to unlock the front door. But it was already unlocked. *Sacré bleu!* Had he even forgotten to turn the key? He pushed open the front door and started to enter. Then he gave a yelp of fright. From the floor, almost to the ceiling, all he could see was a huge heap of earth.

"Police! Police!" he screamed, running down the empty street. He turned onto the Boulevard Jean Jaurès. *"Police! Police!"* Then he sighted an officer strolling toward him. Dumont grabbed him by the lapels. "Something horrible has happened. Come quickly!"

The officer stared dumbfounded at the earth-filled tailor shop while Dumont waved his arms and declared some enemy had done this thing to him. But who? Who could have so hated him?

"M'sieur," the officer said finally, "may I point out that there is no trace of earth on the pavement outside your door. Therefore it was not brought in by this entrance. Is there an alley behind your shop?"

"Of course not! Behind my shop is the rear of the Banque de Nice et Provence!"

The officer's eyes widened. He muttered, *"Mon Dieu!"* and took off on the run.

Ted and Tony Brullov, alerted by a phone call from their store manager, were among the first to arrive outside the bank. Four policemen blocked the entrance and said no one was to be allowed inside. Tony stepped up to the one who seemed to be in charge and said in his best French, "This is an emergency, officer. Please send someone inside to Monsieur Savarin, the vice-president, and tell him that Theodore Brullov must see him immediately." Tony's air of authority had its effect, and in a few moments the anguished-faced vice-president appeared at the door and escorted the Brullovs into the bank lobby.

"It is a nightmare, gentlemen. Unbelievable!" Savarin moaned. "In the sixty years of this bank, we have never been robbed. And now, our whole vault."

"What we want to know," Ted Brullov said grimly, "is what's happened to safety-deposit box two hundred eleven."

"I can't tell you. I understand a few boxes were not opened. I'll take you downstairs and you can ask Inspecteur Vilar."

They descended the marble stairs and went along a corridor to the bank vault. The massive circular steel door was swung back, and inside the Brullovs could see a police photographer shooting flash pictures. In the center of the cement floor there was a jagged hole through which the thieves had gained entrance. All about the floor was a litter of empty safety-deposit boxes and their contents which the looters had winnowed through and cast aside. In the far corner of the vault Inspecteur Vilar, smoking a pipe, was perched on a bookkeeper's high stool, overseeing the work of his subordinates. He was a burly man with piercing gray eyes and a hooked nose of Roman proportions.

"Do not enter," he warned, seeing the Brullovs and Savarin at the door of the vault.

"These gentlemen must have a word with you," Savarin called back. "They are most important customers of the bank. They rent our largest box."

"What is the number?"

"Two eleven," Ted Brullov answered.

Vilar spoke to one of his men, who disappeared from view momentarily, then reappeared. "My sympathy, gentlemen," Vilar said. "What were its contents?"

"Jewels," Ted answered. "One and a quarter million American dollars' worth. Two and a half million at retail."

The size of the figures brought Vilar off his stool and out of the vault. Savarin introduced the Brullovs and added, unnecessarily, that they were of the famous international jewel house.

228

"You may be of assistance, gentlemen," the Inspecteur said. "We have found some items scattered about the floor. You may be able to identify them." The Brullovs said they hoped so, and Vilar asked their patience until his men completed their work inside the vault.

"It was a professional job of the highest order," he went on, almost with admiration. "I'd say five or six men must have been involved to dig a tunnel of such length. One of them had to know the layout of the vault—either a bank employee or someone who rented a box for the sole purpose of mapping the location. At any rate, they knew it would be a long job. We've found beer bottles and cheese wrappings, both in the tunnel and the vault. They used an electric drill to come up through the cement flooring. The electric cable was connected to an outlet in the tailor's shop. The cable is still in the tunnel, which makes me think they left in a hurry. Either their time schedule ran out or something frightened them off. That would explain why a few boxes were left untouched. And where are they with their haul?" Vilar concluded rhetorically. "Certainly not in Nice, and I doubt they would risk the Italian or Swiss borders. They're probably in some fishing boat heading for Algeria."

All the while the Inspecteur was speaking, his subordinates were setting up folding card tables outside the vault and piling them with the scattered leavings from the vault floor—stock certificates, wedding certificates, baby shoes, false teeth, letters, passports, rosaries. There was even a photograph of a naked couple engaged in sexual intercourse, which a detective passed around for the snickers of his fellows, and which Vilar theorized had been kept either for sentimental reasons or for blackmail.

"Aren't you going to check for fingerprints?" Tony asked.

"A waste of time. They were professionals and would wear gloves. Ah! Here is what you've been waiting for," Vilar said, as one of his men emptied a gathering bag onto one of the tables. The Inspecteur fingered through assorted wedding rings, cameos, silver lockets, a rosary with a garnet-studded crucifix, several seed-pearl necklaces and one small unmounted ruby. "Clearly none of these would be your merchandise," he commented to the Brullovs. "Unless—" he said, picking up a large domino-shaped brown stone—"unless perhaps this topaz."

Ted Brullov shook his head. "No. We deal almost exclusively in precious gems."

Vilar frowned at the object in his hand. "There's an inscription on the back. Perhaps some sentiment expressed to a loved one. It appears to be Hebrew—or possibly Arabic script."

"May I see it?" Ted asked. He took a jeweler's loupe from his pocket and held it up to one eye and examined the stone. "It's Arabic," he said. As he handed back the stone, he glanced at Tony with a slight lift of one eyebrow which he hoped the Inspecteur would not notice. "May I copy the inscription?" he asked casually.

"To what purpose?"

"Professional curiosity. I'd like to have it translated by a linguist; it might prove to have some historical interest."

Vilar smiled shrewdly and sucked noisily on his pipe, which had gone out. "In which case you might make an offer to purchase when the owner identifies his property?"

"I see you are ahead of me."

Vilar nodded with self-satisfaction. "If the fingerprint detail were here, they could dust the topaz so the inscription could be read more easily. Perhaps I can oblige you with my own little method."

"Please do."

Vilar knocked the dead ashes from his pipe into the palm of his hand, then pressed a thumb into the ashes, transferred them to the back of the stone and brushed away the residue. Now the inscription stood out with clarity and Brullov inked a free-hand copy on the back of an envelope from his pocket.

"As soon as we have a translation, Inspecteur, we'll get

back to you. And we'll bring along a copy of the inventory for box two eleven."

"That would be appreciated." Vilar nodded. "In the meantime, if the owner of the topaz should claim his property, I'll have his name for you."

The Brullovs did not discuss the matter until they had stepped out onto the sidewalk of the Boulevard Jean Jaurès. Then Tony asked, "You really think it's a brown diamond?"

"Positive. But not until I put it under the loupe. It has almost no fire, because it was flat-cut, without facets—which is why Vilar, and the thieves, probably, thought it was a cheap topaz. About forty carats, I'd guess." Brullov stared absently down the Boulevard toward the ornate pile of the Municipal Casino. "Diamonds haven't been flat-cut in centuries, which means it's too old to have come from the South African mines. It has to be of Indian origin, and the inscription is either Arabic or Sanskrit. My hunch is that it's the name of the original owner. It was a fairly common practice with valuable gems. But now, where do we find a translator?"

"That's easy," Tony said. "The Language Department of the University of Nice."

Professor Lefèvre was an elderly wisp of a man who had undergone cataract operations on both eyes and wore spectacles with thick compensating lenses which gave him the look of a startled owl.

"There are two separate inscriptions," he said, peering at the bad of Ted Brullov's envelope. "The first is a Persian variation of Arabic. It says: 'By Allah's favor, son of Jahangir, Shah Jehan.' " He glanced up at the Brullovs. "Jehan, as you know, built the Taj Mahal."

Ted Brullov strained to keep the excitement out of his voice. "And the second inscription?"

"It is modern Arabic. It says simply: 'Abdul Hamid the Second.' "

"That's all?" Tony asked.

231

Lefèvre nodded. "If you will pardon my curiosity, gentlemen, you say these were written on the margin of a page from an old copy of the Koran?"

"Yes," Ted Brullov lied. "We wondered if it might have some special value."

"Certainly. If one could prove that the names were genuine signatures. But that is very doubtful. Shah Jehan ruled in India in the early sixteen hundreds; Abdul Hamid the Second was Sultan of Turkey at the turn of this century. How would one make a connection over such a span of years?"

"I see your point," Ted said. "In any case, we thank you for your time, Professor."

"It is nothing, gentlemen."

The Brullovs returned to their store on the Promenade des Anglais and retired to the manager's office on the second floor. "We want that diamond, Tony," his father said, "if the owner isn't too stubborn on price. It may be a dull-looking stone, but tie it to Shah Jehan, and it's a piece of romance we could sell in the six figures."

Tony wondered if another jewelry firm, a competitor, might have used the same bank for the safekeeping of his inventory. No, Ted decided; a jeweler with such a diamond would make a public hurrah over his ownership; the jewel industry would be very aware of it. It must be the property of a private collector, who would surely turn up at the bank later that day. Unless, of course, he was traveling and had not yet received news of the burglary. Meanwhile, father and son agreed, they should learn as much as possible about the stone. They owed that to themselves as potential buyers—and to Inspecteur Vilar.

Ted placed a phone call to their Paris store and spoke to Jacques Verdier. He described the brown diamond and gave a translation of the inscription and asked Verdier to check their reference books to see if the diamond was catalogued among the famous gems of history. Verdier said he would call them back, which he did ten minutes later.

Tony listened to the conversation on the extension phone in the next room. " 'It's first owner was Shah Jehan.' " Verdier read from the catalogue. " 'Its weight is forty-four carats. Later it was taken as a spoil of war by the Shah of Persia, Qajar Fath Ali Shah; then it disappeared until in or about eighteen forty, when it was listed among the Treasury jewels of the sultans of Turkey. In April eighteen seventy-seven, Turkey and Russia went to war and Turkey was defeated. The following year, at the signing of the treaty of peace, Sultan Abdul Hamid the Second presented the Turkish Brown to the Tsar of Russia as a goodwill gesture. Thereafter the diamond was part of the Russian Imperial jewels. However, the official Soviet catalogue of the jewelry in the Hermitage Museum does not list the Turkish Brown, and its current whereabouts is unknown.' "

When the phone call ended, Tony rejoined his father, grinning with excitement. "Dad, I remember you telling me that when I was a kid you went to an auction in London where the Soviets were selling off some of the crown jewels. *That's* how the diamond got out of Russia!"

Ted scowled and waved his hand for silence; he was thinking. But Tony rushed on. "It was in nineteen twenty-seven, wasn't it? At Christie's. Whoever bought the Turkish Brown must live around Nice, or at least his heirs."

"Tony, shut up!" his father growled. He rose from the desk chair and stared out the window at the traffic-filled Promenade and the surf breaking on the beach beyond. Finally he spoke. "The Turkish Brown was never at Christie's. I would have remembered anything as unique as a brown diamond shaped like a domino."

"Then why don't the Soviets have it now?"

Ted Brullov swung around, his eyes flaming. "I'll tell you why!" He took a deep breath, as if to steady himself. "When

the Bolsheviks sent the Royal Family to Siberia, to Ekaterinburg, the Tsar's wife and daughters had a fortune in jewels
hidden in their clothing. The Cheka squad that murdered
them and stripped their bodies discovered diamonds and
emeralds and rubies sewn into corsets and the hems of skirts.
It all came out when the White Russian Army took Ekaterinburg and investigated. The Cheka men confessed everything."
Brullov broke off and glared darkly at Tony. "Don't you see?
The Turkish Brown is here in Nice because here in Nice is one
of those cursed murdering Chekas! He could be the very bastard who killed Tatiana, my lovely Tatiana! And if—if we find
him—" There were tears in Brullov's eyes, his voice was chok-
ing, his hands opened and closed in spasms of rage.

Tony listened to his father's outburst in silence. He had all
but forgotten his father's obsession to avenge the murders of
the Romanovs. Finally he said, very quietly, "We're overlooking one strong possibility. That the man who stole the
diamond may have sold it to someone else who knows nothing
of the background. The present owner may be wholly innocent."

His father sighed; the tempest had passed.

"In any case, what do we tell Inspecteur Vilar?" Tony
asked.

"The truth. Up to a point. It's an offense to withhold information from the police; but one need not divulge suspicions.
Whatever, Tony, let me do the talking."

Tony relaxed and laughed gently. "You usually do."

They returned to the bank in midafternoon. The police
guarding the front door were gone and the lobby was filled
with customers transacting normal business. The Brullovs
wondered, as they descended to the vault level, if the Inspecteur had returned to Headquarters. No, there he was,
seated in a corner of the anteroom, sipping coffee from a
thermos as he observed a line of men and women filing up to
the tables where that morning the detectives had deposited the

assorted articles found on the vault floor. One by one, they pointed out their properties to a bank employee, who noted down their claims and sent them to another table where a notary public prepared affidavits of ownership.

Vilar rose and shook hands with the Brullovs. He nodded toward the line of people. "Notice how well-dressed they are. All well-to-do, some even wealthy. Yet, so far, not one has claimed a great loss in gold coins or bullion or franc notes. I'm positive there have been such losses, some very great; but these honorable citizens do not wish to attract the attention of the tax collector. They will take their losses in silence." He placed his index finger alongside his great nose and grinned. "And not one is guilty of an adulterous affair. All those love letters on the tables, some really obscene in their detail, why, of course, they belong to other people."

The Brullovs laughed, and Ted, noting the absence of detectives, said, "I take it you've about finished your investigation."

"This phase, yes. I'm waiting around for the customers who rented safety-deposit boxes during the past month. I have a list of their names from the bank. So far, four have come in and claimed property or reported losses which I consider genuine. But three names have not appeared yet." Vilar paused and offered his thermos to the Brullovs, who declined. "My theory is that if someone rented a box in order to learn the location and layout of the vault, he will do one of two things. He will come in to avoid suspicion and claim that everything in his box was stolen; but he will not say jewels or coins or cash because of fear of the tax collector. He will mention, perhaps, a last will and testament, or some land deeds or business contracts. Then I will know he is lying, because thieves take only articles convertible into cash. The other course is that this person will never appear and that will signal to me that he rented the box under a false name. Then I shall look at the bank's signature card on him and have an analysis made of his handwriting. We will check the physical description entered on the card, which will have to be something close to the truth. Also, we shall know the alias he used—all of which will be forwarded to Interpol." Vilar paused and took a breath. "And now, gentlemen, what do you have for me?"

Ted Brullov handed him a copy of the store's inventory of the contents of box 211, which, he explained, was a duplicate of the one to be filed with their insurance company. Vilar examined the list of diamond earrings and bracelets, ruby rings and emerald brooches, and said he would forward it to the Sûreté in Paris, which would circulate it to the pawnbrokers and those fences who sometimes worked with the Police. But, he warned, the Brullovs should be prepared for disappointment.

Ted acknowledged this and added, "As for that topaz, I presume the owner hasn't come forward as yet."

Vilar shook his head. "And if he had, I regret I could not give you his name as I had promised. The legal department of the bank informs me that the identities of box holders are confidential."

Ted looked carefully at his son; this was the moment for extreme caution. "In any case, Inspecteur, we are not interested in buying it. We have learned it is stolen property."

Vilar's eyes widened. "You have learned?"

"Yes. And it is not a topaz, as I had thought. It is a brown diamond."

"There is such a thing?"

"They are so rare that we jewelers seldom consider that possibility." Brullov then outlined their investigation; the translation of Shah Jehan's name and Abdul Hamid's, and tracing the Turkish Brown to its place among the Russian Imperial jewels. But he carefully omitted his suspicion that the diamond had been taken from the body of a Romanov.

Inspecteur Vilar chewed his lower lip and considered. "This raises international complications. I shall have to take this up with Paris."

There was a glint of anticipation in Vilar's eyes; this new

development would surely rate a departmental commendation and perhaps even a promotion.

"May I make a suggestion," Tony said, speaking for the first time. "I think it would be unwise to mention the diamond to the press. It would frighten off the thief, if he wanted to claim it."

Vilar agreed. "The press has already been and gone, but they'll do a follow-up tomorrow—and I shall know nothing. Also, I'll suggest the same discretion to Paris." He shook hands with the Brullovs again and expressed his gratitude for their cooperation.

It was the opening Ted had been waiting for. "A thought just occurred to me, Inspecteur. I was born and brought up in St. Petersburg, so if you have found any passports or *cartes d'identité* or letters written in Cyrillic, I'd be happy to translate them for you."

Vilar considered. "Cyrillic? Yes. I seem to remember. But not passports. Personal letters. No one here could read them."

"Then let me oblige," Brullov said quickly. "I might be able to help the bank identify which box they came from."

Vilar smiled understandingly. "You are thinking that if a Russian stole the brown diamond, there might be evidence in the letters of his guilt. That would be too incredible. Who would save evidence that could damn him?"

"Why not? He'd certainly never expect the bank vault to be looted."

Vilar considered that point and said he would return in a moment. The Brullovs watched him cross to the tables and sort through the remaining unclaimed properties. When he came back he handed Ted two letters without envelopes. Brullov put on his reading spectacles and examined them. Both were written on cheap notepaper; one crackled with age. "This one," he said, "was written from Moscow. The date is June twenty-first, nineteen twenty-seven. It is addressed to 'My old friend Yuri.' " Brullov ran his eyes over the text. "Translated roughly, it says:

237

In answer to your question, two of our comrades of the night of 7/4 died last year. Igor was killed by some maniac with a knife. Boris drowned in the Volga. Voikov you read about in the papers. In your next letter, tell me more about Marseilles, and how you earned the money to buy that fishing boat.

"The letter is signed 'Sasha.' "

Vilar sniffed noncommittally. "And the other?"

"It is dated October second, nineteen fifty, written from Minsk."

DEAR YURI—*I turn to you as my last hope. Serge has abandoned me and the children. I went to the authorities and they investigated. They tell me that Serge has defected. They traced him to London, where he now lives under the name "Arthur Smith." A Soviet agent has tried to persuade him to return to his family, but he refuses. He says he does not intend to die like all his old friends. Perhaps, dear Yuri, you could visit Serge and ask him to at least send us money. I will write you again, under the same name, Poste Restante, Genoa.*

Brullov squinted at the signature. "The woman's name looks like 'Zinka.' "

Vilar held out his hand for the letters. "So all we have are melancholy stories of deaths and an abandoned family. Nothing but first names, which will be of no help to the bank."

"At least it was worth a try," Brullov answered.

"Indeed. And thank you again for your generous help."

When the Brullovs reached the street, Ted told Tony he wanted to go straight to their hotel room and make notes on the two letters while the wording was still fresh in his mind.

"Then you've learned something?"

Ted's answer was a tight-lipped smile.

"The most important clue," Ted said after he had jotted down the substance of the letters, "was the date mentioned in the first note. Remember the wording: . . . *two of our comrades of the night of 7/4 died last year*. The writer was using the Russian calendar, which corresponds to our July seventeenth. Don't you see, Tony? Don't you *see?*"

"I'm afraid not."

His father sighed with exasperation. "Remember your history! July seventeenth, nineteen eighteen, was the night of the murders of the Imperial Family. This fellow Yuri was writing to find out what had happened to the other members of the Cheka squad. The proof is that line: *Voikov you read about in the papers*—Peter Voikov, the Soviet Ambassador to Poland, who was assassinated in nineteen twenty-seven. Voikov who supplied the acid to destroy the royal bodies!"

Tony caught his father's excitement. "Then Yuri really was one of the Cheka, and he had a safety-deposit box at the bank, just as you said." Then he frowned. "But why in hell would he keep such evidence? That was the point Vilar made."

His father puzzled awhile. "Perhaps it goes back to simple human psychology. He may have kept the Turkish Brown as a souvenir of his crime. A sentimental thing. And the letters, well, they contained information important to him. But he dared not keep them at home where his wife or some household person might stumble across them. The first letter proves that he was anxious; he suspected that he might be hunted— which you and I know was the exact truth." Suddenly Brullov clapped his hands. "Of course! That explains that fellow Kohlski who came to our office in New York and claimed to be a Romanov. He was an agent for this Yuri! He was trying to track down all of us who swore the oath of vengeance in St. Petersburg."

"And wound up getting murdered himself," Tony appended. "But *who* is Yuri? The woman who wrote to him in nineteen fifty, Zinka, said she'd write again, *under the same name*, Poste Restante, Genoa. That means Yuri was using an alias, maybe many aliases."

"For sure," his father agreed. "The important point in that letter is 'Arthur Smith.' He didn't want to leave London and go back to Russia *and die like his old friends*. That phrase links up to the first letter and the liquidation of the other Chekas. So somewhere in London 'Arthur Smith' is sweating out that justice may hunt him down."

Tony looked sharply at his father. "Dad, you aren't going to start that up again. Hate must finally end."

Ted Brullov smiled and patted his son's shoulder. "I was simply putting myself inside 'Arthur Smith's' mind. He must have many a sleepless night."

The following morning the Brullovs agreed that it was time to wind up their business on the Riviera. Ted would rent a car and drive to Cannes and sign the lease on their boutique on the Croisette. He should be back in Nice by midafternoon. Meanwhile, Tony would spend the day at their local store. He would meet the claim agent from Lloyd's who was flying in to verify their loss; and Tony would telephone the branch stores in Paris, Zurich and London and discuss with the managers the items of jewelry which they could spare from their own inventories to replace the goods stolen from the bank.

While Tony was engaged in these matters he received a telephone call from Erin Deering in Monte Carlo. She began on a whimsical note. "Thank you for your advice, Tony, about putting my diamond in a bank vault. One can't be too safe."

Tony laughed. "So you read about it."

"Yes. For really maximum security, I think I'll stash the Rose of India in the soap dish in some public lavatory." She chuckled at her sarcasm and went on, "What I'm calling about, Tony, is to ask your firm to come up with something really smashing in engagement rings. Not just a hunk of ice; something truly imaginative, designed just for me."

"When do you want it?"

"Oh, say maybe in two weeks?"

"I'll talk to our designer in New York. Dad and I are leaving tomorrow."

"It was marvelous to see your father, Tony. Give him my love."

"Will do."

Tony hung up with complicated feelings. Erin could have chosen any of the great jewel houses, yet she had come to Brullov. Quite a tribute. If only it were not an engagement ring for another man to slip on the finger of Tony's former love.

He returned to the Négresco shortly before five o'clock. As he entered the hotel room, he saw a note propped on the dresser.

> TONY—*I've decided we shouldn't overextend ourselves in Cannes at this time. Am flying to New York. As soon as you've wound up business here, join me.*
>
> *Love,* DAD

Tony frowned at the note. Why hadn't he simply telephoned him at the store? His father knew this was to be their last day in Nice—weren't they going to fly home together? Unless, he thought with a twinge of unease, Dad wanted to be on his own. Tony called down to the concierge's desk and asked what time his father had left for the airport. About ten in the morning. Almost immediately after Tony had left for the store. Had the concierge secured a plane seat for him? He had indeed—on the eleven o'clock flight to Paris. Did he arrange for a connection to New York? He had not.

Tony's unease turned to apprehension. He glanced at his wristwatch; there was just time to call the Paris store before it closed. Jacques Verdier came on the line. Why, yes, he said, M'sieur Brullov had dropped by in the early afternoon. Did he say anything about flying on to New York? No. Well, what did he talk about? Nothing, really. Merely, How are you, Jacques? Then he went into the vault.

"Did he say anything about staying on in Paris?"

"In a way, perhaps. I asked him if I would see him tomorrow. He said no, he was leaving for Orly in a few minutes. That was after he came out of the vault."

"The vault?"

"Yes."

"Did he say what he wanted in the vault?"

"No. He was in there only a moment. Is there something wrong, M'sieur Tony?"

"No, no. I was just curious. Thanks anyway, Jacques."

Tony chewed on a fingernail and thought. His father had taken the time and trouble to go from Orly to the Place Vendôme, go into the vault, then back to Orly. Tony did not have to ask himself what was so important in the vault: he already knew. It was Drawer Zero. It contained the button for the burglar alarm and a snub-nosed revolver. Ted Brullov was in London, and his quarry was "Arthur Smith."

Tony telephoned the London store, but there was no answer; the store was closed. He took out his notebook which listed the home numbers of all their managers. John Katchin answered on the third buzz, and Tony asked him to check all the deluxe and first-class hotels where his father might be registered. Yes, Tony would remain in the Négresco until Katchin called him back.

He ordered a double martini in his room, and after half an hour another double martini. Finally the call came. "Your father is not registered at any of the hotels of the class he would choose," Katchin said. "Are you sure he's in London?"

"I think so. Look, if he drops by the store tomorrow morning, have him call me here. Otherwise, I'm coming to London myself."

Tony ordered a light dinner and mulled over the situation. Suppose it was all in his imagination? Suppose his father had *not* gone to Drawer Zero? He could have fallen into conversation with some passenger on the flight from Nice, learned that the passenger was interested in a certain type of jewelry, and gone to the store to get it. Tony had had that experience himself—except that he had taken the customer to the store with him. No, it was unlikely.

He debated whether or not he should leave for London that night. But where would he find his father? He might choose some obscure hotel, or a bed-sitter where there would be no pressure to show his passport.

The important thing was not to panic, he decided. He went to bed and tossed until dawn. The comforting thing, he told himself, was that time was on his side. There must be scores, perhaps hundreds, of Arthur Smiths in Greater London. It would take his father days to check them all, and by then Tony would have found him and argued him out of his crazy scheme. Besides, *the* Arthur Smith might no longer be in London; he could even be dead.

In the morning, while Tony was shaving, a question came into his mind that destroyed his optimism. How, he asked himself, had the Soviet agent tracked down Arthur Smith in 1950? Did he have an informer or some special lead? Then, as he stared into the mirror at his haggard face, he remembered his own training in the OSS. Good God, it was childishly simple! He had even used the trick himself. He had parachuted behind the German lines to make contact with a French intelligence officer who had gone to ground in Stuttgart. Tony knew the Frenchman was using the cover name "Schwartz"; but he had lost the address of his safe house. He checked the Stuttgart telephone directory; there were dozens of Schwartzes; it would take days to cover them all. Then his OSS schooling came to his aid. He dialed each Schwartz listed and said, *"Comment allez-vous, Jean? Ç'est moi."* German after German had grumbled something and hung up. Finally, one man had instinctively replied in French. Tony had his man in less than one hour.

God Almighty! Tony groaned into the mirror. He had even related the experience to his father. If he had remembered it, all Dad had to do was ring each Arthur Smith and speak in Russian, until one of them replied in the same language.

Tony rang the concierge and asked him to book a seat on the first plane out, preferably a breakfast flight. The concierge called back that several package tours were leaving Nice that morning; all space was sold. Would he list as a standby in case of a no-show? Yes!

Tony telephoned the London store as soon as it opened and talked again to John Katchin. "I'm coming to London," he said. "Can't say if it'll be this afternoon or evening; but if Dad drops by the store, tell him I'll be at the Savoy. If they're full up, I'll hang out in the lobby."

It was early afternoon when he finally boarded a Paris flight that connected with London. He reached the Savoy in mid-evening, and there was a telephone message waiting. The envelope was time-stamped 7:22 P.M.

> *Scotland Yard just called my flat. Your father is in St. Bartholomew's Hospital. They ask you to come immediately.*
>
> KATCHIN

Tony found him in a private room. His eyes were closed, his face flushed from the anesthetic. A plastic tube was inserted into one arm, an oxygen tube into one nostril. A Scotland Yard man, a Sergeant Buller, sat beside the bed with a note pad on his lap. An intern was making an entry in the chart at the foot of the bed.

Tony bent over the still form and said softly, "Dad—it's Tony."

The intern shook his head. "The anesthetic hasn't quite worn off, sir. It was a long operation."

"What happened?"

Sergeant Buller answered. "Took some bullets, sir. They say his liver is gone. I'm here in case he comes around and can tell us who got him."

"I'll sit with him. If he says anything, I'll tell your people."

"Sorry, sir. I got my orders."

"Very well."

The intern left. Tony pulled up a straight-back chair and seated himself on the other side of the bed and held his father's hand. The Sergeant sketched what he knew of the case. The "victim" had been found unconscious in a road near the East India Docks. He had been identified by the wallet in his coat; none of the cash had been taken.

"My chief says your father is a jeweler, an important jeweler."

"He is."

"Would he carry the goods on him?"

"No."

"Somebody must have thought he did. My chief thinks he was kidnapped, because no gentleman like your father would have reason to go into that section of London. They probably dumped him from a car."

Tony nodded silently. *They say his liver is gone.* He knew from his wartime experience what that meant. It was just a question of how long.

Two hours passed, then three. The flush had left Brullov's face and now it was almost chalk white. The intern looked in, then went out again. Tony's hand still grasped his father's. Then he thought he felt a slight pressure of the fingers. A moment later it was repeated—this time with emphasis. Tony looked across at Buller.

"Sergeant, do you smoke?"

"A pipe, sir."

245

"Then why don't you step out into the hall for a few minutes?"

"Not allowed to smoke on duty, sir." He hesitated and looked sheepish. "There is one thing, sir."

"Yes?"

"I got a weak bladder."

"Then by all means."

Buller rose with alacrity. "Two minutes, no more," he promised. "If he comes to . . . ?"

"I'm afraid he won't."

They were alone now and Ted Brullov's eyelids flickered. He whispered something; Tony bent down, his ear near his father's mouth.

"The gun . . ."

"Yes?"

"In river . . . it's . . . safe."

Tony moved his lips to his father's ear. "You found Arthur Smith?"

He nodded faintly. "Only . . . Yuri . . . left."

"Forget him."

His father moved his head from side to side on the pillow. "Find him. . . . He's . . . yours."

Tony straightened up. He saw his father's eyes fixed on his face, as if pleading for a promise. Then the eyelids wavered and closed.

Sergeant Buller returned, looking much relieved. "Anything?"

"No."

Shortly before dawn, his hand still in Tony's, Theodore Brullov quietly died.

Fourteen

New York and Nice
First Week of June 1958

AFTER THE inquest Tony returned to New York aboard
the liner *United States* with his father's coffin in the hold.
At the graveside ceremony Ted Brullov was buried beside
his wife, Helen. Tony was astonished by the scores of floral
tributes; they came not only from every store in the Brullov
chain, but from Tiffany's, Cartier, Van Cleef & Arpels and
Harry Winston—and from Erin Deering and Orsino di Ascoli
jointly, and Lisa di Ascoli separately.

Tony's Aunt Ruth, the elder sister of his mother, came up
from Philadelphia for the funeral. Afterward he escorted her

to the apartment off Washington Square where his parents had lived for so many years and which his father had refused to relinquish long after his commercial success would have permitted a fashionable uptown penthouse. Tony had not seen his Aunt Ruth in several years and hoped to spend the rest of the afternoon with her; but she stayed only long enough for tea, insisting that she wanted to return to Philadelphia and sleep that night in her own bed. Tony took her by taxi to Penn Station, then went back to his father's apartment. He told Mary, the housekeeper, to take the rest of the day off; he would fix his own dinner, if and when he had an appetite. "Begging pardon, sir," she protested in her Irish brogue, "a man should be with those close to him on a day like this. Don't stay here alone, sir, with all them memories."

But who was close to him? Memories were the best companions for that day. He wandered about the apartment, so little changed from his boyhood. True, much of the old furniture was long gone and had been replaced by finer pieces and more costly art objects. But the great brass samovar still commanded the sideboard in the dining room. The photograph of Tsar Nicholas and Empress Alexandra still looked down from the sitting-room wall; the intricately wrought icon of the Virgin still gave its benediction to his parents' bedroom. His own boyhood room had become a guest room, with furniture more suitable for an adult. But to Tony it was still his room, his listening post where he had eavesdropped on his parents' bedtime conversations. Why was it, he wondered, that he remembered chiefly the arguments? Never about the business, seldom about the women who "made eyes," as his mother put it, at her husband. But often about his father's bedtime stories for Tony, the Russian fairy tales instead of American or English. Tony could still hear his mother's soprano rising higher and higher as she depicted for her husband the evils of the Romanov autocracy, the corruption of the nobility—and Ted Brullov's baritone booming that this was Bolshevik propaganda. Old Russia—meaning St. Petersburg, with its beautiful women and handsome nobles and splendid balls—was the most magical place in the world. Eden lost was twice Eden.

The Fifth Avenue store of Brullov & Company had closed for the day of its founder's funeral. The next day Tony delayed going to the store until early afternoon, when he gathered the entire staff together and thanked them for their attendance at the church service and for their flowers and notes of sympathy. Then he went directly to his father's office and buzzed for Trisha in the anteroom. She was not to permit any visitors, he said, nor to disturb him with telephone calls or store problems for the balance of the day.

Trisha nodded. "I have one suggestion, Mr. Brullov." (It was no longer to be "Tony.") "Wouldn't you like us to move some of your photographs and trophies in here from your old office. It helps to be surrounded by familiar things."

"But I am, Trisha. Nothing is to be changed in here, nothing added or taken away. I want this room always as Dad left it."

"Yes, sir. I understand."

She closed the door behind her and Tony seated himself in his father's chair and surveyed the familiar old desk with its gem scales in the glass case, the jeweler's loupe and tweezers, the note pad with the last jotting now three weeks old. This desk had been the center of authority for the entire Brullov chain for over a quarter of a century, and yet, sitting behind it, Tony felt no new importance, only a stifling sense of loneliness. He glanced at the framed photographs on the wall above the leather couch: the family portrait of the Romanovs, the separate photograph of the Grand Duchess Tatiana, the view of the exterior of the original Fabergé store on Morskaya Street in St. Petersburg, and the interior view of one of the workrooms with his father, then a young man, standing proudly with folded arms as befitted one of Karl Fabergé's workmasters. How much time, Tony reflected, he had wasted in skiing and sailing and auto racing, time that could have been better spent with his father. No, that was wrong: Dad had encouraged his sports and competition; it strengthened a young man's character, he had said, and every win brought the name Brullov before the public—it was good for business. Even years before that, Tony's wartime service with the OSS had been welcomed by his father, who never conceded the possibility that his son might be killed in action. "You'll learn to think and act on your own, to improvise in sticky situations. You'll come home with the experience and confidence it takes to rise to the top in the business world."

Recalling those words, Tony suddenly sat forward in the desk chair. That conversation with his father had taken place in this very office; it had been Ted Brullov's preamble to a subject which he had never before disclosed to his son. "When you're overseas, Tony, you may find yourself working with agents of our allies. Not only British and French, but possibly even Russian. And if some of them *are* Russian, men in their middle to late forties, be extremely careful. They may have been Bolshevik agents during the Revolution, members of the Cheka."

Tony had been perplexed; this was the Second World War, not the First. Then his father had added to his puzzlement. He drew out the small drawer above the kneehole of his desk, dumped out the drawer and turned it over. Attached to the underside, Tony saw a sheet with a list of names. Most of the names were prefaced by an X or a question mark, but a few bore no markings. Ted Brullov tapped his finger on the latter. "I want you to memorize these names, son. All were members of the Ekaterinburg Cheka or were Cheka accomplices. If you should meet up with one of them during your operations— you must kill him."

Thus was Tony's introduction to his father's secret world.

At first he had been dumbfounded, almost unbelieving. Then his father had pointed to the name "Pyotr Pagodin," the Bolshevik commissar he had eliminated in the Savoy Hotel in

1927, and related the manner in which he had caused it—and the OGPU's retaliation against Brullov's accomplice, Andrei Katchin. Melodramatic as it sounded, Tony accepted it. But as for encountering another member of the Cheka squad all these years later, he knew the chances were absolutely zero. So Tony had thought on that day in late 1942; but now, in 1958, it was a different story.

He sat back in his desk chair and stared at the small drawer above the kneehole. Then he drew it out, emptied its contents, and turned it over. Yes. The list of names were still there. But now some of the question marks had been inked over by X's. Had they died natural deaths? Or during the sixteen years since Tony had last seen that list, had his father's band of avengers done their work? Then Tony's eyes fastened on a name that was still unmarked. Serge Simonov. "Serge" had been the first name of the man who had abandoned his family according to the letter found in the Nice bank vault—Serge who had fled to London and taken the name "Arthur Smith." Yes; it had to be. Tony reached for the desk pen and put an X beside the name, as his father would have wished him to. Then his eyes fell on the one other unmarked name. *Yuri Dimitrovich Solenko.*

At last. He had the full name of the mysterious Yuri. How could his father have forgotten it? Or had he? Possibly he had kept it to himself, choosing to strike down Arthur Smith, whose whereabouts he knew, and afterward to trace Yuri Solenko. "Only Yuri left," he had whispered in the hospital. And then his last dying words: "Find him. . . . He's . . . yours."

Tony slid the drawer back into the desk and replaced its contents. He pressed his hand to his brow; God, what a headache! Then his stomach juices came up sour. He realized the cause. It was anger, hatred, fury, because of Yuri Dimitrovich Solenko. If those cursed letters to Yuri had not been found in the vault, or that brown diamond, Ted Brullov's obsession would have lain dormant. He would be alive today. And Tony would not have to fulfill his unspoken promise to his father.

That thought caught him up short. *Why* must he hunt down this Yuri Solenko? Was he, too, drifting into his father's mad obsession? He surveyed again the photographs on the office wall: the Tsar and his Empress, Tatiana, his beloved father— all dead because of a band of ruthless murderers. No, it was *not* a madness; justice should be meted out. An eye for an eye, a tooth for a tooth. Tony had killed men during the war; he could do it again, and this time with satisfaction. . . .

He left the office and went down the hall to the washroom and found the aspirin bottle in the mirrored cabinet. He swallowed four tablets, returned to the office and stretched out on the leather sofa. Within a few minutes the headache dulled, then faded away. Now he simply felt tired. He sighed and closed his eyes.

He was awakened by the buzz of the desk telephone. He blinked at his wristwatch. Just after four o'clock. The phone went silent. Then it buzzed again. Tony swung himself up from the sofa and growled into the phone, "Didn't I say no phone calls?" Trisha was apologetic. "The floor manager was insistent, sir. He said I should put him through to you." A moment later the floor manager's voice reported, "Mr. Brullov, I thought you'd want to know that Miss Lisa di Ascoli is in the store."

"Oh? Has she asked for me?"

"No, sir. But she did say she was very upset about your father."

"Okay. But don't let her know I'm in the building."

"Very good, sir."

Tony hung up and frowned. He hadn't seen Lisa since the night of that brawl with Erin at the Cannes Film Festival. It might be interesting to catch up on that world, which he had all but forgotten. At least it would take him out of himself for a few minutes.

He found her in the silverware department. She was as stunning as ever, hatless, with her black hair caught in a bun at the neck. Her suit was pale blue; a pair of aquamarines dangled from her earlobes. He came up beside her. "What are you doing in New York?"

She turned, surprised. "Tony!" She gave him a gloved hand. "I thought you might be taking a few days off."

"I am. I appreciate the flowers you sent. How did you know about the funeral?"

"It was in the Washington papers. I came over for the annual reunion of the class from my Swiss school. Each year it's held in a different country. What I'm looking for now, Tony, is a wedding present for one of my classmates. Would you have any ideas?"

"Well, it should be appropriate for the life style of the bride and groom. Will it be simple or formal?"

"Very formal. Very posh."

Tony recommended a silver-and-gold epergne, which Lisa liked and asked that it be gift-wrapped and sent to her hotel, the Plaza. Then Tony asked, "Have you chosen a wedding present for your father and Erin?"

"No. They both have everything; there's nothing I can think of—except perhaps a secondhand chamber pot for Erin." Tony looked uncomfortable; then he noticed that she was surveying him critically. "How long has it been since you've slept the night through or eaten a decent meal?"

"Does it show that much?"

"It does." She put her hand on his arm. "I know what you must be going through. I can't bear to think how I would take it if *my* father died. Like you, I have no brothers or sisters or mother to share the grief. It's a ghastly burden."

She surprised him. He had never suspected that Lisa considered anyone except Lisa. Then she followed it up: "Would you let me buy you a drink?"

Why not? It was near closing time, and Tony was curious to learn if Lisa's visit to the store had an ulterior purpose. Was she the emissary of her father?

253

They walked up Fifth Avenue the few blocks to the Plaza Hotel and went into the bar. Tony noticed the immediate swiveling of heads in admiration of Lisa's beauty. They each drank a martini and then another; but Lisa did not bring up her father's proposal that the Brullov company become an international fashion house. Instead, her talk was in another vein. "I keep watching my father and Erin for a sign of cooling off. It could all go poof, you know."

"Why do you say that?"

"I've had two very stormy scenes with my father about making Erin sign a premarital agreement. I don't intend to see that bitch do a divorce on him and walk off with a hundred million that someday would rightfully be mine. Also, if something happened to Father, I don't intend to have any bitch stepmother giving me orders how to run the business."

"But I don't see either you or Erin *wanting* to run the business. It should be turned over to a board of trustees or directors."

"Perhaps," she conceded. "In any case, I'm hoping a premarital agreement will put a chill on Erin."

"Suppose it doesn't?"

Lisa sniffed disdainfully and Tony went on, "Have they set a date for the wedding?"

"No. Father wants to be married in the Cathedral of Monte Carlo, but Erin is divorced, so that's out. That's what I'm counting on—if there are too many obstacles, Father may say shove it." She laughed. "You see, I'm picking up all the American slang."

Then she switched subjects. "I'm changing the decor of my Paris place. It's going to be all Louis Seize. I'm tired of the Scheherazade bit. It was a bit much, don't you think?"

In every way, Tony thought. My God, the complications which had followed that night. It had been the prelude to the breakup with Erin. And everything that had followed with di Ascoli. Or would it have all turned out that way regardless?

Lisa broke into his thoughts. "I want to see you eat a steak tonight. Thick and blood-rare. And a fine heavy burgundy to go with it."

"Yes, Mother." He smiled. "But this time it's on me."

They walked the few steps to the Oak Room and gave identical orders to the waiter. They dined and made small talk, and Tony, for the first time in over a week, began to feel something like his old self.

During coffee Lisa said, "You've seen how I live in Paris—or the way I used to—but I have no idea how Tony Brullov lives."

"It's not far from here," he said. "If you'd like." He thought gratefully that he understood: she did not want him to spend an evening alone. Nor did he.

He showed her around his apartment and the view of Central Park, both of which she praised. "Now all I need," she said, "is a view of your powder room." He guided her down the hallway, then returned to the sitting room and sank down onto the sofa and lighted a cigarette. He wondered if he should fix highballs. Then he heard her footsteps approaching on the tile flooring. He started to get up. "Don't move," she said, and dropped down beside him. She swung her legs up onto the sofa, kicked off her pumps and curled one arm around his neck. He was conscious of the scent of exotic perfume that rose from the region of her breasts, probably applied when she had visited the powder room. Her green eyes gazed at him solemnly. "Do you want to talk about it? Your father, I mean." He shook his head. "Sometimes it helps." Another head shake. "Very well." She raised her face to his and ran the soft inner side of her lower lip against his mouth.

"Lisa . . ." he sighed.

"I know," she said gently. "You wish it was Erin. But it isn't. So make do with whatever."

"Don't belittle yourself, Lisa."

"I'm not." She took off her aquamarine earrings and dropped them into her handbag. "But I do believe one should take the nearest peach that hangs over the garden wall. I've

certainly enjoyed plenty, including you, and no harm done."
She kissed him again, tracing the tip of her tongue along his
lips.

"That was of another time and place, Lisa."

She laughed softly. "Many times, many places, many ways."
Then she whispered urgently: "Death is an obscenity, Tony.
An obscene lie. Fight against it. Deny it with life." But he was
silent, unyielding. She sighed. "I'm sorry, darling. I only
meant . . ." She let the words trail off and reached for her
handbag and put on her earrings again. She got to her feet and
slipped on her pumps.

"I'll walk you back to your hotel," he said, rising.

"Don't. But to the elevator, if you like." There was no resentment in her voice, no affront, which seemed out of character for Lisa.

They walked down the long corridor and Tony pushed the
elevator button. They stood watching the arrow over the door
creep toward Tony's floor. The arrow stopped and the door
slid open. Lisa moved to enter. He caught her arm. "Lisa!
Please." She gave him a quick look, understood, slipped her
arm through his, and they walked back along the corridor.

The balance of that week Tony's days were devoted to
pressing business at the Fifth Avenue store and meetings with
his father's attorney regarding Ted Brullov's estate and the
filing of his will for probate. On Friday Tony boarded a Pan
American flight for London, where he connected with Air
France for Nice. He checked into the Hotel Négresco and
telephoned the local headquarters of the Sûreté and asked if
Inspecteur Vilar was in. He was, and yes, he would be pleased
to see M'sieur Brullov at two o'clock.

Vilar's office was a small cubicle hazy with smoke from his
omnipresent pipe. He greeted Tony with an elaborate, and
clearly sincere, expression of sympathy for the loss of his father. "When I first read of the tragedy," he said, "it occurred
to me that perhaps your father might have made some impor-

tant discovery concerning our bank theft, and that it had become necessary for him to be silenced. Would that be a possibility?"

Tony said no, and repeated the convenient theory of Scotland Yard: that it was a simple case of murder by some criminal who mistakenly thought Ted Brullov carried valuables on his person. Tony did not mention to Vilar that in New York he had bought copies of the *Times* of London covering the first ten days following his father's death and had scanned every page until he found a small item headed MURDER VICTIM FOUND IN THAMES. According to the brief report, the bullet-ridden body of a man of about sixty years of age had surfaced; Scotland Yard doubted that identification would be possible, due to the length of time the body had been in the water, which was estimated at eight days. Counting backward, Tony concluded the man had been killed the same day as his father; the body was that of "Arthur Smith." Scotland Yard, Tony decided comfortably, would dismiss the case as "just another floater," and would never connect him with Theodore Brullov, the international jeweler.

"What brings you back to Nice?" Inspecteur Vilar inquired.

"Problems at our local store," Tony said. "I stopped by to hear how your bank investigation is progressing."

"Satisfactorily. We have proved that a certain fishing vessel left our harbor a few hours before we discovered the situation at the bank. There were four passengers in addition to the crew. They landed in Algiers, according to one of our informants, and that, I am afraid, is the last we shall hear of them. Their 'booty,' as the reporters like to call it, is now probably spread from Tangiers to Cairo."

"What about the diamond, the Turkish Brown?"

"It is here in our safe. But so far, no claimant. Paris would like to take custody of it, but I am standing on our evidential rights."

Tony frowned with frustration. "So really there's been almost no progress."

257

"*Au contraire*. Every box holder has identified his or her property found in the vault. Even those embarrassing items, the love letters and obscene photographs, were claimed, once the owners were convinced that we would respect their privacy." Vilar pointed his pipe at Tony. "Forgive me. There is one exception. The bank files show that box number fifty-four was rented to a certain Gaston Mercier in February nineteen twenty. At the same time Mercier opened a checking account with instructions that the annual rental on the box should be charged against his checking account. That has been the sole transaction throughout the past thirty-eight years. No new deposits, no withdrawals, except for the rental."

"Then the man must be dead."

"That was our first theory. But consider this. All property has been claimed except for the brown diamond, those two Russian letters which your father kindly translated for me, and three expired passports—one Turkish, one Yugoslavian, one Spanish. Their dates of issue range from nineteen nineteen to nineteen fifty. The intriguing aspect to me is that the passports were issued in three different names, yet they bear photographs which I suspect are all of the same man, taken at different periods of his life. What would that suggest to you, Mr. Brullov?"

"False passports, I'd say. And probably from Gaston Mercier's box."

Vilar beamed approval. "*Exactement!* It suggests also that Mercier has entered his box from time to time over the years. Unfortunately, the bank destroys its entry slips every five years, and in the current five-year period they have no slip signed by Gaston Mercier. Which means that his visits to the vault must have been prior to nineteen fifty-three."

Tony wrinkled his forehead in thought. "Then perhaps he's dead, after all."

Vilar nodded. "Possibly. But criminals—and I believe that Mercier *is* a criminal—sometimes will leave the business, so to speak, for long periods, such as imprisonment, or will transfer their activities to other areas, other countries. In any case, I have circulated copies of the photographs from all three passports to Interpol representatives throughout Europe and South America. If luck is with us, we may come up with an identification."

And if Gaston Mercier is identified, Tony thought excitedly, *he could be Yuri Dimitrovich Solenko.* "Would it be possible, Inspecteur, for me to see those photographs?"

"You have a reason?"

"Yes. Let's assume that this Gaston Mercier is the man who stole the Turkish Brown. Let's assume further that a man who has stolen one diamond has stolen others. He may have fenced them, or even sold them to a legitimate dealer in gems. On that chance, I'd like to send copies of the photos to all the major diamond clubs and ask my fellow members if any of them recognize the man, have had dealings with him and under what names and when."

Vilar knocked the ashes from his pipe and gave a smile of admiration. "You are most ingenious, M'sieur Brullov. Yes, the diamond clubs, by all means." He opened a drawer in his desk and pushed three enlarged photographs across to Tony. The three faces that stared at the camera wore a common expression, a defiant scowl.

In each photograph, the man wore horn-rimmed glasses, his hair was an unruly thatch, the face was half covered by a flowing moustache and a heavy beard—dark in the earliest photo, gray in the second and white in the third.

"An ugly customer at any age," Tony commented. "Assuming, of course, that the beard and moustache aren't fakes."

Vilar conceded the possibility. "However, I remember in my youth, when I, too, wore a beard and a moustache—very small, very neat—but if I spared the scissors, in two months time I might have been this man's twin. It is quite possible, for instance, that this person purposely went to hair, so to speak, at various times for his own purposes. And when those purposes had been realized, when he no longer needed these passports, he trimmed back—perhaps to be photographed for still other false passports of which we know nothing. So you see, we must take nothing at face value." Vilar grinned. "Forgive my little joke, but when one is dealing with an accomplished criminal, one of the highest order, anything is possible. Now, how many sets of these photos would you require?"

"Ten should do it," Tony said. Vilar picked up his telephone and relayed the request to his assistant, adding that each set should be accompanied by a plain manila envelope.

Tony taxied to the Brullov store on the Promenade des Anglais and borrowed the manager's secretary to dictate the circular letter to the directors of the various diamond clubs. While thus engaged, he was interrupted by a telephone call from Monte Carlo. It was Orsino di Ascoli.

"Tony! I just called you in New York. They told me you were in Nice. I hope you are feeling better."

"Better, sir?"

"Lisa told me she saw you in New York; that you were in pretty bad shape over your father. I understand, of course, and you have my deepest sympathy."

"Thank you."

"Any chance you could have cocktails with Erin and me this afternoon? I realize it's very short notice; but it's also a very short drive."

"What time?"

"Five o'clock. At my penthouse. I'll send one of my cars over to pick you up."

"Thank you, sir."

Di Ascoli laughed. "Not 'sir,' Tony. How many times must I tell you, it's Orsino."

On the drive to Monte Carlo in the chauffeured Rolls-Royce, Tony mulled over the purpose of the invitation. Erin's presence would give the semblance of a social hour; but Tony was confident that Orsino would manage to bring up the business proposition which he had put to him on the cruise of the *Diana* and again at the Cannes Film Festival. The time of decision was at hand.

The Rolls descended from the Corniche, glided through the business district of Monte Carlo and pulled to the curb outside the sixteen-story building which was the world headquarters of Di Ascoli Enterprises. When Tony stepped from the elevator on the sixteenth floor, he found himself in a marble foyer more appropriate to a bank than a penthouse. A baldheaded man in a black suit came forward, and Tony remembered him from the cruise; he was Constantine Durer, di Ascoli's confidential secretary. They shook hands and Durer escorted him through a short hallway and across an immense drawing room with picture windows which afforded a panoramic view of the harbor and the hill topped by the palace of Prince Rainier and Princess Grace. They passed through an archway and went out onto a terrace, where steps led down to still another terrace on the floor below. Its dimensions were almost equal to two tennis courts, permitting ample space for a swimming pool, a cabana, an outdoor bar and an ornamental garden dotted with potted palms. Looking down, Tony saw Erin, in a white summery frock, wave up to him, and di Ascoli ascending the steps to greet him. He dismissed Durer and put his arm around Tony's shoulder. "Before we join Erin, please, let's take a moment to dispose of a business matter."

Here it comes, Tony thought—immediate and to the point. "You mean about our floating a stock issue?"

"Exactly. I do not wish to appear unfeeling, considering how recently you are bereaved, but now, Tony, you own voting control of your company. At a word from you we can begin to lay the foundation of the Brullov fashion empire."

"Voting control is still in the future," Tony said. "Until my father's probate closes, his stock can't be transferred into my name."

"I understand. But from a little investigation I had made, it appears you have been named executor of the estate. So all I wish at this time, Tony, is an indication of the executor's intentions. Is he for my proposal?"

Tony hesitated and glanced down at Erin on the terrace below; the butler was filling her glass from a bottle of champagne. This was already her home, Tony thought with a pang of jealousy, and soon, no matter what Lisa had predicted, she would be its legal mistress. His gaze returned to Orsino. "The executor's intention," he said, "will probably be favorable."

Di Ascoli frowned. "*Probably*, you say?"

"I wish first to consult with my Aunt Ruth, who, although only a minority interest, *is* family, and I have not had a chance to talk to her." Tony spoke the truth; but his evasion was more to enjoy the pleasure of keeping a man of di Ascoli's power dangling in suspense. Especially the fiancé of Erin Deering.

Then Durer appeared again and spoke to di Ascoli. "Hong Kong is on the line again, sir. They insist that it's absolutely urgent."

"Oh, God damn those Chinese!" he sputtered. "Excuse me, Tony, I'll join you and Erin as soon as I can."

Tony went down onto the lower terrace. Erin rose and they kissed each other's cheeks. Then she turned to the butler and told him she was displeased with the champagne; would he bring a different vintage?

Now they were alone. They surveyed each other as if it were their first meeting in years. "You're as beautiful as ever," Tony said. "And happy, I hope."

She ignored the last and took his hand in hers. "Tony, my dear," she said sadly, "I want you to know how shattered I was by your father's death. He was more than my first schoolgirl crush; he was a wonderful man, and my feeling for him prepared me for you."

"While it lasted," Tony said dryly, although he was both surprised and pleased.

"Nothing lasts, I've learned," she said wistfully. "But I am grateful for what we did have. From that first meeting at the Casino—after you got rid of that phony beard and moustache

—I was ready for anything with you. My first nude swim with a man, and making love on that float, and all those magical days and nights together—those are memories that will stay with me always."

Tony noted that she omitted Paris, twelve years later. She was still bitter over his betrayal with Lisa. Even so, considering her present position, her words seemed a reckless confession. Or were they a farewell?

"Erin, *are* you happy?" Tony repeated.

She laughed lightly and warned him with her eyes. "Of course, you silly." The butler was returning.

Orsino joined them in a jovial mood, and described for Tony how he had resolved the problem of the coming wedding. Since he and Erin could not be married by a priest, he had persuaded the mayor of the city to perform the ceremony. It would be there on the lower terrace; and the Monte Carlo police band, on the upper terrace, would play the wedding march. The guest list would be as impressive as for a coronation, and afterward the bridal couple would sail on the *Diana* for a cruise of the Greek Isles.

Tony listened politely, but with only half an ear. The words Erin had said earlier to him kept repeating themselves in his brain. . . . *I am grateful for what we did have. From that first meeting at the Casino—after you got rid of that phony beard and moustache—I was ready for anything with you.*

After you got rid of that phony beard and moustache . . . He had forgotten it completely. *Of course!* When he had first entered the Casino, when he had tried, for laughs, to disguise himself and slip past Victor, the *physiognomiste*.

Di Ascoli slapped Tony's knee. "What do you say? Will you give us the pleasure?"

Tony came out of his reverie. "In what way?"

"Stay on for dinner. And afterward, if you like, you could call your Aunt Ruth and explain that matter we were discussing."

"No. She's too hard of hearing. I'll have to write to her."

"Then at least dinner," Erin urged.

"I wish I could. But I've already made an engagement in Nice, one I can't break." Tony looked at his wristwatch. "Good Lord! I've barely got time. Is there a taxi station somewhere nearby?"

"No taxis," di Ascoli declared. "You came in my car, you'll return in my car."

Tony directed the chauffeur to take him to the Brullov store on the Promenade. The store had been closed for two hours, but after repeated knockings on the door, he attracted the attention of the night guard. He hurried upstairs to the office of the manager's secretary. Yes, thank God, she hadn't finished mailing all the letters to the diamond clubs. There were still two sets of photographs of "Gaston Mercier." Tony took one set, slipped them into a manila envelope, returned downstairs and thanked the guard for letting him in.

He ordered a simple dinner at the Négresco and thought out his approach to Victor. It must be uncomplicated and believable. But suppose it was Victor's night off? He tried to remember back to the evening the month before when he and his father had dropped into the Casino. There was a substitute *physiognomiste* that night. Was it a Tuesday or a Wednesday? How in hell could he remember such a detail? He'd have to chance a taxi ride and hope for the best. . . .

Tony bought his ticket at the Casino entrance and went toward the main gaming hall. Yes—there was old Victor's bald head gleaming under the lights of one of the great hanging chandeliers. When he recognized Tony the tic in his left eye gave an extra twitch, as if in greeting. They shook hands and Tony asked, "Victor, could you spare me a minute or two?"

"For you, M'sieur Brullov, of course."

"In private, please."

"There is a problem?"

"Not really. You see, I've made a wager with some friends of mine. They bet me that I cannot identify certain gentlemen from photographs taken many years ago. So far, I've failed. Then I remembered you, the man whose memory is a catalogue of a hundred thousand faces."

"One quarter of a million, at the very least," Victor corrected proudly. "But I do not understand such a strange wager."

"It's a game, really. You've heard of scavenger hunts, haven't you?"

"Scavenger hunts?"

"Yes. At a party the guests are given slips of paper with riddles on them. The game is to solve the riddle, which always describes a place where one will find some hidden object—an old phonograph record, say, or an old-fashioned lady's corset —almost anything. And when one finds this object, there is a second riddle, which sends one off on another hunt."

Victor bobbed his head. "It comes back to me now. It was a game much played before the war. So you have found these photographs, but also you must name the persons in question?"

"You've got it. There's ten thousand francs in it for you."

Victor shrugged. "That is not necessary for an old patron and friend."

"I insist. But I don't want anyone to see you helping me with these." He handed the manila envelope to Victor. "Perhaps you have an office?"

"Certainement."

Tony followed Victor back to the foyer, then down a flight of steps to a lower floor. Victor's office was at the end of a long hall. The room was lined with filing cabinets which Victor said contained the names, photographs and histories of men and women who were known or suspected to be card sharks or gamblers with systems that had caused heavy losses to the Casino, as well as data on pickpockets who might be a threat to the clientele.

Victor switched on his desk lamp and invited Tony to sit opposite him. He removed the photographs from the envelope, took a magnifying glass from a drawer and, his left eye twitching, studied all three likenesses. "In my profession," he said, "I watch first for the shape of the ear and the base of the nose. These never change throughout one's life. Here I see very large ears, which the Orientals believe is the mark of great intelligence." He moved the magnifier from photo to photo again. "And there is a crease in the lobes of both ears. Yes. It confirms . . ."

"Confirms what?" Tony pressed.

"These are all photos of the same man, but taken many years apart."

Tony knew that much. "But the beards and moustaches, are they fakes?"

"One cannot be certain. If so, they are very good." He tapped the most recent photograph. "This one I do suspect. The hair of the head, the moustache, the beard, are white. But the eyebrows are dark gray. It sometimes happens, but not often. All hair should match in a man of this age." Victor pondered a moment. "Would you permit me to use a pencil on this photo?"

"By all means."

He reached for the jar of pencils on his desk and selected one with a worn tip. Then slowly, gently, he darkened the head of hair.

Tony craned to watch from across the desk, but from his position the photograph was upside down and the darkened hair told him nothing. "Do you recognize him?"

"Not yet. Let me do a bit of barbering on the beard." Again Victor applied the pencil, delicately tracing the probable jaw-line and smudging the lead over the flowing beard. Then he smiled and clicked his tongue.

"Yes?" Tony prodded.

"I think . . ." The tic returned to the eyelid. "But one must be positive." Victor penciled out the drooping ends of the moustache, then darkened the remaining white until it matched the skin tones. He glanced across at Tony and grinned. "You will win your wager, M'sieur Brullov."

"His name, Victor. Is he Gaston Mercier?"

He wagged his head. "That is a name I do not place. No. This photo would have been taken a few years ago, but the gentleman has aged very little. He has been a distinguished patron of the Casino for many years. . . ." By now Tony was rising from his chair. "As a citizen of Monaco, he is not allowed to gamble. Instead, he bankrolls his lady friends."

Tony rounded the desk, but Victor, in a spirit of teasing, covered the photo with his hand. "One of those ladies—" he smiled archly—"was once your own."

Tony gaped. "Miss Erin Deering?"

"But of course."

Victor removed his hand from the photo and Tony stared down at the face of Orsino di Ascoli.

Fifteen

Nice
Second week of June 1958

ALL THE pieces of the puzzle now fitted. Orsino di Ascoli was Gaston Mercier who was Yuri Dimitrovich Solenko. And between his present name and his first there were at least three other aliases, those on the false passports found in the bank vault. But why? Why had he kept such damning evidence?

In the taxi on the way back to Nice, and as he lay awake in his hotel room, Tony asked that question over and over. His own father had suggested that it was simple human psychology: the sentimental criminal who held on to souvenirs of his past, just as other box holders at the bank had treasured love letters and baby shoes and false teeth. But to Tony it did not quite wash. There should be a more compelling motive.

Then in the small hours of the morning, as he started to drift off into the sleep of exhaustion, Tony's subconscious mind whispered the answer—the letters which his father had translated from the Russian for Inspecteur Vilar. The letter of 1927 had answered "my old friend Yuri's" questions about their mutual partners in the crime of Ekaterinburg: deaths by knife, by drowning, by shooting. The second letter in 1950, complained that a woman's husband had fled to London, had taken the name "Arthur Smith" and had told a Soviet agent that he would not return to Russia *to die like all his old friends.* There it was. Di Ascoli/Solenko had, like "Arthur Smith," dreaded discovery and vengeance. Behind that façade of power and wealth, there had been the fear of the hunted. If the hour came when he must flee, he was ready with false passports and disguised photographs. Even the dates fitted. The passport of 1927 matched the assassination of Ambassador Voikov in Warsaw and the poisoning of the Soviet commissar in London. The 1950 passport had been issued when di Ascoli had sent "Dr. Kohlski" in search of those Tsarists who might be members of a vengeance squad. He was ignorant of their identities, but he knew they existed and must be liquidated. Instead, it was Kohlski who had been eliminated. As for the diamond, the Turkish Brown had been left in the safety-deposit box because it was too identifiable, too dangerous to sell or even to cut up into small stones. It had slept away the years in the security of the vault, along with the precious passports—until the coming of men with pickaxes and shovels and dynamite and electric drills.

But now the quandary. Until a few hours before, Yuri Solenko had been an abstraction, a name for Tony to hunt down and exterminate. Now he was Erin Deering's lover and husband-to-be; he was Lisa's father; he was the international financier who would join interests with Tony Brullov to build a fashion empire. Tony half wished that he could relive the past few days. He would not have gone to Inspecteur Vilar; he would have known nothing of the false passports; he would not have sought out Victor. The mystery would remain unsolved and Tony would be at peace. Instead he had eaten the apple of knowledge and must act.

He wondered if it would be punishment enough to publicly denounce Orsino di Ascoli. But how could Tony prove his charges? His father, who could add substance to the accusation, was dead. Vilar and the Sûreté would be loath to move against a man of di Ascoli's power. Even the newspapers would be frightened, for many were controlled by banks tied to di Ascoli's empire. And even if Tony's charges found print, they would be discounted as the sour grapes of Erin Deering's former lover. And it would be a disaster for the business of Brullov & Company.

Tony realized that he was becoming unglued. His nerves were giving way under the weight of indecision. Then he remembered that it was Sunday morning. Perhaps he could find solace, or a way out, by attending services at the great Russian Cathedral of Nice.

He stood there among the hundreds of devout and gazed at the magnificent golden and bejeweled icons; he listened to the organlike tones of the choir; he knelt and crossed himself and prayed while the bishops and archbishops in their resplendent robes intoned the mass. He looked around the congregation and saw the faces of old Russia, the refugees from the Bolshevik terrors—men and women who had lost everything except their self-respect and now made do in a foreign land. That much was apparent to anyone there in the Cathedral; but it went farther with Tony. He was not particularly religious, he was uncertain of a hereafter; yet in that hour he felt the presence of his father almost as strongly as if he were physically beside him. He felt, too, the presence of the Romanov princes and grand dukes and their families who had wintered on the Riviera in pre-Revolutionary days and had worshipped in this same house of God. Mystical or not, Tony saw the path he must follow. "Justice" his father had called it, and justice would be done. Orsino di Ascoli ceased to be a man, but a symbol of those who had oppressed, terrorized and murdered. He was more than a Bolshevik killer, he stood equally for the brutal Nazi exterminators against whom Tony had fought in the last war.

But first he must protect Erin. He must get her away from Orsino. In the early afternoon he telephoned the penthouse in Monte Carlo. Constantine Durer answered, and Tony said he wished to thank Miss Deering for the pleasant cocktail hour of the day before. Could he speak to her? Durer said he would transfer the call.

When Erin came on the line he asked, "Are you alone?"

"Yes. I'm sunbathing on the terrace. Why?"

"I've got to see you, Erin. It's extremely important."

"Then come on over."

"No. This has to be very private. Tomorrow morning could you drive to Nice without telling anyone where you're going?"

"Tony, why all this mystery?"

"I'll tell you when I see you. If you can make it at eleven, I'll be waiting in the Flower Market. We'll pretend to bump into each other accidentally."

"I'm not sure I like this, Tony."

"I don't, either. But it's absolutely necessary. But for God's sake, no Rolls-Royce and no chauffeur. And wear sunglasses. Will you do it?"

There was a long pause before she said "yes."

The Marché aux Fleurs is located in the Old City, a square surrounded by shuttered houses and filled with scores of stalls offering blooms of every imaginable color and scent. At eleven o'clock that morning the market was thronged with customers and tourists with their cameras. Tony idled past the vendors crying out their specialties; he obliged a honeymooning couple by taking a photograph with their camera; then he saw Erin, who, despite her sunglasses, was being importuned by a group with their autograph books. Finally she broke away and came toward him. "Well, hello again!" he called out.

"This is a pretty ridiculous way to be private," Erin sniffed.

"Let's wander out of here," Tony said. "I've got a car parked the next street over."

"Where are we going?"

"It doesn't matter, really."

Tony drove eastward toward "Château Hill," so named because it was once topped by a fortress, and now a favorite of the Niçois for picnics, and of tourists for viewing the sweep of the Baie des Anges and the city's harbor. Tony turned up the inclined road to the parking area and led Erin along a tree-shaded path to the easternmost point overlooking the harbor. Erin stared down at a sailboat tacking its way toward the open sea, a sailboat very like the one Tony had rented that day long ago when they had put out into the Baie and made love on its deck.

"It brings back memories, doesn't it?" Tony said.

She nodded. "Is that why we're here?"

"Partly. Erin, I've been thinking about what you said the other day on the terrace. About those good times when we first met. I've never forgotten them, either. Or when we picked up again last year in Paris. I fell in love with you all over again. You must believe that, Erin."

She took off her sunglasses and gave him a troubled look. "I believed it at the time. But I also believed about Lisa."

He pounded a fist against his knee. "Damn it, hear me out, Erin. I was wrong, totally wrong. Lisa was the biggest mistake of my life—but now I want to keep you from making the same mistake. I don't think you're really happy with Orsino. My God, the difference in your ages. You can't be in love with him. There's still time to pull out."

"You're serious, aren't you?"

"Deadly serious. I'm asking you to marry me."

She was quiet a moment. Her blue eyes began to glisten. "You should have come to me like this months ago."

"But it's not too late." He tried to draw her to him, to kiss her, but she pushed him away.

"No, Tony, no. You don't know what you're asking. The price is too high. I've come a long journey, Tony. I've had my fill of struggling. I want security and respect. Orsino gives me that. He's strong, so very strong, and he makes *me* feel strong. You never gave me that, Tony. You're still something of a playboy, an adventurer. Wonderful fun, and a marvelous lover—but I was always afraid that some day you'd grow bored and I'd lose you. Lisa proved that I was right." Tony tried to interrupt, but she hurried on. "I won't be a loser a second time. If I walk out on Orsino now, everyone will say I was a castoff. And marriage with you would be settling for the consolation prize. That's the way people would talk."

"They'll talk anyway. They'll say you're settling for the big bucks."

"Let them. It *is* a beautiful life, Tony. It's every woman's dream." She paused and looked at Tony's defeated expression. "Darling, this isn't the end of the world. I know that you and Orsino are talking about some business together—which makes it seem all the stranger that you should be against him now—but if you go ahead with your deal, you'll be seeing me from time to time. We'll continue to be friends."

"Friends!"

"The best and the closest. That's why I want you in our wedding party. The invitations go out tomorrow."

"Then you've set the date."

"The evening of July seventeenth."

Tony gave a start. "July seventeenth?"

"Yes."

"Who chose that date?"

"Orsino. But why?"

"It just seems so near," he evaded. "Would it be because you're pregnant?"

Erin gave a surprised laugh. Tony was an old granny, she said.

He could not tell her the true significance of July 17. It would be the fortieth anniversary, to the very day, of the murders at Ekaterinburg, the theft of the Romanov jewels, and the beginning of Yuri Solenko's dazzling career. On that date, when hundreds of thousands would be mourning the murders of their Imperial Family, Orsino di Ascoli would be celebrating the spoils. What a satisfaction it would be—secret, grisly, but still satisfying. And from that moment, there with Erin on the hilltop overlooking Nice Harbor, Tony Brullov lost his last qualm over what must be.

That evening Erin and Orsino attended a rather tedious reception at the palace of Prince Rainier and Princess Grace. When they returned to the penthouse Orsino went out onto the terrace for his ritual last cigar of the night and Erin joined him. They made small talk about the guests at the reception and then, abruptly, Orsino asked, "What did you and Tony talk about this morning?"

Erin recoiled with surprise. "How did you know?"

"My dear, you are engaged to one of the world's wealthiest men. You could be a target for kidnappers. Wherever you go, a detective follows—just as with Lisa." He drew on his cigar and waited. "What did you and Tony talk about?"

The actress in Erin came to her aid and she ad-libbed casually. "It was a beautiful morning and I thought it would be pleasant to drive over to Nice. I was wandering through the Flower Market and—and I heard someone call out my name. It was Tony. He said he wanted to buy roses to send to us in appreciation for cocktails the other night."

"I see. And then Tony forgot about the flowers and drove you up onto Château Hill. What did you talk about?"

Erin gave a sigh of surrender. "He asked me to marry him."

Orsino studied his cigar. "That has the ring of truth to it. And what was your answer?"

"I said no."

"It seems a very short conversation."

"It wasn't. I told him to forget everything that there had ever been between us. That I loved you and I was going to marry you."

Orsino returned to his cigar for a moment. "Then you held out no hopes for some future arrangement?"

"I don't understand."

"I think you do. There is an old French expression: 'The old man who takes a young bride kicks his funeral bell with his ass.' You did not discuss this happy possibility?"

"Orsino, please. You're being cruel. You're not old. You mustn't talk like this." She faltered a moment, trying to find words to defuse this confrontation. "My darling, when we first met, you and I, at the racetrack in Paris, it was true that Tony and I were lovers. But my thing with him was just acting out a fantasy of my girlhood when I had a crush on Tony's father."

"I see. Or rather, I do not see. This 'crush,' as you call it, was at what age?"

"Fourteen. I was a lonely kid living on a coffee-and-banana finca in Costa Rica. I've told you about that. And then one day Ted Brullov appeared from somewhere to see my mother. He told her he was looking for a golden mermaid, and then he—"

"Excuse me, my dear. You said—a *mermaid?*"

"Oh, just a piece of jewelry my mother owned. A tiny mermaid of gold holding a beautiful Oriental pearl. Mr. Brullov, Ted, said he had made it himself back in Russia for a girl he loved. But my mother had lost it, or it was stolen, and so Ted spent most of the evening talking to me, a gangling kid, and he made me feel grown-up and worthwhile, and I fell hard. That's how it all began."

When Erin finished, Orsino smiled for the first time; but it was a smile that belied the cold glitter in his eyes. "Thank you, my dear. You must forgive me for my curiosity, especially when it concerns Tony."

"You won't hold it against him?"

"By no means. His proposal to you was a tribute to my own good taste." He put his arm around Erin and kissed her cheek. "You look tired, my darling. It's time we said goodnight."

"You're staying up?"

"For one more cigar. Sleep well, my dear."

The evening was still balmy, yet as di Ascoli gazed out over the lights of Monte Carlo he felt chilled. Almost forty years had passed since he had torn the golden mermaid from the naked breast of the Archduchess Tatiana. And almost as long since Sonya, the Shanghai whore, had stolen it from the cache of jewels he had hidden under the floorboards of her room. But how many hands had it passed through to arrive in Costa Rica, on the other side of the world? And how had Ted Brullov traced it?

He shivered and went indoors. He passed through the drawing room and the library to his private office, where he pressed a button on the intercom system. He pressed three times in rapid succession, which was the "urgent" signal and a warning that there was to be no conversation via the telephone. Then he seated himself and waited until Constantine Durer appeared in dressing gown and slippers. Di Ascoli nodded toward the door. Durer closed it and waited for his employer to speak.

"It is almost seven P.M. in New York City. Do you have a night phone number for our operatives there?"

"I do, sir."

"Then you are to call them at once. Stress that this is to be a most confidential investigation. I want no reports by mail or cable; they are to be telephoned directly here to me."

"I understand, sir. And the subject to be investigated?"

"I wish to know the entire history of Theodore Brullov, the New York jeweler, from the time he arrived in the United States from Russia. I want the names and addresses of all his friends and business associates; where Brullov traveled and the dates and for what purposes."

Durer cleared his throat. "Excuse me, sir, but such a comprehensive study will require some little time. It cannot be hurried."

"It *must* be hurried. I want no excuses. In addition, tomorrow you will employ the best investigators in Nice to follow the activities of Brullov's son, Anton. I want daily oral reports directly to me. When he leaves the Riviera, wherever he goes —Paris, London, New York—you will employ local people to continue the surveillance."

"May I ask a question, sir?"

"Yes?"

"Am I to understand that our previous investigation of Anton Brullov was unsatisfactory?"

"It was very satisfactory. But it concerned only the business operations of his company. Now I want to know everything humanly possible about him. Day by day, night by night. I want to get inside his brain."

Sixteen

Nice and New York City
Third week of June 1958

IN THE afternoon, following his talk with Erin, Tony drove to Monte Carlo and drove slowly about the streets, noting the locations of the police stations, the angles of intersection of the various avenues and boulevards. He visited the harbor area and walked past the *Diana*, which was moored prow to stern behind Aristotle Onassis' yacht, the *Christina*. He drove along the Boulevard Princess Charlotte and inspected the relationship of the headquarters of Di Ascoli Enterprises to its neighbors on either side of the street. Every bit of knowledge would be useful when the time came for action. Where it would occur, and when, Tony did not yet know. The crucial point was how to approach Orsino without danger to Tony himself. A business conference about the expansion of Brullov & Company? No, too risky. Orsino would have Constantine Durer hanging about. And Erin might be present. In his limousine? No, there would be the chauffeur as witness. Orsino was seldom alone; almost always there was a bodyguard hovering in the background, which ruled out the close range of a pistol; and a rifle fired from a safe distance would be too chancey, for Tony was inexperienced with that weapon. His training in the OSS had concentrated on surprise and silence—the strike of a knife, the quick tightening of a strangling wire, the lethal karate chop. Clearly it was going to take much time and thought to evolve a no-fail plan. . . .

The following morning Tony paid a courtesy call on Inspecteur Vilar at Sûreté headquarters. He told Vilar that the circular letters and photographs of Gaston Mercier had been mailed to the diamond clubs, and that any information was to be sent to Vilar, with carbon copies to Tony in New York City.

"Then you are leaving us?" Vilar asked.

"Tomorrow, I think."

The Inspecteur expressed again his gratitude for Tony's help and wished him an enjoyable flight home.

When Tony returned to the jewelry store he found an envelope which had been hand delivered by Orsino di Ascoli's chauffeur. Inside was the invitation to the wedding on July 17th and a separate invitation to a bachelors' party aboard the *Diana* on the evening preceding. Orsino had added a personal note to the latter invitation: "If you should be in New York before these dates, please consider yourself included among our American friends who will be flying over in my private plane. It will leave La Guardia at 9:30 A.M., July 15."

Included with the invitations was a curious document—a printed time schedule covering the bachelors' party, the wedding and the reception afterward aboard the *Diana*. It was as detailed as a military schedule for the invasion of an enemy land. To attend the bachelors' party, for instance, there would be five sailings by launch, fifteen minutes apart, beginning at 9 P.M., to the *Diana*, which would be at anchor outside the Monte Carlo breakwater. And starting at midnight, again fifteen minutes apart, there would be five return launches.

At first Tony was puzzled. Why was the yacht to be outside the breakwater; why not at dockside? Then he remembered— the *Diana* was presently moored alongside Aristotle Onassis' yacht; Di Ascoli had no wish for his guests to be reminded of his arch-competitor. Also, the arrangement implied to Tony that their Serene Highnesses Prince Rainier and Princess Grace might be among the guests, and if so, distance between Onassis and the Prince would be highly desirable, since both men were locked in combat for stock ownership of the corporation which controlled the Monte Carlo Casino.

Tony tucked the schedule into his coat pocket, left the jewelry store and strolled along the beach side of the Promenade. Problem solving always came easier to him with a walk in the open air. Orsino's detailed itinerary intrigued him; somewhere in all those scheduled minutes and hours there might be the opportunity Tony needed. "Punctuality is the pride of princes" was Orsino's favorite saying, and punctuality just might be his undoing. . . .

As Tony strolled eastward he gazed at the girls in their bikinis stretched out on the uncomfortable pebbly beach and wished that he too had no greater concern than to acquire a suntan. Beyond the surf he saw speedboats dashing over the shimmering blue and water-skiers testing their skill. All those carefree people depressed him; they underscored his own aloneness. There was no one in whom he could confide. In high school and college Tony's coaches had directed him; in business, his father had advised him; in the OSS the station chiefs had ordered him. But now he was totally on his own.

Tony realized that he was hungry. He crossed the Promenade and wandered up a side street until he found a restaurant. He paused to read the menu posted in the window. Good, they specialized in seafoods. He entered, chose a table next to a window and asked the waiter to bring him a lobster salad and a glass of chablis. He lighted a cigarette and glanced out the window. A man was studying the menu posted on the glass; then he peered through the window and met Tony's eyes. He turned and walked away.

The lobster salad proved to be delicious and Tony decided it called for a second glass of chablis. As he looked about for the waiter he saw the man who had stood at the window; now he was seated at a table in a corner, facing toward Tony. He seemed vaguely familiar, Tony thought; there was an English look to his face. A young face, no more than thirty. He wore white slacks and a red-and-white striped shirt open at the neck. Then Tony placed him—when Tony had come out of the jewelry store, he had been admiring the pieces in the display window.

The waiter came and took Tony's order for a second chablis and Tony took out di Ascoli's schedule and ran over it again. Nothing was listed for July 17 until 3:30 P.M., when Orsino and Erin would go to the City Hall and sign the civil registry for their marriage. Then more blank hours until the music prelude at eight-thirty, which would be played by the Monte Carlo City Band on the terrace of the penthouse. The wedding ceremony would begin at nine, and the reception on the yacht at nine-thirty. Di Ascoli had penned a note: "You and Lisa will be in the first boat behind the bridal launch."

Tony left the restaurant feeling pleasantly fortified by the food and wine, and retraced his steps to the Promenade. Behind him an auto backfired so explosively that Tony turned around. But it was not only the auto that caught his attention —there was the man in white slacks and the red-and-white striped shirt, who suddenly turned into the entrance of a shop. An alarm bell sounded in Tony's brain. Was it a coincidence, or was he being followed? Like most professional jewelers, he had trained himself to observe people around him. His father had schooled him in the dangers that attended his profession. Never enter an elevator when there was only one other passenger, male or female. Never walk alone in an unfamiliar neighborhood. Never share a taxi ride with a stranger. Jewel thieves were endlessly patient; if they had reason to believe a man carried the goods on him, they sometimes tracked a jeweler from city to city and even country to country, until the right moment. Tony's OSS training had stressed the same precautions, as well as how to flush out a tail. Very well—Tony would put him to the test. He followed the Promenade to the next intersection, then turned inland until he came to a department store. He entered and idled from counter to counter for a good ten mintues. From time to time he glanced about casually. Not a red-and-white shirt anywhere. He relaxed; it had all been in his imagination. He turned and made his way toward the street entrance. Then, out of the corner of his eye, he saw him. He was trying on a beach robe and inspecting himself in a mirror. A nice bit of camouflage for that striped shirt.

So it was more than imagination or coincidence. The next step was to learn if the man was working alone or with a partner. Tony walked rapidly back to the Promenade and westward to the jewelry store, where his rented Fiat was parked. He nosed out into the traffic, turned the corner, proceeded to the Rue de France, then west toward Cannes. He kept his eye on the rearview mirror, but the traffic was too heavy to single out any one particular auto that might be following him. He reached the turnoff for Cagnes, swung onto it and passed through the town and then onto the winding road which led up to the village of Vence. There were still too many cars on the road behind, for Vence was a favorite tourist attraction. Tony needed a truly quiet road. At Vence he chose the road that climbed upward through the mountains to Coursegoules. The road was narrow and tortuous, with many switchbacks. Finally he reached a turnout and pulled to the edge of the road and looked down. On the switchback below him he sighted a tan sedan and behind it a blue convertible; and still farther to the rear a black van. The road to Coursegoules was remarkably popular. He gunned the Fiat up the grade, then down through a gorge, and up again toward another switchback. Ahead of him he saw a man waving a baton topped by a disc with the word HALT. Tony killed the engine, got out and walked toward the signalman. Was the road closed? he asked in French. "For a few minutes," the man replied in a thick Provençal accent. A steam shovel was maneuvering around the next bend; a construction road was being built up to the mountain peak where there was to be a new radio-telephone relay station to link Nice with the cities to the north. All the way to Paris, the Provençal added proudly. He had barely finished when there was a loud booming sound which echoed through the hills. The signalman grinned; it was *un explosif à haute puissance* to blast an opening for the steam shovel.

Tony turned and walked back to his car. Behind him the tan sedan had stopped, and behind it the blue convertible and the black van. Tony lighted a cigarette and strolled past all three vehicles. There were two men in the tan sedan, beefy peasant types; the driver of the blue convertible was a blond young woman who rapped her fingers on the steering wheel, impatient at the delay; it was more difficult to view the driver of the black van, for its seat was placed high and over the engine. From Tony's angle of view he could see the man's chest and shoulders; he was wearing a sweater and a beret. But beneath the beret was the face with the English look.

A whistle blew in the distance, and the signalman waved to Tony. The road ahead was clear. Tony put his car into low gear and moved up the grade; then into second gear when he rounded the bend in the road. Off to his right he saw the steam shovel biting into the jumble of rock released by the blasting, and above and beyond a work shack with a red flag fluttering from the roof—a warning that it stored high explosives.

Of course! Tony smiled to himself. Why hadn't he thought

of it? He had remembered all the means of self-defense in his OSS training—but he had forgotten the purpose of most of his missions: to blow up enemy railroad bridges and power stations. Dynamite was the answer.

Tony reached the mountain village of Coursegoules, where the tan sedan pulled in at a garage. Tony continued westward on the road to Gréolières, followed by the blond in the blue convertible, and the black van. Shortly before Gréolières he picked up an intersecting road which circled back to Vence. There was more traffic now, and the convertible and the van dropped back, spacing themselves three and four cars apart. So they remained through Vence, onto the Corniche and back to Nice, where Tony pulled up outside the jewelry store.

Louis Dubois, the manager of the Nice branch of Brullov, was the younger cousin of Jacques Verdier, who ran the Paris store, and bore a certain family resemblance. But in contrast to the solemn, middle-aged Verdier, Dubois was a blond curly-haired enthusiast who reveled in the resort atmosphere of Nice. On this particular afternoon his natural good spirits deserted him when Tony, arriving back from his drive, reported, "I've got two tails on me" and related his experiences from lunchtime onward. He led Dubois to the second-floor window and pointed to the van and the convertible parked on the Promenade, a discreet hundred yards apart.

Dubois clucked his tongue. "Then we must act at once. I'll phone the police and have them picked up."

"Not yet," Tony said. "If they're jewel thieves, they've got to be caught in the act. I think this afternoon all they wanted was information." Tony consulted his wristwatch. "You'll be closing in thirty minutes. Can you get an extra night guard for the store in that time?"

"Assuredly."

"Okay. After that, call the police and ask for a patrol car to check the store all night long. And tomorrow put on an extra day guard."

"This all goes back to the break-in at the bank," Dubois

said ruefully. "There was so much publicity about our loss, it's alerted every jewel thief on the Riviera. They think now we keep our best goods here in the store safe."

"Which we do," Tony said. "So go make those phone calls."

Just before the store closed, Tony had a second conversation with Dubois. "Tell me something about your apartment house, Louis. Does it have a back entrance?"

"A service door, yes. It opens into an alley."

"But you can get to it from every floor?"

"Indeed."

"Would it be possible for you to invite me to your apartment this evening?"

Dubois' jaw sagged with surprise; then he recovered. "But of course. It would be a pleasure. I'll call Nicole and tell her you're dining with us."

"Thank you. And later, I'd like to borrow your car." Tony saw Dubois' look of bafflement, and he laughed. "You forget I'm a bachelor. I've met a certain young lady. I'd rather not visit her with jewel thieves on my heels. It could complicate the evening."

Dubois gave a conspiratorial smile. "Then I am at your disposal. I shall not park my car in the apartment garage. I shall leave it one block over."

"Perfect. One last thing—do you have a raincoat, a dark one?"

"It is navy blue."

"Waterproof?"

"But yes." The bafflement returned. "But the weather is so fine. It could not possibly rain tonight."

Tony smiled and patted Dubois' shoulder. "I see you have never visited a young lady with nosy neighbors and a husband who works nights. In the war, we called it camouflage."

"Ah-h-h! I see."

Nicole Dubois, an attractive brunette, was somewhat flustered to have her husband's employer for dinner. She apologized for the simplicity of their fare (which was altogether delicious) and the poor manners of her six-year-old twin sons (who were models of politeness). However, she was pleased that M'sieur Brullov admired the view of Nice, which repeatedly drew him to the parlor window. Tony failed to mention that his real interest was the black van parked catercorner across the street from his own car.

At eight-thirty the twins were put to bed, and half an hour later, Tony finished his brandy and took his departure with the keys to Dubois' car, its license number and instructions on where to find it. Dubois' raincoat was slung over one arm, and in Tony's trouser pocket was the service-door key to let himself back into the building when he returned.

Before starting the small Renault, Tony opened the trunk and saw with satisfaction that it was equipped with tools for roadside emergencies and a flashlight. There was nothing he need buy at a service station.

He drove about the city for a few minutes, watching the rearview mirror for any suspicious car. When he was satisfied, he set off on the same route he had taken in the afternoon— west toward Cagnes, then north into the hills to Vence and onto the mountain road leading to Coursegoules. From the time he left Vence, he sighted the headlights of only one auto, and it was headed in the opposite direction. Finally he rounded a bend and sighted the entrance to the construction road and, in the light of a half-moon, the silhouette of the steam shovel a short distance up the grade. He turned off his headlights and surveyed the area for a lantern or other evidence of a guard. Nothing was visible, which meant his work should be easy.

Tony pulled up the road and parked in front of the steam shovel. He opened the car trunk and took out the flashlight, a screwdriver and a tire iron, and trudged uphill toward the work shack. In addition to the red flag on the roof, which now hung limply in the breezeless air, there was a warning painted on the door: DANGER! EXPLOSIFS! The door was secured by a formidable padlock. Tony focused the flashlight on the hinges and grinned; the hinges did not match the security of the padlock—they were fastened into the wood with ordinary screws. A few turns of Tony's screwdriver and the hinges came free.

He shone the flashlight into the interior. There were the expected pickaxes and shovels and two wooden boxes containing red sticks of dynamite. Tony chose six sticks and shoved them into his trouser pockets. On a shelf he found a carton of detonating caps and a coil of thin electric wire which was used to connect the blasting agent with a battery and plunger, both of which were far too heavy for his use; but he would need several feet of the wire. What else? A shovel. Nothing remained now but to close the door and screw the hinges back into place. . . .

He drove slowly back down the mountain road in the direction of Vence, watching carefully for some identifying mark which could be remembered easily. Tony had gone a little over a mile when his headlights picked up the burnt stump of a pine tree emerging between two boulders on the downslope from the road. He stopped the car and wrapped Dubois' raincoat tightly about the dynamite sticks, the detonating caps and the electric wire. He scrambled down the hillside, counting off twenty steps from the burnt pine stump, and shoveled a hole several feet deep and buried his cache. Tomorrow, he reminded himself, he must be sure to pay Dubois for his "misplaced" raincoat and think up some believable explanation.

Constantine Durer escorted a blond young woman and a man with an English cast to his face into the private office of Orsino di Ascoli, who sat expectantly behind his desk.

"This is Mademoiselle Annette Pelletier and M'sieur Paul Radlett, sir," Durer said, and then withdrew to a seat in the corner.

"What have you so far?" di Ascoli asked Radlett.

"To begin with, sir, the subject was aware that he was being followed. He is a jeweler and so is on guard against possible holdups such as cost the life of his father. Also, you will remember, he was with the American OSS during the war, and that has also sharpened his eyes."

Di Ascoli glowered. "I did not hire you for excuses. I hired you to tell me his activities."

Radlett and Pelletier exchanged uncomfortable looks and then took out their notebooks. The day before, "the subject" had lunched at a restaurant on the Promenade, he had visited a department store, he had driven to Vence and Coursegoules and then circled back to Vence and returned to Nice and the jewelry store.

"We knew by then that he was testing us," Annette Pelletier added, "because he made no stops except when a signalman halted him because of road construction. It was what the Americans call a 'joy ride,' but for a purpose."

Di Ascoli grunted his displeasure. "What about last evening?"

Radlett brightened. "It was more interesting. Annette rented a different auto but I kept with my van, and we followed the subject to the apartment of M'sieur Louis Dubois, who is the manager of the jewelry store. We believe the subject dined with the Dubois and stayed on for a very long time. The lights went out in their apartment at ten twenty-eight P.M., but the subject did not leave until three-ten this morning."

"What do you make of that?"

Annette Pelletier suppressed a smile. "We suspect that he slept with Madame Dubois, or perhaps with M'sieur Dubois, or perhaps with both."

Di Ascoli broke into guffaws. "Do I detect a note of envy?" Then more seriously: "And today?"

Radlett checked his notebook. "The subject left the Négresco at ten-twenty, drove to the jewelry store, then to Monte Carlo. He parked on the Quai Antoine and talked to a man who was fishing from the breakwater jetty. We questioned the man afterward, and he said the subject had simply asked him the species of fish which one might expect to catch. Then he drove back to the Négresco and left with his bags for the airport. He took the three-o'clock Air France flight to Paris."

"Did you find out if he was taking a connecting flight to somewhere else?"

Annette spoke up. "I talked to the concierge at the Négresco. He said the subject had left a forwarding address for his mail. It was to be sent to him care of Brullov and Company on Fifth Avenue, New York."

Di Ascoli turned to Durer. "Alert your people in New York to begin surveillance."

"May I make a suggestion, sir?" Durer replied. "If Mr. Brullov was aware that he was being followed here, would it not be better for New York to delay action for a few days? It might tend to relax his guard." He glanced at Radlett. "Would you agree?"

"Completely. We strongly recommend it."

Durer showed the investigators out and returned to di Ascoli, who asked for his reactions.

"I doubt we shall learn anything of importance, sir. Mr. Brullov seems an innocent enough gentleman."

"So it seems. My real interest is in his late father. When can I expect a report on him?"

Durer hunched his shoulders. "To reconstruct a man's life over nearly forty years requires much time. New York suggested to me at least three weeks, perhaps longer."

"*Paw!* More excuses. All right, you may go." Then, as Durer opened the door, he called him back. "One thing bothers me. Why was Tony Brullov interested in the type of fish in our harbor?"

"I really can't imagine, sir."

Seventeen

New York City and Nice–Monte Carlo
June 23–July 17, 1958

O**N HIS** night flight across the Atlantic, Tony slept the
sleep of exhaustion. Once or twice he awakened and
stared out the window at the stars and wondered at himself.
Was he a complete lunatic? The project he had committed
himself to could be, *would* be, more dangerous than any
operation he had undertaken in the OSS. That, of course,
was its attraction. It would be the great adventure. It would
make world headlines—yet he would never be able to claim
it as his handiwork. . . .

Due to the time differential between New York and Paris, which he had left at sundown, he arrived at La Guardia shortly after 10 P.M. His stomach was still on Paris time, so he ate "breakfast" at the airport restaurant, then taxied to his apartment. More sleep was impossible, so he fixed a pot of coffee, opened a fresh pack of cigarettes and stretched out in his lounge chair in the living room. Now was the time for thinking and imagination.

He reviewed the techniques he had been taught by the OSS. When he had blown up railroad bridges and power stations, the dynamite had been detonated by one of two methods: either an electrical line two or three hundred feet long connected to a battery and plunger, or, if it was important to be far away when the blast occurred, then a clock was added, which closed the electrical circuit hours after Tony had rigged it. But the Monte Carlo operation, as Tony conceived it, required arming his device at least nineteen hours before the explosion. Clocks were limited to a twelve-hour span. If, for instance, he set the alarm clock at 1 P.M., it would be operational at any time up to 1 A.M. the following morning. But not a single second beyond.

He considered the possibility of using two clocks in tandem. The first clock would run for twelve hours, then trigger the second clock to run until the required moment of explosion. But Tony failed to see how a windup clock could trigger a second clock; they would have to be electrical clocks, connected by a circuit. But that, too, was out, for electrical clocks required more voltage than an easily portable battery could deliver. How was it to be done? How?

Shortly after three in the morning, Tony gave up. He took a sleeping pill and crawled into bed. He set the alarm for ten o'clock, when he intended to call Trisha and tell her not to expect him at the store until the next day; he would say he had personal matters which required his attention.

At ten o'clock the alarm buzzed, and in Tony's dulled ears, it reminded him of a different alarm, one he had not heard since his college days when he had been a camera fan. Was it possible? he wondered. He rolled out of bed, made his phone call to Trisha, fixed himself another breakfast and mulled over the idea. Yes, he decided, he was on the right track.

His first stop was at a downtown camera shop, where he bought a small darkroom timer—which was nothing more than a windup clock with a range from one second to one hour and was used by photographers who developed their own negative film. A sturdy lever projected from the side of the clock. When the lever was pushed down, the clock began to count the seconds and minutes required to develop film in its solution; at whatever time required, up to one hour, the clock would buzz and the lever would snap upward.

At Hammacher Schlemmer he bought a reel of fine-gauge fishing line. At a radio-television store he asked the clerk for a powerful battery to operate a portable radio which he said he was taking on a hunting trip. At an electrical-supply store, he bought a small circuit relay switch, a voltmeter, a soldering iron and silver solder, an electrician's pincers, a roll of electrical tape and a few feet of electric cord. Finally, at a hardware store, he purchased a length of waterproof tarpaulin and a tube of waterproof cement.

He returned to his apartment, carried his purchases to the kitchen and began his work, following from memory his training in the OSS. First, he attached the voltmeter to the battery and satisfied himself that its strength would activate a detonator cap. Then he opened the back of the photographic timer and soldered the circuit relay switch to the clapper of the alarm. Next he soldered the electric cord to the circuit relay, punched a hole in the back plate of the timer and threaded through the electric wire. One section of the wire he clamped to the battery, another section he attached to the voltmeter. Finally, he drilled a hole in the lever on the side of the timer, ran the fishing wire through the hole and tied it. Now he was ready. He wound the timer and set the alarm to go off in three minutes. He tugged the fishing line and the lever moved to "on" position. He stared anxiously at the face of the timer as the second hand began to circle; at sixty seconds, the minute hand moved forward. One minute . . . then two . . . then three. At exactly three minutes, the needle on the voltimeter jumped across the dial. It worked!

All that remained now was to make a carrying pouch from the tarpaulin. He placed the timer and the batteries inside the pouch, making sure there remained enough room for the six sticks of dynamite. He pricked a tiny hole in the side of the pouch and threaded through the fishing line to the outside. Then, before sealing the pouch with the waterproof cement, he emptied half a can of talcum powder into the bottom of the pouch.

Nothing more could be done until the cement seal hardened, so Tony went out to dinner—a "victory" dinner he told himself—at his favorite French restaurant on Fifty-fifth Street. Then, glowing with the warmth of red wine, he returned to his apartment. He carried the pouch into the bathroom, filled the tub with cold water, and watched the pouch settle to the bottom.

The next morning, before showering, he removed the pouch from the tub, cut it open and examined the talcum powder. Damnation! The powder was gummy. Moisture had seeped through the hole provided for the fishing line. The pouch had to be bone-dry or the electrical circuit would short out and the sticks of dynamite would be soggy and useless. How to solve it?

Tony went to his office on Fifth Avenue in a state of perplexity. He listened to the report of the store manager on sales while Tony had been on the Riviera, and dictated answers to the letters Trisha had accumulated during his absence. He handwrote his acceptance of the invitations to di Ascoli's bachelors' party, the wedding and the reception and instructed Trisha to dispatch it by airmail. Business behind him, he wandered into his old office and gazed at the shelf of trophies he had won in twenty years of competitions. He had always been

293

a winner, he reminded himself; he had never turned aside from a challenge, nor would he this time. Somehow he would find a way to make that damned pouch watertight. . . .

At noon he told Trisha that he had a business luncheon which would last at least two hours. In reality he ate a sandwich in a drugstore and went to the Athletic Club. He swam the length of the club's pool ten times; then, underwater, the width of the pool ten times. His wind, he realized, was not what it used to be when he had captained the swim team at prep school. He would have to cut out cigarettes for at least the next few weeks. And to tone up his muscles, he'd need at least a daily hour in the gym.

On his way back to the office Tony chanced to stop for a traffic signal alongside a woman with an infant in a baby buggy. He watched her bend down and coo at the infant and adjust the bottle of formula which had slipped from its mouth. "By God! A *nipple!*" Tony exclaimed out loud. The woman stared at him. "Beg pardon?" He smiled back. "I said that's a beautiful baby you have there. Very beautiful." "Why, thank you, sir."

At the next drugstore which he passed he went in and asked a clerk for half a dozen nipples for a baby bottle, the kind that allowed the fluid to flow out but prevented air from being sucked into a baby's mouth.

That evening, in his kitchen, Tony made a second pouch from the rest of the tarpaulin. He scissored a small hole in the side, inserted a nipple and cemented it. Again he placed the timer and battery in the pouch, with more talcum powder, ran the fishing line through the nipple and sealed the pouch with cement. When it had dried, he filled his bathtub once more and dropped in the pouch. The next morning he removed it, slit it open and inspected the talcum powder. It was as dry as a desert wind.

The last week of June passed and the first ten days of July. Tony desperately missed his cigarettes, but he had come to look forward to his daily workout at the Athletic Club. He had increased his swim to thirty laps the length of the pool and twenty laps underwater across its width. He was close to top form physically—but mentally was another matter. Every day his nervous tension grew. He snapped at Trisha and was caustic at sales meetings. He even thought, several times, that someone was following him on Fifth Avenue. But that was nonsense, he told himself; it was simply a carry-over from his experience in Nice.

Every day now the New York newspapers were carrying items about the coming "Wedding of the Year." Hollywood stars and producers and their London counterparts saw to it that their press agents told the public that they were invited guests. Gossip columnists reported that the rooms in every deluxe and first-class hotel in Monte Carlo, Nice and Cannes had been booked solid by celebrities and press and television personnel. Tony had foreseen this and had telephoned Louis Dubois and asked if he could be put up in the Dubois' apartment. "But of course," Dubois said, "Nicole will send the twins to visit their grandmother. You will have their room, if you do not mind sleeping on a rented bed." Tony did not mind; now he could escape the watchful eyes of a hotel concierge.

On July 14, Bastille Day in France, he took the night flight to Paris. He refused to let the stewardess hang up his raincoat lest she become curious about the unusual weight caused by a photographic timer and a bulky battery. The baby-bottle nipples were all that he entrusted to his luggage; they would scarcely raise the eyebrows of French Customs.

In Paris, on July 15, he spent the morning buying another length of tarpaulin, more waterproof cement, scissors, a new reel of fishing line and a pair of swimming goggles. Everything fitted snugly into a small grip which would not be opened by Customs at Nice since he would be deplaning from a domestic flight.

That evening Louis Dubois met him at the airport. As they

walked through the passenger lounge, Tony noticed a blond young woman suddenly become interested in reading a newspaper. Tony excused himself from Dubois for a moment; he had to make an important phone call. He found a telephone, dialed a random number and spoke a few words to a bewildered child. He glanced over his shoulder; the blond was watching him. So it was beginning all over again. But why?

Tony returned to Dubois. "I want to rent a car here at the airport," he said. "I'll meet you at the apartment."

"But Nicole has dinner waiting. A very elaborate affair."

"I'll be less than ten minutes," Tony promised. "And when you get home, would you mind parking your car one street over, and let me use your garage?"

Louis Dubois rolled his eyes. "The same young lady?"

"I just called her. Her husband won't be home until three."

"She must be most remarkable."

"*Magnificent* is the word." Tony winked.

Nicole had truly outdone herself. The dinner was superb and the wine was a First Growth Bordeaux. During the meal, Tony asked Nicole if she might be able to take his tuxedo to be pressed in the morning in preparation for the bachelors' party. She could, indeed; she would take it along on her daily food shopping. And would she forgive him if he went out this evening for a while? He had promised to see a friend. She smiled quickly at her husband; he had made her privy to Tony's rendezvous.

"In that case, you may wish to sleep late," Nicole said, "so I shall go out early and there will be nothing to disturb you. I'll leave coffee and croissants for your breakfast."

"You are an absolute jewel," Tony declared and kissed her hand.

Tony followed the same routine as he had the first night with the Dubois. He let himself out the service door into the alley, found the Renault and drove about the city streets until the rearview mirror satisfied him that he was not being followed. Then he took the highway westward to the turnoff for Cagnes and Vence and onto the mountain road for Coursegoules. Finally his headlights picked up the construction road leading up to the new radio-relay station. He turned around and retraced his route for a mile until he recognized the burnt stump of the pine tree wedged between two boulders. He clambered down the hillside, counting off twenty paces, and located the shovel which he had hidden under some scrub brush. He could not remember exactly the spot where to dig, and it was not until his third try that he unearthed Dubois' raincoat wrapped about the dynamite and detonator caps.

Tony returned to the apartment house shortly before 2 A.M. A lamp had been left burning for him in the parlor; he switched it off and stepped to the window and looked down. The black van was parked across the street. They were most persistent jewel thieves, Tony thought. Or were they something else? He would worry about that later; for now, he would hide the dynamite under his bed and hope for the restorative of sleep.

He awakened a bit after nine. He went to the kitchen and found Nicole's coffee and croissants, which he consumed with gusto. Now he felt clearheaded for the work ahead. He brought the raincoat containing the dynamite and detonator caps to the kitchen, along with his grip, and began making another tarpaulin pouch. That done, he set the timer at four minutes, connected the battery to the timer and then to the detonator caps, wedged them among the sticks of dynamite, and inserted the assembly into the pouch. He threaded the fishing line through the nipple, and paid out twenty feet of line, which he judged would be more than enough. He closed the pouch, cemented it, placed it in the grip and returned it to the closet. From start to finish, it took just forty-five minutes.

Now it was time to attend to that van and the blond. He took the elevator down to the garage and his rented car and drove boldly down the street. His route was random, through one of the residential areas, then down to the beachfront. By the time he had reached the Promenade he had identified a Citroën coupe driven by the blond, and a few cars behind her, the black van. He swung off the Promenade and headed for the headquarters of the Sûreté and a talk with Inspecteur Vilar.

Orsino di Ascoli took the telephone call from Annette Pelletier in his private office. He listened impatiently to her account of following Tony Brullov from the Nice airport, of Radlett's all-night stakeout at the Dubois apartment, and following Tony in his rambling drive about Nice until his arrival at Sûreté headquarters. What she said next brought a scowl to his face.

"M'sieur Radlett and I have broken off contact, sir. We are resigning the case."

"What are you talking about, woman?"

"We believe the subject must have reported us to someone at the Sûreté. When he left and we began to follow again, we saw a police car trailing us. We have no wish to be questioned by the Sûreté, who might believe that we are jewel thieves who use our investigative work as a cover for jewel thievery. So we have gone our separate ways and hope we shall not be questioned."

"Then I'll hire another agency," di Ascoli snapped.

"I strongly recommend against it, sir. The Sûreté is now protecting the subject, and they will pull in anyone you hire."

Di Ascoli slammed down the receiver. He had spent thousands of dollars to shadow Tony Brullov and what had he learned? From the New York agency only that Tony spent hours every day at the Athletic Club and had dined a few evenings with various friends. The Paris coverage had been abysmal: the agent had lost Tony in the traffic between the airport and the city. All that was known was that he did not visit the shop on the Place Vendôme or register at any leading hotel. If there had not been a second agent stationed all day at the airport, even Tony's flight to Nice would have gone unreported.

Di Ascoli mulled over what he had learned from the separate investigation of Tony Brullov's father. The investigation was still in progress, but from the details already reported di Ascoli had been able to winnow out certain facts of importance. Brullov had been active in White Russian emigré organizations from the time of his arrival in New York in 1919. He had been in London in 1927 when the Soviet auction had been held at Christie's and one of the commissars had died mysteriously. In 1950 he had warned the New York Diamond Club of a visit by "Dr. Serge Kohlski," who claimed to be of Romanov blood and was likely a confidence man and jewel thief. Kohlski would not have called on Brullov unless he had strong suspicions that he was a threat to di Ascoli. Most important of all—and, of course, unknown to the New York investigators—Ted Brullov had traced that golden mermaid to Erin Deering's mother in Costa Rica. How much of all these matters did Tony know? Father and son had been remarkably close to each other. Everything, di Ascoli decided, kept coming back to Tony. He had had an affair with Lisa—but was it for pleasure or a means to get close to her father? And he had tried to persuade Erin to break off her engagement. Possibly jealousy, possibly something else. Now he was dragging his feet on the proposal to link Brullov & Company with Di Ascoli Enterprises. Why was Tony holding back? And finally, had Tony learned something from the Sûreté in the investigation of the looting of the bank vault—the very place where di Ascoli had secreted those damned passports and letters?

Nothing was provable, but there were far too many coincidences. Orsino di Ascoli had learned through the years to be ever suspicious, to trust his instincts. Better that Tony Brullov were not around.

Di Ascoli sat back in his chair, folded his hands behind his head and came to a decision. Tony Brullov must be a guest on the honeymoon cruise.

For the first time since Tony's return to Nice he felt at ease. Inspecteur Vilar's cooperation had ended the worrisome trailing of the blonde and the black van. He could go anywhere with freedom, and so now he drove to Monte Carlo, detoured around the Casino and descended to the beach road. He went slowly westward past the beach hotels, noting the various walkways which led down over the rocks to the waterline. As he approached the harbor proper he saw the *Diana* at anchor outside the breakwater. Tony pulled out onto a small promontory where a group of fishermen were casting from the boulders below. He tried to judge the distance out to the *Diana* and estimated it to be about four hundred yards. The two motor launches of the yacht were plying back and forth between the vessel and a landing platform inside the harbor—undoubtedly ferrying out provisions for the bachelors' party in the evening to come. Tony set the stopwatch mechanism on his wristwatch and timed each trip from the landing platform in the harbor to the float alongside the *Diana*. Six minutes, ten seconds; six minutes, twenty-five seconds; six minutes flat. In each case the launches moved very slowly inside the harbor, observing the speed limit set by the port authorities, then on passing the twin jetties, they opened throttle and flew over the water.

Tony studied his stopwatch. Just over six minutes, average. He had set the photographic timer at four minutes, which was cutting it rather fine. He wished that he had allowed a little more variable, and had programmed the timer for three minutes. But he dared not change the timer now. The bomb was armed; if he opened the pouch, the slightest slip of his fingers would be the end of Tony Brullov. No. Let well enough alone.

Now it was back to Nice and Nicole and Louis' apartment and, with luck, a long nap before the evening's work.

That evening Tony, dressed in his tuxedo, bid the Dubois goodnight and explained that the grip he was carrying down to his car contained a wedding present for Erin and Orsino. He locked the grip into the trunk of the car and set off again for Monte Carlo. When he reached the harbor *quai* he saw the long line of limousines and taxis and decided to park immediately and cover the distance to the loading platform on foot. This was no night to entrust his car to a parking attendant.

He descended the steps to the boarding float and recognized the second mate of the *Diana*, who appeared to be in charge of loading the launches. "Quickly, m'sieur!" he called out to Tony. "There is room for one more."

Tony looked at the launch and saw that the metal canopy covering the passenger seating was not the green and gold that distinguished di Ascoli's personal boat. "I'll take the next one," Tony answered. "I'm waiting for a friend."

"As you wish." The second mate blew a whistle, a crew member cast off the line and the launch growled into motion.

Tony was the first aboard the owner's launch. The passenger area under the canopy was exactly as he had remembered when it had picked him up in Geona, on the *Diana*'s cruise of last fall. Padded leather seats lined the port and starboard sides, while others backed against the engine housing. Under each seat there was a locker containing a life jacket. In the semicircle of the stern was di Ascoli's seat, which had two armrests; to one side there was a boxed telephone for him to communicate with the helmsman forward in the bow cockpit. It was this seat of di Ascoli's which Tony chose for his own.

The last tuxedoed passenger clambered aboard, the mate's whistle blew, and the launch moved away from the platform. Tony started his stopwatch. Shortly before they reached the jetty, still cruising slowly, and while the other passengers were talking and joking and oblivious of him, Tony unlatched the locker beneath him and felt inside. Thank God, there were no inner walls separating the lockers; the seats were bolted to the hull and the uprights to the decking.

Six minutes and twenty seconds later, by the stopwatch, the launch nosed alongside the *Diana*'s float steps. Tony stared upward at the spectacular sight. The *Diana* blazed with lights; pennants flew from bow to stern and somewhere an orchestra was playing show tunes.

"Welcome aboard!" Captain Cipriani greeted each guest as he stepped onto the deck. "Welcome aboard!" Orsino di Ascoli repeated, shaking each guest by the hand. "Welcome aboard, Tony," he said, with less enthusiasm.

"Thank you, Orsino. Where's the bar?"

Di Ascoli laughed. "So it's going to be one of those nights, is it? Three bars inside, three on deck. Take your pick."

Tony chose the nearest, in the main lounge, and ordered champagne. He judged there were already well over a hundred guests aboard, and more still to come. Some of the faces were familiar—Aly Khan, Rubirosa, several of the Rothschilds, an English former Prime Minister, a French elder statesman; and among Erin's actor friends, Gary Cooper, Charles Boyer and Boris Karloff. Guests bantered in every continental tongue and solemn-faced bankers and industrialists tried to top each other as to which was the most intimate friend of Orsino di Ascoli.

Tony circulated for a while, made small talk when it was called for and ordered glass after glass of champagne, which he stealthily emptied into the nearest vase of flowers. Finally he strolled out onto the aft deck, where he saw di Ascoli chatting with Aly Khan. When they separated, Tony approached his host. "Orsino, I'd like to tell you about my wedding present," he began, carefully slurring his words.

"Ah, it's magnificent!" di Ascoli interrupted. "Erin opened it this afternoon."

"I mean the *real* one. Your proposal to join forces with the Brullov Company. It's a deal."

For a moment di Ascoli was taken aback. His face registered more than surprise—he wore a look of bewilderment. "You are sure, Tony? This is definite?"

"Absolutely. Let's announce it here and now."

"No. Let's put it into the works first; after that we'll choose the right psychological moment." Then di Ascoli beamed and embraced Tony. "I can't tell you what this means to me, boy. You and I, partners."

It had the desired effect. Di Ascoli introduced him around to the bankers and industrialists and described Tony as his "dearest friend. A young man to watch." And watch they did, as Tony appeared to be taking on more champagne than he could handle. It was important, it was absolutely necessary, that there should be gossip that reached di Ascoli's ears. *Your young friend seems to be taking your capture of Miss Deering rather hard.* That would tickle his vanity and make Tony's actions later on seem harmless.

At midnight, the launches began to ferry the guests back to shore. Tony delayed until the last launch, then weaving noticeably, he sought out di Ascoli again. "Thank you for a wunnerful evenin', Orsino. Sorry I got sloshed. Always was a poor loser. Don't . . . tell Erin."

"It's between us, boy." Di Ascoli grinned.

"And—and there aren't any changes for tomorrow? Everything on schedule?"

Di Ascoli's expression changed. "Why? Problems?"

"Oh, no, no. I just wanted to be sure about the reception. I'm to be Lisa's escort in the second launch."

"Right. Goodnight, Tony."

" 'Night." Tony weaved off in the direction of the deck.

Di Ascoli watched him with a thoughtful frown. Then he hurried after him. "Tony. I almost forgot. I want you to come along on the honeymoon cruise. A whole week in the Greek Isles."

"Oh? But I don't have cruise clothes with me."

"Buy them in the morning. I'll send a car for your bags. Say, about three in the afternoon."

"Well . . . I dunno."

Di Ascoli clapped Tony's shoulder. "I have it! I'll invite Lisa, too. That sound better?"

"Much. 'Night again."

Once ashore, Tony was instantly sober. He walked the distance to his car and drove it along the waterfront until he passed the eastern jetty of the breakwater. There was still light traffic along the beach road, and dance music coming from the hotels fronting onto the water. When in hell would everybody go to bed? He turned up the grade into the city and then idled westward toward Nice. He pulled off the road for a while and listened to the late radio programs, then turned back toward Monte Carlo. A few minutes past 3 A.M. he reached the beach road. It was deserted now and the beachfront hotels were dark. Tony parked on the small promontory where the previous afternoon he had seen the fishermen on the boulders below. He stripped off his tuxedo, all of his clothing down to his shorts, and stowed them in the car trunk and took out the grip with its lethal contents. He made a belt of his spare fishing line, tied it about his waist and paid out ten more feet and fastened it around the tarpaulin pouch. He slipped the swim-goggles over his eyes and then, very gingerly, carried the pouch down over the boulders until he reached the lapping water. He gazed out past the breakwater toward the position of the *Diana*. It was blacked out except for one green and one red light and a safety flood on the float where the two launches were moored. Thank God, Tony thought, there was no fog, or it would be hopeless. He took a deep breath, wished himself luck, and waded in.

He swam leisurely to conserve his strength. The pouch trailing beneath him exerted very little downward pull because of the trapped air inside and the buoyancy of the salt water.

When he had covered what he thought to be a hundred yards,
he trod water and checked his position. He was too far to
seaward, and he corrected his course. Another hundred yards
and he trod water again. He had overcorrected. Another hundred yards. And another. The *Diana* was farther out than he
had estimated. Then, on his fifth check, he sighted the
launches and the floating platform. They were dead ahead not
more than fifteen yards. He filled his lungs and dived beneath
the surface. After a few moments he could see the glow of the
safety light on the platform filtering down through the water.
Then his head collided with something solid. He surfaced. It
was one of the launches, the wrong one. He pushed the goggles up onto his forehead and scanned the decks of the *Diana*.
Where was the night watch? He shook the water from his ears
and listened. Not a sound except water lapping against the
platform. He submerged again and swam along the side of the
launch until he made out the shape of another hull. The owner's launch. Again he surfaced, pushed up his goggles and
cleared his ears. This time he heard the tread of footsteps on
the deck above. The sound faded off. The watch was circling
to the far side of the *Diana*. Tony grasped the stern line of the
launch, pulled himself up and dropped into the passenger
compartment. Now the overhead canopy would shield him
from view. He hauled up the tarpaulin pouch and untied it
from his waist. He crawled to the seat with the two armrests,
opened the locker underneath, pushed the life jacket to one
side, and positioned the bomb. He ran the fishing line which
would trigger it under the next seat where Erin—supposedly
—would be seated; then under the next and the next, the
fourth seat from di Ascoli's. He tied a large loop at the end of
the line, threaded it between the locker door and the seat, and
hid the loop under the cushion. One hard tug on the loop and
it would act exactly as a lanyard on a cannon.

Tony sat back on his haunches and surveyed the result.
Unless one knew where to look, the several exposed inches of
fishing line would be invisible. Then he saw the deck flooring

and groaned. He had dripped water everywhere. He pondered a moment; what could he use to sop up the water? Then he saw the owner's flag hanging limply from the stern pole. He unfastened it and mopped it over the deck. He wrung it out over the side, and repeated the operation until the decking was barely damp. He wrung out the flag once more and refastened it to the stern pole. By dawn and the first few minutes of sunshine, the flag would be dry again.

He heard the footsteps of the watch returning. Then they stopped. Tony held his breath. Was the watch coming down onto the platform? Then another sound. The watch was blowing his nose. The footsteps resumed, grew faint; then silence. Tony put on his goggles, lowered himself over the side, filled his lungs and submerged. His mission was all but complete.

The bedside alarm went off at 9 A.M. Tony dragged himself from the bed and shaved and dressed. He was bone-weary from the night's work, but he had to appear bright and chipper when he sat down to Nicole's breakfast. That behind him, he drove downtown to Nice's main department store and bought two changes of cruise clothing and deck shoes. The clerk was mystified when Tony would not bother to try them on for fit. He returned to the Dubois apartment, packed his purchases in his suitcase and the now empty grip, and asked Nicole to give them to di Ascoli's chauffeur when he called in the afternoon. If he was supposed to be going on that cruise, he had to make it look convincing.

"I think I'm coming down with the flu," he told Nicole. "Would you mind if I spend the afternoon in bed?"

"Ah, you poor man! And tonight is the wedding!"

"I'll make it. A long sleep will put me in shape."

"I do hope so. I'll have some broth for your lunch. And dinner will be something very simple."

"Thank you, Nicole." He started toward the bedroom.

"Tony—while you were out, I saw your tuxedo. How did you get it so wrinkled?"

"Cheap material, I guess." Nicole's attentiveness was grating on him.

"But no. It is of the best. In any case, I shall have it pressed again. You must look your absolute best tonight. This will be the wedding of the year, you know."

It was one of those summer evenings for which the Riviera is famous. The golden twilight was fading and the azure prelude to night crept up the hills and mountains behind Monte Carlo. On the great terrace of the penthouse the lanterns began to glow and the potted trees and bushes twinkled with thousands of tiny lights. At the far edge of the terrace, in the exact center, a gazebo twined with orchids awaited its moment as the setting for the ceremony to come. A green-and-gold carpet, di Ascoli's colors, led away from the gazebo, dividing the seated guests, and up the stone stairway to the upper terrace, where the Monte Carlo Police Band softly rendered the theme music from Erin Deering's major films.

Tony Brullov chose one of the folding chairs on the aisle and gazed about at the assembling guests. "A veritable Almanach de Gotha of finance and industry," someone murmured in French behind him. And of show business, too, Tony added mentally—movie stars, producers, studio heads from two continents. He felt a tap on his shoulder and looked up. It was Lisa, dramatically simple in a salmon-colored gown. She smiled at him and took the aisle seat directly across. *Tonight*, Tony thought, *I'll make you one of the richest young women in the world. And Erin one of the wealthiest widows.*

The band segued from motion-picture themes to the somber yet soaring aria from *Tosca: E lucevan le stelle*—"And the stars were brightly shining." Erin's favorite. But, like *Tosca*, the stars no longer shone for Tony. His palms were damp, his forehead pounded, his throat was constricted. Suppose something went wrong? Not failure of the bomb to go off; Tony's expertise from the OSS assured success in that quarter. But something else, something unforeseen. Orsino di Ascoli was not a railroad bridge. He was a killer himself. He was famous for cunning and ruthlessness. Tony's mind raced back over the bachelors' party of the night before. Why had Orsino watched him so closely? Why, at the last minute, had he invited Tony on the wedding cruise? It was unnatural. And his odd reaction when Tony had asked if there were any changes in tonight's schedule. Everything he had said seemed strange in retrospect, everything rang false. Tony felt on the verge of panic.

Di Ascoli suspected him. That explained why he had been trailed all over Nice; those people were detectives, not jewel thieves. Tony clenched his fists, digging his nails into his palms. Snap out of it. No one had trailed him last night; no one knew about the bomb. He was simply suffering from what Erin called "opening night jitters." Then a new fear. Erin. How could he be so certain that he could separate Erin from di Ascoli in time, that she would be safe? For weeks Tony had been so confident of his strategy; he had banked everything on surprise and confusion—the technique of the terrorists. But suppose di Ascoli was not surprised? Or suppose there were a bodyguard on that bridal launch? No, Tony must add another element; he dared not try to swing it by himself. He glanced across the aisle at Lisa, so beautiful, so responsive to him. Yes. She was the answer. She was his guarantee.

He was aware that the music had ended, that people were turning in their seats and looking toward the upper terrace. Orsino and Erin were descending the steps—he in a cutaway coat, she in a floor-length gown of ice-blue. They advanced along the green-and-gold carpet toward the gazebo and the mayor took his position before them. It was certainly an unorthodox wedding, Tony thought: no bridesmaids, no best man, no ushers. But then, they were an unorthodox couple.

The mayor began reading in French the words of the civil wedding ceremony. Then he paused and asked a question of Orsino and Orsino said *"Oui."* He repeated the question to Erin and she said *"Oui."* Orsino removed the wedding ring from his waistcoat, slipped it onto Erin's finger, and they kissed. Trumpets blared the opening fanfare of Mendelssohn's Wedding March.

Orsino and Erin, arm in arm, walked rapidly up the aisle, smiling at the standing assemblage. Just before they reached Tony, Erin winked at him—and threw her bouquet at Lisa's feet. Lisa, stone-faced, did not look down.

Tony was one of the first to step out into the aisle. He picked up Erin's bouquet and thrust it at Lisa. "Carry it," he ordered. "No. I won't touch it!" He pushed the bouquet into her hands. "Do it. For my sake." Lisa gave him a startled look and obeyed.

The cavalcade of limousines wound through the narrow streets which were lined with people waving and shouting their good wishes, then along the *quai* toward the launch landing. Tony and Lisa were in the second limousine with Aly Khan and Porfirio Rubirosa sitting on jump seats. The bridal limousine halted. Orsino and Erin stepped out and were immediately surrounded by photographers and men with microphones. Tony and Lisa joined them and were bombarded with brazen questions: How did Miss di Ascoli feel about her new stepmother? Did she believe the girl who catches the bouquet will be the next to marry? Any comment on that, Mr. Brullov?

Tony ignored it all. His attention was on the sailing platform at the bottom of the flight of steps. Who were those men standing beside the launches? He recognized the uniforms of Captain Cipriani and the crewmen waiting by the mooring lines. But who were the two in civilian dress? Stocky men with roving eyes. Then, as if in answer, the two separated, went to the two launches and dropped down into the bow cockpits alongside the helmsmen. Bodyguards, for sure. Tony turned cold. Better to forget the whole thing: scratch it and wait for another chance. But how? When? Perhaps never. . . .

Orsino and Erin broke away from the news people and went down the steps to the sailing platform, followed by Lisa and Tony. Captain Cipriani saluted the bridal couple and escorted them toward the owner's launch, which was in lead position, engines thrumming. Tony studied the distance between the cockpit, where the bodyguard sat, and the passenger compartment. Fifteen feet or more. At least that was something. The bodyguard would have to crawl back over the engine housing, which had no handrails. Slippery business when the launch was at full speed with the bow tilted upward and half out of the water.

Captain Cipriani handed Erin down into the launch, then di Ascoli. Tony nudged Lisa and whispered, "Are you game for some fun?"

"Always. But what?"

"Just do as I say."

The di Ascolis waved to the people crowding onto the platform for the second launch. The mate blew his whistle and a crewman cast off the mooring lines. The engines growled and the launch started to edge away from the platform. Tony shouted to Lisa: "Let's join them. Come on!" With that he jumped, pulling Lisa after him, across the widening water and tumbled down onto the seats.

Orsino half rose, his face suddenly white. "No! You're in the second launch!" He picked up the telephone to call the helmsman.

Tony caught his arm. "Please. Don't split us up." He raised Lisa's hand with the bouquet. "You know what this means. We're all going to be one family."

Orsino hesitated, then returned the phone to its cradle. He gestured to the bodyguard, who was standing up in the cockpit and staring back, that it was all right.

Erin smiled tightly at Tony. "You seem to be in a proposing mood these days. When did it happen?"

"Right now. This second. Orsino, I'm asking for your daughter's hand."

The di Ascolis did what Tony had counted on—they stared

at Lisa. Just long enough for Tony to feel down the side of the cushion for the loop of fish line and jerk it sharply.

"Lisa, is this what you truly want?" di Ascoli asked.

"I don't know. . . . yes! Yes, it's what I want." She turned to Tony, who was looking at his wristwatch. "I hope you're not just caught up in the spirit of the evening. That you truly mean it."

"Will this convince you?" Tony pulled her onto his lap and kissed her.

One minute passed. All four were laughing and babbling at each other, half shouting to be heard over the rumble of the engines. *One and one-half minutes.* Tony glanced back at the second launch, which was cutting through the water a hundred yards behind. In the distance he saw the lights of other launches that di Ascoli had hired to bring all the guests to the reception in the shortest possible time. Behind them, fanned out, were scores of small pleasure craft filled with spectators. Overhead a helicopter clattered. Reporters and photographers, Tony guessed.

They passed the jetties of the breakwater and the launch surged forward, roaring and canting its bow upward. Erin peered out from under the canopy. "What a magnificent night!" she shouted over the engines. "The stars, the lights of Monte Carlo—and look! *Look!*"

Skyrockets were shooting up from the *Diana* and bursting into blossoms of red and green and yellow and blue.

Two minutes. Tony jumped to his feet. "Damn. It's time I kissed the bride."

Erin held up her face expectantly. Tony's arms closed around her waist, pulled her to her feet and flung her, shrieking, over the side.

Lisa screamed and di Ascoli seized the telephone and bawled, "*Raul!* Reverse engines! Reverse engines!" A second later the bodyguard came out of the cockpit and started to crawl back over the engine housing.

Tony seized Lisa. "Now you. Jump. Jump!"

"Father! He's insane!"

"No. I am justice!" Tony shouted wildly. "I am the executioner of a mass murderer! The man you call Father is Yuri Dimitrovich Solenko, killer of the Romanov family! Remember that before you testify against me in court!"

For a moment Orsino cringed at the accusation, then he roared, "I knew I should have killed you!" and lunged at Tony. Tony threw himself sideways, evading him, and picked up Lisa bodily, intending to hurl her overboard. Then her father caught Tony's neck in a stranglehold and Lisa fell to the deck. "So it's a bomb, is it?" he hissed. "Then we go together!" And to Lisa: *"Jump, darling! Jump!"*

But Lisa seemed turned to stone. Tony wrenched and struggled, unable to break Orsino's grip. Then he saw the bodyguard coming at him with the raised butt of his pistol. Tony spun Orsino to meet it; the pistol crashed against Orsino's skull and he slumped to the deck. Tony seized Lisa once more and dragged her to the side of the launch. She flung out both arms and locked them around one of the canopy posts. "Father! Father!" she shrieked. The bodyguard threw himself at Tony again, just as he went over the side and caught Lisa by the legs. His sheer weight, he hoped, would break her hold on the post. But time had run out. With a thunderous roar, a great orange ball of fire, the launch heaved upward and dissolved into the night.

Erin Deering, dripping and shivering but unhurt, stared across the water from the *Diana*'s second launch. Searchlights from the launch, the Harbor Patrol and other craft, were playing over the black water; but all that was visible was floating debris. The Harbor Patrol came close and someone shouted through a bullhorn, "We have a woman's body and part of a man. Or maybe two men. What about you?"

"One survivor," the helmsman called back. "Madame di Ascoli."

The launch began another circle, then the engines cut back to idle. The helmsman shouted to the Harbor Patrol, "Ready with your boat hook!"

Erin watched the two craft closing the water between them, then the searchlights converged on a floating object. A sailor lowered the hook over the side. It was Tony, floating face upward. Erin gazed down at him and thought, No. It's not his face. It's another man. The face of a man standing on a veranda in Costa Rica with the rain pouring off the eaves behind him. Ted Brullov was smiling at her and saying, "Forget the violin, my dear. Your fame and fortune are on the stage."

The limp body was transferred to the launch and stretched out on the floorboards. Erin knelt beside him and cradled his head in her lap. Then there was a gurgling sound and seawater spewed from Tony's mouth. Instantly Erin's fingers went to his neck. Yes. There was a faint pulse. "Tony!" she cried. "Oh, Tony, my dearest!"

The afternoon was bright and warm and Tony Brullov was grateful that Erin had moved his wheelchair into the sheltering shade of the potted palm tree on the penthouse terrace. He would be even more grateful, he thought, when the doctors could remove the turban of bandages from his head and the damned plaster cast on his left leg, which was now propped on a padded footstool. Erin, seated beside him, put down the magazine she had been reading aloud and watched the approach of Constantine Durer.

"Madame, an Inspecteur Vilar of the Nice Sûreté wishes to speak to Mr. Brullov." Durer gestured toward Vilar, who was waiting in the shadow of the terrace staircase.

Erin turned inquiringly to Tony, who nodded consent and waved to the Inspecteur.

"My apologies for intruding," Vilar said, coming forward. "I trust you are well on the mend, M'sieur Brullov."

Tony nodded. "Coming along. What brings you to Monte Carlo?"

"A visit as a friend. A friend with a possible solution to the tragedy of last week."

"A solution?"

The Inspecteur turned to Erin. "Madame, would it offend if I smoked a pipe?"

"Of course not."

"Thank you." He dug into his breast pocket, tamped his pipe full of tobacco from a pouch, lighted it and sent aloft a great puff of aromatic smoke. "I am here unofficially; but I have discussed my theory with my opposite number here in the Principality. M'sieur Brullov, you recall that some days ago you stopped by Headquarters and told me you were being followed about by a black van and another car?"

"Certainly."

"I have questioned the persons involved—one Paul Radlett and one Annette Pelletier. It seems they are private investigators who had been hired by the late lamented Orsino di Ascoli. I have confirmed that fact with Mr. Constantine Durer." Tony and Erin looked at Durer, who hovered uncomfortably in the background. "This information," Vilar continued, "immediately cast a beam of light into the dark mystery of what was to follow. Radlett and Pelletier, M'sieur Brullov, were in effect your bodyguards. For some reason, Mr. di Ascoli was displeased with their services and discharged them and said he would employ others in their place. But why bodyguards? you may ask. The answer is that we in police circles have known for years that Mr. di Ascoli employed agents to protect his daughter from kidnapping and, if you will forgive the implication, from blackmail. Now we come to my theory. According to Mr. Durer, you, M'sieur Brullov, were about to merge your business with the Ascoli enterprises. Therefore it would be natural that Mr. di Ascoli would wish to extend protection to his new associate, especially an associate who was romantically linked with his daughter. Do you follow?"

Tony nodded. "Completely. In fact, I had proposed to Lisa and she accepted me with her father's blessing. Madame di Ascoli was a witness."

Vilar's eyes saddened. "Then my sympathy is compounded. Also it adds substance to my theory. In the world of criminals, there are those who are ever alert to the possibility of gaining a great sum of money. The Algerians who looted the Nice bank, for instance. It is my contention that some group, learning of the coming marriage of Mr. di Ascoli and Mademoiselle Deering, demanded that he pay them what is commonly called 'protection' money. Mr. di Ascoli refused them; instead, he added extra bodyguards at the wedding and on the launches going out to the yacht. This was a challenge which the terrorists could not tolerate. They would kill everybody aboard that launch as a warning to future victims. Pay or die."

Erin shuddered. "What sick minds!"

"And all too common," Vilar agreed. "But there is one aspect which I cannot explain to myself. How was it, madame, that you went into the water just before the explosion?"

"I've already explained that to the Monte Carlo Police. I was standing up, the launch hit a swell, I lost my balance."

"For which we must all thank a merciful Providence. Unfortunately the Monte Carlo authorities have indicated to me some doubt." Vilar paused to suck on his pipe. "To put it bluntly, madame, it has been suggested that you and M'sieur Brullov, who had once enjoyed a . . . shall we say, a tender relationship, might have intended to share Mr. di Ascoli's inheritance."

Erin exploded. "That's monstrous! Tony is wealthy in his own right. My God, he almost drowned, and look at his condition now. Besides, Orsino and I had signed a prenuptial agreement. Mr. Durer was a witness. Ask him."

Vilar turned toward di Ascoli's confidential secretary. "Would you be so good?"

Durer swept a hand over his perspiring bald head. "The terms, sir, were that in the event of a divorce, Madame would

315

receive a certain sum; if the marriage succeeded until Mr. di Ascoli's death, Madame would receive a specified percentage of the estate; but the great bulk of it, by far, would go to his daughter and to her legitimate children, if any."

"You see," Erin said triumphantly, "Mr. Brullov had no motive whatsoever."

Inspecteur Vilar glowed with satisfaction. "Then the structure of my theory is founded on solid rock. It *was* indeed the work of terrorists. Yes. I shall communicate this to the locals and to Interpol." He shook hands with Tony, wished him a speedy recovery, bowed to Erin, and Constantine Durer escorted him from the terrace.

Erin watched their departure and then looked at Tony. "I wonder what the Inspecteur and the Monte Carlo Police would say if they knew that you had thrown me overboard."

"You could have repeated exactly what I told you—that I heard a strange ticking noise in the launch and remembered what it meant in the old OSS days. I wasn't about to take a chance."

Erin sighed. "If poor Orsino had only believed you . . ."

"And poor Lisa."

"Yes. Lisa. Would you really have married her, Tony?" He shifted uncomfortably in his wheelchair and grimaced at the weight of the plaster cast. "Would you?" she repeated.

"I proposed, didn't I?"

She shrugged. "I thought it was a case of rebound. Vanilla ice cream when you couldn't have the chocolate. Was I right?"

"Well . . ." Tony smiled. "For some time now, chocolate has been my favorite."

Erin considered his words solemnly, then moved her chair closer to Tony and they clasped each other's hands and gazed contentedly at a flight of pigeons wheeling in the cloudless sky. In a few minutes it would be time for tea.